Surviving Serendipity

By

Jacquelyn Sylvan

QUAKE

SURVIVING SERENDIPITY

A Quake Book

Shakin' Up Young Readers!

First Quake paperback printing / January 2008

QUAKE

is a division of

Echelon Press, LLC

9735 Country Meadows Lane 1-D

Laurel, MD 20723

www.quakeme.com

13-Digit ISBN: 978-1-59080-586-2

10-Digit ISBN: 1-59080-586-0

Library of Congress Control Number: 2007942635

PRINTED IN THE UNITED STATES OF AMERICA

10 9 8 7 6 5 4 3 2 1

To my husband, Martin, who was the first to see where this was going, and gave me the gift that made it all possible...not to mention hundreds of hours spent propping up my self-confidence. I couldn't have done it without you, my love.

Oh, and Merry Christmas, Danny.

June rushed from the bathroom to the bedroom, narrowly avoiding a high-speed collision with the coffee table. She hurriedly kicked off her slippers (wincing slightly as one flew hard into the wall, leaving a dark smudge) and rummaged through the bottom of her closet, picking through the debris of clothing that had wilted from the hangers onto the floor. At last she came up with not just one, but both, high-heeled boots, which, after a few minutes' struggle and a minor fall, ended up in their proper place on her feet. Panting slightly, June moved in front of the mirror for inspection.

Not too shabby. June nodded in approval at her reflection. *Kyle's going to be upset he didn't try harder to get out of that little sales conference when he sees pictures of tonight.* She fluffed her wavy dark hair, shivering as it tickled the bare skin between her shoulder blades, and did a slow turn, trying to take an objective look. The dark, fitted jeans and sparkly gold top made the most of her figure, showing her curves without making her look chubby. Her dark mascara and eye shadow contrasted sharply with her glacier-blue eyes, so they practically glow, and a dab of blush had given her pale skin just enough color to keep her from looking like the recently departed.

The door buzzer went off, startling her, and with a last check to make sure she had nothing hanging out of her nose and hadn't slopped toothpaste on her shirt, she grabbed her purse and hurried out of her apartment.

Ashleigh had already gotten back in her little blue VW beetle and sat waiting for June as she dashed out the front door of the building. June leapt into the car, closing the door so quickly she almost caught her long hair in it. "Hi," she said, breathlessly. "Sorry I wasn't out front."

Ashleigh snorted.

"Like I expected you to be, rather than standing in front of the mirror checking to make sure your ass doesn't look fat," she said, with a knowing smirk, and June made a face as she dug in her purse for her cigarettes.

"Thanks for being designated," June said, cracking the window just enough to let the smoke out and not mess up her hair.

"Well, you've done it for me for three months now, time I

returned the favor," Ashleigh said, tapping out her own cigarette and handing it to June to light for her.

"You say that like I had a choice in the matter," June said, handing the lit cigarette back, "considering I haven't been legal."

"Whatever," Ashleigh said, "if we start trying to go tit-for-tat here, we'll be at it all night."

"Yeah, fifteen years of it, we would be. And add Shannon to the mix..." June made a little *pbbt* sound with her lips. "Forget it." She sighed, letting her head flop against the headrest, and Ashleigh glanced at her.

"Did Kyle call today?"

"No, I guess the conference stuff usually goes late, like seven or eight, and they always hang around and b.s. for a while after." June began twisting her engagement ring on her finger, the only piece of jewelry she ever wore.

Ashleigh looked at her watch. "And it's what time now?" she asked, pushing her wrist toward June, who raised her eyebrows warningly.

"Eight *Vegas* time, sweetie. We're on Eastern Standard. Quit it."

"Whatever," Ashleigh muttered, and June looked at her sharply.

"Oy," she said, trying to make a joke out of a very sensitive subject for her. She pointed a finger at her own chest. "Birthday girl! No picking!"

Ashleigh gave a long-suffering sigh, blowing her feathery bangs off her forehead, but didn't say another word about Kyle.

The subject of Kyle was really the only source of contention between June and her friends. She'd met him about two months after her parents died, and they'd gotten serious quickly; Kyle moved into June's small apartment in a matter of a month or so. He was a great guy, no drug or alcohol problems, no compulsive gambling, no history of womanizing, no question about his sexuality. Lily-white. But not exactly the most doting or appreciative guy. And yes, from time to time it bothered her–today, for instance–but for the most part June could overlook a minor flaw in an otherwise perfect stone. Her friends could not.

Shannon sat waiting in a corner booth when June and Ashleigh arrived–she lived two blocks from the bar, and parking was more of a hassle than just walking. As soon as she saw them, Shannon waved exuberantly, and hugged June as she slid into the booth.

"T-minus one hour, birthday girl," Shannon said, tossing back her bright red hair, a devilish grin on her freckled face. "God, I can't wait, we are going to get you *sooo* plastered..."

"Like you haven't seen me plastered before," June said, rolling her eyes.

"Yes, but this is the first time we get you *legally* plastered," Ashleigh said, joining them after having stopped to talk to the bartender. "And out in public, too, with more people to point and laugh."

"Oooh, remember at Jimmy's party, junior year in high school?" Shannon said, still grinning.

"No, actually, I don't," June said, feigning annoyance to cover her embarrassment, "but everyone else does."

"How could anyone forget the now infamous panty-dance?" Shannon said, cutting her eyes to Ashleigh, who had been crumpled up with laughter, but now sat upright, eyes wide.

"Haha, not only do I remember," Ashleigh said, rummaging in her purse, "I brought the picture!" June made a wild grab for the photo, but missed–Shannon managed to snatch it over June's head.

"Hey everyone," Shannon yelled, standing up on the bench (June buried her face in her hands, mortified but shaking with hysterical laughter) "Anybody want to see a picture of a hottie in underpants?" A few rough-looking guys in the next booth looked over and cracked up, catching sight of the picture of June, drunk as a skunk, doing a Rockette-style dance on Jimmy's coffee table with a pair of his mother's voluminous underpants on her head. Satisfied, Shannon plopped back down next to June and handed the photo back to Ashleigh, who tucked it neatly in her purse.

"I know where you hide your key, you know," June said, glaring good-naturedly at Ashleigh. "Don't think I won't break into your house and steal that damn photo."

"Wouldn't do you any good," Ashleigh said primly. "I have the negatives in my safe-deposit box."

"So how's work?" Shannon said, changing the subject before June could retort. "Did they do anything for you for your birthday?"

"Yeah, the girls got me a card and a little cake," June said. "Nobody's really in the mood to celebrate, though, since we got that complete jerk Dr. Dence. God, I can't stand her. I'm thinking maybe it's time to look for another job."

"But you love that job," said Ashleigh, shocked.

"Yeah, I *loved* that job, until *La Femme Hitler* arrived on the scene."

"Can't you say anything to Dr. Zalzin?" Shannon asked.

June shrugged. "It wouldn't do any good. She brought a lot of patients with her, and yeah, I'm a great employee, but medical assistants are a dime a dozen. I'm replaceable. Josephine Stalin, M.D.? Not so much." She shrugged again, tucking her hair behind one ear, and her black look made her friends quickly change the subject.

The conversation drifted merrily on, aided by Ashleigh's amusing anecdotes about her husband, Jared. They were laughing so hard that they didn't even notice Chuck, the bartender, standing over them with a tray lined with three shots of tequila, three lemon slices, and a shaker of salt.

"Compliments of the house," he said, smiling, as he set them out before the girls.

"Join us?" asked June, smiling invitingly, without even wincing when Shannon kicked her hard in the ankle. Shannon had a big-time crush on Chuck, who was undeniably crushable. Unfortunately, Shannon's crush robbed her of all capacity for coherent speech, so usually she ended up keeping her mouth shut around him.

Chuck looked around at the barroom, which was slow for a Friday night. He pursed his lips as he considered the invitation.

"Promise we won't tell your boss," said Ashleigh, smiling. Not only was Chuck the owner of the Merry Widow, but Shannon was too far away to kick *her* ankle.

"Yeah, sure, why not?" he said, and went to the bar to get his own shooter. Shannon glared at June and Ashleigh, whose faces bore the beatific, innocent smiles often found on Virgin Mary statues. Chuck returned with his drink and slid in next to Shannon. June tried hard to keep a straight face as she watched Shannon struggle for composure, and she felt, rather than saw, Ashleigh's amusement next to her. Chuck sprinkled salt on all of their hands, and raised his glass. "To the birthday girl."

"Hear, hear," said Ashleigh. Shannon, lips pressed tightly together to avoid embarrassing logorrhea, merely nodded, and held up her glass. They all watched as the second hand of the Budweiser clock above the bar twitched to midnight. June licked the salt, tossed back her shot, sucked the lemon slice fiercely, and slammed her glass down bottom-up as the others did the same.

"So, no Kyle tonight?" Chuck asked. June shook her head and put on her best diplomatic smile, trying to keep her face clear of emotion. "No, not tonight, but he promises to make it up to me when he gets back, in a big way."

"Well, he'd better," Chuck said, as he got to his feet. "That guy doesn't know what he's got." He smiled quickly then, the smile of someone who realizes they might have put their foot in it. "Another round, ladies?"

"No more tequila tonight," June said, letting Chuck's comment pass with another too-sunny smile. "I'll have a beer. What do you guys want?" Ashleigh and Shannon placed their orders, and Chuck walked back to the bar.

"He doesn't, you know," Shannon said quietly.

"Who doesn't what?" June asked, smiling, already feeling the tingle of the liquor.

"Kyle. Doesn't know what he's got."

June looked from Ashleigh to Shannon, both of whom wore serious expressions. Her shoulders slumped in exasperation. "Guys, he's *working*. It's not like he doesn't *want* to be here." Ashleigh merely nodded, but Shannon made a very unconvinced-sounding *hmm* noise.

June opened her mouth to argue, but Chuck returned with their drinks, and afterward the conversation turned to quiet berating of Shannon over her 'Chucky-love'.

As she listened to the back and forth between her friends, her thoughts turned inward, examining the strange feelings the simple movement of the clock hand had awakened in her. She felt suddenly twitchy and restless, like a dog before a thunderstorm. The talk about Kyle had irritated her, as well. *You'll see him Monday,* she thought, soothing her inner petulant child, currently ranting about the unfairness of having her fiancé halfway across the country on this milestone of birthdays.

Ashleigh dropped June off at her apartment around 2 a.m. "You sure you're alright to get up the stairs on your own?" Ashleigh asked. "You have your keys and everything?"

June, more than a little tipsy, jingled her keys. "I've crawled up steeper stairs before," she said, giggling.

"Yeah, I know," Ashleigh said. "That's why I asked. You fail to remember that I was behind you most of those times, pushing you up." They laughed, and June waved Ashleigh off as she turned to walk toward the door. She stopped midway, though, and watched Ashleigh drive off, taillights bright in the gloom.

It was eerily quiet as she stepped inside her apartment building, especially for a Friday night, and tonight the hallway lights only seemed to darken the shadows by contrast, rather than chase them away. Determined not to let the horror-movie setup creep her out, June squared her shoulders as she turned the key in the lock.

The door opened on darkness, pierced only by a small red light, flashing in the gloom. That would be Kyle's message on the answering machine, wishing her a happy birthday. *See, he remembered to call,* she thought, as she made her way across the room.

She'd made it halfway there when her inner alarm system stopped her dead in her tracks, raising every hair on her body with a prickling thrill. Heart racing, her blood pulsing a dull *thump thump thump* in her ears, she turned to meet the intruder.

He stood in the entranceway from the kitchen to the living room, not moving; June would never have known he was there, had some primitive sense not alerted her. Her mind raced. Was he here to rob her? Rape her? Should she run, scream? Should she try to reason with him? As she stared at him, silhouetted by the nightlight above the kitchen sink, he surprised her by reaching over and flipping the wall switch, bathing them both in incandescent light.

June blinked in astonishment, then bit back an inappropriate urge to laugh. Well, maybe not entirely inappropriate.

He was swarthy-skinned, wearing baggy, bright purple pants tucked into the tops of knee-high black riding boots and held up by a wide black belt, with a vest which matched his pants over a very hairy chest. The biggest surprise, though, was his hat. Looking like a squashy orchid cushion, it boasted a long green feather at least a foot and a half long. Long jet-black hair flowed from under his hat and over his shoulders, the same color as his mustache and goatee. Icy blue eyes stared into hers from under bushy eyebrows.

They watched each other for a moment, June still fighting an unreasonable urge to laugh that she was pretty sure had to do with the plume. Finally, unable to stand it any longer, she broke the silence.

"I don't know what you're here for, but the television and stuff are right here, and there's a CD player and some spare change in the bedroom. Whatever it is you want, take it, but that's all there is, I swear," she said breathlessly. "I won't say anything, I promise, I'll just stand here, I won't try anything..."

June trailed off, feeling that her slowly closing throat wouldn't allow her to talk much longer, anyway. Shakily, she forced herself to take a deep breath, trying with all her might to fight the encroaching panic squeezing her with sharp claws, breaking down her capacity for rational thought. It was also increasing her urge to collapse into hysterical laughter, and she really didn't think it would be a good idea to laugh in the face of a potential maniac.

The pirate/genie regarded her quietly for a moment, then spoke. "I am not interested in your possessions."

June's desire to laugh dried up instantly. Shivering, she tightened her hand on her purse, feeling the strap give under her grip. All she had in there were her wallet, cell phone, and a couple packs of cigarettes, but if she managed to get a good shot across his nose... She took a half step backwards, squaring her shoulders.

"If it's me you want," she said, voice trembling slightly, "you're going to have a hell of a fight on your hands." June brandished her shiny satin purse as threateningly as possible. The pirate/genie smiled faintly. She didn't like his smile.

"Forgive me, please," he said, with a slight bow. "You misunderstand my intentions. I am here for you, but not in the way you th–" He broke off as June whirled on her heel and made a break for the door. Her hand had just grasped the doorknob when–

Suddenly, she found herself racing through blackness at incredible speed. She couldn't even understand how she knew she was moving, since there were no points of reference and no wind, and no up or down, which was fairly nauseating. What frightened her the most, though, was the feeling of endless space, all around her, and the unaccounted-for knowledge that if she got lost here, she would never, ever find her way back out again.

After what seemed like hours, but could only have been a few moments, there was a blinding white flash, and June found herself standing knee-deep in reddish grass in the middle of a field, still clutching her purse to her chest. Whirling around, dizzy and disoriented, she found the pirate, smiling his faint, creepy smile.

Backing up, she looked wildly around her, searching for–what? Help? A landmark, to let her know where she was? The only things she saw were an imposing forest far to her left, and a small cottage, smoke curling from the chimney, on a hill about a quarter-mile away to her right. June looked from pirate to house and back again. She'd never make it, even in her non-smoking days. Strong as she was, she was never what you'd call a fast runner. And what if the cottage didn't contain help, but someone else who meant to hurt her? What then? She had nowhere to run, and the dusk was deepening around them.

The only option currently available to June was fainting, and she took it, gratefully.

～2～

When June woke, she found herself in a very strange place. First, rather than a bed, she lay in a hammock. The ceiling of the room peaked above her, bisected by rough wooden beams, from which dusty bunches of dried plants hung. The walls were of the same wood, and covered by shelves, upon which a number of objects rested. She spotted corncob pipes, bottles of colored liquids, and bones she definitely didn't recognize from Biology 101.

Huge slabs of sand-colored stone made up the floor, covered here and there with fur rugs, and a few weak shafts of sunlight trickled through the boards nailed across the room's only window. June stared as particles of dust swirled slowly in the thin rays, losing herself in their waltz.

Then she remembered how she'd gotten here. Heart in her throat, she leapt out of the hammock with catlike grace (surprising, given her usually klutzy nature) and began searching the room for an escape route. Only two, window and door.

Preferring a stealthy exit to a violent escape, June went to the window and tugged experimentally on a board. It didn't budge. She could probably pry them off, but that would take time, and she'd make a hell of a racket.

The door, then. Before she tried, she scanned the shelves for a suitable weapon as she quietly slipped off her boots and placed them in the hammock. Settling on a large femur-ish bone lying on a shelf next to a very strange skull which might have had three eyes in life, she crept to the door and tried the knob, half-expecting it to be locked. It turned easily, however, and heart pounding, she opened the door and stepped out into the hall.

The narrow corridor was walled and floored with the same materials as her room. The stone floor made things easier; creaking floorboards might have given her away. To her right, the hallway ended in a closed door. She heard voices speaking in low tones to her left, where the hallway opened into a larger room. June stood for a moment, trying to slow her breathing and deciding what to do. Running away would be futile, since she had no idea where she was or how to get out of the house. Sooner or later, there would have to be a conflict, and she might as well get it over with.

Brandishing her bone, she moved toward the voices, pressing herself lightly against one wall for cover. As June stepped into the open, she nearly dropped the femur in astonishment.

Five men sat on benches at a long picnic-style table in a primitive kitchen. "Primitive" because as far as she could see, there were no light fixtures, appliances, wall outlets, or plumbing; simply a table, an enormous wooden hutch at least five feet wide, racks of pots and pans hanging from the ceiling beams, and a large cast-iron stove, putting off the pleasant odor of wood smoke.

More astonishing than stepping into an apparently Amish kitchen were the men sitting around the table, one of them the pirate/genie who had abducted her. Although June had already met him, his appearance still jolted her. The other four men, however, made the shock of a purple pirate kidnapper compare with the surprise of winning $1 on a scratch-off lottery ticket.

They were blue. Not blue as in depressed, but...blue. Their skin was actually a brightish slate blue. In every other respect, they looked like perfectly normal men in their twenties. But–blue? It had to be makeup, had to be, but as far as June could tell, it wasn't.

In addition to the millions of other questions racing through her mind, June now questioned her sanity.

One of the blue men, with chestnut-brown hair, glanced up and found her watching them, bone still raised threateningly. He leapt to his feet, standing almost in an attitude of military attention, then bowed as deeply as the bench and table allowed. The other three blue men did the same, as did the pirate, although he got to his feet more slowly. June, startled by their movement, jumped backward, knocking over a previously unnoticed chair and nearly falling over it.

Regaining her balance, she stared in ever deepening astonishment, fighting between impulses to laugh or cry. At least they had better clothing than Mr. Purple Pants–simple buckskin-looking trousers, off-white linen shirts, and moccasin-like boots, with clean-shaven faces and short hair, also unlike her abductor. Better, but still very 1700's.

She lowered her femur-bone slightly from its threatening position, feeling a little encouraged by their behavior. Strange as it was, she didn't think people who bowed to her seemed likely to attack. Then the pirate/genie smiled, and she raised her guard and her bone.

"Welcome home," he said, with another bow. June opened her mouth, made a small sound, then closed it.

"My name is Halryan," he continued, ignoring her distress. "I am about to tell you something you will no doubt find hard to believe. I assure you, however, it is all true." He gestured toward the table, inviting her to sit.

June made no move to join them, however; she righted the chair she had knocked over and perched stiffly on the edge, feet flat on the floor, ready to run if the need arose. All four of the blue men waited until she sat before returning to their seats; Halryan remained standing.

June and Halryan stared at each other, barely blinking. He made no move to speak again, and the silence became nearly unbearable, but June had the strangest feeling that if she spoke first, she'd be losing some kind of battle. So she resisted the urge to fill the void, and kept her gaze locked with Halryan's. Finally, he cleared his throat and cut his eyes away to the wall behind her. June exhaled quietly as Halryan began to speak, realizing she'd been holding her breath.

"As I have said, I am called Halryan. This is Errigal and Feoras—" he gestured to two very dark-haired men to his right, who nodded. June noted with a start they were twins, only distinguishable by a thin vertical scar down the left cheek of one of the men. "Minogan—" the serious-looking man with chestnut-brown hair who'd bowed first to her nodded solemnly, "and Koen." The man closest to her, with light sandy-brown hair, almost blond, was the only one to offer her a smile, which she returned reflexively, if weakly.

"They belong to a race known as the Valforte, recognized for their skills as warriors, and will assist us in our quest," Halryan continued.

"Quest?" June interjected, failing to keep a nervous squeak out of her voice.

"Yes, a quest," Halryan answered. He straightened slightly, a pompous expression on his face.

"We must save the world."

Serious as the situation was—either June *had* lost her mind, or she'd been kidnapped and transported to an alternate reality—she just couldn't hold back the snort of laughter. Halryan looked distinctly ruffled and drew himself up further.

"This is no laughing matter!" His indignance made laughing even harder to avoid, although she managed it by pressing her lips tight between her teeth. "Your mother, the queen—"

"Wait, wait, wait," June interrupted, putting up the hand still holding the bone. "My mother is from Connecticut. There is no royal family in Connecticut."

"The man and woman who raised you," Halryan said, slowly, with his version of sympathy, "were not your parents."

June reached the end of her patience.

"I'm sorry, but that is complete bullshit," she said, (pausing mentally for a split second of triumph in Halryan's shocked expression over her foul mouth) "I have a birth certificate, baby pictures out the wazoo, and my father's nose. There is no way I'm adopted."

"There was no 'adoption'," Halryan continued, trying but failing to hide his annoyance at the repeated interruptions. "The people who raised you had no idea you were not their daughter–"

"BULLSHIT," June yelled, leaping to her feet. She shrank back, momentarily feeling threatened, for the other four men had also risen, but not in a menacing way. In fact, the expressions on their faces seemed sympathetic. She turned back to Halryan in a fury. "I don't know what the hell you're trying to pull, kidnapping me and dragging me to God only knows where–"

"Have you looked in a mirror lately?" Halryan interjected mildly.

"Wha–no, I–I–what does that have to do with anything?" June stuttered. Halryan picked up a tarnished silver hand mirror from a shelf in the kitchen and came toward her. June rocked slightly onto the balls of her feet, ready to run.

"Everything," he said, and held the mirror in front of her.

June gasped and spun around, looking for whoever stood behind her, for the face looking back at her certainly wasn't hers.

There was no one there.

"What..." she said, weakly. She looked at Halryan, who wore a smugly triumphant expression. He jiggled the mirror slightly in front of her. Slowly, feeling dazed and dreamlike, she reached out and took the mirror from him. The bone fell to the floor, forgotten, as her hand came up, exploring the new lines of her face, confirming what she saw in the mirror.

A face of astonishing beauty stared back at her. The eyes drew her first, still her own light, clear blue, but almond shaped now, almost exotic, striking in a face now much darker, a rich golden bronze, rather than her usual pale Anglo-Saxon coloring.

She looked down at her arms, the same color, gone unnoticed in the fright of waking in a strange place. She licked a finger and scrubbed at her arm, thinking the color had to be makeup, or dirt. It reddened slightly under her rough touch, but even with the scrape of a fingernail, the color stayed.

The other contours of her face had changed, too, her nose now straight and regal, but delicate, her cheekbones high and refined, lips a full sensual bow.

Her face?

"It's a trick," June said, looking at Halryan. "It has to be. Not even plastic surgery could do this, it's impossible." She turned the mirror over and looked at the back, feeling the edges for a telltale crack where some kind of electronic device could have been hidden. *Just an ordinary mirror.*

"You will also notice," Halryan said, smugness creeping into his voice, "you are speaking your native language, Prendarian."

"That's ridiculous," June scoffed. "How could I–" She broke off, panic swirling like ice cubes in her stomach. Because, since he had called attention to it, she realized she *was* both speaking and thinking in something which certainly wasn't English. And Halryan hadn't been speaking English, either.

June's lungs stuck together like wet garbage bags as she tried to inhale. Halryan folded his arms across his chest, evidently very pleased with himself. If she hadn't been so concerned with breathing, June probably would have hit him. She must have paled alarmingly, for the light-haired blue guy, the one who had smiled at her, leapt forward and took her by the elbow (June flinched back, but his hands were gentle), and guided her back to her seat. They all watched silently as she put her head between her knees, drawing deep, shuddering breaths. Finally, the spinning in her head slowed to an occasional wobble, and June looked up at Halryan.

"Start talking," she said.

And he did, standing as though he were giving a presentation (the blue men had retaken their seats). "Once more, my name is Halryan, and I am a sorcerer."

June was so deeply shocked, she didn't even react to this ridiculous revelation, merely nodding for him to continue.

"Some time ago, you were born as part of a set of twins. As the kingdom was under threat, a recommendation was made by the Sorcerer's Guild, which advises the royal family, to send one of you away, and keep the other here. That way, if something should happen to either your mother, Queen Taharia, or your sister, you would be protected, safe on the other side of the universe.

"We (for I am, of course, a member of the Guild) transported you to what you call Earth, placing you in the crib of an infant, a girl-child, who had unexpectedly died moments before. Through enchantments, we concealed your appearance so even as you grew, you would resemble the child whom you replaced.

"In the meantime, the Eid Gomen, an evil race that also inhabits Thallafrith, have discovered and awakened an ancient magic which is even now unraveling the threads of power that hold this world together. In order to keep it from being destroyed, another, even more ancient magic must be invoked, to stop the destruction and repair the damage. Thousands of years ago, this magic was written on a stone tablet, the tablet broken into pieces, and the pieces hidden throughout the kingdom. Only a member of the royal family can activate the spell written on the pieces.

"Unfortunately, your mother, Queen Taharia, died three years ago, and your sister, Queen Morningstar, a few weeks ago. This leaves you as the sole surviving member of the royal family, and the only person who can stop the world from ending."

June took a deep breath, puffing out her cheeks as she slowly exhaled through pursed lips. She sat back in her chair, running her hands over her face as she tried to absorb what she had just heard, and sighed once more. Finally, she leaned forward, resting her elbows on her knees and clasping her hands together.

"So, you're saying I'm not even on Earth anymore?" June said as she waited for her brain to catch up.

Halryan shook his head. "You're in the kingdom of Prendawr, on the planet Thallafrith." June nodded quietly and bit her lip.

"How am I supposed to activate spells if I'm not even...magical, or whatever?"

"Oh, my lady," Halryan said, in a 'silly girl' tone of voice that made June want to hit him a lot more than she already did, "Given your parentage, and some simple tests at your birth, I'd venture to say you are the most powerful sorceress this world has ever seen."

"How is that possible?" June said, frowning. "I've been alive for twenty-one years, and I've never done anything like magic. I even tried when I was a kid. I find it very hard to believe that all this time I've been a sorceress and haven't known it."

"The atmosphere on Earth is not conducive to magic," Halryan said. "It took the combined efforts of six sorcerers to perform the simple charm to disguise you as the deceased child, when it could easily have been done here by an apprentice. And you, alone and untrained, would not have known what to look for. Besides," he said, smiling his nasty superior smile, "How else do you explain that you're suddenly fluent in Prendarian, so fluent you didn't even realize you were speaking it?"

June thought about it for a moment, then realized doing so was giving her a headache, and moved on. "Okay, what about the tablet?" she said. "How many pieces are we talking here, and how far?"

"There are three pieces," Halryan said, (here June breathed a sigh of relief; she had been envisioning hundreds of pieces scattered everywhere) "but as for their locations, all we know is they are somewhere within the boundaries of the kingdom."

"Oh, okay," June said, feeling better. How big could a kingdom be? The way the stories read from feudal times in England, they really didn't seem to be bigger than a county, or a small state. She caught the blue men trying unsuccessfully to hide smiles. "What?" June asked, suspicious.

Halryan, too, was trying to hide a smile at her obvious relief. "Prendawr," he said, "is about the size of your America."

June sighed again. "Great," she said sarcastically. "But all I have to do is find those pieces, put them together, read a spell, and I'm done?"

"Well, you still must regain your throne..." Halryan stopped as June shook her head.

"Uh-uh, no way," she said. "I find your rocks, I save your world, and then I am *leaving.*" Halryan opened his mouth to protest, but she cut him off. "I have a life at home, and I'm not going to give it up to settle here in Prendower, or whatever." *Listen to yourself! Are you seriously considering this? Not only considering it, but actually accepting it?*

Oddly enough, she was. Even though it sounded like the plot of some low-budget movie, even though she kept waiting for Halryan to point to the ancient cast-iron stove and say, "Smile...you're on Candid Camera," even though she wanted more than anything not to believe him, somehow she knew Halryan was telling the truth. Or, he was so dangerously delusional he really believed it was the truth. Given those two options, June wasn't sure which she preferred.

"Prendawr," Halryan corrected, but he made no move to argue further. June found it surprising he ceded the point so easily, but she'd never been one to look a gift horse in the mouth.

"When do we leave?" June asked.

"Tomorrow," Halryan said. "After the midday meal."

June nodded slowly and stood. All four of the men at the table sprang up, which irritated her for some reason.

"I'm not going to run off on you or anything," June said, "but you just dropped a lot on me here, and I need to sit down and work it out by myself somewhere. Is that the door to the outside?" Halryan nodded, reluctant to let June go, but she hurried out before he could protest.

The sun was just going down, and June realized she'd been unconscious all night and all day. Looking to her left, she saw a wooden bench facing the sunset. She sat down Indian-style, rubbing her hands over her strange, dark arms.

Unable to look at herself any longer, she directed her gaze across the landscape. Despite the fact that her entire existence had been turned upside down, and she could no longer trust her eyes, ears or any of her senses, she couldn't ignore the beauty before her.

The cottage sat on a hill, looking down on the field she had first appeared in, carpeted with tall reddish grass rippling in the breeze. A deeply rutted dirt road wound through the grass and off into the forbidding wall of trees. From her higher vantage point, June could see that it was an immense forest, the end of which extended completely beyond her range of vision. The sun slowly sank behind bluish mountains so distant, the peaks blurred into the sky. Watching the sun sinking below the horizon, June herself sank into the quagmire of emotion that had threatened to engulf her since waking an hour before.

She thought about Ashleigh and Shannon, calling this morning to mock her hangover, worrying as the day passed with no return call. Letting themselves in the building with the emergency key June had given them, finding her door open, apartment empty, no note, no trace, answering machine still blinking. Kyle, returning home to a police investigation, utterly bewildered at her disappearance. How would she feel, if something similar had happened to him, or Shannon or Ashleigh?

At least her parents wouldn't be worrying. For the first time, she found herself relieved they were gone, happy she didn't have to picture them standing together in the middle of her apartment, clutching each other, their eyes searching for some clue to where June had gone.

Happy, too, they had died never having to question if the daughter they raised was the daughter they had borne.

June sank deeper into her reverie. She'd come out here, meaning to work out all the information she'd been given, formulate a plan...but every time she tried to lay it out in a way that made sense, her house of cards collapsed in fluttering chaos. Finally, she gave up and let her brain sink into disjointed confusion.

As the dusk deepened and stars winked out above her, June stared ahead, almost as unaware of the change from day to night as of the tears flowing down her cheeks. Suddenly, a hand on her shoulder jerked her from her trance, and she leapt off the bench and whirled around with a squawk to face the intruder.

"Your Highness, I..." One of the Val-whatevers stood behind the bench, the one who had helped her to her seat, an expression of mixed alarm and dismay on his face. "I'm sorry–I called out..." June, meanwhile, had collapsed on the ground, trying in vain to massage the pins and needles out of her legs, which had fallen asleep after too long in one cramped position.

"It's okay," she said, through gritted teeth, kneading her calves. "I was just–thinking really hard, I didn't hear you. Not your fault."

The prickling sensation began to subside. Leaning back on her hands, she straightened her legs to encourage circulation and wiggled her feet. She rubbed one hand over her face to try and wake herself up, and found her cheeks damp. After regarding her wet hand stupidly for a moment, she wiped it on her pants and looked back up at her visitor, who eyed her cautiously, like a bomb that could go off any minute.

"Halryan asked me to come check on you, since–" he gestured up at the night sky, "and to see if you needed anything."

"No, I think I'm okay...what's your name again?" June asked, flexing one leg experimentally and wincing at a fresh spike of pain.

"Koen, Your Highness," he answered, with a small bow. June tried not to laugh.

"Okay, well, my name's June. Not 'Your Highness,' just...June." He bowed slightly to acknowledge her, and she closed her eyes and sighed.

"Look, I don't mean to be rude or anything," she continued, trying not to offend him, since he was obviously trying to be polite. "I don't think anyone's ever bowed to me before, and it makes me really uncomfortable. Just treat me like you would anyone else. Please." June watched him struggle to restrain himself to a simple nod. She tried not to smile at his effort, but couldn't help it. He noticed her grin and returned it sheepishly.

"So, uh, June, is there anything I can get for you?" Koen asked.

"No, thank you. Oh, wait, yes, actually. You know the bag I had when I got here? Do you know where it is?" Koen nodded. "Can you bring it out here to me?" With another barely restrained bow, he turned and trotted back to the cottage. While he was gone, June got to her feet, walking creakily in a circle to work out the last few kinks. She interlaced her fingers and pushed her palms up over her head, feeling the stretch in her shoulders.

Tilting her head back, she gasped as she caught sight of the sky, a velvety bluish-black, filled with millions of stars, shining brighter than she'd ever thought possible. To her further amazement, she saw two moons, in slightly different stages of wax and wane, shedding an eerie silvery light on the red grass of the field. She plopped back down on the bench, unable to take her eyes off the sight even as Koen returned with her purse.

"Is the sky always like this?" June asked, and from the casual way he looked up, she knew it was.

"Like what, Your–June?" he asked, puzzled.

June smiled. *Imagine having something like this to take for granted.* "Never mind." Tearing her eyes away from the sky, she took the proffered purse and dug furiously for her cigarettes and lighter. Pulling a cigarette out, she flicked the lighter and was about to bring the flame to the tip when Koen gave a gasp of astonishment.

"What?" June said, jerking the cigarette out of her mouth and looking around in alarm. Koen, however, pointed a finger at her.

"You *are* a sorceress," he said, sounding slightly awed.

"Pardon?" asked June, confused.

"The fire," he said, still pointing. "You made fire in your hand."

"Ohhh," she said, understanding. "It's not magic, it's a lighter. Here, watch." Replacing the cigarette in her mouth, she first held up the lighter and then lit it by exaggeratedly flicking the wheel. Sucking smoke gratefully deep into her lungs, she handed the lighter to Koen to try. He peered curiously at it, spinning the wheel experimentally, and jumping when it threw a spark.

"Careful, don't burn yourself. Here," June said, leaning over and showing him how to flick the wheel while making sure the thumb depressed the butane pedal. After only two tries, Koen succeeded in sustaining a flame, which illuminated a delighted smile on his face. June smiled back. "Pretty cool, huh?" she said.

"But how does it work?"

"Well, the metal wheel strikes against a tiny flint inside," she said, taking the lighter from him and flicking the wheel without activating the butane so he could see the spark, "and there's gas inside, that the spark lights into fire." Here she pressed the lever only, so he could hear the hiss of escaping gas.

"Gas?" he asked, brow creased.

"Yeah, gas, like, um..." June's hands waved, trying to think of a way to explain gas to someone who had obviously never taken Earth Science. "Like a fart," she finished finally, and was amused that even in the darkness she could see his face darken. "But a different kind of gas." She gave him a moment to get his face rearranged properly and concentrated on her cigarette. After he got himself back under control, she patted the bench beside her. "Have a seat," she said, and after a nervous glance back at the cottage, he did, although as far from her as possible.

Without being too obvious, she took a moment to study him. He was short, at least by Earth guy standards, perfectly level with her five-two when standing. Earlier, when they were all standing at the table, his companions had been approximately the same height, so June guessed this must be a trait of the race. Other than that, he seemed a perfectly normal man, and actually a very attractive one, fit, with strong, handsome features and nicely shaped eyes, the exact color of which she couldn't make out in the moonlight. Perfectly normal, except for...

"I hope you won't think I'm being rude or anything, I'm just curious, but—your skin, is it really..."

"Blue? Yes," he said, but June thought she suddenly detected bitterness in his tone. "Why, don't you have blue people where you grew up?"

"No," June said. "Brown and black and red and yellow, but no blue." She smiled, trying to lighten the suddenly tense atmosphere. "I think out of all the colors, though, blue is definitely the most interesting."

Koen was silent for a moment. "Do they get along?" he asked quietly.

June snorted. "No," she said. "Not by a long shot."

Silence fell between them once again. Unable to think of anything to say, June lit another cigarette.

"That's an interesting way of using tobacco," Koen said, his tone of voice once more light and conversational.

"Most people where I come from use it this way," June said, thankful to be back on steady ground with him. She held the cigarette in front of her, contemplating its glowing tip in the darkness. "It's not very good for you, but," she shrugged, "even living will get you killed sometime."

Koen laughed. "That's very true," he said, smiling. They fell into a much more comfortable silence than a moment before. June looked up at the sky, and Koen pointed out some of the constellations for her and shared their legends. When she stomped out her second cigarette, Koen looked toward the cottage.

"You may want to get some rest," he said. "We won't leave till after midday, but we have a lot to do in the morning."

June nodded and followed Koen back to the house, exchanged polite goodnights with the rest of the men and Halryan, and went to her room. *This is pretty silly,* she thought, as she lay down on the hammock. *Like I'm really going to be able to get to sleep after all these goings-on.*

An instant later, she was out.

~3~

A soft knock on the door the next morning awakened her. Panicked, unable to remember where she was or how she got there, June made to leap from the hammock, got her legs tangled, and landed on the floor with a bone-crunching *thump*! Thankfully, no one seemed to have heard the noise in the hallway, and she got to her feet, slightly bruised, but without the indignity of witnesses. June brushed herself off, (getting a small jolt at her appearance) finger-combed the tangles out of her hair, and marched down the hall into the kitchen.

First she noticed Koen must have passed on the no-standing, no-bowing message, for two of the men began to rise, but stopped themselves, doing a sort of silly hop in their seats. Koen caught her eye, smiled, and shrugged, as if to say, *well, they're working on it.*

June hung in the doorway, unsure what to do next, but the man next to Koen, the one with the dark reddish-brown hair, beckoned her with a polite nod. "Have a seat," he said, indicating the empty bench beside him. "You must be hungry."

June's stomach gave a ferocious growl in answer, and she had to restrain herself from running to the table. As she sat down, she realized she hadn't had a thing to eat in over twenty-four hours. It seemed like a lot more than a day—more like a million years.

Looking at the table, however, her stomach lurched with both hunger and dismay. Except for the bread, she recognized nothing. Bowls and plates full of strange fruits and what may have been cheese covered the tabletop, but she had no idea how to eat any of it, or how it tasted. Fear of embarrassment overcame her ferocious hunger, and she reached out and put a single slice of bread on her plate, regarding it mournfully. Consoling herself that she'd been meaning to drop five pounds anyway, she ripped the bread into small pieces and chewed slowly, in a futile attempt to convince her stomach she was feeding it more than she actually was.

The man beside her (M-something?) offered her a bowl full of unfamiliar fruits.

"Please, help yourself," he said. June, smiling nervously, selected a red fruit out of the bowl and placed it on her plate. She regarded it dubiously, painfully aware of being watched. The skin was textured, like an avocado or orange, but softer. Should she cut it?

Peel it? June had herself quite worked up when one of the men, the one with the scar on his cheek, selected another of the same fruits, and with a meaningful glance at her, bit straight into it.

June exhaled, giving him a grateful look, and did the same. It was the best thing she'd ever tasted, *but then*, she reflected, *that may be because I'm starving*. Now, however, the ice was broken, and they all had a wonderful time watching June eat the exotic (to her, anyway) foods. All were tolerable, most wonderful, with the notable exception of Eckthrop cheese. Her gagging reaction had the men nearly rolling on the floor, as June attempted to drink a cup of water to rinse her mouth while trying simultaneously not to vomit or giggle.

Between bites, she managed to memorize their names. The dark-haired twins were Errigal and Feoras, Errigal being the one with the scar on his cheek who had shown her how to eat the fruit. Minogan was the one who had beckoned her to sit, and Koen she already knew.

After June proclaimed she couldn't eat another bite, the men got up and began clearing the table. She tried to help, but they respectfully shooed her away, so she walked into the sitting area, near the front door, examining objects on shelves and peering out the window. As she circled, June spotted the mirror, face down on the seat she'd occupied the previous afternoon. Unable to stop herself, she picked it up and sat down to examine her face once more.

She felt a sense of loss. Every trace of the family who had raised her was gone from her features. June realized she would never see her mother's chin or her father's nose again, at least not here. It removed them from her even further than their deaths had. Suddenly, they were just strangers, linked by nothing but circumstance.

June also had the sense of being violated, of something private and valuable being stolen from her. It may not have been the prettiest, or the most unique, but it was her face. She'd had it from childhood, watched it grow and change, and had no reason to expect she wouldn't continue on for the rest of her life with it. Closer than the closest friend, it had been with her through everything, every hour, every day. June watched tears stream from her oddly shaped eyes, down over foreign cheeks and chin. She looked up to see Koen standing in front of her, head cocked to one side, a sympathetic expression on his blue face.

"I can't even imagine how strange that must be," he said softly.

"Stranger than anything so far, if you can believe it," June said, laughing through her tears. She held the mirror up once more and sighed. "The hair is the same," she added, pulling a curl of her dark hair straight, then releasing it, watching it snap back in the mirror. "Probably the only thing I would have been happy to change, too."

"My sisters would have killed for hair like yours," Koen said. "They used to wrap it up in rags at night, to try to get it curly."

"Ha," said June, raking her fingers through her hair, "I give them a week with this mop. The novelty would wear off real quick, I assure you." She looked back up at Koen, meaning to continue, but stopped, momentarily startled. She hadn't really gotten a look at his eyes earlier, had just assumed they were brown or hazel or something similarly mundane, but they were a startling, vibrant sea-green. Koen cleared his throat and shifted his weight, confused by her stare. June shook herself, speaking quickly to cover her embarrassment. "So, you have sisters, huh? How many?"

Koen opened his mouth to respond, but an interruption in the form of Halryan swooped through the front door, carrying a large cloth-wrapped bundle, which he deposited at June's feet. She barely restrained a moan of disappointment at his appearance—she'd already learned Halryan equaled unpleasantness. June could feel a sobering of spirits in the others, who stood stiffly, facing Halryan as he bowed to her. Obviously, he'd missed the memo on bowing.

"Your clothing, my lady," he said, waiting expectantly.

"My what?" June asked, leaning over and prodding the package.

"Your clothing. I thought you might require something more appropriate to wear for travel, perhaps something that wouldn't raise so many questions."

June looked down at the sleeveless, sparkly, very low-cut shirt she'd chosen with such care the night before last, then the skin-tight jeans, and she felt her face flush. *Oh my God*, June thought, *what did they think of me when I showed up? They must have thought I was a hooker or something.* "Okay, um, I'll go change."

She left the mirror on the chair and returned to her room. With a baleful glance at the hammock, remembering her less-than-graceful dismount this morning, she set the package down on a stool and began unwrapping it.

Nearly half an hour later, she emerged, strode into the kitchen to face Halryan, and said angrily, "I am not wearing this." Koen and the others turned to look at her, and with the exception of Halryan, their jaws dropped.

The lower half of June's body was smothered in two layers of thick skirt, a petticoat, and a dark brown overskirt. The top of the outfit, however, was the real problem.

It had taken some time for June to figure out how all the pieces went together, since she wasn't used to such complex layers. When she had finally figured it out, she couldn't believe it. In fact, she was sure she had it on backwards, until she realized that turning it around wouldn't have done any good.

June wore a corset-like garment, like a tank top, with a lace up front and boning, over a peasant blouse. Both the items were so low-cut that no matter how loosely she tied the laces, her breasts, already fairly large (her curves, like her hair, had stuck around), spilled precariously over the top. June knew without trying that raising her arms would court disaster. Between fighting indecent exposure and trying not to trip over her full skirts, she could barely move.

"Is there a problem?" Halryan asked impassively. Behind him, Feoras gave a small snort, which earned him a sharp glance from Halryan. June blinked at Halryan, stunned incredulity on her face.

"A problem?" Her eyes widened. "Yes, there's a problem. I look like a prostitute."

Feoras, Errigal, and Koen were all clearing their throats, eyes averted–Minogan was apparently checking the ceiling for leaks.

"I am sorry you feel that way, my lady," Halryan said, now radiating annoyance, "but there is no time to get you garments that are more to your taste."

"Halryan," June said, using every bit of self-control she had to keep her voice calm, "I can't move. I can't breathe. Look," she said, raising her arms as far as she dared (the Valforte, having just dared to glance back at June, started in alarm at the sight of her rising chest and quickly turned away again). "How am I supposed to travel in an outfit like this? And forget walking, with these skirts." She looked thoughtfully at the Valforte. "Are there any spare clothes like that around?" she asked, thinking their clothing was the closest she'd get to jeans and a T-shirt around here.

"My lady," Halryan said, with an air of long-suffering patience, "putting you in men's' clothing would be entirely unacceptable."

"Why?" June asked, a note of challenge in her voice.

"Because, my lady, we are undertaking a dangerous mission which must be completed with utmost discretion, and a woman traveling the countryside in men's clothing would attract an unwanted amount of attention."

"Helll-oooo," June said, pointing at her chest. "You don't think this is going to attract attention? Especially when I go to scratch my head and my entire chest pops out? Look, I'll wear a loose shirt, I'll keep my hair tied back, and if we know we're going to be near people, I'll put the skirt on." Seeing Halryan's face still stony and unimpressed, she added sarcastically, "Besides, no one's going to take their eyes off your outfit long enough to even notice whether I'm a boy or a girl." Halryan's eyes narrowed and his nostrils flared as all four Valforte burst once more into coughing fits.

June one, Halryan zero, she thought, as Halryan snapped at Errigal to go and check for spare clothes.

Comfortably outfitted in trousers, linen shirt, and ankle-high moccasin-boots, June rejoined the Valforte in the kitchen, and together they headed outside.

"Can you ride?" Minogan asked as they walked toward a barn behind the cottage.

"Well, yes..." June said apprehensively. She'd owned her own horse up until college, but she had reason to be a little worried....

They rounded the corner, coming into full view of the paddock, which held half a dozen horses and mules.

"Oh thank God," June said, with a sigh of relief.

"What's wrong?" Koen asked.

"Oh, just glad...nothing, never mind," She'd been concerned ever since peering out a window earlier and seeing a goatlike creature with three humps, like a camel, tied to a shed. Thankfully, the horses were just...horses. Halryan ducked through the fence into the paddock.

"I procured these horses early this morning, for our journey," he said, (June wondered fleetingly if he ever spoke without the disgusting self-important tone), "and I took special care to select a suitable steed for you." Weaving into the herd, he grasped the halter of the largest animal and led it forward.

"Oh," said June. "Oh, my." The enormous grey horse blinked benignly down at June from about three feet above her head. Well over six feet tall at the shoulder, the animal reminded her of a medieval war charger, with dinner-plate sized feet supporting a solidly muscled frame. It had a torso so thick she'd practically have to do a split to get her legs around it. And as good a rider as June was, and as gentle as he looked, if she and the horse had a difference of opinion on speed or direction...

June slipped through the fence and approached the horse, hand out, palm down and fingers dangling. The horse reached forward and sniffed her hand, meek as a kitten, and June turned her hand over flat and allowed it to lick the salt from her palm as she reached up (way up) to scratch its neck. With a sigh, she turned back to Halryan.

"Halryan," she said, slowly, "I'm really sorry, but...I can't ride this horse. He's way too big for me. I won't be able to get on him without help, and I'll be in trouble if he decides to bolt." June waited for a moment as this sank in, Halryan's nostrils flaring as reality struck home.

"He's a really beautiful animal, though," she said, hurriedly, "and he's got a great temperament. Maybe you could ride him?" June suddenly felt bad for Halryan. In the past hour, he'd offered her two things, clothing and a horse...and she'd turned down both.

Releasing the grey with a pat on the shoulder, she watched him trot slowly back to the herd, and scanned the other animals. One in particular caught her eye, a mule, but a small one, nicely proportioned, with a shining coat and clean, strong lines. June walked around it, looking up and down for flaws.

"This little jenny should be good," she said, scratching the bay between her ears, which June could actually reach.

"That," said Halryan, "is a mule."

"Which is perfect, since we're going on a long-distance trek. Is she saddle-broke?" June's eyes flicked to Minogan, who nodded. "Perfect. This is our girl, then." Halryan's eyebrows furrowed, though, and June looked to him with a sigh. "What?" she asked.

"Do you really think it's appropriate for a princess to go traipsing around the countryside on a mule?" he asked, voice dripping with incredulous snobbery.

"What's wrong with a mule?" June asked, confused. "It's just a long-eared, sturdier horse."

"My lady," Halryan said, with a tone of condescension in his voice that immediately got June's dander up, "I know you were raised as a peasant, but there are certain rules of decorum you must consider for a woman of your status."

June's guilt for treating Halryan badly evaporated like a water droplet on a hot griddle.

"Well, unless you want to go back wherever you 'procured' these horses and get me another one that's actually my size, she's going to have to do," She patted the mule, who she had mentally dubbed Rosie, and headed out of the paddock.

This should be interesting, she thought. *The guy's already on my last nerve, and I've got to travel God knows how long and far with him.* June sighed, glancing over her shoulder at the boys, who still stood at the fence, exchanging amused glances. At least she seemed to have allies in them.

The next few hours passed both too slowly and too quickly. Halryan had disappeared yet again, and the boys were packing supplies into saddlebags and sacks and piling them outside by the paddock. They moved quickly, but carefully, checking and double-checking supply lists. June supposed if they forgot something, it would be a long time before they'd get to a town to replenish supplies. She was frustrated, though—no one would let her help at all, waving her politely away any time she moved to carry or pack anything. Apparently the rules could be bent on stuff like bowing and titles, but they wouldn't let a princess fetch and carry. Which was unfortunate, because considering her current state of mind, she really could have used the distraction.

So she ended up back on her little bench, watching the bustle from afar, peering curiously down at the small village off in the distance behind the hill the house sat on, smoking too many cigarettes (she was trying to ration—by a stroke of luck she'd gotten a buy-two-get-one-free deal in the afternoon before her little trip, and she'd only smoked a few, but still, she needed to be careful) and trying very, very hard not to think too hard about the goings-on of the past day-and-a-half. And sighing. She was doing an awful lot of sighing.

Finally, Feoras called her for lunch, and she went in to join the others. The mood at the table was grimmer than it had been this morning; for the most part, everyone just kept their eyes on their plates. And, despite the lunch spread being even more impressive than breakfast, everyone just played with their food, unable to bring themselves to eat.

June was getting very nervous. No one seemed to want to leave the table, though they'd all obviously lost their appetites. After a lot of uncomfortable shuffling, Minogan cleared his throat and stood. This seemed to be the signal, and everyone stood and began clearing the table. Once more, June tried to help, but was politely shooed away.

So she went outside for another cigarette, to give her trembling hands something to do. The emotional tightrope she walked was getting shakier and shakier. Not for the first time today, she wondered exactly how much a person could take before they lost their mind.

June was so lost in thought, she didn't even notice Halryan standing in front of the bench until she almost ran into him. He regarded her coolly with his icy-blue stare, but she refused to drop her gaze. For the second time, she felt as though this was a battle she had to win. Finally, Halryan spoke.

"Do you have any questions?" he asked.

June did in fact have one question, but she hesitated to ask it. She looked past Halryan, off into the trees, considering. Then she turned back to the sorcerer.

"What if–" June paused, licking her lips nervously, "What if I refused to do this? Just said flat-out no?"

"Then every living thing on this world would be destroyed." Seeming to read her mind, he nodded over her shoulder. "Including them." June looked at her feet, biting her lip, and nodded.

"Anything else?" Halryan asked, and June shook her head. Without another word, he moved past her and went inside the cottage.

June sat down on the bench and lit a cigarette with shaking fingers. "Damn," she said under her breath, "*damndamndamn*." She watched as Minogan, Koen, Errigal, and Feoras all walked out to the paddock and began loading the packs onto the animals, but turned away quickly, unable to look at the kind strangers whose lives were now her responsibility.

June tilted her head back and exhaled a cloud of smoke straight up into the air as she watched a few wispy clouds drift by in a sky just the perfect shade of blue, and wondered in amazement at how quickly life can drop one on one's head. The day her parents had died felt similar to this...but at least then, she had some familiar things to cling to, like her friends. Now she felt like some kind of cosmic castaway, shipwrecked and alone, expected to survive in a world–and a reality– completely foreign to everything she'd ever known.

June dropped her chin to her chest, and for maybe the millionth time today, sighed. She tried to reconcile herself to the task at hand, to convince herself this whole situation was like a giant bandage; the sooner she got it done, the less painful it would be. But she didn't want to rip off the bandage, and she didn't want to go on a quest.

What she really wanted to do was crawl into her own bed, pull the covers over her head, and take the longest nap in history. Or, as a second option, throw herself down on the grass and have a screaming, kicking tantrum. She most certainly did not want to traverse the kingdom of Prendawr on muleback in search of ancient bits of rock.

Stomping her cigarette out violently, June looked over at the paddock. It looked like they were ready to go. The pack animals were fully loaded, the riding animals saddled, including June's small mule, and the Valforte stood back surveying them, hands on hips, looking for anything they had missed. June swiped her face clean of tears, took a shaky breath, and got up.

As much as she dreaded this trip, her journey into the unknown, she was glad it was finally time to go, because at least she'd be doing something. All this sitting around invited deep thoughts and pity parties, none of which were doing her any good. *Just get moving, get it over with, and then go the hell home.*

June had packed her personal effects in a small saddlebag. Sadly, all she had were her cigarettes and lighter, and two pictures, one of Shannon and Ashleigh, another of Kyle. Everything else she left behind, other than the engagement ring which never left her finger. She didn't think anyone would need to see her driver's license, she hadn't seen any ATM's, so she could leave her check card, and she definitely had no use for her cell phone (although she had checked to see if it had service, just for giggles–obviously, it didn't).

Halryan had insisted she bring the horrible clothes he had bought, and she grudgingly acquiesced, mainly to avoid more conversation with him. Her dislike of him was more than just a matter of clashing personalities; it was something deeper, a visceral reaction that occurred every time he walked into her range of vision, every time she even thought of him. Maybe it was just the fact it was he who had disturbed her existence, by whisking her across the universe to this godforsaken place, but June felt fairly sure she wouldn't be warming up to the man anytime soon.

As they began mounting their horses, Koen offered her a leg up, but June waved him away politely, swinging with practiced ease onto Rosie's back. As she adjusted her stirrups, her knee bumped into the sword and scabbard attached to the front of her saddle. Despite her protestations, since she had no idea how to use a sword, they had still insisted she carry it. June didn't like it; its presence on the saddle reminded her of the impending danger. At least they didn't try to press bow and arrow on her, like they carried. Smart move, too, considering the whole of her archery experience consisted of an hour at Girl Scout camp when she was nine.

Koen, now mounted, pulled his horse up alongside hers.

"Are you all right?" he asked, peering into her face. "You look pale." June shot him an "oh come on" look, and Koen grinned sheepishly. "Well, okay, I guess you're a little nervous," he said, shrugging. June raised her eyebrows, but said nothing. Her mouth was so dry, she didn't dare speak.

Koen himself wasn't exactly looking relaxed, either; his shoulders were tense, and when he looked away from June, his expression hardened into one of grim determination, mirrored by the other three Valforte.

Halryan, on the giant grey horse intended for June, waited at the head of the line for everyone to finish adjusting their reins and saddles. When Minogan nodded to him, Halryan turned back and urged his horse forward, and they all fell in behind him. June, who was wondering if a stress-induced heart attack was possible at her age, hummed "We're off to See the Wizard," under her breath, trying to lighten her mood.

It didn't work.

Down the hill they went, to meet with the road June had noticed earlier, the one leading into the woods. They had fallen into formation now; Halryan at the head of the column, followed by Errigal and Feoras, riding abreast, then June, then Minogan and Koen, also abreast, with the pack animals on long leads behind. The protective nature of the formation was not lost on June, and she shivered, goosebumps up and down her arms despite the warmth of the day.

The closer they came to the woods, the taller the trees towered. When at last they entered, each tree stood at least as high as a twenty-story building, with possibly sixty-foot circumference trunks, and June was fairly sure that wasn't hyperbole.

Normally, she loved trees, and went walking and hiking as often as she could. But as the forest closed in around them, womblike, she realized she had never been in a forest like this before. A quarter-mile in, the light dwindled to a deep greenish dusk, though it was only around two in the afternoon. And the silence pressed in on them from all sides, so the sound of a small animal rustling in the leaves made them jump like a gun had gone off.

June twisted around in her saddle to look at Minogan and Koen's faces. They sat straight in their saddles, eyes darting to and fro (though Koen gave her a quick smile when he saw her looking at them, which she returned) but they didn't seem nervous, just watchful, so June allowed herself to relax a bit as the hours passed.

As night began to fall, a sudden noise to June's left made her pull Rosie to a halt. The others had heard it too, and stopped as she did. From the woods, about a hundred yards from the road by June's guesstimate, came the sound of a child, crying as though his heart would break.

Bewildered, June looked to the Valforte for an explanation. The men, however, were busy notching arrows to their bowstrings, and Halryan backed his horse away from the sound, behind Errigal and Feoras.

"What–" June whispered, but Minogan held up his hand,

gesturing for silence, never taking his eyes off the woods. They all sat motionless as the child's crying intensified to a keening wail, pain evident in every note. It sounded as though someone had red-hot pokers pressed to the bottoms of the poor thing's feet. Finally, June could no longer stand it.

"For God's sake," she said, swinging her leg over Rosie's back, feet landing in the dirt with a thump, "are you going to do something, or are we just going to sit here and listen to it get killed?" Without giving anyone a chance to respond, she strode purposefully toward the source of the sound.

"June, don't," cried Koen, and something in his voice stopped her dead in her tracks. Staring into the gloom, she gasped as a pair of eyes glowed suddenly in the shadows, locking with her own. Green, piercing eyes, huge, advancing on her slowly, like a tiger stalking a deer. Whatever this was, though, it was bigger than a tiger...judging by the distance between the glowing eyes and the ground, at least the size of a bear.

Then it stood up.

June stumbled backwards, bumping into Rosie, who snorted, but held her ground. Sheer terror wiped every thought from her head as the creature continued to advance. As it emerged from the gloom, June's terror slipped sideways into something as yet unnamed.

The creature stood upright, like a man, but there all resemblance ended. All twelve feet of it was covered in shaggy grayish-black hair, and a stench of rotting meat preceded it. The back legs were like a dog's, with paws rather than feet, between which a tail, also doglike, waved slowly.

Its massive torso widened to a barrel-shaped chest, and its arms were taut with ropy muscles, ending with three cruelly hooked claws. The head rose straight from the shoulders with no defined neck, topped with rounded ears, like a lion's.

The face was the worst, though, for it was wolflike, with a tapered snout, but completely without skin, leaving all the tendons and muscles clearly visible, tensing and tightening as the jaws flexed. But most horrible of all was the sound pouring forth from the mouth– the sound of a crying child–as it continued to advance on June.

Without warning, four arrows struck the beast in the neck and chest. It screamed in its sickening child's voice, causing June to clap her hands over her ears, unable to take her eyes away as the monster rounded on her companions. Errigal, looking for a better shot, had edged around behind the animal, and he became the creature's target.

It charged.

"NO," June screamed, and it froze, turning to look at her once more. This time, however, she swore she saw fear in its eyes as it dropped to all fours. June forced herself to hold eye contact, focusing on the uncertainty in the animal's unnatural face. The Valforte had frozen as well, their eyes fixed on the silent drama now unfolding.

June's mind whirled with uncertainty as she tried to think of what to do next. The only remotely similar experience she'd ever had was at the age of twelve, walking home from Ashleigh's house. She'd surprised a stray dog, all bones and dirty fur, nosing in an overturned garbage can, and it had turned on her, hackles raised and teeth bared.

Maybe....

"Bad dog," June shouted, trying to force anger and dominance into her voice. She stepped forward on shaking legs and drew herself up to her full height. "Bad dog! Bad! Geddoudahere! Git!" She clapped her hands loudly at the creature, which flinched and lowered its head warily. "SHOO! Bad dog!"

Gaining confidence, since she hadn't been eaten yet, June picked up a stick and waved it threateningly. "Git!" She hurled the stick, which struck the beast on the shoulder. It yelped, a child's exclamation of pain, turned tail, and sprinted off into the forest.

There was a full minute of stunned silence before anyone found their voice again.

"Huh," said June. She stared, blinking, at the trees where the creature had disappeared. Shaking herself slightly, she turned to see if everyone was all right. Everyone looked fine, except for their jaws, which seemed to have come unhinged. Even Halryan's face was white and shocked.

"What?" said June, uncomfortably, as they all stared. It was a stupid question, she knew perfectly well what.

"Four arrows." Minogan shook his head, without taking his eyes off her. "Four."

"And you threw a stick at it," said Feoras, his voice full of awe.

"Well, maybe it had some kind of childhood trauma involving a stick," June said, trying to be funny and break the mood. "Oh, c'mon, guys, it probably just never had anyone yell at it before. Or I smell funny, because I'm from someplace else. Animals are weird."

"Actually, draeks like it when you yell," Koen said. "The more you scream and carry on, the harder they come at you."

"Was that what that was?" June asked. "A draek?" They all nodded, grimly.

Halryan cleared his throat. "We may as well camp here," he said. Looking around, June realized the forest had gotten darker, the faces of her traveling companions blurry in the dim greenish light.

"What if that thing comes back?" June asked

"Keep a stick handy, just in case," said Koen, smiling, and the others laughed. June tried not to smile, but her face betrayed her. The men began to make camp, unloading cooking and sleeping supplies from the animals and gathering firewood. June tried to help once more, but was politely but firmly rebuffed, and sat huffily on a nearby log to watch.

She soon became aware, however, that Halryan stood nearby, watching her. Her still-frayed nerves left her in no mood for his head games tonight.

"What?" June snapped, turning to face him.

The sharp tone of her voice did nothing to diminish the smug look on his face. "You do realize why the draek turned away, don't you?" he asked, and June shrugged, feigning nonchalance.

"I've never been one to look a gift horse in the mouth," she lied. Actually, she was very curious. She didn't know much about this world, but she did know there was no logical reason that animal should have backed down from her.

Luckily, Halryan was on a roll, and paid no attention to June's comment. "It saw you for what you are," he said.

He was being (June thought) deliberately mysterious. She really didn't want to play along, but if she wanted answers, she'd have to give a little.

"And what am I?" she asked, trying to keep the annoyance out of her voice with little success. Thankfully, Halryan wasn't very sensitive to nuances.

"A sorceress," he said, and June snorted. "You may scoff," he continued "but the draek heard the power in your voice. It didn't dare disobey."

God, did he actually just say 'scoff' out loud? "Whatever," June said. She'd been hoping for something new, rather than the same 'you are the chosen one' b.s. She undid her braid, turning her head upside down to fluff out her hair.

"My lady, you must begin to take this power seriously. Practice, train yourself, or when the time comes—"

June whipped her head up, tossing her hair back, and looked at Halryan. "I said whatever," she said, coolly, cutting him off. Miffed, he strode off without another word. With a small ember of satisfaction glowing in her chest, June began combing her hair with the carved wood comb Koen had given her before they left.

The smile slowly faded, however, as once again she slipped deep into thought. She really hadn't paid this sorceress thing much attention. She'd been too busy dealing with having been kidnapped and given a new face and language. *No way am I a sorcerer,* she thought. *No way. I'd have found out by now. I would have conjured a roll of toilet paper when I was stuck on the john or gotten Ruben Stiles to ask me out in 8th grade. Something would have happened.*

And yet, a little voice inside her said, softly, *here you are, on another planet, princess of a kingdom you'd never laid eyes on. Everything you've ever known has been a lie. You are not the person you thought you were. Can you really say you would know? When for most of your life you haven't even known you?*

Koen rescued June from her inner torment by bringing her a cup of tea. He gestured to her log. "May I?" he asked.

"Please," she said, and he took a seat on her right. They both stared into the new fire for a few moments, sipping their fragrant herb tea in comfortable silence.

"We're sorry we didn't tell you about the draek," Koen said finally, looking at his cup. "We just–when you've lived somewhere for your whole life, you don't think that things might be strange to someone. You take for granted that everyone has the same as you."

"I'm not mad," June said. "I'm a little embarrassed, but not mad."

"Why are you embarrassed?" Koen said, cocking his head to the side.

"Well, I probably should have known something was up when you guys were drawing your weapons against the sound of a crying child," she said. "And I put everyone in danger, because I didn't pay attention."

Koen sighed, rotating his cup in smoothly calloused hands. "I've grown up with stories and warnings about draeks. I've even had cousins killed by them." Koen acknowledged June's exclamation of sympathy with a nod before continuing. "But, when I heard that crying this afternoon, I had a hard time stopping myself from running into the woods to save a child that I knew didn't exist. So did the others. That's why draeks never go hungry." He turned to look at June once more, his eyes a deep emerald in the firelight. "And also why you shouldn't be embarrassed. You wouldn't have any idea that noise was something other than a child in pain."

They both looked up to see Errigal, nodding in agreement with

Koen. June patted the log on her other side, and he sat, a mug of tea in his hand as well.

"I want to thank you for what you did today," Errigal said, a little self-consciously, his blue face darkening. "I'm sure my wife will be pleased I didn't manage to get myself killed the first day out."

"Well, I'm not actually sure I did—wait, you have a wife?" June asked. She hadn't seen any females in the cottage, and had just assumed that all the men were single.

Errigal smiled. "Feoras, too," he said, smiling. "To twin sisters."

June groaned. "Oh, God, what a cliché," she said, laughing.

Feoras, hearing his name, looked over from the fire. "Telling her about Mara and Sara?" he asked, pronouncing the names MAWra and SAWra. Errigal nodded, and Feoras chuckled. "I can always tell by the reaction," he said, turning back to stir the pot simmering over the flames.

Feeling emboldened by the good-natured vibe of the group, she asked, slyly, "So, is there ever any trouble telling each other apart?" Both brothers ducked their heads in embarrassment, and Koen shook with suppressed laughter beside her.

"I, um, I think it's better if we don't answer that one," Feoras said.

June shrieked gleefully as both Feoras and Errigal turned deeper shades of blue.

The laughter slowly died down as Feoras served the stew, hunger not allowing them to concentrate on anything other than stuffing their faces. After finishing her meal, June was broadsided by a leaden wave of exhaustion. *And no wonder*, she thought, thinking about the day she'd had.

Minogan brought her bedroll, which actually turned out to be just a blanket, barely big enough to wrap herself in. She lay down and closed her eyes, but something nagged at her, and try as she might, June couldn't get to sleep. It was the stupidest urge, but—

Kicking off her blanket, June stomped over to the fire, annoyed for actually giving in to this. She withdrew a fairly long, thin stick, waved it to extinguish the flames, then walked out just past where Minogan lay, his place being furthest from the fire. Pressing the charred end of the stick into the ground, she drew a circle, counterclockwise, by walking backwards around the campsite, making sure the horses were inside. When she came back around to the beginning, she connected the ends of the line, so it was one solid circle (or oval), then drove the stick into the point where she'd begun and ended her circle.

June stepped back momentarily, looking over her work, then walked slowly back to her blanket. She wasn't sure what exactly she had just done, but somehow, she knew everyone would be safe tonight. Looking across the fire, she saw Halryan was awake, watching her, that same smug look on his face. June pretended she didn't see him as she rolled herself back up in the thin wool.

He looks even stupider without the hat, June thought, and fell immediately to sleep.

~4~

June woke the next morning with a groan, both at the dawning awareness of her surroundings and her physical state. Every square inch of her body screamed obscenities. Her legs ached from grasping the horse, and her ass felt like raw hamburger. And her head–oh, her head–felt ready to split like an overripe pumpkin.

After laying for several moments with eyes closed, daggers jabbing the back of her eyeballs, she thought her head splitting might not actually be the worst thing in the world. It would take care of everything, anyway.

June listened to the others moving around her, and she knew she couldn't feign sleep much longer. She pushed herself into a sitting position, drawing her knees up to her chest. Moaning softly deep in her throat, she took another minute, resting her head on her knees.

She heard a soft noise next to her, and cracked an eyelid, tilting her head to see a cup now sitting beside her, full of steaming tea. She picked it up and took a few gulps. The bitter liquid revived her somewhat as it slid down her throat and into her stomach. She continued to sip for a few moments until the pain in her head subsided to a dull ache, with an occasional sharp stab if she moved her head too quickly. June finally stood up and stretched as much as her knotted muscles would allow, then pulled her hair back in a low, loose ponytail.

Everyone was already up, busily packing and loading the animals. She thought she'd missed breakfast, until she spotted a plate with a lump of cheese and some odd-looking cracker things balanced on a nearby log. She just barely managed to restrain herself from stuffing it all in her mouth at once. *God, I'm starving.*

Just think of all the calories you're burning, riding all day, June thought in a weak attempt to look at the bright side. Still, she supposed most people, having woken up on the forest floor of a distant planet, cold, soaked with dew, and in excruciating pain, wouldn't have bothered with the effort.

"Need help?" June called out to Feoras, who rushed by carrying a saddle.

"No, you just rest," he called back. June washed her last bite of cracker down with the dregs of tea, shuddering at the bitterness of the leaves which had fallen to the bottom of the cup. Halryan stood by his still barebacked horse, reading a piece of parchment, which left the four Valforte men to saddle and pack all six animals.

"Oh, screw this," June said, setting her cup down hard on the log and standing up. She walked over to Rosie, whose tack and saddlebags lay next to the tree she was tethered to. She spotted a currycomb and rag near a pile of supplies, and set to work, her practiced hands neatly grooming Rosie in less than five minutes. She found a short, stout stick on the forest floor, and had just begun to pick Rosie's hooves when Halryan rushed over.

"My lady," he said. "Please, this is not appr–" He stopped dead at the look on June's face as she straightened up to face him.

"If you'd like to get underway by noon," June said, steel in her voice, "then they need help. I've been taking care of horses all my life. I assure you, it doesn't bother me in the least."

"But if someone *saw* you, the princess, *cleaning hooves*..."

June looked around the clearing, deserted except for their party and flanked on every side by silent forest, and shook her head in exasperation before resuming her efforts, ignoring Halryan's continued protests. She had finished with all four hooves before he finally went away. As she arranged the saddle on Rosie's back, she became aware of all four of the Valforte watching her surreptitiously. With a sigh, she turned and faced them.

"Look," June said, "I appreciate that I'm supposed to be royalty or whatever, and I'm not supposed to be doing anything as far as work goes. But I've never had a servant before, and as nice as the idea is, it makes me uncomfortable. So, from now on, I'll take care of my own horse and some of the others if you're busy. And, for crying out loud," she said, "if I ask if you need help, and the answer is yes, then *please* give me something to do!"

Not waiting for a response, she turned back to Rosie and finished tightening the girth, then slipped the bridle on, adjusting the mule's forelock so the straps didn't pull the animal's hair. After a quick check to make sure everything was tight, without pinching or rubbing uncomfortably, she looked around at the boys.

"Need me to do anything?" June asked. They glanced nervously over at Halryan, who was distractedly saddling his horse while trying to watch June. She looked past them at what still needed doing. Two horses stood without saddles, and one needed its pack. "Whose horses are those?" June asked. Minogan and Koen raised their hands slightly. "Okay, how about you saddle your animals, Errigal and I finish packing this horse, and Feoras helps Halryan?" They all nodded and set to work, grateful, June thought, that they hadn't actually had to tell her to do anything.

Fifteen minutes later, they got underway. June could tell as she settled herself in the saddle that she had a long day ahead of her. No matter how she sat, she pressed on something bruised or chafed. Finally, around mid-morning, she gave up and dismounted stiffly, choosing to walk alongside Rosie and rest her tush. As she walked, she imagined being back home after this was over, scrubbing thick yellow calluses off her behind in the shower with a pumice stone, and smiled at the mental picture.

The smile soon faded, however. Thoughts of a hot shower led to thoughts of home. She couldn't help but picture Kyle and her friends talking to the police, giving a report, putting up "Missing" posters all around town. June could only imagine how they felt—she knew how she'd feel, were it one of them. Guilt overwhelmed her, even though it wasn't her fault, Kyle, Shannon, and Ashleigh were doubtless worried sick over her.

June returned to the present when Rosie stopped to avoid running into the backsides of the horses in front, which had also stopped. She stepped out to the side, looking past Errigal's horse. All she could see was Halryan, standing beside his mount, peering down at a small stream which crossed over the road they followed.

"Why did we stop?" June called out to Halryan. He turned to face her.

"My lady, would you be so kind as to tell us if this stream is safe?"

June narrowed her eyes cautiously. "Safe for what?" she asked, leading Rosie up to Halryan.

"Safe for drinking, so we may fill our waterskins," he said, like it was obvious. June looked at him, brow furrowed.

"And how do I do that?"

"By checking for poison and enchantments," Halryan said, again as if it were apparent.

"And how do I do that?" June asked again, voice carefully controlled, close to losing what little patience she had.

"You're a sorceress, my lady." The infuriating smug expression returned to his face. June rolled her eyes, shaking her head in disgust.

"Fine, whatever," Dropping Rosie's reins, she approached the stream. Feeling very self-conscious, with Halryan and the Valforte watching her, she knelt down and stretched a hand toward the water.

She'd meant to put her hand *into* the water, but it froze a few inches above the surface. A strange feeling came over her, and she turned her head to one side, trying to listen to the stream.

June closed her eyes, and her mind filled with an image of black and red, swirling together, like dye dropped in water. The colors *spoke* to her, if that were possible. *Death,* they said. *Pain. Madness. Death.* She watched the colors, fascinated, listening with an inner ear she'd never known she possessed.

A hand on her shoulder made her open her eyes, and she looked up to see Halryan hovering over her, a hungry gleam in his eye. June shrugged his hand off and stood, trying to hide how shaky she felt.

"Don't drink the water," June said, aiming her comments at the group in general. "Don't even touch it." Mounting Rosie quickly, she trotted her back to the end of the line, then turned toward the stream once more, urging her into a canter, which forced the mule to leap the stream.

June pulled Rosie up short on the other side and turned, nodding to the others, who followed her example. Once everyone was on the other side, they shuffled back into their original formation. June carefully avoided Halryan's gaze. *He did that on purpose. He knew perfectly well what was going to happen.*

The next several days passed without incident. They traveled at a steady pace, stopping for lunch, dinner, and sleep. June could see she was becoming less of a burden to the Valforte, and more of a companion. They opened up about their families, their lives, and childhoods.

Koen and Minogan, she learned, were cousins, and best friends since their births a few months apart, twenty-six years before. The twins were June's age, twenty-one, so before maturity closed the age gap, the four hadn't spent much time together as a group. Now, however, they were great friends, and spending time with them reminded June of Shannon and Ashleigh; lots of laughter, with a deep undercurrent of trust and respect.

June learned more about Halryan, too, but not through pleasant fireside conversation. Listening to him talk, the way he reacted to her and the Valforte, she found him a man governed by fear. Fear of embarrassment, punishment, death, pain, the unknown, life in general. And that worried her. She'd always been pretty good at figuring people out, at understanding what made them tick. If Halryan had just been a jerk, well, it would be annoying, but she could deal with it. But a coward like him could be volatile and dangerous, willing to do anything and sacrifice anyone to keep from facing his fears. Being forcibly tied to someone like him made her nervous.

She also thought constantly about home. How would she get back, and what would she find? And how in the world would she explain her disappearance? What could she possibly say that wouldn't raise suspicion, either with the police or with Kyle? She had to tell Ashleigh and Shannon the truth; they'd known her since grade school, and she couldn't lie to them. And she thought they'd believe her, too.

But Kyle...Kyle was a different story. He liked his facts cold and hard. June just didn't think he had the imaginative capacity to wrap his mind around a story like hers.

But here was the conundrum. The only story she could tell him and the police, without raising too many questions, is that she'd run away, stayed in a hotel under a false name or with an old made-up friend. If she said she'd been kidnapped, there'd be an investigation, and sooner or later they'd realize she'd lied. But to do that, to say she'd run away, would be to say she'd run away from *Kyle,* and she had a hard time believing he'd take that easily. It seemed even if she did make it back, she still ran the risk of losing him.

About seven days after leaving the cottage, the landscape began to change. The trees thinned, and the road appeared more worn, with smaller roads feeding into the one they followed. Toward late morning, Halryan turned his horse around to ride alongside June.

"We are coming up to Meckle, a good-sized town–" Halryan began, and June squealed with delight, cutting him off.

"A town? Oh-please-tell-me-we're-staying-overnight-I-need-a-bath-so-bad," June babbled, overcome with excitement. Halryan held up his hand, and June cut herself off.

"We will be staying overnight in Meckle," he said, ignoring June's happy squeal, "but you must wear a skirt." June frowned.

"Just the skirt?" she asked dubiously.

"Just the skirt," Halryan answered.

"'Kay," June said, and she dug the skirt out of her saddlebag, leapt off Rosie and ran into the bushes to change.

Riding with the skirt required some adjustment, since June had to go sidesaddle to preserve modesty (she didn't care, really, but she had a feeling the villagers would), but it was hard to get upset over a little balance issue when visions of hot baths, fluffy towels, and soft sheets danced in her head.

Her excitement continued to build as proof of the proximity of the town showed itself in the form of various villagers, leading oxen-drawn wagons full of burlap sacks, bushels of produce, and crates of fowl. They all gave June's motley crew strange looks, but after all, their group had a single woman between five very well-armed men. It drew attention.

The Valforte's behavior, however, concerned June. As they approached the village, their faces became drawn with tension. She tried to catch Koen's eye, but his gaze remained fixed on his horse's mane, brow furrowed and jaw clenched. Between excitement about the village and nervousness at the Valforte's behavior, her inability to sit still made sidesaddle even more of a challenge.

Finally, the trees parted completely, and June looked down at a small village nestled in a sunlit valley. From what she could see from her vantage point, the town spread out in a wheel shape from the "hub," a grassy square in the middle of town.

Entering the town was like walking into the American Colonies of the 1600's. The houses were all wood and stone, populated by people who looked as though they'd stepped straight out of 'The Scarlet Letter', only darker-skinned, like June. Looking down, she was enchanted to see the streets were paved with actual cobblestones.

June looked around at the Valforte to see their reactions to the town. Rather than amazement, or simply interest, they had become even more tense, hunched over in their saddles with eyes cast downward.

What's going on here? June thought, trying to catch the eye of one of her companions. But they simply refused to look up.

Halryan brought his horse up alongside June's. Withdrawing a small sack from his saddlebag, he pulled out a handful of something and poured a number of strange coins into her palm.

"To pay your room, my lady," Halryan said, before leaning back to hand several of the coins over to Minogan, who pocketed them.

"But–wait, isn't anyone coming with me? I don't even know where the hotel is!" Panic seized June unexpectedly, as the thought of being left alone turned the town from a cheery whirlwind of people to a dangerous den of thieves and criminals.

"No, no, the Valforte will accompany you," Halryan said, in what he must have considered a soothing voice. "You'll have to pay for your room yourself, though, it wouldn't be proper otherwise." June nodded, even though she didn't really understand. *What wouldn't be proper? Is it because they're men?* June wondered. She began to wish they were back in the woods. She had finally started to feel somewhat secure, but this had scrambled it all up again.

Halryan nodded respectfully, then turned his horse and spurred it down a side street, disappearing from view. *Never thought I'd see the day I was actually sorry to see him go,* June thought, with a wry smile. It was true, though–he was the only one acting normally. Well, normal for him, anyway. Feoras glanced quickly behind, to make sure she was following, then turned as they continued.

They finally found the inn, which a shingle hanging from a post out front announced as *The Drunken Sow.* They all dismounted, and Minogan took Rosie from June.

"Just ask for the innkeeper," he said, (and she wasn't imagining it now, he was deliberately avoiding eye contact with her) "and tell them you want a room–and a bath, they charge extra for that, sometimes. We'll come get you for dinner." June nodded, and without a backward glance, they all led the horses off, leaving her feeling abandoned at the front of the inn. She felt almost as scared and alone as she had when she first came. Coins sweaty in her palm, June took a deep breath and pushed open the door.

It was exactly what she'd expected, dimly lit, all dark wood, a faint smell of stale alcohol and leather in the air. A few woebegone chairs formed a lopsided half-circle to the left of a massive stairwell. A grubby looking man with thick stubble lay slumped over in one of these 'conversation area' chairs, snoring wetly.

The sound of clinking glassware floated out from a doorway on the same wall as the staircase–*must be the barroom*, June thought.

She didn't have to wait much longer. A bony woman with lank blonde hair pulled tightly back in a bun emerged from the barroom, wiping reddened, chapped hands on her apron.

"Room?" said the woman, sharply, and June nodded.

"Please," she answered.

The woman held out her hand. "25 denats."

June looked down at the fistful of coins she held. *Hmmm.* "Um, is a bath extra?" June asked, trying to buy herself more time, shifting the coins in her palm and trying to differentiate.

"5 denats extra," said the woman. "Eight, we give you a nice bar of scented soap."

"So, that would be...33 denats?" June asked, still struggling to see a number on the coins, but all they showed were lumpy-looking people in profile.

"Yuh," said the woman, now looking at June with suspicious interest. Giving up, June decided honesty would have to be the best policy.

"Look, this is really embarrassing, but...I'm not from around here, and I'm not quite sure which of these are denats. Could you, um..."June held out her open palm, hoping the woman would be honest. She shuffled forward, peering into June's hand.

"Not from around here, eh? Where you from, then?" the woman asked, as she picked through the pile of coins with fingers like twigs.

"Oh, um...somewhere else," June said weakly. The woman's eyes flicked up to her face, but she didn't press. She bounced the coins she had chosen from June's hand once on her palm, then turned sharply on her heel.

"This way," she called over her shoulder as she climbed the steps, and June scrambled to keep up. They walked down a hallway, floor to ceiling the same dark wood as the downstairs, but eerily quiet.

Finally, the woman stopped before a door with a tarnished brass '5' nailed to it. Pulling a large ring of keys from behind her apron, she detached one and unlocked the door with it. She showed June inside to a small, bare room, furnished sparsely with twin bed, table, and chair. The table had a chipped basin and pitcher resting on its surface. But what mattered most to June was the enormous clawfoot tub resting in the corner, a privacy screen partially obscuring it from view.

"Lucky," she said. "This is our only room with a tub in it, you'd have had to come downstairs to the bath room else." She handed June the key, then turned to leave. "I'll send my girls up directly with the hot water." She meant it, too–minutes later, two girls had filled the massive tub with steaming water. The last girl left a basket of towels and soap.

June barely took time to lock the door before stripping and practically leaping into the tub. She lathered herself three times, basking in the scent of the soap, sweet and feminine and so much different from the greasy yellow stuff they'd been using in the woods. She closed her eyes and soaked for a bit before she nearly fell asleep and drowned herself, then pulled her clothing into the tub and scrubbed it, too.

With the water cooled and her clothes clean, she got out, wrapped herself in a towel, and wrung out the clothing, hanging it on the privacy screen to dry. June drew the curtains, dropped her towel, slipped under the covers, and went to sleep.

A knock on the door woke her with a start. Looking around at the light in the room, she realized it must be nearly sunset; when they had gotten here, it had been just past noon. "Who is it?" she called out, clutching the covers to her chest.

"You have visitors," a strange female voice said from the other side of the door. "Downstairs."

"Oh, um, thank you," June called, grabbing the towel off the floor to cover herself and crossing the room to where her clothes hung, giving the fabric an experimental squeeze. Thank God, everything was dry.

She dressed quickly, checked her reflection in a spotty mirror behind the door—once again shocked by her new appearance—fluffed her freshly clean, shiny hair over her shoulders, and hurried downstairs.

Minogan, Koen, Errigal, and Feoras stood just inside the front door of the inn, looking painfully uncomfortable.

"Hey, guys," June started, uncertainly, "you didn't have to send the maid up. You could have come up, I wouldn't have minded."

Feoras gave what sounded like a derisive snort, and she looked at him sharply, but he wouldn't meet her gaze. None of them would. As much as she really didn't want to call them out in public, she'd have to confront them soon and figure out what exactly was going on here. Had she done something? Said something?

"Um, well, do you want to grab something to eat?" she asked, nodding her head toward the barroom, from which the delicious smells of roast meat and wine wafted. Minogan started, as though something had stung him; the rest shifted uncomfortably. Finally, Koen spoke.

"We can't go in there," he said, a bleak note in his voice. "We have to go in there." He nodded toward a door at the back of the room, past the stairwell.

"Why can't we go in there?" June asked, looking at the barroom entrance.

"Not 'we'," Minogan said, his voice hard. "You can go in there, that's where you eat. The rest of us have to go in there." He pointed to the door Koen had indicated.

A horrible revelation began to dawn on June. "Why can't *you* eat in here?" she asked, afraid she already knew the answer.

"Because we're Valforte," Koen said quietly, "and you're Andrian."

The buzz of noise coming from the barroom seemed very far away, as June looked from face to miserable blue face. Now everything made sense. They were ashamed, and angry. And on

June's behalf, they had been forced into this place, sheep in the lions' den. Horrified, she stood for a moment, not sure what to say.

"Oh, guys," she said, misery in her voice, "I'm so sorry. If I'd have known..." Koen shrugged.

"It's all right. You had no idea, and we weren't about to tell you. But for now, you have to eat in there," he nodded toward the barroom door, "and we have to eat there." All four began to walk slowly toward the door at the back of the room.

"Hey, guys, no, wait a sec," June said, circling around so she stood in front of them once more. "Okay, so you can't eat in the main barroom, but is there any rule that says I can't eat with you in your dining room?" All eyes widened in shock.

"Uh," said Koen, "I don't think it would be a good–"

"I don't care," June said slowly. "I don't care what people will think, I don't care what's appropriate and what's not appropriate. What I want to know is, can I eat with my friends without anyone getting arrested or lynched?" The Valforte looked at each other with guarded expressions.

"I suppose so," Minogan said, slowly, "but–"

"Perfect," June said. She stepped off to the side to allow them to pass. "Lead the way." The Valforte's shoulders slumped in defeat, and together they pushed open the door to the segregated dining room.

It was dimly lit, but not in the same way as the foyer–that was a soft light, which brought the dark wood of the room to life, giving it warmth. This room was dark simply because of a lack of candles, as though whoever had set up the room thought there was nothing in here worth seeing. Bits of dirt and old crumbs littered the scuffed floor and scratched tables, and some of the slats on the backs of the chairs were broken or missing.

Only two other people sat in here, a Valforte couple at a table by the wall. They looked up as June's companions entered the room, smiling, but their eyes widened in shock when they spotted her. June smiled warmly at them and nodded, and they returned the smile, if a little warily.

They sat at a table in the center of the room, the only one large enough to accommodate all five of them. A barmaid stuck her head out of a door in the corner of the room, an unpleasant look on her already unattractive face. Her mouth dropped as she caught sight of June, but she quickly narrowed her eyes in an expression of distaste.

She ducked her head back in, only to re-emerge a few moments later with five tankards on a tray. She thumped a tankard down hard in front of each of them, causing the liquid inside to slosh over the sides.

"Thank–" June began, but the barmaid's large posterior had already disappeared into the door she'd come out of. "You," June finished quietly, to herself.

Feoras picked up the tankard and took a sip, then grimaced. It smelled like some kind of cousin to beer, but the odor was unpleasantly sour, and June pushed hers away toward the middle of the round table, wiping her hand on her skirt.

"So," June said, clearing her throat, "where'd Halryan disappear to?"

"He wasn't very specific," Minogan said softly, checking over his shoulder for eavesdroppers. "He said he had some contacts here that might be able to point us in the direction of the first piece."

June nodded, and was about to continue when the barmaid approached once more with a tray. This time, she slammed a plate of food down in front of each of them, laden with some sort of carved meat, small, slimy potatoes, and a stringy cabbagey-looking vegetable. The food stank of grease, and the meat was more than half fat. *Guess we don't get to see a menu,* June thought ruefully.

"Filthy barbarians," the barmaid muttered, as she dropped the last plate disdainfully in front of Feoras, then turned to leave. June's jaw dropped, and the barmaid was halfway across the room before June could bring herself to react.

"Excuse me?" she said, unable to believe her ears.

The barmaid turned back to face June, one hand on her overgenerous hip. "You heard me," she said, cockily.

June stood up slowly, her hands on the table, eyes never leaving the barmaid. "I just want to make sure I heard you right," June said, voice shaking slightly. "Say it again."

The Valforte couple sitting near the wall had ceased their quiet conversation and were watching the unfolding drama with rapt attention.

The barmaid smirked, pushing a greasy tendril of hair which had come loose from her bun back from her face. "Fil-thy-bar-bar-i-ans," she said slowly, fat jowls quivering as she enunciated each syllable.

Koen's hand reached for June's across the table, but she jerked it away, and walked slowly around the table to within inches of the barmaid's jutting shelf of a bosom. Shivers of adrenaline shot from the soles of her feet to her scalp, making her limbs feel rubbery and tense all at once. Over the sound of the blood pounding in her ears, she heard one of the twins asking her to forget it, telling her it wasn't worth it.

But June was already past the point of walking away. Once, in seventh grade, a ninth-grade boy had made fun of Shannon's cheap generic backpack as they stood waiting for the school bus. One look at Shannon's crumpled face had sent June flying at the boy, three years older and sixty pounds heavier than her. June got some split knuckles and a week's suspension from school; the boy got expensive orthodontic reconstruction, and the lasting shame of having been beaten up by a little girl.

It was a very bad idea to insult June's friends.

"And why would you say a thing like that?" asked June, her voice dangerously calm, eyes flashing like hazard lights in the dark. Unfortunately, the barmaid wasn't heeding the warning.

"'Cause they are," the barmaid said, mouth turned up as though she'd just swallowed a lemon. "Coming in here and bothering decent Andrians. If it were up to me, they'd eat in the barn with the pigs, where they sleep."

June's lips curved in a nasty smile. Deliberately looking the barmaid up and down, her eyes finally rested on her face, fat pink cheeks now flushed with excitement.

"How *nice* of you," said June, vicious sarcasm dripping from every word, "to invite my friends to eat with your *family.*" Smiling, she waited for her comment to sink in, relishing the sight of the blood fading from the barmaid's face, leaving her flesh looking like lumpy bread dough.

WHAM! June rocked back from the force of the punch, vision exploding with tiny pinpoints of light, floating up and popping like soap bubbles. She hadn't expected her to be so quick.

Not as quick as June, though, who dodged the woman's next punch, catching her forearm as she did so, relishing the look of surprise and dismay on the woman's face.

The next thing she knew, she was being pulled off the barmaid, who lay on the floor, sobbing, her face covered in blood. June still struggled to get at her, though, her sight obscured by a reddish haze of rage.

"June, stop–oh for God's sake!" Koen's voice, in her ear, as he and the other Valforte fought for control of her arms and legs. Finally, June gave up, and allowed herself to be dragged out a side door and into the fresh night air.

~5~

"I don't believe it," said Halryan, pacing back and forth in front of her. They'd all gathered in an empty box stall in the barn, June sitting on an upturned wooden bucket, a cold cloth held to her eye. All four Valforte stood behind her, with the exception of Koen, who stood directly to her left. As innocuous as their positioning may have been, it gave June a pleasant feeling, as though the guys were literally backing her up.

"I leave for a few hours, and return to the innkeeper and his wife, screaming about how you accosted and insulted their niece, and you, in the barn, covered in blood and ranting about 'segration,' whatever that is!" Halryan's hands went to his temples in a gesture of anguish.

"Segregation!" June's hand, holding the cloth, fell to her lap. "And number one, she hit me first, and number two, she insulted us. Do you expect me to just take that?"

"Yes," Halryan said, turning on her with renewed vocal vigor. "You shouldn't even have been–" he must have seen a dangerous gleam in June's eye, for he quickly changed direction.

"You are a *princess*," he said, his voice lowering to a hiss, "you cannot be rolling around on the floor in brawls! We will be meeting some very important people in a week, and I hardly think they'll be impressed by a princess with a black eye!"

"Who are we meeting?" June asked, eager to change the subject. Halryan regarded her coolly for a moment, as though trying to decide whether she deserved to be told.

"The leaders of the Sidhe," Halryan said, his deliberate gravity almost comical. Behind her, she heard the sharp rasps of indrawn breaths, and Koen started slightly beside her. June's brow furrowed; something about the name sounded familiar.

"Isn't that..." She trailed off, not wanting to say what she was thinking out loud, afraid of being laughed at.

"You know them on Earth as faerie-folk, or elves," Halryan said.

"Wow," June said. "Wow."

"My sources tell me they may have information regarding the location of the first piece of the tablet. It is a very difficult journey, however, and dangerous. The woods between the Sidhe city and here are full of Eid Gomen."

"Pshaw," June said, smiling impishly. "I am June, conqueror of barmaids. Lemme at 'em, I tell ya." Halryan wasn't amused, but she heard Feoras and Errigal chuckling behind her, and Koen turned to hide a badly suppressed smile.

"We should all sleep," Halryan said, clearing his throat. "We leave at dawn."

"Thank God I left my stuff out with you guys," June said, standing. "I don't have to go back to the room."

"What do you mean?" Halryan asked, scandalized. "Surely you don't mean–"

"Oh yes I do," June said. "If you think I'm sleeping in there, with those ignorant bastards, you are sadly mistaken. Besides, this is still way better than the woods." She walked over to the pile of saddlebags in the corner and began to rummage, coming up with her own bag with a small triumphant sound. Halryan, who seemed to be learning, gave a long-suffering sigh.

June walked outside into the cool night air and sat under a tree a good distance away from the barn. Lighting a cigarette, she let her head flop back against the tree trunk and lost herself in the beauty of Prendawr's night sky.

The fight and its aftermath had an unexpected effect on her; confidence. Throughout the week, she'd felt storm-tossed, simply waiting for the next wave to come and carry her along, with no say in her destiny or direction. Now, though–she had done something, fought and won.

The ferocity of her feelings when the Valforte had been insulted surprised her, too. Shannon had been her friend since kindergarten, nearly eight years when the bus stop incident happened. She'd only known the Valforte for a week. Still, she reasoned, they'd been eating, sleeping, and traveling together, day in and day out. A recipe for quick bonding if she'd ever heard of one.

Two cigarettes later, she went back into the barn, re-entering their 'room' for the night. Everyone had already bedded down, so June settled down as quietly as she could, wrapping herself loosely in her woolen blanket.

"I'm sorry you didn't get to sleep in a bed," Koen's voice whispered from her left. June got up quietly and turned around, laying down on her stomach, propped on her elbows, so their heads faced each other.

"It's okay," June whispered back, smiling. "I got a bath and a nap. I'm good." She paused, frowning. "I'm sorry too," she said. "I think you tried to tell me, the first night, but I didn't understand."

"Yes, well," Koen said, looking down between his own elbows, "now you know." He grinned suddenly. "Where'd you learn to fight like that?"

June smiled. "I don't really know, to be honest," she said. "I've only ever been in one fight before tonight. I had an ex-boyfriend who was in the Army, he taught me some self-defense stuff, but I think it's just me getting pissed off, honestly."

Koen lowered his head and chuckled, running his hands through his sandy hair. "Well, I'm very impressed." His face grew serious suddenly, as though he was struggling with something. "Thank you. For coming in with us, for sticking up for us–"

June rolled her eyes, shaking her head dismissively as she turned on her side. "That's what friends are for," she said, pillowing her head on her arm and falling asleep before her eyelids even closed.

June awoke with a gasp, hands clutching wildly, disoriented from the feeling of being dropped from one world into another. She'd been dreaming of Kyle. They'd been laying in bed, spooning, Kyle behind her, her backside snugly pressed against his hips, his chest and stomach firm and warm against her back. His arms were around her, his fingers interlaced with her own. He had kissed her on the neck, and she could still feel the ticklish warmth of his breath, and the moisture from his lips. Smiling, she'd turned to face him–

A stalk of hay stabbed her in the spine as she rolled over, jerking her back to reality and consciousness. Shaken, she sat up, rubbing her hands over her face, heart pounding, sweat pooled in the small of her back and between her breasts. *I can smell him,* June thought, and held a lock of her hair to her nose, inhaling deeply. There really did seem to be a familiar manly smell, just underneath the scent of hay and the flowered soap from yesterday's bath. June exhaled slowly, trying to center herself, and shook herself mentally, looking around as she did so.

Feoras knelt in a corner of the stall with his back to her, packing something into a saddlebag, and the other three Valforte sat eating a breakfast of bread, cheese, and hot tea. Seeing her awake, Koen smiled and pushed a cup of tea toward her. June thanked him absently, twisting her engagement ring on her finger, her mind still on the dream, feeling embarrassed and exposed, as though her traveling companions could see her dreams.

She stretched, wincing at the prickle of hay inside her clothes. Even though she woke up in almost the same position she'd fallen asleep in, somehow, during the night, a large quantity of straw had worked its way inside her clothing. June also wished she'd braided her hair before going to sleep; she spent breakfast eating with one hand and picking hay out of her curls with the other. Still, this was pure luxury compared to waking up on the hard forest floor.

"Not bad," Errigal said, squinting at her face, as they all sat on the floor of the stall, finishing their meal.

"Well, um, thanks," June said, smiling bemusedly at him. He shook his head and laughed.

"I meant your eye," he said. "I thought you'd have a real nasty bruise, but it's just a little yellow underneath. You wouldn't even notice if you weren't looking for it." June reached up and touched her cheekbone. Sure enough, it wasn't even tender. Amazing, for a hit that had nearly knocked her out.

Disconcerted, she got up and went to a nearby watering trough for a closer look. She couldn't even see the yellow Errigal had described in the poor reflection. Her face looked as normal as ever, considering the drastic change it had made last week.

That's not right, June thought. *I shouldn't even be able to see out of this eye today. Errigal's right, it looked way worse last night.* She shook her head, and quickly pushed this into the already enormous mental file of *Things not to think about.*

June turned back to the others, attempting to distract herself. "So, where's Mr. Personality this morning?" she asked, and tried not to wince at the strange sensation which jolted through her. Sometimes, when she'd try to use a common American euphemism, her brain wouldn't stop at translating the word, but would use a more socially appropriate combination of words, which resulted in what June thought of as 'mental double vision.'

The others tried to mask wry smiles, unsuccessfully.

"He said he had a few things to finish up," Minogan said. "He'll be back soon."

"Oh, *good*," June said, rolling her eyes, causing the boys to deliberately avert their eyes. It was strange, their relationship with Halryan. On one hand, they took orders from him without question, unless June herself said something contradictory, and they never spoke ill of him. On the other hand, they obviously held the same disdain for him as she did, only they took much greater pains to hide it. Was Halryan paying them? He had to have something over their heads, because it certainly wasn't friendship that sponsored their loyalty.

Speak of the Devil, she thought, as Halryan rode dramatically up at full gallop, sharply reining his horse to a halt in front of the stable door. June winced as she saw the animal flex its jaw in protest of the harsh bit.

At once, their relaxing morning became a frenzy of activity as they prepared themselves and their animals to leave. June brushed her teeth with a chewed twig from a minty-tasting shrub the men had shown her. She'd been pleasantly surprised by the hygiene habits of the Valforte; judging by the amenities of the house they'd begun in, she hadn't expected much, but they all carefully brushed their teeth, washed, and shaved each and every morning. Halryan, on the other hand...

As she washed her face, neck, and arms in a bucket of *really* cold water behind the stable, June remembered a part in the book *The Once and Future King,* where young Wart breaks the ice in the basin to bathe himself in the morning, and shuddered, hoping she wasn't still here when winter rolled around.

Come to think of it, she wasn't really sure what time of year this was for them. It felt to her like early summer, longer, warm days with only the smallest chill in the early morning. Did they even have the same seasons here? Snow? She'd save those questions for later. It seemed like segue to a nice conversation to break up the monotony of a long day on horseback.

An hour later they were well underway, back in the forest on a different trail this time, traveling to the southeast. June had actually approached this leg of their journey with something like optimism, thinking herself pretty well accustomed now to 'roughing it.'

The next day, however, June was thinking longingly of their journey to Meckle; she'd never experienced such misery as now. They had entered a much more dangerous section of woods, and Halryan, worried a fire would draw the Eid Gomen, wouldn't even allow a small camp oven. So their diet consisted of cold-steeped tea, which was the very definition of nasty, and stale or soggy (or, both) bread, dried meat, and cheese.

To top it all off, it was raining. Not very hard, barely a mist, but consistently, and as they rode the under the trees, fat cold drops fell from the canopy, down the back of their necks or on the crowns of their head, where they trickled icily down their scalp, greasy and fragrant with plant oils.

At night, they rolled themselves in their woolen blankets, the same blankets they'd used as cloaks all day, so they really were good and soaked. They laid down in as mudless an area as they could find, and tried to sleep, damp bodies aching with chill. Every one of them kept a handkerchief clenched in their hands to wipe away the constant trickle of snot that dripped from their noses. They couldn't even find comfort in each other, because everyone was tired and cold and wet and cranky and had no patience for anything or anyone.

And so they rode, heads bowed, the only sound the constant whisper of rain in the trees, and the occasional trumpet of a nose being blown.

Finally, on the fourth morning, the rain quit. Lunch was still very no-frills, including the disgusting cold tea. The tentative rays of sun filtering through the treetops brought a sense of well-being to the group for the first time in days. June left the boys to finish their meal and wandered a short way down the stream they had stopped beside (which she'd already 'checked'), looking for a nice private place to pee and wash.

She wandered a fair distance before she found a clump of bushes to conduct the first part of her business in, and then knelt down by the stream to deal with the second. After washing, June simply sat for a second, head tilted back and eyes closed, basking in the weak warmth the sun sent down through the canopy, enjoying the soft red light filtering through her eyelids.

A sound snapped her back to reality, the sound of a large animal trying to move stealthily through the forest. June sat still and watchful as a deer, remembering the last large animal she'd unexpectedly encountered in the forest. There, another sound. Something was definitely coming. Slowly, warily, she got to her feet, eyes searching the trees before her for whatever was making the noise.

And then she saw it.

It stood about three and a half feet high, naked of hair, or clothing, apparently sexless, since June could make out nothing to tell her one way or the other. Its gray skin blended well with the tree trunks–if it hadn't moved just as she'd looked at it, she'd never have seen it. One four-fingered hand tightly grasped a weapon, a cross between an axe and a spear; a large, curved blade on the end of a pole the height of the creature, coming to a sharp point, so it could be used to stab or slash.

It was thin, very thin, which made its already oversized, slightly triangular head appear even more so. If there was an expression on its face, June couldn't tell; its huge eyes were black from lid to lid, with no whites or iris, and slits for its nose and mouth.

June stood, frozen, unable to move in her terror; fortunately, the creature hadn't noticed her. It turned its back now, showing a backside with no cleft, merely a single lump of flesh at the base of the spine. She shuddered, unable to turn away, her breath coming in shallow, rapid gasps. It was looking for something, and June knew that it was looking for her. And if it found her...

A hand clapped over her mouth, and a strong arm gripped her around the middle, pinning her arms to her sides, and dragged her backwards, swinging her behind a tree. Already on adrenaline overdrive, she began to struggle violently.

"*Shh*," Koen whispered in her ear, and she sagged back against him, choking back a sob of relief. He dropped the hand over her mouth so his arm fell across her chest, still gripping her tightly to him. His breath was also ragged, and she could feel the tension in his body. June closed her eyes, trying to dam the tears leaking from her eyes. *Go away,* she thought, in a senseless litany. *Go away go away go away go away...*

After what seemed like an hour, Koen relaxed, and abruptly released June, who turned to face him.

"Gone," he said, his face paled to a slate gray color, pointing in the direction away from their camp. He looked at her closely, sea-green eyes full of concern. "I'm sorry I scared you. I didn't hurt you, did I?"

"No, no, I...thank you," June said, hugging herself against a sudden chill from within. "I don't know what I would have done if...thank you," she finished lamely.

He nodded, seeming embarrassed. "Come on," Koen said, taking her arm gently at the elbow, "let's get back. That was just a scout. If we hurry, we might be able to get out of the area before they realize we're here." They half-ran back in the direction of the camp.

"Was that an Eid Gomen?" June asked quietly, as they hurried forward.

"Yeah. Creepy things, aren't they?" Koen asked.

"Sure are," June said softly. She was lost in thought, as this latest mind-blowing revelation vibrated through her like the aftershocks of an earthquake. How many times had she watched the SciFi channel, and seen black eyes like the creature's she'd just encountered staring at her from an investigative documentary? How many movies, how many books, created by directors and writers captivated by the elusive mystery? She'd even seen those eyes on a child's Halloween mask.

Because, no matter how she tried to reason with herself, to deny what she'd seen, she knew she'd just encountered what almost anyone would immediately recognize as an extraterrestrial. An alien.

June's head felt as though it would split open and spill her disjointed thoughts on the forest floor as Koen quickly caught the others up on the incident by the stream. None of this made any sense. Faeries? Sorcerers? *Space aliens?* Once the initial shock had worn off, she'd actually accepted the whole idea of blue people, sorcerers, and faeries pretty darn well. This, however, was the absolute last and final straw. What next? The Abominable Snowman? The Easter Bunny?

June felt as though the world was swathed in fog as she mounted Rosie, her hands slack on the reins. Rosie, well accustomed with the way things worked by now, moved to her proper place in line, and picked up the slow galloping pace set by the others as they tried to put distance between them and the Eid Gomen. After a time, they slowed back to a walk, but June barely noticed.

"June? *June?*" She blinked as her eyes focused on Feoras, twisted around in his saddle to face her. "Halryan wants to continue through the night, to stay ahead of them." June nodded mutely. Feoras looked as though he wanted to say something else, but changed his mind, turning back around and nodding to Halryan.

As night fell, June worried she might nod off on Rosie's back and fall off. As the darkness deepened, however, her fears proved groundless, and she began wondering if she'd ever sleep again. She simply couldn't wrap her mind around the matter of the Eid Gomen. What were they doing here? What were they doing on Earth? What were they? Try as she might, she couldn't come up with anything close to a reasonable explanation.

Absorbed in her cheerful thoughts, June didn't even notice the light until well after sunrise. She realized suddenly she could hear the constant *shh* sound and smell the fishy scent of a moving body of water.

Soon, they could see it, a large river, coffee-colored with disturbed sediment from the rain, cutting its own path through the trees. Halryan led them off the trail and onto the sandy, pebbled bank alongside the river. The water was running very fast, with lots of tree branches and other flotsam speeding along its surface like paper sailboats. Halryan pulled up his horse and dismounted, and they all followed suit.

"I believe it is safe to stop here for a short time," he said, looping his horse's reins around a small tree. June did the same for Rosie, and loosened her girth. *Now remember you did that,* June chided herself. A few days before, she'd forgotten she'd loosened the strap holding Rosie's saddle, and tried to mount, resulting in June landing flat on her back between Rosie's legs and the Valforte (and June, once she recovered from her shock) crowing with laughter, probably the only time any of them had laughed since leaving Meckle.

Everyone scattered among the rocks beside the river, taking care of business that needed attending after so long on horseback. June took her own potty break quickly, then hurried down the beach in the direction she'd seen Halryan head. As much as she disliked talking to the man, she needed answers about the Eid Gomen, and she knew he'd have them.

June met him coming back to where they'd left the horses, adjusting his flamboyant purple pants. He looked mildly surprised to see her; she didn't usually seek him out for conversation. Not bothering with small talk, June stopped in front of him.

"I want to know about the Eid Gomen," she said, crossing her arms across her chest. Halryan smiled slightly.

"They frighten you badly, don't they, my lady?" he asked, an odd expression of amusement on his face.

June merely raised her eyebrows. "The thing is," she said, "I've seen them before. Home. On Earth." Halryan's head jerked in surprise as June continued. "Only in drawings that people have made, though. Not everybody believes they're real."

"Well, the name, Eid Gomen, isn't actually what they call themselves—no one knows that," Halryan said, moving into Professor Fathead mode. June repressed a sigh and tried to concentrate on what he said, rather than getting irritated by the way he said it.

"It is from an ancient language, and means World Eaters." He paused here, fixing June with a serious stare. "And that's exactly what they are, world eaters. They travel from planet to planet, scout it for sometimes hundreds of years, find a way to destroy it, and then consume the energies of the destroyed lives, and of the planet itself. They've been here for quite some time, but in recent years their numbers have multiplied a thousandfold. They're moving in for the kill."

June paused for a moment, as this information sunk in, gnawing absently at a hangnail on her thumb. Behind her, well down the shore, she heard a splash and a whoop of laughter.

"So they're doing that at home, too? Planning to destroy Earth?" June asked, suddenly realizing once she was done here, she might be returning to a planet as doomed as this one.

"It's puzzling," Halryan said. "Normally, the planets the Eid Gomen target are worlds in which magic is a large part of life. It makes for...a better meal, I suppose." He paused for a moment, staring off into the distance. "I cannot think what they could be doing on Earth."

Seeing June's face, he inclined his head toward her. "However, if there are so few of them the general population has not acknowledged the truth of their existence, I can assure you with almost complete certainty Earth is in no immediate danger."

Suddenly, he looked up sharply, an expression of alarm on his face, eyes fixed on something over her shoulder, and June whirled around.

Minogan raced up to them, and the sheer panic on his face made June's heart drop into her stomach like a hot stone. Panting, he pointed over his shoulder toward a large outcrop of rock jutting out into the river.

"He–he fell," Minogan said, between gasps. June looked in the direction he pointed, where Errigal and Feoras stood waist-deep in the river, looking frantically out into the water.

Koen was nowhere in sight.

June was sprinting along the shore before her mind had consciously made the decision to run, scanning the roiling surface of the water frantically as she did so. She stopped suddenly, feeling as though her whole body was a divining rod, quivering and straining toward a point out in the river. She looked out into the water. Directly perpendicular to the point at which June stood, a twig stuck up above the surface of the river.

He's there, said a voice inside her, and without hesitation, she ran full-tilt into the water, pausing only to kick off her shoes. She swam out into the water, skin contracting palpably from the bitter cold. The current pulled so ferociously she needed to swim diagonally against it to continue in a straight line.

Here, said the voice again, when she had nearly reached the twig, and June filled her lungs and dove. Her body spasmed as the frigid water closed over her head. Eyes open or closed, it didn't matter–she couldn't see a thing. She frog-swam down and down, frantically waving her arms in front of her, fingertips searching for skin, hair, cloth, anything. *Please,* she thought, desperately, *please, please.*

Then fingers brushed fabric, and her hand closed on an arm, floating limply in the current. *God,* she thought, not knowing whether it was succor or exclamation, as she threw her free arm around Koen's chest. Her legs scissor-kicked ferociously, but Koen's body didn't move. June struggled, lungs straining painfully against themselves. A few more seconds, and they'd both be in trouble.

Let GO! June thought. Suddenly, Koen's body floated free in her arms. With the last of her strength, she dragged them both to the surface, throat closed tight against the breath her body struggled to take.

Her head broke the surface, and June gasped, dizzy for a moment from the sudden availability of oxygen. One arm tucked under Koen's armpits, she swam backward with her legs and free arm, keeping his head above water by pillowing it on her chest, as she'd seen in a lifesaving training video, trying not to think about Koen's lack of movement. He was textbook dead weight.

June's eyes fixed on the cloudy sky above them as she paddled backwards. *God, please,* she pleaded with the clouds, *don't do this. I can't take any more.* But the clouds floated on, wads of dirty wool, indifferent to June's struggles.

Then hands grasped at her and Koen, pulling them toward the shore.

"Him," June gasped weakly, groping with her feet for the river bottom. "Just get him..."

The three Valforte left her then to drag herself out of the water, all of them necessary to support his limp body. Halryan watched from the shore, his expression inscrutable.

A burst of adrenaline surged through her body, and with renewed strength, June charged up to where they had laid him on his back.

They all stood back, surveying his still form, silently, mournfully. June dove down in the sand next to him, skidding the last few inches on her knees. She struggled with him, trying to turn him over. It felt as though he had turned into a giant lump of modeling clay, with no bones at all—her hands simply sunk into his yielding flesh.

"Help me!" The Valforte merely looked at her, not comprehending. They'd already begun mourning Koen, but June hadn't given up yet.

"Now," she barked, no room for disobedience in her tone. Errigal and Feoras dropped next to her and helped to flop him on his stomach; Minogan, meanwhile, sat down hard in the sand, his hands covering his mouth and his eyes blankly staring in horror.

"Lift his legs up, quick. No, higher than that, higher!" June herself grasped Koen around the hips and lifted, widening the angle between his torso and the ground. Tea-colored water poured from his nose and mouth, soaking into the sand in amounts that put a knot in June's already tense stomach.

"Flip him again," she said, and Errigal and Feoras quickly complied.

June dug under Koen's jaw for a pulse, dropped her head to his chest, seeking the sound of a soft rush of air filling lungs. Nothing. His skin was gray, waxen; his handsome face a ghastly shadow of its former self. Without hesitation, she tilted his head back, pinched his nose shut, and administered two full breaths; difficult, since between her sprint, her swim, and the overall power of terror shooting through every molecule of her body, she could barely catch her own breath.

June moved to his chest, seeking the right place with her fingertips, remembering the feel of the rubbery Resurrection Annie in her CPR class. Lacing her fingers, she gave fifteen compressions, counting under her breath. "One and two and three and four and five-"

June didn't know how long she continued, aware of nothing but Koen's inert body and her own counting. Once, June heard a rib crack as she compressed, and she winced, but didn't stop or slow. She was Koen's only hope–she couldn't stop. There were no paramedics coming, no ambulance, no hospital with oxygen and defibrillator. There was only June, standing between Koen and oblivion.

Suddenly, Koen's body gave a great spasm, and he coughed, sending a spray of river water into June's face. This time, she could turn him over herself, and moved up so she supported his back with her knees, keeping him propped on his side as he violently vomited river water. She heard the gasps behind her, an unintelligible cry from Minogan.

June dropped her forehead onto Koen's shoulder, closed her eyes, and took a deep breath. *Thank you,* she thought, *thank you, thank you.* She swallowed hard, then took a deep breath and straightened up.

"We need blankets," she said to Errigal and Feoras. "Sugar, salt, honey. Get a fire going, quick, and boil some water." They raced off. June looked to Minogan, who looked back, completely bewildered.

"Help me," she said, ripping at Koen's shirt. "We've got to get him out of these wet clothes, quick." She looked over toward the horses. "I need those blankets," she shouted. Minogan was tugging at Koen's shoes.

June looked down at Koen and took his pulse. Rapid, but strong and steady. His eyelids fluttered weakly, but a tinge of blue was returning to his face. *And that's a good thing,* June thought.

"Koen?" June said, taking his face in her hands and turning him toward her. He didn't answer, and the moment of triumph faded. It had just occurred to her Koen had been a very long time without any oxygen. What about brain damage? What if she had saved him, only to condemn him to the life of a vegetable?

"Hey, Koen," she said again, slapping his face gently.

His eyes flew open, pupils expanding and contracting within his sea-green irises as he struggled to focus on her face. "Yeah," he said softly, squinting with the effort of concentrating. June closed her eyes and just barely contained a moan of relief.

"What's my name?" June asked.

"June," Koen said, with an obvious effort.

"What's his name?" June asked, pointing at Minogan.

"Melonhead," Koen said. June smiled uncertainly and looked at Minogan, who smiled back and nodded. That would have to do—June didn't actually know what year it was here, and there wasn't a president. She turned back to Koen to find his eyelids drooping.

"Hey, Koen, listen," June said softly, "I know you feel like shit right now, but you have to stay awake, okay? No sleeping. We're going to get you warmed up and get something hot to drink, but right now you—hey!" June slapped him lightly again as his lids began to close—at her slap they flew open again, blinking. "*Stay awake.*"

"Chest hurts," Koen said weakly. June hissed between clenched teeth as she laid one of her hands down lightly on his bare chest, where a greenish bruise was already forming.

"I know, Koen, I'm sorry." As she touched him, she became aware that her own body was tingling—probably adrenaline leaching out of her muscles. Errigal had returned with the blankets and June looked back at Minogan, who had removed all but Koen's undergarments.

"Cold," Koen said softly, an occasional shudder rippling through him. He was getting shocky—his body didn't even have the strength to shiver properly.

"All his clothes," June said, ignoring the scandalized looks on

Errigal and Minogan's faces. "Sorry, guys, this is no time for modesty." June continued to wrap Koen's upper body in blankets as the Valforte tried to preserve Koen's modesty while they removed his underwear. Watching them out of the corner of her eye, June had to suppress a smile. She tossed blankets down to Minogan as she began rubbing Koen's arms briskly to restore circulation. Minogan and Errigal, catching on, began doing the same to Koen's legs.

Within no time, Feoras had a roaring fire going, and a kettle full of hot water. June mixed the sugar, salt, and honey into a mug with the hot water. The sugar and salt idea she had gotten from a wildlife refuge, to keep some baby squirrels who had fallen out of a tree alive long enough to make it to the shelter. She remembered reading something about honey, too, something to do with electrolytes. Either way, it couldn't hurt.

June tried some of the concoction and made a face. *Better him than me,* she thought, and began forcing the mixture, sip by sip, down Koen's protesting throat. Luckily, shock kept him weak, so he didn't fight much. Within moments, though, the drink began working; an alert light shone from his eyes where there had only been a dull gleam moments before. June laid the back of her hand gently on Koen's arm, hand, and foot and was relieved to find warmth had returned to his extremities. She finally felt safe enough to breathe a sigh of relief and to turn her attention to other things. Halryan, for instance.

He'd been pacing back and forth at the edge of her vision since June had given the instructions to light a fire, and his impatience had become more and more evident with every moment. June sighed, then looked up at him.

"Problem?" she asked.

"My lady, we cannot tarry here," Halryan blurted, obviously having waited a very long time to speak. "It is not safe, we do not even know where the Eid Gomen are or how close, and we light a fire, to guide them straight–"

"The fire was not an option, it was a necessity," June said, feeling no inclination to move away from the fire; her own clothes were still soaked and clinging to her body like cold fish skins. "And as for not 'tarrying' here, well, that's not an option either. We have to stay, at least for a few more hours."

"Hours? *Hours?* My lady, by that time the Eid Gomen will be upon us," Halryan cried, his eyes wide and disbelieving. "We must go at once!"

"He can't sit a horse," June said, her voice rising sharply in volume. "Do you know how dangerous it would be to move him now? Just because he's out of the water doesn't mean he's all right!" Halryan looked at her, a strange expression on his face, then cut his gaze away quickly. June started as comprehension dawned on her.

"You want to leave him," June said, incredulous.

"We put ourselves in danger if we stay," Halryan said in a near-mumble.

"And we put Koen in even greater danger if we go," June said, her eyes blazing.

"June, it's okay, I can ride," Koen said, pushing himself up on his elbows.

"Shut up, nobody asked you," June snapped, pushing him back down without taking her eyes off Halryan. "If you want to go so bad, then go. We'll catch up with you."

Halryan paused, biting his lip and looking across the river. He stood this way for a few moments, then muttered something June couldn't hear.

"What?" June said, making no effort to mask the irritation she felt.

"I cannot leave you, my lady," Halryan repeated, turning back toward her.

"Well, then why don't you make yourself useful and go fling a few protective spells around," June said, turning her back on Halryan as she poured herself some tea. "You keep telling me you're a sorcerer, but I haven't seen you so much as pull a rabbit out of that stupid hat of yours." A pause, then the sound of Halryan's footsteps retreating through the sand.

June sighed and raked her hands through her soaking wet hair. She was angry, and not only because of Halryan. She felt the kind of anger that makes mothers, reunited with a child who wandered off in the mall, slap their offspring, then clasp them to their breast, the kind of anger that comes on the heels of a terrible fright.

The very pregnant silence surrounding her was also wearing her nerves. Errigal, Feoras, and Minogan had all kept silent during the argument with Halryan, and continued to do so now, but the air thickened with their unspoken words.

"That's the second time you've stuck up for us," Feoras said finally.

"Yeah, well, maybe if you'd stick up for yourselves, I wouldn't have to," June said, and instantly regretted it. "Sorry," she muttered, feeling her cheeks darken, and turned back to Koen for a diversion.

"How's your chest?" she asked.

"My chest? It's fine." Koen's brows curved down over his brilliant eyes as he looked up at her, perplexed.

June made a scoffing noise.

"Koen, it's okay to say if it hurts," she said. "You've got a broken rib, remember?" Now it was Koen's turn to snort.

"I've had broken ribs before. I don't have one now," he said.

Shaking her head, meaning to show him the bruise and prove it, she peeled back the layers of blanket covering his chest. The bruise was gone. June pulled the blanket back further, thinking she had misjudged the area of the break, but she hadn't. His chest was smooth, with no hair to hide discoloration. She laid her hand down in the exact spot she had before, pressing gently and looking at Koen's face to gauge his reaction. Nothing. He gazed down at her with a mixture of amusement at her confusion and embarrassment at her intimate touch. June replaced the blankets and stood up, turning away from everyone in an attempt to hide her face. Not, however, before she met Minogan's eye.

I heard it too, his face said, as clearly as if he'd said it out loud. *I heard the rib crack when you pushed on his chest, and I saw the look on your face when you did it.*

June's knees were shaking badly, and she had broken out into a cold sweat.

"I'm going to walk a little ways," she pointed downstream, her voice trembling. "If you need anything..."

She walked off, her steps uneven; it felt like her knee joints had been removed. She clenched her fists at her sides, nails digging into the soft flesh of her palms. Finding a likely spot, June flung herself down behind a rock, mind racing. *It was broken,* June thought. *I heard it. I saw it.*

You laid hands on him, another voice answered. *You healed him.*

Not possible. I've never done anything like that before in my life, and I've touched a lot of sick people at work.

It's all different here, though, the voice said. *Halryan says you're a sorceress. And as much as you hate the guy, everything he's told you so far has been true.*

June unclenched her hands to run them through her hair. As she did so, she noticed the smears of blood around the tips of her fingers, and saw she'd squeezed her fists so tight she'd drawn blood from her palms with her nails. She studied the cuts for a moment, trying to judge their depth. And watched them close up before her eyes.

June licked her thumb and rubbed away the blood on one hand, not trusting her eyes. Sure enough, the cuts that had been there just a few seconds before were gone. A sickening cold feeling spread through her stomach and lower body.

Feeling disconnected, as though in a dream, she watched her right hand pick up a sharp shard of rock from the beach and draw it across the skin of her left arm, leaving a trail of blood beading up behind the point. Watched as, just as quickly, the cut sealed itself, leaving only the drying drops of blood as proof it had ever been there.

I'm a sorceress, June thought, and began to sob. Harder, even, than she'd cried when she got here, hard enough for the wracking sobs to bring on dry heaves. She felt as though she'd turn inside out with grief. Because, for the first time, it was clear no mistake had been made. With some work, an explanation could have been found for the other things, like her face and the language–hypnotism or something, maybe.

But this–this made it real. She, June, had made things happen, amazing things. It was no longer happening *to* her. This was the moment when she understood she really was the person everyone claimed, a princess, a future queen, and the possible savior of the world.

The weight of it nearly crushed her.

June grayed out for a while, her body carrying her across the tumultuous waves of emotion. When she came back to herself, she lay on her side, curled up in the fetal position. She slowly sat up, brushing off the pebbly sand where it had imbedded itself in her cheek. Her face was covered with tear tracks in various stages of drying, and (*ew*) mucus which had apparently been running freely from her nose.

Shakily, June got up and went to the river, kicked off her shoes, and waded in. Her clothes were still wet; no point in rolling her pantlegs up. The cold water around her ankles gave her a sense of reality, of being a part of the world again. She bent over and splashed water on her face, washing away the grime of her outburst.

June combed her wet fingers through her hair, breathing deeply into her stomach. She dried her hands on her pants, then ran her hands over her face, checking for any crusts of grime she'd missed. Her skin was clean and smooth, with just a few slight indentations still from the pebbles on one side of her face.

June took one last deep belly breath, with her head tilted back and her eyes closed, and then waded back out of the water. As she put her shoes back on, her mind reached out to the revelations of the past few hours, then recoiled, her chest tightening. She shook her head. *No,* she thought, *you're going to have to start coming to terms with things. Your little breakdown just now probably wouldn't have happened if you'd dealt with things as they came.*

June had acquired a peculiar skill after her parents died. Suddenly, not only had she been all alone in the world, without adult guidance (even though she was nineteen when they died, she still needed them, very much) but faced with a whole new set of responsibilities, decisions, and truths. So, June had developed a very hard shell between the outer portions of her awareness and the inner. This meant she could deal with the fallout of their deaths, the arrangement of their funerals, the endless lawyer and insurance agent meetings to tidy up their financial affairs, and the sale of the house, but these things never actually penetrated to the vulnerable part of her consciousness. She dealt with everything, and dealt with it well, but never with any emotional awareness or acceptance.

That strategy having been so successful before, she had done it again here, without actually making a conscious decision to do so. The problems here, though, were infinitely nastier than simple bereavement. June had left things alone without dealing with them for too long, and with this terrifying day, her shield had failed, and everything had come tumbling in at once, like a heavy snowfall caving in a roof.

So, June sat for a moment, one shoe half-on and forgotten, and dealt. She'd cried her tears, yielded to her terror. Now all that was left was to stop fighting the truth and simply accept it.

"I am a sorceress," June said, softly, tasting the strangeness of the words on her tongue. "I am a princess. I'm here to save the world." Her fingertips slid gently over her face, feeling the strange contours that were finally becoming familiar. She sat, thinking over her words. Said them again. And again.

Finally, she knew it was true. She *was* a sorceress. She *was* a princess. And she *was* here to save the world.

June, the sorceress, the princess, put on her shoes and stood up, brushed sand and stones off her behind, then went off to save the world.

~6~

When she returned to the fireside, Koen was sitting up, talking quietly to the others, still wrapped in a mountain of blankets, holding a steaming mug. Halryan paced near the treeline.

The Valforte looked up at her approach, then cut their eyes away. *Guess my eyes are still pretty red,* she thought, sitting beside Koen and accepting a cup of tea from Minogan. Clearing his throat, Koen continued, and June lit a cigarette as she listened.

He'd been telling the others what happened at the river. After relieving himself, he'd climbed a high outcrop of rock overhanging the river, to get an idea of the surroundings. He had stepped too close to the edge, and slipped on a patch of moss. As he fell feet-first into the water, he struck the back of his head on the rock.

Stunned, he sunk like a stone to the bottom, carried by the current until his feet caught in a waterlogged tree. By the time he regained the use of his limbs and faculties, Koen was in a panic, unable to free himself, and blinded by the muddy depths.

"Then everything started to go peaceful," Koen said, his voice softening as he stared into the flames of the small fire. "All of a sudden, getting out of the water wasn't so important. And then I started to remember things, from when I was a child. I almost felt...happy." He turned to June. "The next thing I knew, I was on the shore, with you slapping me." Koen smiled, but it didn't touch his eyes. June suspected everything was still just a bit too close and raw.

Minogan, Errigal, and Feoras all shook their heads. Minogan looked especially upset.

"We saw you fall, but we didn't realize...God, we laughed!" Minogan pounded his fists angrily against his thighs. June reached for him, but he pulled away. "And then you didn't come up. We waited..."

"Hey," June said. "It's not your fault. Koen can swim, and if you didn't see him hit his head, you'd've had no reason to be worried."

Minogan shook his head dismissively.

"He's fine," June pressed. "Everyone's fine. It was a scary accident, but it's over." Minogan had looked away, but June leaned into his line of sight, and he nodded, if a little grudgingly.

Now came June's turn, and, flicking her cigarette in the fire, she explained the mysteries of CPR. She left out the parts about his rib and how she'd managed to find him, though–they could draw their own conclusions.

When she finished, June sat back and sipped her tea. The liquid woke her empty stomach, and hunger hit her like a Mack truck. "Is there anything to eat?"

Feoras handed her an apple-like fruit, a lump of cheese, and a chunk of bread, and she wolfed them down, pausing occasionally for a sip of tea. As the blood rushed to her now-full stomach, her eyelids drooped. They'd traveled for eighteen hours without rest or food, June had performed a water rescue and had a fairly good-sized nervous breakdown–not surprising she'd crave a little nap.

She looked at her companions. All four Valforte, especially Koen, had dark circles under their eyes, and stared bleary-eyed and slack-jawed into the flames. June glanced over her shoulder for Halryan. Still wandering around, muttering, and waving his hands, casting spells. At least she hoped that's what he was doing.

"I have a suggestion," June said. The Valforte turned to her, blinking themselves out of their trances. "We're exhausted. Let's camp here, get some rest, and start again in the morning."

Minogan opened his mouth, but was distracted by something over June's shoulder. June heard footsteps scuffing quickly in the sand. *Damn his ears,* she thought, closing her eyes and praying silently for strength.

"My lady, we cannot tarry!" Halryan's dissonant squawk made June wince. "If we stay, we will lose all the ground we put between ourselves and the Eid Gomen, and more!"

"Are we even sure they're chasing us?" June asked, speaking down at the pebbly sand as she rested her forehead in her hands, knowing she couldn't look at Halryan without leaping at his throat. "They may not have realized we were there. We only saw one scout."

"We must assume they are. We have already stayed too long, and we have advertised our position with the fire."

Halryan waited impatiently for a response, shifting from foot to foot–she could hear the rustle of his silly pants. June bit her tongue hard to keep from making a sharp retort. Taking a deep breath, she ran her hands through her hair and looked up at the Valforte.

"What do you guys think?" she asked, and all their eyes widened in surprise. "Can you make it?" They glanced at each other.

"Come on, I need an answer here." June said. "An honest one."

An entirely wordless conversation began taking place right in front of her. June, Shannon, and Ashleigh used to do the same thing, saying volumes with mere glances.

Now, Minogan leaned back on his hands and stared off to the side, lips pursed, mind a thousand miles away. Then he looked at June and nodded.

"He's probably right," Minogan said. "Even if they aren't on our tails, if we stay here much longer, they will be. Maybe we can rest a little further down the trail, but for now, we should get moving."

June looked at Halryan, his light blue eyes narrowed. He seemed torn for a moment, then nodded and stalked off toward the horses.

"God, I wish I knew what his problem is," June said softly, remembering Halryan's excellent hearing.

"Well, right this moment, it's because you went on our word that we should leave, and not his," said Koen, his voice equally soft. "Probably that you even asked us."

June just snorted and shook her head. The other Valforte got up and began to pack things up and put out the fire. June looked at Koen.

"So, how are you feeling now? Really," June said, knowing he'd try to say, 'Fine,' even if he wasn't. Koen smiled sheepishly, aware he'd been caught.

"I'm pretty good, considering," he said, "Just my head, where I hit it on the rock." June reached out and gently touched the back of his head, and found a very large, hot goose egg, sticky with blood. She only hesitated for a moment before pressing her fingers more firmly against the lump and concentrating. She felt the bump cool and shrink, smoothing itself against his skull, leaving behind nothing but a smear of drying blood.

Her body tingled strangely, as it had before, when she'd mistaken the sensation for adrenaline. Something told her the job was done, and June pulled back, noting with amusement but not surprise the blood coloring her fingertips was blue. Dizzy and exhausted from her efforts, she closed her eyes and sat down hard next to Koen.

Koen's eyes widened. He reached up and felt the back of his head. June shifted uncomfortably and looked at the ground.

"Yeah, I know. Weird, huh?" June said. Tears again welled up in her eyes, as reality hit her with its big, ugly stick. *I thought we worked through this already today,* she chastised herself. June ducked her head to hide the tears, too late.

"What's the matter?" he asked softly. June shook her head, not trusting herself to speak. "What?" he probed, leaning forward to try and meet her downcast eyes. June wiped her face on her sleeve before she looked up at him, his eyes full of concern.

"I still–before today I didn't..." June trailed off, sighing. Koen's eyes stayed on her face. "I was still thinking that all this was a mistake, or a trick," June said after a moment. "Now, though–I have proof. I can't fool myself anymore. I have to deal with it."

"Was it the rib?" Koen asked, and June nodded. "The others told me, when you went for a walk. They all heard it crack. I didn't really remember." He smiled wryly, and June joined him, shaking her head.

"That, and how I found you underwater, and got you untangled from the tree."

"And brought me back to life?" he asked quietly.

"No, that was strictly the CPR." June said.

June suddenly became aware that she and Koen were very, very close to each other. And that Koen had no clothes on under those blankets. Without her permission, her mind began using information about Koen's body she'd gained while stripping the wet clothes from him. Things which weren't really appropriate for an engaged woman to be thinking about a man who wasn't a) her fiancé, or b) Brad Pitt or comparably yummy and unattainable celebrity. Clearing her throat, she stood, feeling a familiar heat in her belly which reached down between her legs. A breeze blew over her too-sensitive skin, and she barely suppressed a shiver.

"You'd better change," June said, smiling, but looking away to (hopefully) hide the redness of her cheeks, "and I should help pack up." Koen nodded, but looked confused by her sudden mood change. Before he could ask her anything, she hurried off toward the horses, barely restraining herself from breaking into a run.

What is wrong *with me?* June thought, as she tightened girths and straps. *After the day I've had, being awake for–God, I've lost count of how many hours–seeing that creepy alien guy and realizing that the creepy alien guys are on Earth, probably planning to destroy it, saving a friend from drowning, finding out I can do magic...and now I'm* horny? June stepped back from the last horse, checking the load distribution, her mind still on Koen.

"God damn," she said under her breath, twisting her engagement ring absentmindedly on her finger. Minogan looked up sharply at her. She met his glance, and he raised his eyebrows inquiringly.

"Do we have anything stronger than tea?" June asked impulsively. Minogan blinked, but dug into his saddlebag and pulled out a fairly large animal-skin bag more than three-quarters full and offered it to her.

She took it, pulled the cork, and sniffed. Her eyes watered from the smell–like whiskey, but stronger, more raw. Just the ticket. June brought the bag to her lips, took three healthy swallows, and lowered it, gasping as the alcohol burned its way down her throat and smoldered pleasantly in her chest and stomach. She wiped the last few drops from her lips with the back of her hand and sucked them off her skin as she handed the bag back to Minogan, who looked fairly impressed.

"Thanks," June said. "I needed that."

"Anytime," Minogan said, as he corked the skin and replaced it in his saddlebag.

"Oh, you don't want to say that," June said, smiling. "I'll have your jolly juice bag empty in three days, tops."

Koen joined them, back in his dry clothes with an armload of folded blankets. Minogan took them from him and left; Koen turned to June, his face serious. "I don't think I thanked you for saving my life," he said, looking embarrassed. "Thank you."

June's mouth twisted in a wry grin. "You're very welcome," she said. "Thank you for being my friend. I seem to have a shortage of them lately." Almost subconsciously, she looked around for Halryan, and found him standing off to the side, letting everyone else do all the work again while he fooled around with a map or something.

They stood for a few moments in uncomfortable silence.

"Well," Koen said, unable to find words to finish his sentence.

"Well," said June, a good deal calmer, Minogan's moonshine having evened out her nerves. *Guys are guys, no matter what planet they're on,* she thought. *Fish out of water with feelings.*

"Go get on your horse, you big dork," she said good-naturedly, swatting at him, Koen grinning as he left. Watching him go, June couldn't help but notice the clean, strong lines of his shoulders, and the way the muscles of his back suggested themselves through his shirt. *Good lord,* June thought as she mounted Rosie tipsily. *If we don't get you out of here, girl, you're going to get yourself in trouble.*

June woke when Rosie halted, jolting her back to awareness. She spit a few hairs of the mule's mane out, her face having been pressed to the animal's neck, and sat up and blinked, confused. June had no memory of falling asleep, or even of laying her head down on Rosie's neck. *It's a miracle I didn't fall off,* June thought. Thinking of what she'd learned about herself in the past day, however, she decided it probably wasn't all that surprising.

Everyone was dismounting and unsaddling their horses. June

sleepily did the same, quickly drew her nightly circle around the campsite, then took her blanket and saddlebags and headed to where the others had settled themselves, sitting on the ground with a *thump.*

They weren't making a fire, and June sighed at the thought of cold yucky tea again, thinking longingly of the fire a few hours ago. They shared out (*surprise!*) more bread, cheese, and overripe fruit. June thought longingly of pizza as she bit into the stale bread. *Too bad my cell phone doesn't work here,* June thought with a smile. *I could call for delivery.*

Her smile dried up as her mind wandered back to the new fears the day's events had brought. She'd found out the bad guys threatening Thallafrith were threatening Earth as well, but surprisingly, the Eid Gomen didn't weigh on June's mind the most.

Koen's accident had made her realize something much more disturbing. If they got in trouble, she couldn't just run to the nearest phone booth and call 911. If one of them got sick or hurt, there was no hospital, no doctor, no antibiotics or store-brand cold medicine. And if they ran out of food, there were no burgers down the road at the drive-thru. They'd starve.

June looked over her shoulder at the Valforte, understanding for the first time how much she needed them. If she got lost here, or if something happened to them....

"Is everything all right, my lady?" June whirled around mid-shudder to find Halryan peering down at her.

"Yeah, yeah. Everything's fine," June said, taking a discreet breath to steady herself. "I was just wondering–how much longer before we reach the Sidhe?"

"To be honest, my lady, I have no idea," Halryan said.

"What do you mean?" June asked, confused. With all the time he spent poring over pieces of parchment, you'd think one of those pieces was a map.

"The Sidhe keep the location of their city secret, to discourage unwanted visitors," said Halryan. "The city is not on any map, and no non-Sidhe knows the location."

"So, how are we supposed to find them?" June asked. "How do we know we're even on the right road?"

"Oh, that much we do know," Halryan said. "We simply travel on this road until the Sidhe contact us."

"But what if we miss them?" June said. "What if we just walk right past them?"

"They'll find us."

"But what if they don't?"

"They *will*," said Halryan, in a tone of finality. He bowed and retreated. June watched him go, shaking her head in disbelief and annoyance, and, deciding she'd had enough for one day, shook out her blanket, pulled it up over her head, and fell asleep.

June dreamed of Judy Garland dressed as Dorothy Gale, sitting on a high branch in a tree, Toto clutched under her arm, kicking her legs teasingly and giggling. On her feet were a pair of bright red sneakers, which June kept leaping off the ground to try and catch. "I need those shoes," she yelled. "I have to get home!"

"They're mine, though," Judy/Dorothy said, still giggling. "Besides, even with these, you'll never catch up to him." With the hand not clutching Toto, she pointed off into the distance, and June turned to look.

A dirt road ran behind June, and up a distant hill. On the top of the hill, silhouetted by sunlight, stood Kyle.

"Kyle!" June ran as fast as she could toward him. He waved to her, but rather than getting closer as she ran, he got farther away. She pushed harder, digging her toes into the road as she ran, but still the gap between them widened.

June woke with a start, gasping as though she really had been running. Both moons were on the wax, and moonlight coated the trees with a silvery sheen. Shaking and sweating, she reached for her saddlebag, thinking to light one of her well-rationed cigarettes–and stopped dead, the hair on the back of her neck prickling ominously. Something was wrong. Very wrong.

June looked around slowly, afraid to move too much and make noise. She thought of her sword, still attached to the saddle, on the ground near the horses. *Damn,* she thought. Looking around for the closest Valforte, she spotted Errigal, propped against a tree, bow, quiver, and sword in his lap. Too far away to reach, though. She slipped quietly free of her blanket and crept toward him. At her light touch, he snapped awake, and one look at her face told him all he needed to know.

As he leapt to his feet, the woods exploded with light and noise. The horses whinnied in terror, shying and pulling at their bonds, bouncing off one another in their struggle to flee.

A circle of Eid Gomen, two rows deep, surrounded them. Each held a torch in one hand, and a wicked-looking axe-spear–like the one June had seen the scout in the woods carrying–in the other. They stood, perfectly silent, the fire from their torches making their overlarge eyes glitter like polished onyx.

The rest of her companions had woken in seconds, swords drawn before they were on their feet. June grabbed a stout branch lying on the ground and held it in front of her with both hands like a baseball bat. The Valforte and Halryan encircled her, facing outward, like buffalo protecting their young.

The Valforte stood as still as the Eid Gomen, reminding her of deer on the edge of a field, eyes watchful, bodies strung tight. For the first time, it really hit June; these men were *warriors,* in the truest sense of the word.

Between the Valforte's shoulders, she saw the front line of the Eid Gomen part. One of the creatures shouldered through the gap, naked and armed as the rest, but this one exuded an aura of leadership.

"Surrender," it said, in a horrible clicking voice which made June shudder. "We want only the Princess. The rest may go unharmed." The Valforte shifted in response, squaring their shoulders and hoisting their weapons a few inches higher.

June looked at the faces of her friends, set in grim determination. There were at least a hundred of the Eid Gomen, and only six of them, June and Halryan included. They'd never survive. And June saw, as she studied their faces, that they were perfectly aware of this fact, and didn't care. They meant to die today. *We want only the Princess,* the Eid Gomen had said. *The rest may go unharmed.*

"Is that a promise?" June yelled, surprised her voice sounded so strong, since she had been expecting it to come out a tinny little squeak. Between the shoulders of the Valforte, she watched the Eid Gomen leader nod, its lipless slit of a mouth twisted in a grotesque mockery of a smile.

"No," Minogan said. "As noble as your intentions are, if you die, or you surrender, we all die. You have to get through, no matter what. If we don't make it, keep going on the road we've been traveling. The Sidhe will find you."

"No, no way," June said, shaking her head violently from side to side. "I'm not leaving you, I'll fight—"

"June," Koen said, softly, and she looked at him, meeting his eyes as he looked over his shoulder at her. He said nothing more, just her name. His eyes said far more.

"God damn you," June said, softly, tears spilling down her cheeks. She looked around at the other Valforte, all with similar expressions on their faces, expressions which said, *We're making this sacrifice so you may live. Don't let it be for nothing.*

June's shoulders slumped in defeat, and the Valforte turned back to the circle of enemies surrounding them. June's gaze flicked to Halryan. His face shone with sweat, and he looked ready to run.

"Send her out, sorcerer," the Eid Gomen clicked again. There was a pause, and the Valforte turned toward Halryan, whose eyes were glazed, his mouth working without sound.

"Come and get her, filth," said Minogan, after assuring himself Halryan wasn't going to regain his voice.

And without warning or sound, the Eid Gomen charged, spears raised, their silence terrifying. June saw the Valforte shift, bracing for the impact; she herself settled her feet more firmly in the ground. But then–

WHAM! Something hit June with the force of an NFL linebacker; she staggered back with a cry, dropping her stick and falling into Errigal, who started, having braced for a frontal attack. On her knees, June gasped for breath, and shuddered at the sensation of hundreds of needles pricking her skin.

June looked down, expecting to see blood, but there was nothing there. Suddenly she looked up, alarmed; shouldn't the Eid Gomen be on them by now? But the Valforte were looking outward, their swords lowered in their amazement. And peering through their legs, June understood why.

Several of the Eid Gomen lay on the ground, looking as surprised as possible with their expressionless eyes. The rest poked their spears in the air at some invisible barrier separating them from their prey. June looked at the sharp tips of their spears, then down at her skin in sudden, horrible comprehension. Apparently, drawing the circle hadn't been a silly impulse after all.

But this wasn't going to last. June could feel her energy draining from the power required to hold the barrier. Soon, she'd be tapped, and then what? They'd all be killed, June captured, game over. She had to do something else. But what could kill a hundred Eid Gomen, bent single-mindedly on killing the six of them?

Suddenly, a lightbulb clicked on. June wasn't sure where this insane idea came from, but she knew she could do it.

June sat down, Indian style, in the center of the circle the Valforte and Halryan made around her. Closing her eyes, she took a deep breath...and flew out from her body.

Suddenly, she was flying through the trees at immeasurable

speeds, solid and liquid and gas all at once. The sensation made her giddy, euphoric–she could split apart in a thousand shards and be everywhere all at once, she could shoot straight into the stars, dance on the treetops, even go belowground and explore an ant colony.

June didn't have time to revel in the feeling, though; she had business to do. And luckily, she didn't have to go far to do it.

The draek slept in a hollow formed by a fallen tree a short mile from their campsite. June reached out and touched its mind gently to wake it. Startled, it recoiled warily.

Blood, she told it, in some strange mental language which didn't require words. *Meat. Come.* It cowered before her, unsure, only knowing it couldn't bite or kill her to defend itself. June persisted.

Meat, she told it again. *Blood. Come.* She could feel it responding to her, its tongue flicking ropes of saliva from its mouth. *Come,* June said, more urgently. Between the astral projection or whatever she was doing and the shield around the Valforte, she couldn't hold on much longer.

Thankfully, the draek needed no further convincing, and followed her as she led it swiftly through the trees. Her power began slipping away, and she struggled to hold on, squeezing like a child's fist around a slimy frog. Just a moment more–

And then June landed back in her body. She fell heavily to her side, panting as though she'd just run a marathon, and watched as the draek unleashed itself on their enemies.

The carnage was ungodly. Koen had been right, the draek did like screaming. And scream the Eid Gomen did, high-pitched, chittering cries which echoed through the forest and fueled the creature's blood lust.

It slashed with claws and teeth, not stopping to feed, just killing as many as it could, reveling in the bloodshed. A few spears flew at the draek, but for the most part the attack took them by surprise, and the Eid Gomen either fled into the darkness or were split open like so many November jack o' lanterns.

An eerie silence descended. The bodies of the Eid Gomen lay scattered on the road, their torches burning beside them, huge eyes gazing sightless at the moonlight filtering down through the leaves. The smells of blood and fear hung thick in the air. The call of a distant night bird and the soft, sloppy chomping noises of the draek served only to outline the quiet.

"June?" Minogan looked down at her, face full of wonder and concern. She pushed herself up weakly, her head whirling. Attracted by the movement, the draek looked up from where it had been nosing in the abdomen of an Eid Gomen, mouth full of gore.

No, June told it. *I gave you plenty. You don't touch these. They're mine.* The draek considered her a moment, eyes glinting in the guttering torches left by the dead and the fleeing, chewed its mouthful, swallowed, and then turned back to its meal.

Halryan looked down at her, awestruck, apparently at a loss for words.

"We have to go," she said, attempting to get up, but losing her balance and falling hard on her behind. The sudden movement caused her vision to waver sickeningly, and she moaned, putting her head between her knees. God, what she wouldn't give for a warm, soft bed, and a day to lie in it.

"You need rest," Feoras said.

June shook her head, trying to move it as little as possible to avoid another dizzy spell.

"No time," she said, struggling to her feet, successful this time with the help of Errigal and Koen. "They're going to be back, and I'm fresh out of tricks."

The Valforte looked at her dubiously. June forced a smile, trying to convince them.

"Hey, I'm okay," she said. "I just need a little help getting on the horse." She nodded toward the draek. "He should leave you alone, but give him a wide berth, just in case."

The men got the horses ready in record time. As they galloped along the dark trail, June thanked whatever powers there were she had such a sensitive animal to ride. Rosie seemed to know how weak June felt, but rather than take advantage of it, she kept a perfectly smooth pace, taking pains not to turn or shift her weight sharply. June, normally a good rider, especially lately, with all the practice she'd been getting, let the reins go and clung to Rosie's mane, lower body limply draped over the saddle, feeling as wobbly as a newborn foal.

June must have passed out or fallen asleep, for she woke once again spitting Rosie's hair out of her mouth. She sat up and stretched her shoulders, lacing her fingers behind her back and pushing down as she rotated her neck to soften the tight muscles.

Looking around, it appeared she was the only one who'd gotten any rest. The Valforte had dark circles under their eyes, and their faces were a lighter blue than usual. She twisted around in her saddle, caught Minogan's eye and smiled; he nodded in response. Beside him, Koen stared off into space. June turned back around and pursed her lips, thinking. She closed her eyes and sent herself off once more, in search of the Eid Gomen. She found them, about fifteen miles back, in hot pursuit.

June snapped back into her body like a rubber band. She was torn between exhilaration at her new trick, and trepidation at her heretofore-unknown power. What else didn't she know about herself?

June shook herself, and glanced around once again at her companions. They looked completely exhausted, all of them, nearly spent. Even Halryan, who usually looked crisp and well rested, drooped in the saddle. June steered Rosie around Errigal's horse and up to speak to Halryan.

"My lady," he said, bowing slightly in his saddle, "The Eid Gomen are–"

"About fifteen miles behind us, I know," said June, without impatience. He nodded.

"Can I make a suggestion?" June asked, and continued without waiting for a response. "Everyone's exhausted, but the Eid Gomen are too close for us to stop. Can we maybe do shifts, so that people can get some rest?"

"That is an excellent idea, my lady," Halryan said, with some obvious relief. "Shall I take the first shift?"

"No, no, I slept some already, I just woke up. Why don't you and some of the Valforte rest, that way, there'll be a sor–one of us awake who can check a bit farther for threats." Halryan nodded once more, and June rode back to see who wanted to stay awake. They decided June and Errigal would take the first shift, one at the head of the line and one at the back, tying the horses in the middle together so they wouldn't wander or stop to graze. As they took their positions, something occurred to June.

"Halryan," June said, "what's my name?" Halryan, slow on the uptake from fatigue, looked at her blankly.

"They named me something when I was born, right?" Comprehension slowly dawned on Halryan's face. "So, what's my name?"

"Ah, my lady," Halryan said, with the air of one about to reveal a wonderful surprise, "your name is Princess Ulfhilda."

Dead silence.

"Princess Ulfhilda?" said June, mortified. "My sister gets Queen Morningstar, and I get stuck with *Ulfhilda?*"

Halryan looked affronted. "You were named for your grandmother, a noble and honorable queen who–" June waved him off, an expression of despair on her face.

"God hates me," she said. "He really, truly hates me. Plops me down on a planet that hasn't invented toilet paper yet, and then he crowns me *Ulfhilda*. Of all the..."

She heard a snigger and whipped around, but all the Valforte had rearranged their faces into innocent stares. Errigal's mouth twitched, though, and Koen and Feoras's faces were much darker blue than usual.

Shaking her head, June pulled Rosie up to the front of the line, and they started off again. Within a few moments, everyone had either dozed off or lost themselves in thought, the only sounds being small animals rustling in the underbrush, and June, muttering, "Ulfhilda–God!"

~7~

Halryan and June kept a close inner eye on the positions and speed of the approaching Eid Gomen as the days passed. They rotated frequently to keep everyone rested. They munched wild greens and berries to supplement their dwindling supplies, and stopped as long as they dared to rest the animals, who felt the strain just as much as their two-legged counterparts.

June was actually grateful for the long, unbroken travel, because it gave her ample time to mull over everything she'd been pushing aside in the name of denial. She'd never been what she'd call a *believer*. Unless she could see, touch, taste, or smell it, she wouldn't believe it. A skeptic to the core.

Events, however, had forced her to re-adopt the mentality of her childhood, when faeries hid behind every tree, and she rushed to bed on Christmas Eve, so she wouldn't scare Santa Claus away. *Jeez, I hope he's not here,* June thought with a wry grin. *Even with all the stuff I've been through so far, I think that'd push me right over the edge.*

Soon, though, her mind became too occupied with worry to commit it to idle thought. Despite their best efforts, the Eid Gomen kept gaining. They had to stop occasionally to rest the horses, and the poor animals were still ready to drop, and skittish and ornery to boot. Even June's sweet Rosie was having fits of the stubborns.

Sometimes, for a break, June played mental games to keep her occupied. She'd sing all the songs she could think of by a particular pop artist, and name all the cast members of her favorite TV shows. She couldn't think about the serious stuff all the time, especially when her mind kept creeping back to Kyle, Ashleigh, and Shannon.

And then one morning, just after the sunrise, as June tried to recite the Pledge of Allegiance backwards in her head, her subconscious bristled, like a dog scenting danger on the wind. June pulled Rosie sharply to a halt.

She tried to send herself out to check the area, but couldn't, and felt oddly claustrophobic not being able to leave her body. The tickle of suspicion quickly descended into fear, and June whipped around to face her companions, drawing her sword for the first time (and nearly dropping it).

"Wake Halryan, qui–" June didn't have time to finish the sentence, for several figures stepped quietly out of the trees, so smoothly they appeared to materialize out of thin air.

At least a dozen of them, dressed similarly to June and the Valforte, with linen shirts and animal-skin pants, surrounded them; tall, willowy figures, whose grace was apparent even when they stood still. Silvery blond hair flowed over their shoulders and down their backs. Their eyes tilted sharply, almost Asian looking, but with startling pale gold irises, set in faces which looked carved from polished ivory.

All had bow and arrow trained on June and her companions.

The Valforte had reacted instantly, even Minogan and Feoras, who had been asleep, drawing their swords and clustering around June as they had during the Eid Gomen attack. Halryan, however, started in surprise, but relaxed as his eyes focused on the strangers.

"Ah, Lagart," he said to one of them, a pleased expression on his face. All of the strangers lowered their arrows and bowed respectfully. Halryan returned the bow from his saddle, looking significantly over at June and the Valforte. Reluctantly, June sheathed her sword, and the Valforte did the same.

"The Queen expected you yesterday," said the Sidhe.

"We had some unexpected delays." Halryan's lips tightened as he glanced at Koen. "We haven't a moment to lose. The Eid Gomen are close."

"Your Highness, I am Lagart, captain of the Sidhe guard." He bowed so deeply his nose nearly touched his knees, as did the other elves. "I must ask that your escorts allow us to blindfold them. The location of our city is secret, and none but the Sidhe may know its location." He paused, bowing slightly again. "And you, of course, Your Highness."

"Oh," June said. "Um..." She looked at the men, eyebrows raised. *Okay with you?*

Minogan gave her a humorless grin, and raised one shoulder. *What choice do we have?*

"Yes, that's fine," June said, turning back to Lagart. Five of the Sidhe stepped forward with white cloths, and the Valforte leaned forward in their saddles to allow them to be tied on. June noted Halryan's offended look with amusement; apparently he didn't think the Sidhe would blindfold him too. Once everyone but June had been securely blindfolded, a guard came and took the bridle of each of their horses, and led them off deep into the woods.

If June was a little surer of her company, she would have joked that not being blindfolded didn't make a difference. She'd never be able to find her way back; she couldn't see any sign of a trail. Something made sense to the Sidhe, though, for they led them on a weaving path through the forest, occasionally turning sharply for what seemed to June no reason at all. And then–

Suddenly, an immense wall loomed up out of the trees, continuing horizontally in both directions as far as the eye could see, made of brown and grey stone. Armed guards patrolled the ramparts at least a hundred feet above them. A drawbridge descended over a great black moat at a shout from Lagart.

June was grateful the Sidhe guard held Rosie's bridle, for her hands were shaking and slippery with sweat, making it impossible to hold the reins steady. She looked around at the Valforte, who must have been even more nervous, not being able to see what they were walking into. They sat stiffly, lips pressed together in thin lines. Only Halryan seemed calm, if still a bit annoyed.

The horses' hooves struck the wooden drawbridge with a hollow sound which only intensified June's apprehension. She resisted the urge to bite her nails, and instead twisted her fingers into Rosie's mane. She curled her toes in her boots so she wouldn't jiggle her feet in the stirrups.

A disquieting thought struck her. Lagart had mentioned 'the Queen.' Was the Queen here? Was June about to meet her? What should she say? How should she act? *Damn Halryan,* she thought, panic beginning to seize her, *what the hell is he here for, if not to coach me through this stuff? What if I screw up, say something stupid or offensive? Is it 'Off with their heads?'*

As they moved through the stone arch, inside the walls, June took a deep breath, trying to slow her pounding heart. *Try not to freak out until you have to,* she thought. *Save your energy.*

Inside the walls, a large, clean cobbled courtyard met them, smelling of hay and grain and fresh horse manure. Lagart stopped, and the line following him did, also. Unsure of what to do, June glanced back at Halryan, whose blindfold had just been removed by a guard. Halryan dismounted, as did June, and the Valforte, once their eyes had been uncovered. Grooms led their horses away, and June's eyes followed Rosie.

Lagart, catching her look, said, "Never fear, Your Highness. Your animals will have the best care we can give, and your belongings will be taken to your quarters immediately."

June nodded, biting her lip. Just then, she heard a fanfare being played, and June looked to her left to see a procession, led by elves playing slender silver trumpets, approaching them swiftly.

June drew herself up, with another conscious effort to slow her heart. The trumpet players stopped abruptly, then stepped off to either side, facing one another. As they blew a variation of the fanfare they'd played during their approach, a woman like none June had ever seen stepped forward.

There was no other way to describe it; she *glowed*. A halo of light radiated around her form. Her porcelain face, around which gorgeously wild waves of pale hair flowed, held a set of brilliant gold eyes burning with intelligence. Clad in a shimmering gown, also of gold, she was a spectacularly awe-striking figure.

Lagart bowed deeply, as did the rest of the Sidhe. June glanced at the Valforte, who seemed as flummoxed as she, and at Halryan, who bowed as deeply as the elves. Feeling very stupid, as she wore pants, June curtsied. To her surprise, the Queen returned her gesture, then stepped forward and clasped June's hands.

"May I present Her Royal Highness, Queen Mab," Lagart said, bowing once more.

June's face went blank with shock. Queen Mab? *The* Queen Mab, mentioned in practically every single Irish fairy tale ever? The Queen smiled benignly at June, ignoring her shock.

"The very image of your mother," Queen Mab said, eyes soft, as she stood back from June and looked her over. "The eyes are different, but otherwise...."

June was painfully aware of her appearance—her river-rescue of Koen had been the closest she'd come to a bath in the past few weeks, and she was dirty and sweaty.

I can't believe she's standing so close to me, June said, eyeing the Queen's immaculate appearance. *I must smell like a pigpen.* The Queen appeared to take no notice, however, and gestured to two willowy blonde women clad in white gowns behind her. They stepped forward and curtsied deeply to June.

"This is Lesai and Nemura," Queen Mab said. "They will be showing you to your quarters and caring for you while you stay with us." The Queen squeezed June's hands warmly and released them, stepping back. "You must be exhausted. Go and rest," the Queen said, "and perhaps you can join me later."

"I look forward to it," said June, mustering all the self-composure she could. As suddenly as she'd arrived, the Queen retreated to the renewed sounds of the trumpets, leaving the courtyard almost deserted, and June feeling bewildered. Smiling at her obvious befuddlement, Nemura and Lesai beckoned her forward.

The courtyard they stood in was actually an enormous raised platform of earth cobbled with stone. June went to the edge of the platform and gasped audibly at the sight. Rather than the grubby wooden homes and dusty streets of Meckle, an immaculate expanse of short, velvety green grass spread before her as far as the eye could see. And pushing the grass up in numerous places were–

"Fairy mounds," June whispered, heart full of sudden inexplicable emotion. Of all shapes and sizes, round and oblong and even snakelike, covered smoothly in the emerald green grass, except for arched doorways and porthole windows set in the sides. All reminded her of mysterious mounds found on Earth.

Nemura and Lesai led her down the stone steps. June stopped, and looked over her shoulder at the Valforte. They were being led off with Halryan, in a different direction, looking around with awestruck expressions. Despite trepidation at being separated, June turned and continued to follow the two Sidhe onto the grass.

Even through her shoes, the grass felt wonderful, cool and springy, and June had an urge to take them off and run barefoot. Nemura (or was it Lesai?) turned back toward June, looking amused, and June wondered for a moment if they could read minds.

They came finally to an oblong mound, the entrance set far to the right, and one of the women held the door for her as she stepped inside.

It was possibly the most warmly inviting room she'd ever been in. Wood the color of strong tea made up the walls and floor. Soft fur rugs were liberally scattered at her feet, and the walls sported beautiful woven tapestries depicting various aspects of Sidhe life, colored in what June thought of as fall tones, dark red, brown, and gold. Three plush chairs sat in the corners, looking so soft she felt an actual, physical ache to sit in one.

June already felt like she'd fallen into the happy ending of a fairy tale, when she walked through an arched doorway to her left–into paradise.

An enormous four-poster canopy bed, mahogany with white gauzy drapings and gold silk comforter and pillows dominated the room. Several more cushy chairs, the kind which cry out for a book, a cup of hot chocolate, and a rainy evening filled the corners. A beautifully carved dressing table with an ornate gold mirror stood against the wall, near a huge cast-iron bathtub, behind which an elegant privacy screen stood, a velvety robe hanging from one corner. Tendrils of perfumed steam curled lazily from the surface of the bathwater. June barely suppressed a moan of longing.

Nemura and Lesai stepped in behind her, and without asking, began to undress her. Ignoring her feeble protests that she could do it herself, they stripped her entirely nude and led her to the tub. As she lowered herself into the water, June couldn't remember anything having felt better than the warm liquid against her skin. The tub's depth allowed her to sink completely up to her chin.

The Sidhe women, whom June could still not tell apart, split up; one went to the foot of the tub, one to the head. The one at her head extracted a delicate-looking blue glass bottle from a basket by the tub and poured some of its contents onto June's head, massaging it into her scalp. The one at the foot of the tub took a cake of greenish soap and a cloth and began to wash June's body, starting with her legs and working upward.

June, normally a very modest person, and not one to be waited on, submitted with a surprising lack of argument. The hands on her scalp and tired muscles felt so good, the water so warm and soothing, she just couldn't work up the energy to argue.

Half an hour later, scrubbed, rinsed, and dried, Lesai and Nemura dressed June in a soft nightgown and tucked her between the cool sheets of the four-poster bed, where she fell instantly asleep.

June dreamed she was in a tiny rowboat, far out in the middle of the ocean, surrounded by blank sky and endless stormy sea. Up and down the swells June and her boat went, the water a sinister bluish-black, promising monsters with sharp teeth waiting in its depths. As she crested the next wave, she saw another boat, like hers, bobbing in the water.

Kyle, Shannon, and Ashleigh were all in it.

June yelled, standing up in her boat and waving frantically, but her boat sank into a trough and she lost sight of them. Her stomach dropped when the next swell carried her to a good vantage point, for they were floating away.

June grabbed for the oars, meaning to row after them, but they were the size of Popsicle sticks, and she angrily flung them into the water. Looking up, she saw a massive grey thunderhead bearing down on her. June continued to wave her arms, trying to get the attention of Kyle and her friends in the boat, but the wind carried her voice away, and they drifted still farther, oblivious to her voice.

June woke with a start, but relaxed as she remembered where she was. Smiling, she pressed her face into the pillow and stretched her legs, delighting in the smoothness of the sheets against her skin, and the softness of the mattress as it gave under her weight. She heard quiet movement in the room, and peeked out of her warm nest to see Lesai/Nemura setting a tray of food and drink on a small table next to the bed. Food. June emerged from the covers, eyes on the tray.

"Mmm," said June, grabbing the tray and pulling it into her lap, trying to staunch the flow of saliva springing from beneath her tongue. God. Fresh fruit, fragrant soft cheese, and warm bread, dripping with butter and honey. *Hot* tea with *milk*. June ate like a wolf at a caribou carcass, to the delight of the Sidhe who had brought it.

When June had stopped just short of wetting her finger to pick up the crumbs of food still left on the tray, she set it aside with a deep, satisfied breath and leaned back against the pillows to sip her tea. They'd never exactly been starving, but she hadn't been really full since leaving the house they'd begun in. God, she'd missed it.

"The Queen requests your presence, as soon as you are able," Lesai or Nemura said, and June jerked upright, nearly spilling her tea.

"Why didn't you say so?" June said, sitting bolt upright, voice shrill, as panicked thoughts of the Queen holding a sharp axe and looking impatiently at a clock rose to her mind. "I could have hurried!"

"At your leisure, she said, Your Highness. At your leisure."

June relaxed slightly, but still set her tea aside and got up, looking down at the nightgown she wore, then around the room.

"Um, where did you put my clothes?" June asked, and Lesai/Nemura pulled a light blue gown and a corset-like undergarment from the other side of the privacy screen.

"I'm afraid those clothes have seen the end of their usefulness, Your Highness," she said, "but the Queen would like you to accept this with her compliments." June took the dress with a smile, silently hoping they planned on giving her some *riding* clothes when she left.

Someone had an expert eye for size, for when June put on the light blue dress and stood before the mirror, her jaw dropped in shock. She hadn't seen her whole self since leaving Earth, and what a difference a few weeks hard riding and meager diet had made.

The dress, made of a soft cottony fabric, hugged her new, slimmer curves like it had been made just for her. June twisted and turned to see herself in the mirror, happy with the way her body looked, fit and voluptuous all at once, but sad, because now, she could see almost *no* physical resemblance between herself and the person she'd been for twenty-one years. It was like staring at a stranger.

Swallowing hard, she fluffed her clean hair over her shoulders and turned back to the Sidhe women, who smiled in approval.

"Lovely, just lovely," one of them said, arranging a tendril of June's hair across her shoulders. "The Queen will be delighted."

They led June out of the mound and across the grass once more, heading further in toward the center of the city. As they walked, June wondered how they managed to keep this place a secret. It was *huge.*

At last, half an hour after setting out from the mound, they arrived at an enormous mound, the biggest June had seen so far, one she assumed was the palace. Lesai and Nemura, smiling encouragingly, left her before an ornately carved door. After she'd watched them retreat into the distance, June turned, grasped a huge brass knocker, and let it fall with a resounding *boom.*

The door swung inward, and June stepped inside, heart pounding. Awe took the place of trepidation, however, as she looked around, eyes wide. And she'd thought *her* mound was nice. Mahogany walls arched high above the glossy marble floor, meeting in a vaulted arch high above her head. Three chandeliers, each holding hundreds of candles, hung gracefully in the entrance hall.

Another tall, willowy male Sidhe stood before her, dressed in a green silk tunic and pants which reminded June of a pair of Chinese-styled pajamas her mother had worn. He smiled and bowed as she met his eyes.

"I am Soltis, the Queen's advisor. How are you finding your stay in Lumia?"

June smiled nervously. "Oh, it's beautiful, thank you for asking."

"I'm glad to hear it, very glad. The Queen is anxious to speak with you. Shall we go?"

Without waiting for a reply, Soltis turned crisply on his heel and led her down the hall and through an archway to the right, into another, smaller hallway, lit by elegant oil lamps. They passed several doorways on either side before he stopped in front of one on the left. He stood there, silently, without moving. June had begun to wonder if she should poke him or something, when the door swung open.

"Enter," called a lilting voice.

Soltis stepped off to the side and bowed, gesturing for June to go in. She entered the room and the door shut behind her with a dull *thud,* making her jump. She'd entered a royal parlor, with soft armchairs upholstered in rich browns and pale golds, an enormous woven carpet covering the floor from wall to wall. June was so absorbed in her surroundings, when she finally spotted the Queen, sitting quietly in an enormous throne-like armchair, she jumped again.

"Good afternoon," said the Queen, rising and giving a deep curtsy which June returned (much more gracefully, now that she had a dress on). "How are you enjoying your stay in Lumia?"

"Oh, it's wonderful, thank you. Thank you so much for having us." June took a subtle, steadying breath to stay the encroaching wave of panic. The Queen gestured to a seat near hers, next to a table holding a tea set.

"Do come and have some tea," the Queen said, and June nervously tripped over her dress in her hurry to cross the room. They both took a seat, and June stared stupidly at the tea set. Was she supposed to pour, or the Queen? She couldn't imagine it would be proper for the Queen to pour her own tea, much less June's.

Just then, a green-gowned Sidhe emerged from the shadows, poured two cups of tea, and then disappeared just as quickly as she'd come.

"Well, you've had quite a journey so far, haven't you?" said Queen Mab, picking up her saucer and cup and holding them in her lap.

"It's been an adventure," June said, fighting a nervous giggle as she picked up her own cup and saucer, aping the Queen.

"Well, unfortunately, it is just beginning," said the Queen, taking a sip of her tea. "We've finally been able to divine the location of the first tablet piece. It's somewhere on Fire Mountain, which is up in the northeast corner of the kingdom."

June raised her eyebrows, then smiled sheepishly. "I hope you don't think I'm stupid," she said, "but I'm really not sure where I am now. I've never seen a map of Prendawr."

The Queen gave a soft laugh, then set her tea down on the table and got up, walking across to a chest of drawers across the room.

"I'm sorry," she said over her shoulder, as she opened one of the drawers and extracted a hard leather tube. "It's easy to forget you've only been here a short time." The Queen sat down once more and twisted off the top of the tube, sliding a roll of parchment out and handing it to June, who unrolled it.

June's eyes widened as she looked at the map; Prendawr was

huge. She found Fire Mountain first, up in the corner, where the Queen had said it would be, and then Lumia, way down in the bottom. The worst part came when she located Meckle, and realized that, compared to what lay ahead, their nearly two-week trip from the town to here had been like a stroll to the corner store.

June sighed, letting her hands and the map drop into her lap; looking at their upcoming journey had exhausted her again. Heavy-hearted, she rolled the map back up and handed it to the Queen, who slid it back into the tube and handed it to June.

"You'll need a good map," Queen Mab said.

June nodded and murmured thanks.

The Queen's expression became dark and grave, and June drew back, alarmed.

"Now, for the unpleasant part of our business," Queen Mab said.

Oh my God, June thought. *Am I going to be doing some kind of negotiations here or something?* The Queen looked neither angry nor upset, just melancholy, which was somehow worse. June wanted to clap her hands over her ears and run out of the room. Whatever the Queen wanted to tell her, June didn't want to hear it.

Queen Mab sat back down, reaching over and patting the back of June's hand comfortingly, which only alarmed June further. With a deep sigh, the Queen began to speak.

"Something very disturbing has recently come to my attention, something which affects you deeply. You know who sent you to Earth, correct?"

June swallowed, trying to force some saliva into her dry mouth. "Um, Halryan, and the rest of the Sorcerer's Guild, right?"

The Queen nodded. "I was also part of that decision. Now, when the time came to retrieve you, Halryan volunteered, and no one argued, since the trip to Earth is a difficult one, and dangerous, since Earth's atmosphere prohibits magic."

"Why is that?" June asked, happy for an excuse to sidetrack Queen Mab from whatever she was about to tell her.

"Electricity," said the Queen. "It fouls up the atmosphere and makes it next to impossible to do any magic. In fact, that's why the Sidhe left Earth. It was either that, or give up magic forever." The Queen smiled, straightening in her chair, but June saw a flash of something behind her smile she didn't like. Before she could consider it, though, the Queen continued.

"Now, Halryan went to bring you back to Thallafrith, alone. There were things he should have told you, though, things we all assumed he would tell you, but he didn't. And it is now my duty to tell you these things."

Queen Mab rose, and beckoned June to follow her. She walked over to a curtain-covered wall and pulled a gold tassel next to it, drawing back the curtain to reveal a full-length, oval mirror.

"Do you know what this is?" Queen Mab asked.

June thought she did. "A–a magic mirror?" she asked, and the Queen nodded in surprise.

"You've seen one before?" she asked.

"Kind of," June said, smiling a little, since watching Snow White probably didn't count.

The Queen studied June for a moment, then took her gently by the arm and guided her squarely in front of the mirror, facing it.

"Tell me what you see," said the Queen, and June looked into the glass.

Whitish-grey mist clouded the surface, but quickly cleared, and an image slowly came into focus, like a television set being switched on.

An old man sat in one of several Adirondack chairs on a patio. An old woman and what appeared to be the couple's adult children and grandchildren occupied the other chairs. Although there was no sound from the mirror, all the faces were full of laughter.

"I see an older couple, and their family," June said, looking at the Queen, who was looking at June with disquieting intensity.

"Look again," said the Queen, and something in her voice made June's chest tighten. "Look closely."

June obediently squinted at the scene, bringing her face close to the mirror. Maybe the background? All she could see was a nice, green lawn, and the back of some neighbors' houses.

Her gaze returned to the people in the foreground. There was something familiar about the older man, and a younger man in a chair beside him, but she couldn't put her finger on it. June leaned in still closer, until her nose almost touched the mirror's surface. It was right there, just beyond her grasp. If she just looked a moment more...

And then it hit, with all the subtlety of Hiroshima, and the air seemed to go out of the room. *No,* thought June. *No, no. Not possible.* Her eyes frantically scanned the scene, trying to find something to tell her she'd come to the wrong conclusion.

It was like one of those magic eye paintings, though—once the hidden image has been revealed, it's impossible to view it as it was before. Try as she might, she couldn't help but see the image of her memory juxtaposed over the one right in front of her. Couldn't help but see the young, strong shoulders, now stooped with age, or the same soft brown eyes now peering out beneath grizzled brows. The liver-spotted hands, joints twisted with arthritis, once smooth and supple, which had caressed her body.

The old man in the chair was Kyle.

June backed up from the mirror as if it were a snake, nearly falling over a footstool behind her. The image in the glass melted away, to be replaced again by the serenely swirling miasma.

"No," she said, out loud, shaking her head back and forth without stopping, eyes still on the mirror. "That can't...how...?"

"Time does not pass on this planet as it does on Earth," Queen Mab said softly. "We chose the place as much for this reason as for its remoteness."

Realization crept over June, making her feel as though she were slowly being immersed in icy cold water. "So– so my mother...?"

"Died about a week before you arrived back to Thallafrith. I am so sorry, my dear."

~8~

June made it halfway out of the mound before she even realized she had run out of the Queen's chambers. She flung open the door with an enormous *bang* and raced outside. The sun had set, and stars were just beginning to appear. June wasn't thinking about the sky, though–she could only think of finding Halryan.

June sprinted across the grass, gown billowing behind her, until her feet carried her to the mound she somehow knew Halryan and the Valforte shared. Bursting in the front door, she found Halryan sitting in an armchair directly in front of her. As soon as he saw June, he froze, his face a flashing neon sign of guilt.

Without pause, June stalked straight up to Halryan's chair and socked him in the jaw. He rocked back from the force of the blow, and both he and his chair fell over backward. June was about to leap on top of him when out of nowhere, Koen and Minogan appeared, apparently woken by the commotion and clad only in long underwear bottoms, and grabbed her arms, restraining her.

Halryan scrambled to his feet and pressed himself up against the wall, face pale under his swarthy skin, holding his jaw.

"HOW COULD YOU DO THIS?" June screamed, struggling wildly against Minogan and Koen, who, despite the fact that they each outweighed her by about forty pounds, were having a great deal of difficulty holding on to her. "HOW? YOU BASTARD, I'LL KILL YOU!"

"My...my lady," Halryan stuttered, his lips white. "You must understand..." Feoras and Errigal had appeared in the doorway, also in nighttime garb, swords in hand, looking bewildered.

"June, *what* is going on?" Koen edged around in front of June, trying to meet her eyes, but she wrenched her arm from his grasp and Minogan's, backing away.

"Don't you *dare* try to act like you don't know," she said, eyes full of tears as she looked at Koen. "I *trusted* you. All of you. I thought you were my friends. Especially you. The least you can do is stop playing games."

The Valforte looked bewildered; Koen opened and closed his mouth a few times, running his hands through his already disheveled hair, apparently at a loss for words. "June, we haven't done anything.

I swear to you, I have no idea what you're talking about. And I don't think anyone else does, either."

June snorted in disbelief, swiping angrily at the tears running down her face.

"Ask your fearless leader, then," she said, her eyes returning to Halryan, who remained flattened against the wall with the side of his face cradled in one hand.

"Go on, tell them," June said, her eyes burning into Halryan's, and he pressed himself still closer to the wall as she began to walk toward him. "Go on," she prompted, her voice a steely dead calm. "Tell them."

Halryan's eyes began to scan the room like a mouse cornered by a cat, looking for an escape route or a rescuer. Without warning, June scooped up a vase off a nearby table and whipped it at Halryan's head, where it caught him just below the hairline and shattered. Halryan's knees buckled and he slid down the wall, the hand not cradling his jaw now trying to staunch the flow of blood coming from the cut the vase had left.

Koen and Minogan both rushed forward once more; Koen caught her wrist, but she wrenched it from his grip.

"You touch me again," June said to him, her voice cold, "you are going to be the sorriest man on this godforsaken planet. I swear it."

Koen looked uncertain and dropped his hands slightly, but held his ground. Minogan, on the other hand, backed off a few paces, exchanging glances with Errigal and Feoras. June returned her gaze to Halryan, who flinched as her eyes fell on him.

"Are you going to tell them?" June asked, and Halryan began to babble.

"I–I don't–I didn't..."

"Don't make me ask you again." June began to advance on Halryan once more, but Minogan held up his hands placatingly to her and turned to Halryan.

"Why don't you just tell us what's going on?" Minogan asked quietly, and Halryan's shoulders slumped in defeat.

"I–the main reason the planet Earth was chosen for her protective exile is because of the–the time."

"The time?" Minogan raised his eyebrows questioningly. Halryan gulped, made a small whimpering noise, then continued.

"Princess Ulfhilda is not Queen Morningstar's sister. She is her daughter." The Valforte gasped audibly, but June's eyes never left Halryan's face. "Queen Morningstar died giving birth to the princess.

We sent the princess to Earth, partly for her protection, and partly so she would be ready to assume the throne in a matter of weeks, not decades."

The Valforte looked at Halryan in silence, expressions of dawning horror on their faces.

"If the princess was born when the Queen died..." Minogan said slowly, glancing sidelong at June.

"Then everyone I've ever known is dead or dying," June finished, still looking straight at Halryan. "My home is gone, my friends are gone, everyone I've ever loved is gone. You had no right. *No right.*"

"It was the only way," Halryan said, eyes wide as he pushed himself up into a standing position, looking around the room for support. The Valforte stared back in disgust. He turned back to June and continued.

"The kingdom was under attack, the Queen was dead, something had to be done..."

"So you decided to play God with my life?"

"The lives of an entire world were at stake!"

"YOU NEVER ASKED ME," June yelled. "Did you think after all this was over, when I'd saved your planet for you and was ready to go home, you'd just tell me, 'Oh, well, everyone you ever knew is dead, so why don't you just hang out here and be the Queen?'" June laughed bitterly. "And that I'd be like, 'Oh, well, that's a real bummer, thanks for the invite, I guess I will?'"

June swayed slightly, dizzy with emotion–Koen moved to help her, but she pushed him roughly away.

"Well, you can forget it," June said. "Deal's off, the whole thing. You made your bed, now lie in it." June turned to walk out the door.

"Are you forgetting you'll die too?" Halryan said, a touch of his old cockiness coming through. June whirled around to face him and he flinched back again.

"I'm already dead," June said. "Everything I was, my past, my present, my *future,*" she swallowed hard, hand closing spasmodically over her engagement ring, "is gone. You left me with nothing. I'm just returning the favor." June began to turn away once more.

"And will you condemn them to death?" Halryan said, striding forward and grasping Koen by the shoulder. Koen pulled away, a look of revulsion on his face, but Halryan ignored him, focused on June, a desperately eager look on his face. "These men, who fought for you, nearly died for you? They had nothing to do with the decision to send you to Earth, nothing to do with the deception. Would you condemn them and the rest of this world for the sins of a small few?"

June looked around the room at the Valforte. None of them would meet her eyes; they all looked at the floor, faces intentionally blank, as though trying not to influence her decision.

She was desperate for revenge, to destroy Halryan, leave him with nothing as she'd been left with nothing. But could she sentence them all to death? Because *her* life had been destroyed, *her* heart broken, did the whole world have to pay for it? In terms of ratios, one life certainly was payment for a whole world. The cost was harder to reconcile when you were the one paying, though.

"You're right," said June. "I can't make others pay for your sins." Halryan's shoulders slumped in relief. "But I can make you pay for your own." His eyes snapped up to hers, and it gratified her to see the fear in them.

"You have a choice," June said, walking slowly over to where Errigal and Feoras stood. "You can leave the kingdom, tonight, and never come back, or–" June met Feoras' cautious eyes as she took the sword from his grasp, "I can kill you now." June turned back to face Halryan as she raised the sword up before her.

"You pick," she said, her eyes on the sharp shining edge of the steel.

Halryan paled once more and swayed on his feet. No one reached out to help him.

"I...I will leave, my lady," he said, softly.

The sword fell to the floor with a clang, and June walked out into the night.

June wandered aimlessly through the mounds until she found a solitary place, an orchard against the wall of the city. Mindlessly she gathered fallen branches from the fruit trees into a small pile at the edge of the trees. Thankfully, she'd stuck her cigarettes and lighter between her corset and shift when she got dressed that afternoon, and she used the lighter first to make a small campfire, then to light a cigarette.

June sat for a long time, staring into the flames and smoking. Just as she flicked her butt into the fire, she heard footsteps approaching.

"June?" She looked up to find Koen, dressed now, looking down at her with a cautious expression on his face. From behind his back, he produced a familiar skin bag, sloshing with liquid. "Minogan said to give this to you," he said, holding it out to her. "He thought you might need it."

June looked at Koen, then took the proffered bag, pulled out the cork, and took a long, deep drink, her eyes watering at the sting of the home-brewed alcohol. She lowered the bag, wiped her mouth, then took another drink, ignoring Koen's raised eyebrows. Her insides burning with a comforting heat, she corked the drinking bag and set it alongside her, then looked up at Koen.

"Was that all?" June asked, unable to keep a stinging note from her voice.

Koen sighed. "June, you have to believe I didn't know. None of us did. I would never...how could you think after everything, the fight in the inn, you saving me from drowning, saving us all from the Eid Gomen, that we would have continued to lie to you?"

June's eyes filled with tears once more, and she lit another cigarette to give herself something else to concentrate on.

"No offense, Koen," she said, exhaling smoke as she stared into the fire, "but I'm having just a little trouble figuring out what's fact and what's fiction here. First, I find out my whole life's been a lie, then I find out I was lied to about the supposed truth, and simultaneously find out that what was my life has been stolen from me. So pardon me if I'm not real clear on exactly where the lines are."

Koen was silent for a moment. "Do you want me to go?" he asked quietly, and June raised one shoulder.

"If you want," she said.

"That's not what I asked," he said. "Do *you* want me to go?"

June's throat felt very, very tight, and her head pounded from holding back tears. Even though she knew in her heart Koen didn't have anything to do with this, she hated the universe right now, and she wanted to hurt someone, to lash out, so they felt as badly as she did. But she didn't want to be alone.

"How about this," Koen said, walking over and sitting down beside her. "I'll hang around for a little while, and if you get sick of me, just say the word, and I'll leave. Okay?"

June nodded, not taking her eyes off the patch of ground between her feet, afraid to look Koen in the face and show him how broken she was right now. She raked her hair back from her face, leaving her fingers entangled in the waves at the back of her head.

As they sat in silence, reality hit June afresh. *Everything was gone.*

Her whole body began to shake; the more she tried to control it, the harder she shook. Her breath came in gasps, and sweat dampened her forehead, despite the cool night air.

"June? You okay?" She nodded, despite it being fairly freaking obvious that she was not, in fact, okay.

"Hey." Koen placed his hand on hers. "Look at me. June? Look at me." June shook her head *no*, her chest hitching as her lungs fought to catch a fulfilling breath of air.

Then Koen put his arm around her and pulled her into his chest, and June gave in to her grief's nauseating roller-coaster ride. It felt as though she cried for hours, harsh, wrenching sobs that threatened to snap her in two. Koen's arm stayed around her, though, his hand stroking her back comfortingly, and somewhere in her subconscious, a glimmer of hope flared. She'd lost everything, a whole life on Earth—but it seemed she had at least one friend here. And that was a start.

When the storm of tears finally subsided, June sat up, sniffling and wiping her eyes. She smiled sheepishly at Koen, then brushed at the front of his shirt.

"I got you all wet," she said, with a weak grin. Koen glanced down and shrugged, smiling.

"It'll dry," he said. "Feel better?"

June met Koen's eyes. "I do," she said. "Thank you for—for staying with me. I'm sorry I was such an ass." Koen waved his hand in a gesture of dismissal, then turned and looked into the fire.

"Are you going to finish the quest?" Koen asked, after a minute's silence.

June nodded.

"Yeah, I guess I am. Like it or not," her throat tightened threateningly again, and she swallowed hard, "this is where my life is now. And I can't punish the world for Halryan's sins."

Koen nodded thoughtfully. Then, without looking away from the fire, he said, "You know that *we're* not leaving, right? That me and Minogan and Errigal and Feoras, we're going to see you through this thing, as long as it takes?"

June closed her eyes against a trickle of fresh tears. "I think I did know, yeah," she said. "But it's nice to hear you say it."

They sat in silence for several more minutes, staring into the fire. June tried to ignore the ache in her chest, like an amputee's 'ghost pain,' only instead of a limb, she'd lost two decades of her life. But oh, how it hurt.

"You want me to walk you back to your place?" Koen asked finally, breaking the silence, and June shook her head as she reached for her cigarettes.

"I think I'm just going to stay here, watch the sun come up." She gestured with her head toward the lightening sky.

"Do you want me to stay?"

"No, I'm okay. Thank you, though." Flipping open the cigarette pack, June made a small noise.

"What is it?" Koen asked, and June picked the cigarette out with trembling fingers.

"Last one," she said, holding it up. She studied it for a moment, twirling it between thumb and forefinger.

"Maybe we can get a pipe or something," Koen said, and June smiled genuinely for the first time since she'd left the Queen's chambers, a brief image of herself in a wooden rocking chair, overalls, and a straw hat, smoking a corncob pipe, floating to the surface of her mind.

"No," she said, as the smile faded from her face. "I think it's better, this way." *Out with the old world, in with the new.* Koen, with a last, long look at June, turned and walked off between the rows of trees. June, turned so she faced the west, toward Thallafrith's rising sun.

As she watched purple ribbons streak across the sky, June wondered about Kyle, how long it had taken him to move on, what the rest of his life had been like. *He looked happy. Hell, maybe I wasn't even the one for him. Maybe I'd've screwed his life up if I'd stayed.*

She wondered, too, about Ashleigh and Shannon. Had Shannon found *The One?* Maybe even married Chuck? Did they have kids and grandkids like Kyle? Were their lives happy, or tainted always by the strange disappearance of their friend?

A thought hit June with a jolt, cramping her stomach with a sickening sensation of hollowness. In about a week, or maybe less, Kyle would be dead. If Shannon or Ashleigh were still alive now, they were old, old women...they didn't have much time left, either. And June's few remaining relatives had been at least twenty years older than her, so they were worm food by now, for sure.

Which meant in just a few weeks, no one would be left alive who remembered June. Any old pictures of her would be thrown out when relatives went through their belongings. No one would remember. No one would care. No one would miss her. It would be as if she'd never existed.

The bright colors of the sunrise bent into still more beautiful rainbows in the prisms of June's tears.

When the sun had risen, and her fire had burned out, June made her way back to her quarters, weaving through the mounds, surrounded by the quiet sounds of the Sidhe awakening, emptying their chamber pots and rustling around in the kitchen. The good smells of cooking wafted around her, and June's stomach protested at having been neglected so long.

Thankfully, no one was at her mound when June arrived. A hot cup of tea and a large tray of food sat on the table next to her bed. *They must have seen me coming and cleared out,* June thought. *Bad news travels fast.*

June slipped the gown over her head and dropped it to the floor. Grass stains streaked the rear of the dress, and several rips fringed the hem, but June could have cared less. Although Queen Mab had filled her in on Halryan's omissions, she'd still been a part of the original conspiracy, and June couldn't forgive that so easily.

June contorted herself into some highly improbable positions, trying to get to the corset strings in the back, before a thought struck her. *Duh,* she thought, shaking her head. *You have got to be the worst sorceress ever.*

Smiling humorlessly, she closed her eyes, concentrated, and sighed as the corset loosened. Easily unlacing the now-untied strings, she dropped the undergarment on top of the discarded dress. She looked down at her feet and wiggled her dirty toes, realizing she'd lost her shoes at some point.

Now, clad only in a fitted shift, she sat on the edge of the bed and picked up a piece of bread. She'd taken only a few bites before realizing, hungry as she was, she simply couldn't get the food down. Setting the bread aside, June opted for the hot tea with a little more cream and sugar than usual.

She was about halfway through the cup when exhaustion sandbagged her. Unable to sit up anymore, June scooted to the middle of the bed, sinking into the feather mattress. Despite her fatigue, though, she couldn't fall asleep.

June thought she knew now what a slave felt like. To not be viewed as a person, but merely a means to an end. She could understand why the Sorcerer's Guild had done things the way they had. They did, after all, need an adult queen. But had anyone stopped to think June would come to consider Earth her home and resent being ripped from it?

Halryan had. And that's why he hadn't told her. June could eventually forgive Queen Mab, for maybe it was ignorance which made her send June away to a foster family, a foster world. But Halryan knew exactly what June was going to think when she found out, and he'd deliberately kept it from her, to make his job easier.

June had to wonder, though, whether things would have been different, had she known. If Halryan had come to her and said, 'Look, millions of people will die if you don't come with me and help me save this world,' would she still have come? Would she have sacrificed her life, her happiness, for the lives of strangers?

The thing was, June thought she *would* have. It would have taken some pretty convincing evidence, and she might have needed a few days to think it over (*and Earth-days* are *a blink of an eye in this world*) but June really, honestly believed she would have come. And that's what upset her the most. If they'd been honest, maybe zapped her off to another part of Earth to make her listen, make her believe, the end result would have been the same. She'd've been here, helping save their planet, leaving her life behind. But she'd never been given the choice.

Maybe I just have a high opinion of my moral values, June thought, as her eyes finally closed.

When June woke from a heavy, dreamless sleep, it was morning–again. She'd slept all day and all night, and woken with the dawn. Another tray with steaming hot tea and food sat on the table next to her. *How do they know when I'm about to wake up?* June wondered. *Or is there some kind of spell on the cup that keeps it hot?* June thought Lesai and Nemura were just eerily attuned to her mood and sleep pattern; the cup didn't feel enchanted.

A dark blue dress with slipper shoes had been laid out for her on a nearby chair. With no destination in mind, but unable to sit still, she dressed and went out.

Even with her current mental state, she couldn't help but revel in the morning, crisp and fresh and fragrant, the sun slowly strengthening to warm her skin. Once again, June heard the Sidhe in the mounds waking and beginning their day. The grass, wet with dew, sent up clouds of its green fragrance as the stalks crushed beneath her feet. June wondered how they managed to keep the grass from being worn down by foot traffic.

June wandered around Lumia, threading aimlessly in and out between the mounds, when she spotted Minogan and waved at him. He raised his hand in response and waited for her to catch up, but it looked as though if given the chance, he would have pretended not to see her.

"Good morning," said June, smiling as best she could.

"Good morning to you," Minogan answered, looking wary.

"How are you?" June asked, struggling to maintain the conversation.

"I'm very well, thank you." Uncomfortable silence.

"Halryan leave?" June asked.

Minogan nodded. "About ten minutes after you did." More uncomfortable silence. Minogan had always been a tough nut to crack, but June thought after all they'd been through, he might have started to warm up to her a tiny bit. Still, except for sending her the rotgut last night, Minogan was nothing but business when it came to her.

"So, when do you think we should get going?" June said finally, breaking the silence.

Minogan blinked in surprise. "Do you know where we're going?" he asked.

"Fire Mountain, Queen Mab said." June had to think hard to recall the name; a lot of the other night was rather fuzzy. Minogan shook his head.

"Never heard of it."

"Well, the Queen gave me a map. I think I might have left it at her place, I'll have to ask for it again. Are you guys rested enough, though, or do you want to stay another day? Or a few days?" Minogan shrugged, looking nonplused.

"Whenever you think is best," he said, and June barely repressed a sigh of annoyance.

"It's still fairly early," she said, looking at the sky, where the sun was halfway to apex. "If we hurry, we could make it out by noon. Unless you want to stay."

Minogan shrugged again. "Sure," he said, and June clenched her hands behind her back.

"How about we leave at noon, then," she said, steadying her voice with an effort, "unless anyone has any objections?"

"As you wish," he said, and this time June couldn't suppress the sigh.

"All right," she said. "Why don't you get the guys together and pack up, and if there's any change of plans stop by my place. If not, I'll meet you about an hour before noon at the stables." Minogan nodded respectfully, then turned toward the gate, to his own quarters.

June stomped back toward her mound, annoyed. She didn't want an all-out pity party or anything, but it would have been nice if he could at least have acknowledged the events of the night before last. *Just a simple, "Hey, sorry your life got ruined," would do it,* she thought. *Don't have to get me a card or anything.*

And the "as you wish," crap. If there was one thing she hated, it was people who refused to make up their—wait. She slapped herself in the forehead, cursing herself for her stupidity.

Of course Minogan wasn't going to tell her what he wanted to do. With Halryan gone, she was the leader. And Halryan had never exactly been open to suggestions. She stopped walking, with half a mind to turn around and tell them to rest a few more days.

Then again, June wasn't exactly sure how much time they had before the world ended, so maybe they shouldn't procrastinate. And with everything she had on her mind, the distraction would be welcome. Twisting her engagement ring on her finger, she turned back and headed for her mound.

Lesai and Nemura had already begun packing for her when she returned, not that she had all that much. God, this ESP thing creeped her out. June forgot the creepiness, however, when she saw the surprise they had for her.

The Queen had traveling clothes made for June, two pairs of pants and three shirts, but more tailored than the men's clothing she'd been wearing. The pants fit better in the waist and leg, with enough give for freedom of movement, and the shirts looked more like a tunic than a man's castoff shirt.

Her underpants and bra had both fallen apart from weeks of hard wear and frequent washing. June really didn't think she'd miss the underpants; after all, they really just got in the way when you were trying to pee in the woods, and the elves gave her a girdle-like device for when she got her period. For a bra, they figured out a way to tie a wide strip of cloth around her breasts, like a halter-style bikini top, to achieve the same effect, effect of course being not hitting oneself in the chin while riding.

Minogan, Koen, Errigal, and Feoras were already waiting at the stables, along with Soltis, the Queen's advisor, and Lagart, captain of the guard. As she approached, flanked by Nemura and Lesai, who had insisted on carrying her one dinky saddlebag for her, Soltis stepped forward and bowed low.

"Your Highness," he said, stepping back slightly. "The Queen regrets she was unable to see you off herself, but she had urgent state business to attend to. Are you sure we cannot convince you to stay a few days longer?"

June shook her head, glancing at the men, whose faces remained carefully blank.

"Thank you very much," she said, "but I really think we should be going. Thank her for everything for me, her hospitality, and the clothing." Soltis bowed once more and stepped back, to be replaced by Lagart, who also bowed, making June feel momentarily like she was in a yard full of chickens pecking the ground. Very tall, skinny blonde chickens. Lagart handed her a familiar leather tube.

"Your map," Lagart said, and June slid the map out and unrolled it for the Valforte. Lagart also looked over the map, and nodded.

"Right here." Lagart indicated a road on the map, leading (in a meandering fashion) from Lumia to Fire Mountain, following parallel for a short time to the route they'd followed to get here. "Our intelligence indicates this to be a fairly safe route. It does not appear that there are any Eid Gomen settlements in this area." June looked to the Valforte to see their reactions; their faces, however, remained carefully impassive.

"Whatcha think?" she asked, and they all shrugged noncommittally. *Just as I suspected,* June thought. She put the map away, then tucked it into her saddlebag, which Lesai had set down nearby. She turned back to Lagart. "You'll show us which way to go, once we get back on the road?"

"Of course, Your Highness."

June caught sight of Rosie, tethered to a fencepost nearby, already saddled and bridled, and walked over to the animal, throwing her arms around the mule's neck. She hadn't realized how much she'd missed her.

"How you doing, sweetie?" she murmured, forehead pressed against the animal's neck. Rosie nickered softly, turning to nudge June in the shoulder. Apparently, the feeling was mutual.

They set out half an hour earlier than expected, since the grooms had packed and saddled their animals for them. They said their goodbyes to Soltis, Lesai, and Nemura. Everyone was silent, contemplating what lay ahead, as they followed the Sidhe through the woods, the Valforte blindfolded once more. June had barely gotten through half of the things which could possibly go wrong before they met the road.

"The road you want to take will meet this one on your left, a few miles ahead," Lagart said, pointing. "Safe journey."

With a bow, he and the rest melted away into the trees, leaving June mouthing wordlessly, uncomfortably aware of the sudden responsibility she now held. And how terribly alone they were in the forest. Swallowing hard, she turned Rosie in the direction Lagart had indicated, and the Valforte followed.

As promised, they found the path recommended by the Sidhe. June pulled Rosie to a halt as it came into sight, and the rest did the same.

"Are you sure you want to go this way, guys?" June asked, turning to the others. More noncommittal shrugs and blank expressions. June sighed and closed her eyes, letting her head flop back in a gesture of supplication to the heavens. She took a deep breath through her nose before lowering her head and looking squarely at the Valforte, who looked at her expectantly.

"Listen, I know Halryan was a dick, but I'm not Halryan. I don't give orders or commands or edicts. From here on out, this is a democracy–" June felt a jolt as 'democracy' came out in English, and clapped her hand to her mouth, as if she'd just cursed accidentally.

"What's a dem-ok-cras-ee?" Feoras asked, rolling the unfamiliar word off his tongue. June felt a surge of pity; they'd lived all their life in a world where there was no word for democracy.

"A democracy," June said, enunciating carefully, "means that everyone gets an equal say in decisions. For example, if you and I said we wanted to go this way," June pointed up the road Lagart had shown them, "and Minogan, Koen, and Errigal said they wanted to go that way," she pointed back the way they'd come, "then we'd go the way they wanted, because they're the majority." They stared at her, stunned.

"But you're the Princess," Errigal said, sounding scandalized.

"Not out here, I'm not," June said. "And it would be stupid to put me in charge, anyway, considering that you've lived here all your lives and I haven't even been here two months." June paused. "Every single decision that gets made from here on out could cost us our lives," she said, her eyes traveling over each of their faces. "No one person should have that power."

"You will, though, someday," said Koen, his face serious. June had a sudden vision of herself as Queen, and shuddered.

"We'll cross that bridge when we come to it," she muttered.

"Now, I'm going to withhold my vote until you've voted, so I don't influence your decision." She saw the corner of Errigal's mouth curl in a slight smile. "All in favor of going down this way?" June pointed down the road Lagart had shown them. They exchanged glances.

"Oh," June said, forgetting they'd never done this before. "If you want to go this way, raise your hand." All four hands went up.

"Well, okay then." She turned Rosie down the path they'd chosen.

"Wait," said Feoras. "You didn't vote."

June smiled. "Doesn't matter," she said. "Majority rules."

Since they had started out late in the day, they had a small meal on the run (June didn't have much of an appetite, but she tried to force some food down, for appearances' sake) and made camp at sunset. Democratic process worked against June here, for even in Halryan's absence, the Valforte still refused to let her do anything past caring for the horses, no matter how much she protested.

As night fell, the Valforte talked among themselves good-naturedly as they ate, with occasional sidelong glances at June, who sat quietly, staring into the fire, twisting her ring on her finger.

A lull in the conversation brought her back to the present, the sudden silence louder somehow than the men's voices had been, and saw them laying out their blankets in preparation for sleep. Errigal had drawn first watch—he sat with his bow on his lap, leaning against a tree. June wrapped herself in her blanket and lay down on her side, eyes still on the flickering orange of the fire.

June woke with a start, shivering and covered with sweat, her face wet with tears and her throat aching. It was dark, and the fire had burned down to coals. She sat up and wiped her face, glad she hadn't cried out, or the Valforte would have been on their feet, swords drawn.

"I wasn't sure whether I should wake you or not," Koen's voice said, from where Errigal had sat earlier in the evening. "I didn't want to scare you."

June nodded silently.

"What did you dream?" he asked.

June took a deep breath, trying to slow her pounding heart. "I don't remember," she said, truthfully. Then she gave a small snort, looking at her hand, gleaming in the moonlight with the tears she'd wiped from her face. "I think I could probably take a wild guess, though."

Koen nodded.

June stared at the shimmering coals, twisting her ring absently, trying to decide whether to stay awake and stoke up the fire, or try and go back to sleep.

"Did he give that to you?" Koen nodded toward her hand, and June nodded.

"My engagement ring," she said.

"You were going to be married?" His tone was conversational, but June thought she saw his eyebrows raise in the dark.

"Yeah," June said. "In three months." She snorted again. "Or fifty years ago, depending on how you look at it." She stood and walked over to the fire.

"Tea?" she asked, and Koen went to get up. "Oh, sit down, will you? Let me do it for once." Koen looked like he wanted to argue, but sat back down, a disapproving frown on his face.

June threw some wood on the coals, where it immediately caught and blazed up, then set the teapot, still half full of water, on to boil. As got the cups, she noticed her saddlebags laying on the ground, and fished out her pictures of Kyle, Ashleigh, and Shannon. She put a spoonful of tea leaves into each cup and went back to the fire, where she beckoned Koen to come and join her.

She handed the pictures to him and he nearly dropped them in shock.

"They're called pictures," June said, and gave him a brief, sketchy explanation of photography (since she really had only the sketchiest understanding of photography herself).

"Amazing," he said, handing them back to her. "It must be nice, to carry this with you."

"In this case, no," June said, studying the pictures. Then, without any forethought, she flicked them onto the fire, where they immediately curled and shriveled.

"No!" Koen made a grab to rescue them, but June grabbed his arm.

"Don't," she said.

"But..." Koen gestured toward the fire.

"No." June stared at the two lumps of black ash, still diminishing in the flames. "If I were at home, and they had died, or something...." June rubbed her hands over her face before continuing. "I'd have time to mourn. But I don't, here." She shrugged helplessly. "I can't fall apart. As much as I would love to just lie down and close my eyes and not get up again, ever," her eyes stung, and her throat began to ache again, "I can't. The whole frigging world needs me to be

Superwoman. And if I looked at those pictures every day, I'd always be looking backward." She swallowed hard. "I'll always remember them, always, but that part of my life is over, and nothing will ever change that."

"And that?" Koen said, nodding again at her hand, where she'd been fiddling with her ring again.

June smiled humorlessly, looking down at her hand.

"Yeah, well, I can't go completely cold turkey." Wrapping a rag around her hand, she lifted the teapot full of now-boiling water off the fire and poured them both a cup of tea. They sat in silence, sipping their drinks and watching the sun come up, until the others woke and swept them into the bustle of the day.

This journey was much more pleasant than the one from Meckle to Lumia. The flat terrain made travel easier for the horses, and fresh green meadows full of singing insects and birds broke up the monotony of the trees. Abundant game meant the Valforte could frequently augment their supplies of dried food with fresh meat. They found much better grazing for the horses, which meant they could travel longer distances, and preserve the grain stores.

Despite the gorgeous surroundings, easy travel, and lightness of mood she attributed to Halryan's absence, June struggled to keep going. Some days she had to break it down as far as one foot in front of the other. It was exhausting to continue, and even more exhausting to put on an act for the others, pretending she was fine, that every second of every day she wasn't praying something would swoop down and kill her quickly, so finally, in death, she could lay down all her burdens.

After several days on the road, the trees parted, revealing the bluest, most beautiful lake June had ever seen. Even the Valforte couldn't mask their amazement as they stepped onto the shoreline for a better look. Its crystalline waters seemed to beg June to jump in. Looking down the shoreline, she saw a small tree-covered peninsula jutting out into the lake. If she went around that bend–

"All in favor of taking a break?" Now perfectly comfortable with democracy, all four men raised their hands.

"Perfect. If you don't mind, I'm going down there," she pointed to the peninsula, "to take a bath. So you might want to stay here, unless you want an eyeful." All four Valforte blushed blue, and June smiled wryly as she turned Rosie down the shore.

June found a perfect little beach on the other side of the peninsula, like someone had left it here, just for her. She dropped

Rosie's reins, knowing the mule well enough now to be sure she wouldn't go anywhere, and stretched, facing the water and tingling with anticipation.

With a little thrill of exhibitionism, she stripped off her clothes and waded into the water. It felt even better than she'd imagined, cool and refreshing, not cold. She remembered she'd forgotten to grab her soap, but the water was too nice to get out just now. She'd get it in a minute.

Strangely, though, she couldn't relax. The water was perfect, the air warm and fragrant with forest smells. Maybe the quiet was what bothered her. Stubbornly determined to relax in the idyllic setting she found herself in, she floated on her back and closed her eyes.

And opened them wide again, standing up in the water as a knife of panic flashed through her chest. Something told her she needed to get back to the Valforte, right now. She lunged toward the beach and dressed as quickly as she could, leaving her shoes and pulling her shirt on as she ran through the trees, twigs prickling the soles of her feet, leaving Rosie to stare after her.

She broke out of the trees and stopped dead in horror. The beach was deserted, the lake smooth and empty, like they'd never been there at all. A second, crueler stab of panic hit as she envisioned herself abandoned in a strange world, forced to complete the quest alone. *They didn't,* she thought, gasping. *They* wouldn't…

"Guys?" June shouted, whirling around. "Guys!"

She turned, just in time to catch a glimpse of a triangular grey head, black eyes glimmering soullessly. A flash of pain, bright red, a sound like roaring wind in her head, and the world went black.

~9~

"I think–did she move?"

"I can't tell; it's too dark in here."

"Her breathing changed, I think."

"There–she moved again."

Whispers surrounded her, swelling and fading like ocean waves. As she floated toward consciousness, she became aware of excruciating pain in her head, like nothing she'd ever experienced. It didn't feel like June even had a head anymore; just a bloody, pulpy mass at the end of her neck. She wanted to slip back into the black, into the quiet, where it didn't hurt. But she could hear the fear in the voices of her friends, knew it was for her.

With a supreme effort, she forced her eyes open, blinking rapidly, trying to focus on the shadowy forms hanging over her.

"June?" Koen's voice, sounding worried. All the parts of her mouth were sticking together–she struggled to moisten her tongue so she could move it.

"Yeah," she breathed finally, amid gasps and exclamations of relief. Her head throbbed rhythmically in the midst of a thick fog. Her limbs felt like wood. With another huge effort, she lifted a hand to her right temple, the epicenter of the pain, sticky with blood and swollen to an unbelievable size.

Nausea overwhelmed her suddenly, and she managed to roll over on her stomach before vomiting, pulling her knees underneath her and pushing up with her elbows to get off the floor. She retched with such violence June thought her head would split open. The fog began to close in on her again, dragging her down into a darker and darker grey which would undoubtedly become black.

"I think she's passing out again," someone said, and June felt someone's arms slip around her chest and waist and pull her into his body for support. The sensation of contact brought her back toward consciousness, and she pushed for the surface once more. This time, she felt as though she passed through an invisible membrane, behind which the fog lay trapped. Ribbons of too-bright color swirled sickeningly behind her closed lids, but she didn't think she would pass out again.

"I'm okay," she whispered, then, more strongly, "I'm okay." She pushed herself up off Koen's lap, where he'd pulled her to keep her from hitting the floor, wiping her mouth.

"Did I get puke on you?"

"Wha–no, no, you didn't," Koen looked utterly nonplused, as if she'd just asked him if he knew how to waltz. June looked up, ignoring the indignant stab of pain in her head as she moved too quickly.

"Everyone else okay?" They all nodded. Their faces shone pale in the darkness, and they had some scratches and bruises, but no major injuries. June looked past them at the room.

They were in a small dungeon, floor-to-ceiling stone, with an iron-barred door and a smattering of straw on the floor. A wooden bucket stood in the corner, exuding an odor that made clear its purpose. Firelight flickered dimly from the hallway, making the shadows in the corners seem eerily alive. June was very glad they hadn't decided to put her in a cell on her own.

"What happened?" asked June, and Minogan snorted.

"We were stupid, that's what," he said. "We let our guard down, and about five minutes after you left our sight, those grey bastards surrounded us, told us they had you already, and if we put up a fight you'd be dead. Of course," his jaw muscles flexed as he ground his teeth in anger, "they *didn't* actually have you yet, and if we *would* have fought, we'd have been able to save you and ourselves, but we didn't." Minogan turned and kicked the stone wall, a murderous look on his face.

June was taken aback. She'd never seen Minogan lose control, and it unnerved her. That, and the shouting hurt her head.

"Minogan, don't," June said, as he loaded his leg to kick the wall once more. "We'll get out of here, don't worry."

"How?" asked Errigal, a sour look on his face.

June took a deep breath, then slowly got to her feet. The Valforte stood also, Koen holding his hands out cautiously toward her, afraid she'd pass out again. It was a near thing.

"*Mmm*," she said, swallowing hard as another wave of nausea hit. It passed quickly, though, and June walked over to the bars to look out.

Torches burned in sconces along the narrow stone hallway, which ran perpendicular to the cell. She leaned forward and grasped the bars to try and get a better look and nearly fell over as the door swung open, spilling her out into the hallway.

June paused for a moment, brow furrowed, then poked her head back in the cell, where the Valforte stared open-mouthed at her.

"Did you even *try* the door?" June hissed.

"Of course we did," Minogan hissed, looking offended.

"Well, um...it's open now," she said.

The Valforte took the exact same formation as when they rode as they filed quietly out of the cell, two in front, two behind, making a June sandwich. She made sure to close the door to their cell, thinking if someone walked by, an open door would attract more attention than a closed one.

"Which way?" she whispered, and Minogan, who, unlike June, had been awake when brought in, pointed to their left.

They traveled at a slow jog, which made June's head ache as her feet hit the stone floor, sending a jolt up through her body. Her head was clearing quickly, though; feeling it experimentally, she found the lump had already shrunk to half its size. The way she'd been hit, on the temple, she knew she was lucky she hadn't been killed. If luck actually had anything to do with it.

Benefits of being a sorceress, June thought. *Then again, if I weren't a sorceress, creepy alien guys wouldn't be chasing me around bonking me on the head.*

The Valforte's memory amazed June; they must have been paying close attention when they came in, for they seemed certain about the path they took as they wended their way through the tangled corridors which made up the Eid Gomen's dungeon.

Suddenly, every hair on June's body stood up. "Hide," she whispered urgently, "Quick!" The Valforte doubled their speed, but even so, June heard footsteps behind them. Then, suddenly, they found a door, and June was pushed roughly in and the door shut, all four Valforte pressed against it in preparation for attack.

June, however, had stepped further into the room, and gazed starry-eyed at the contents.

"Jackpot," she whispered, and the Valforte turned to look.

The room was piled high with weapons and armor. Crossbows, swords, knives, shields, mail shirts...heaped together, as though discarded. Quickly, the Valforte surged forward, grabbing swords, bows, and arrows and strapping them on.

June chose a knife on a studded belt–she wanted something smaller, and didn't know how to use a sword, anyway, other than swinging the pointy part at the bad guy. As she strapped it around her waist, she noticed reddish-brown stains on the belt, and suddenly understood why these weapons had been thrown carelessly into piles.

She caught Errigal's eye, a similarly stained strap of leather in his hands, and they looked at each other for a moment in mutual understanding. June rubbed her thumb gently over one of the stains, then straightened, mouth set.

They looked at one another, somber determination in each face. June looked at their clenched jaws and squared shoulders, and was grateful for their presence. If anyone could get them out, these men could.

The footsteps passed the door, and echoed off in the distance. Minogan looked at June and raised his eyebrows. *Ready?* June nodded crisply, faking a confidence she didn't feel.

Silently, they crept out of the discarded weapons room and continued on the way they'd been going, at the same slow jog, careful to keep their swords and such from clanking and giving them away. June tried to send herself out, to scout for Eid Gomen, but something was interfering–she couldn't get more than a few corridors away. Still, they managed to stay out of the Eid Gomen's way. For a while.

Then the inevitable happened, when June felt the approach of the Eid Gomen, and there was nowhere to go.

June sensed relief among the Valforte as they stood, shoulders squared, between herself and the six Eid Gomen who blocked the corridor, and understood it, even if she didn't share it. At last, they had their enemy in front of them. June drew her knife from her belt, weighing the heft of it in her hand, hyperaware of the textured stiffness of the rawhide-wrapped handle as it shifted against her palm. *I hope you give me better luck than you did your last owner.*

The Valforte touched their swords briefly together, like a toast, and charged.

June had gotten a sense of the Valforte's talent as warriors when they'd last stood against the Eid Gomen. She'd noticed a certain quick preciseness to their actions which belied an athlete's familiarity with his body and its capabilities, but she'd never seen them fight, never so much as a friendly spar among themselves. She'd seen sword fights in movies, but she'd never seen anything like this.

The Valforte moved with exquisite grace, never wasting a stroke, working together seamlessly, as though by some form of telepathy. If there wasn't so much carnage, she might consider it beautiful. Insanely, it reminded her of a cook she'd seen on television once. The man seemed to merely pass his knife over an onion or a clove of garlic, and a split second later the unfortunate vegetable lay in tiny squares on the cutting board, diced to perfection. Well, the

Valforte were the cooks, and the Eid Gomen, the onions.

Within seconds, the passageway was clear, and June stepped over the bloody remains of their attackers to follow the Valforte as they sped along the passageways. None of the Eid Gomen had escaped to raise the alarm, but it wouldn't be long before more of them came across the remains of their companions.

Suddenly, the corridor opened into an enormous room, the size of two football fields, dwarfing the Eid Gomen guards who stood ready with spears. At the other end of the room stood a giant archway, cut into the stone wall. Their way out.

They sprinted across the open room. June was terrified, for now they were open to attack from all sides. Guards advanced on them from the back, side, and front, and more emerged from the shadows, converging on them with terrifying silence and speed. The Valforte, though, sliced through their opponents with the grace of an Olympic diver knifing splashless into the water. Before she knew it, they'd made it through the archway, and outside.

What she saw nearly stopped her in her tracks, if Koen and Feoras, behind her, hadn't urged her on.

The building they'd escaped wasn't *made* of stone; it was carved from it. One single, solid piece of stone. As were the buildings, shapeless lumps of rock with doors, lining a stone avenue three times the width of a football field and continuing lengthwise as far as the eye could see. Trashcan sized indents had been gouged out of the road, and fires within them dimly lit the way. Above them, instead of sky, was a convex expanse of stone, like an inverted bowl.

They were under the lake.

They ran flat-out down the center of the avenue, heading for some distant point June couldn't see. A horrible, discordant gong began to sound, like a warped church bell, nearly causing June to falter. As did the sight of hundreds of Eid Gomen pouring from the entrances of the crooked buildings and heading straight for them.

"Shit," gasped Feoras behind her.

June could now see their goal. The ground rose straight ahead, but rather than cresting, it met the ceiling of the gigantic cave where it dipped down to meet the ground. A tunnel had been cut where ceiling and floor met, and June prayed it lead outside.

Even if they made it to the opening, June couldn't see any hope for escape. The Eid Gomen trailed them, their thin grey legs pumping in hot pursuit, axe-spears raised in savage excitement. She doubted the Eid Gomen would give up the chase once they got out. There wasn't enough space to lose them, and too many of them to fight. The Valforte had done their part...now it was June's turn.

They had reached the tunnel. As Minogan and Errigal ducked through, June darted off to the side, slamming herself flat against the wall, so Koen and Feoras continued for several feet past her, unable to stop.

"Hey," Koen yelled. "What the hell are you doing?"

"Get back," June shouted over her shoulder. She had turned to face the terrifying wave of grey bodies and sharp spears rushing toward her, trying to slow her pounding heart with a deliberate, deep breath. She focused her eyes on the ceiling above them.

"June," Koen shouted again

"Get back, I said!" June's voice left no room for argument. Her limbs began to tremble as she summoned every bit of strength in her body into a thick, hot ball just below her rib cage. This wouldn't have been easy in normal circumstances, but there was something here interfering with her magic.

She closed her eyes, trying to find some inner, quiet place, far from the cries of the Valforte and the disturbing war whoops of the Eid Gomen, who had nearly reached her. June envisioned a caged tiger, crouching, every fiber of its being focused on its unsuspecting prey.

Her eyes opened, focusing once more on the portion of the ceiling farthest from them. The tiger sprang, and with an earsplitting crack, the stone buckled and collapsed.

Billions of gallons of lake water, cold and foaming and angry, dropped onto the Eid Gomen, crushing some, drowning others, sweeping with terrifying speed toward the place where she stood.

June had just a moment to take this in before her knees gave way and the darkness swallowed her once again.

June woke to water trickling down her throat. She coughed weakly, then harder as the water went down the wrong pipe. She opened her eyes, blinking against the sunlight.

Koen, Minogan, Errigal, Feoras. They had all made it. June smiled at the welcome sight of their blue faces peering with concern into hers. She shifted slightly against the tree she'd been propped against and the bark caught at her hair. When she lifted her hand to untangle it, it felt as though she had twenty-pound weights tied to her wrist. God, she was weak.

"We made it," she croaked, and they all nodded.

"Yeah, barely," Koen said, shaking his head in disapproval, but unable to mask a slight smile. "Next time, could you stand a little further back if you're going to do something like that?"

"Oh, next time, he says. Such a freaking comedian." June said sarcastically, just before a wave of dizziness hit. She took a deep breath and blew it out through pursed lips.

"Is there anything to eat?" she asked. She needed sugar or something before she passed out. Luckily, Feoras had picked some berries in anticipation, and she popped the entire handful in her mouth, chewing thoroughly, sucking every drop of the tart juice out. She swallowed, and felt an instant glow of warmth radiate out from her belly to the rest of her body, and her head cleared. Looking around, she saw nothing but trees, with no sign of the lake or the road anywhere nearby.

"Everybody okay?" June asked, and Minogan cocked his head toward Errigal, who sat behind everyone else, face pale. Feoras had been standing in front of him, but as he moved to the side, she could see Errigal was shirtless, said shirt being soaked with blue blood and pressed to his left forearm. June sucked her breath in between her teeth, hissing softly. She scooted over to Errigal, unmindful for a moment of her own discomfort.

"Let me see," she said, softly, and Errigal held his arm out without hesitation. June carefully pulled back the shirt, and bit her lip in order to not make a sound.

The back of Errigal's arm had been slashed from elbow to wrist, the bluish-white of bone clearly visible deep in the wound. Drops of blood pattered onto the dead leaves from his fingertips in a sickening tattoo.

"How did this happen?" June asked.

"When we were coming out of the dungeon, in that big room. One of the guards got me with his spear." Errigal grimaced in pain as he recalled the strike. *And he still fought the whole way,* June thought, shaking her head. *My God.*

June pressed the cloth back to the wound and sighed. Something had to be done, but she just didn't have the physical energy to heal him; if she tried now, she'd very likely kill herself. As she sat back to think, she brushed up against Feoras, who stood behind her, and felt an odd tingle throughout her entire body that made her gasp. She looked up at Feoras thoughtfully.

"I think I can do something," June said. "But I need help. Are you feeling pretty good?" Feoras nodded, clearly puzzled.

"I'm not strong enough to do this, not right now, and if we let it go longer–" she glanced at Errigal, then back to Feoras, who lifted his chin in understanding.

"What do you need me to do?"

"I need to borrow some of your...strength, I guess you'd call it," June said. She patted the ground next to her, in front of Errigal. Feoras squatted down where she'd indicated.

June reached out for Errigal's arm again, uncovering the wound. Errigal averted his eyes–obviously, he didn't much care for the sight of his own blood.

"Ready?" she asked Errigal, and he nodded, teeth gritted, his expression anticipating pain. She turned to Feoras, the same question on her face, and he nodded as well.

"Give me your hand," she said, and Feoras did. Gently, she laid her other hand on Errigal's slashed arm and closed her eyes.

It was an interesting sensation, challenging, like directing traffic in New York City. Feoras grunted in surprise, and she felt the flow of his energy stall, and her own energy sap into Errigal.

"Please don't fight me," she murmured, almost a moan, and he relaxed, allowing her to take what she needed. Weak as she was, she managed to channel all of what she took from Feoras into Errigal, without keeping any for herself.

A few seconds later, she got a sensation of fullness from Errigal's arm, and she released them both. Errigal looked down at his arm, skin smooth and unbroken, with blood still drying from a wound that no longer existed.

"Wow," he said, then turned his head away and threw up. Koen put a steadying hand on his shoulder, and Errigal clapped his over it in acknowledgment.

Feoras had fallen back, gasping when June had released him, beads of sweat standing out on his forehead, his face ashen. "My God," he half-whispered, voice awed, "is that what it's like for you every time?"

"Mm-hmm," June said, without looking up. She sat Indian-style, elbows on knees and head in hands, trying to keep from passing out for the third time today. It wasn't working, so she flopped down on her back, hands over her eyes, breathing deeply. She'd been able to use Feoras's energy for most of the healing, but she'd still had to use some of her own, and she didn't have any to spare.

"Can you walk?" Minogan asked her quietly.

"Uh-uh," June said, shaking her head the slightest little bit in the negative. She heard Valforte talking quietly among themselves from what seemed like very far away. She'd heard it wasn't possible to pass out when you were laying down; however, she had a feeling she was about to disprove the theory.

"We have to go, there had to have been some survivors, they'll be looking for us..."

"Well, obviously, but what are we going to do? She can't walk..."

Suddenly, she felt herself being lifted, and opened her eyes to find herself in Koen's arms. He jerked his head in a 'come on' gesture to the other Valforte.

"Koen, no, I'm too heavy..." she protested. "Just leave me here."

"That would make the quest kind of pointless," Koen said, with a smile in his voice. "And you are not too heavy. In fact," he bounced her gently in his arms, "you're too light. You need to start eating more."

"Koen, please..." she said, although her head had already flopped onto his chest.

"*Shh*," he said. "Just go to sleep. I've got you."

And with the comforting thump of his heart in her ear, she did.

When June woke up, it was dark. Koen felt her stir, stopped, and set her down on her feet, one hand still on her back in case she fell over. She didn't. In fact, she felt pretty good. "How long have I been asleep?" she asked, stretching.

"Oh, about five hours, maybe," Koen shrugged.

"Five *hours*? You carried me for *five hours*?"

Koen shrugged again. "Well, you got passed around some," he said, smiling.

June groaned, embarrassed. "I didn't drool on anybody, did I?" she asked. Errigal raised his hand, an evil grin on his face. June glared at him, wiping her mouth self-consciously.

"Feeling better, I see," she said to him, and he dropped his foolish grin and smiled in earnest, rolling back the sleeve of his bloodstained shirt.

"Good as new," he said, flexing his hand and wrist.

"So, how are we doing?" June asked the group at large.

"Well, we've got no food, no water, no horses, and we're fairly sure we're being pursued," Minogan said, sounding aggravated. June's stomach dropped sickeningly at the mention of the horses, thinking of her Rosie.

"What happened to the horses?" she asked, a slight tremble in her voice.

"Oh, I'm sure they're fine," Minogan said, "they're just not *here.*"
The weight in her chest lifted.

"I could probably fix that," June said, plopping down cross-
legged on the ground, preparing to send herself out, like she had for
the draek. Koen eyed her dubiously.

"Am I going to have to carry you again?" he asked.

"Thought you said I wasn't heavy," June retorted, glaring good-
naturedly up at him. Koen just rolled his eyes.

She found the horses easily, since they hadn't moved far from
the lake shore, and June and the Valforte hadn't traveled far on foot.
She felt Rosie's presence and gave a sigh of relief as she called her
and the rest of the animals to her. She pushed out further, trying to see
the Eid Gomen, but something blocked her, and she could feel the
drain on her energy already.

"The horses are coming," she said, snapping back to herself and
shaking her head to clear it. "And the Eid Gomen are around, I just
can't get a clear picture of them." She slammed her fists into her
thighs angrily. "Why can't I see them? I could see them before, so
why not now?"

"The Eid Gomen are powerful magicians," Minogan said. "If
they're in their home territory, they're even more powerful. And they
know you're looking for them, so they're on their guard."

"Well," June said, taking Koen's proffered hand up, "the horses
are on their way. We can still keep walking; they'll find us."

"Hopefully before the Eid Gomen do," Minogan said.

June looked at him sharply. "We're in a lot of trouble here, aren't
we?" she said. He nodded as they began to walk again. June made a
sound through her nose.

"Okay, so here's another thing I don't get," June said. "How the
hell did the Sidhe not know about this? That little town the Eid
Gomen have–or had–couldn't exactly have been built overnight. So
how did they miss it?" The Valforte all exchanged cautious glances.

"Do you think we were sent here deliberately?" June asked
warily.

"The idea came up," Minogan said, his voice carefully neutral.

"So you think it was on purpose, then." Minogan paused,
seeming to make up his mind about something, then nodded.

"So is it just a small group, or is it all of the Sidhe?" June
pushed, trying to catch someone's eye; they all looked at the ground,
faces blurry in the starlight.

"It might just have been an accident," Minogan said. "The Eid Gomen are very powerful. Maybe they really didn't know if the Eid Gomen had their location well hidden."

"But you don't think it's likely," June said, her eyes traveling again from face to face.

"No, we don't think it's likely," Feoras said finally, ignoring a sharp glance from Minogan.

June gave an exasperated sigh. "I know you don't want to falsely accuse anyone, especially anyone as powerful as the Sidhe, and I know that you," she turned to Minogan, "still don't trust me, but you're going to have to start. We're all we've got, and as long as you stay with me, my enemies are your enemies. So let's figure out who they are, exactly." June looked at Minogan again. He looked back with a very strange expression on his face. "What?" she asked hotly.

"'As long as you stay with me'? What does that mean, exactly?"

"It means that Halryan's gone, and I don't have any claim on you," June said, forcing nonchalance into her tone, getting angry for no reason at all. "So anyone who wants to go home, can. At any time." Minogan stared at her, expression full of almost scornful disbelief.

Looking at his face, so shocked by her statement, despite having made it clear they were her friends, not employees or slaves, something in June snapped. Anger bubbled in her chest, white-hot, and she stepped right up to Minogan, who held his ground with some difficulty.

"How many times do I have to tell you that I am *not* Halryan?" June said, her voice rising dangerously. "I am very sorry I was born with this," she pointed to her face, at her skin, "but it's not my fault. Neither is the fact that I was born who I am. Or that the people who look like me treat you like shit. Most especially, it is not my fault that your people have *let* my people plow over you without lifting a finger to fight it, which I don't understand after watching you fight today." Tears streamed down her face, hot and oily, as her temper spiked. She stepped back from Minogan.

"I've fought for you. I've saved all of your lives together three times. I saved his life," she pointed at Koen, "and I'm fairly sure I saved his life today." She pointed at Errigal. "I have been ripped from my home, lost my future husband, my friends, my *life,* and still I have kept moving forward to save a world I don't even feel is mine, mainly on your behalf. So my question to you is, what exactly *do* I have to do to get you to say, 'Hey, I think she's all right!'" June kept her eyes on

Minogan, who was now staring at the ground, jaws clenched.

"If you don't trust me, or like me, then why don't you do me a favor and go the hell home?" she asked, choking back a sob and wiping the tears from her face with her sleeve.

Just then, the horses trotted up, and June turned and swung up on Rosie, urging her into a fast canter away from the Valforte, who stood stunned as they watched her go.

"June! *June!*" She heard Koen's voice behind her, peppered with his horse's galloping hoofbeats as he raced to catch up with her. He pulled up alongside her, squinting in the dusky twilight to see her face.

"Hey," he said softly, leaning out of his saddle toward her. "Are you okay?"

"Oh, sure, peachy-freaking-keen," she snapped, and Koen recoiled slightly.

"I'm not the bad guy here," he said. Then, after a long pause: "Or am I?"

June raked her hands through her hair, taking a deep, ragged breath.

"No, you're not. I'm sorry." She sighed again, thinking she'd never sighed as much in her whole life as she had here. "I should probably try not to alienate the only friend I have."

"That's not true," Koen said. "You have Feoras, and Errigal."

"That's different, and you know it," June said, picking a leaf out of Rosie's mane. After a small silence, Koen spoke again.

"Minogan's father was killed in front of him when Minogan was ten, beheaded, by an Andrian who wanted his ox and cart."

June closed her eyes, torn between sympathy for Minogan, and hurt that he would equate *her* with those kinds of people.

"And I'm sorry for it, but I can't go back in time to fix it. And I think I've proven I'm not that kind of Andrian." June's voice began to rise dangerously again, and Koen held his hands out in a placating gesture.

"I didn't say he was right to feel the way he does, I only told you so that you could maybe understand a little more about him."

"And why would I want to understand him when he makes no effort on my part?" June asked hotly.

"Because despite the way he's been treating you, he's really a good guy," Koen said, and June remembered this was his best friend. They heard hoofbeats approaching swiftly behind them, and Koen's hand went to his sword hilt, then relaxed as Minogan, Errigal, and

Feoras trotted up on their horses, with the pack animals in tow. June turned quickly back around to face front, not wanting to look at Minogan.

Minogan thwarted her plan when he pulled up alongside her horse, sandwiching her between himself and Koen. She kept her eyes down, ripping the leaf she'd pulled from Rosie's mane into teeny bits, but she felt Minogan watching her. Finally, grudgingly, she lifted her eyes to his face.

"There's something you need to know," he said, a strangely vulnerable note in his voice, and June's eyes narrowed. For the first time, she felt she was seeing Minogan himself, and not what he wanted her to see.

"I told her," Koen said. "About your dad."

Minogan stiffened slightly, but didn't take his eyes off June's face.

"That wasn't what I was planning on telling her, but I'm glad she knows," he said. "It might make this next part a little easier to understand." He dropped his eyes, and June glanced at Koen, who shrugged, apparently lost. Errigal and Feoras, however, wore expressions similar to Ashleigh's dog when it had made a mess on the carpet.

"I didn't take this journey on for the money, or for our people's safety," Minogan said. "Neither did Errigal or Feoras. We took it so we could kill you."

"WHAT?" Koen's face went grayish with shock, but June held her hand up.

"Go on," she said.

"We planned on taking you through to complete the quest, and once you'd saved the world, we'd kill you, and try to take control of the capitol. Obviously, Koen wasn't in on it. He thought maybe once you got to know us, you could be convinced to change things when you were queen. He'd never agree to an assassination."

"You're damn right I wouldn't! What the hell were you—" June held up her hand once more, and added a warning glance this time.

"Keep going," she said, turning back to Minogan.

"After a few weeks, though, Errigal and Feoras dropped out. They said they liked you too much, that they couldn't go through with it anymore."

"But you could," June said, and he nodded.

"All I had to do was remember my father's head lying in the dirt, his eyes still on me," Minogan swallowed hard, "and I knew I could do it. All I had to do was to keep from getting fond of you. But it started getting harder after Lumia." June's gaze stayed on Minogan's face, unmindful of the slight golden glow lighting the forest as the sun began to rise. "Seeing what you were going through, and how you respected us...."

"Really had to put your mind to hating me, huh?" June asked, and Minogan nodded.

"I always had doubts after something happened, or you said something that made me think you might actually fix things when you became queen, and it got harder to stay focused, but I managed."

"Until a couple of minutes ago," June said, and Minogan nodded.

"I was acting like an Andrian," he said. "Hating you because of what you are." He laughed bitterly. "Not to mention you're probably the best chance my people have.

"So I'm sorry, for the way I've treated you, for what I planned to do...everything." With a deep breath, Minogan turned his horse away and began to ride back the way they came.

"Minogan, wait." He reined his horse in and turned to face her, his face dark and full of shame.

"Where are you going?" June asked.

"Home," he said, looking away.

"Why?"

Minogan looked at her, incredulous. "Because I—well, you—" He shrugged his shoulders helplessly.

June looked at the sky for a moment, palest blue in the morning light, then back at Minogan.

"If you're leaving because you don't want to do this quest, then I won't stop you," she said, "but if you're doing it because you're ashamed or embarrassed, don't be. Stay."

Minogan blinked, surprised, and opened his mouth to speak, but Koen interjected.

"What do you mean, 'stay'?" he asked, astounded. "He was going to kill you!" He glared angrily at Minogan, who turned his head, unable to meet Koen's stare.

"He did no less than I would have done, Koen," June said, and Koen stared at her wide-eyed. "Your people are in a hell of a lot of trouble, and he was planning to do what he could to save them with the resources he had. I might have done the same, if I'd've been smart enough to think of it in the first place."

Koen continued to stare at her in disbelief. Words failing him with June, he rounded on Minogan.

"How could you?" Koen's voice was low and dangerous. "How could you plan something like this, then keep it from me? *Me?*"

"Visions of a reaction like this, for one," Minogan said, regaining some of his composure. "And I knew you'd never agree, and you'd talk the others guys out of it, and I couldn't let that happen."

"War is one thing," Koen said, voice rising, "but you were planning murder. You'd be no better than the Andrian who killed your dad."

"Koen," June said, trying to slow his momentum, but this time Minogan held up his hand to silence her, eyes still on Koen.

"No better, even if the end result was freedom for our people?"

Ignoring this last statement, Koen kicked his horse over to Minogan's. "What I don't understand is how you could do this, keep this up, when you *knew...*" Koen cut himself off, nostrils flared angrily. Pulling his horse around, he spat on the ground between himself and Minogan.

"We're done, you and I," he said, glaring at Minogan with a look of pure hatred. "Finished."

Koen made as though to gallop off into the woods, away from them, but June anticipated this and turned Rosie quickly around to block his horse. He glared at her, but she merely raised her eyebrows and shook her head.

"Oh no you don't," she said. "You are going to stay right the hell here while we work this out." Koen stuck his chin out in defiance, eyes narrowed, and began to gather the reins up again. June gave him a piercing look and stuck one hand on her hip.

"Don't make me knock you off your horse," she said. Koen snorted in disbelief and started to turn his horse once more.

June flicked her eyes upward, searching. She quickly found a likely looking branch that wasn't hanging over anyone's head, and with a burst of power, snapped it off at the trunk. She noted happily it hadn't taken much energy to do it. Seemed as though this magic thing was like a muscle—the more you worked it, the stronger it became.

The branch came crashing down through the tree limbs with a tremendous noise, causing all of the horses to shy slightly. When he'd gotten his horse under control, Koen looked at June again, still angry, but with a touch of uncertainty in his eyes.

"Oh, can't I?" she said, and he jerked his head away. "Now," June continued, "explain to me what you're mad about."

Koen rolled his eyes in an *isn't that obvious* expression, but June stared at him steadily and he saw he wasn't getting off so easily. He exhaled sharply, shaking his head at the ground. "Okay, fine," he said. "I'm pissed off at you, because this bastard was going to kill you, and you act like it was the most natural thing in the world for him to do. As for him, he lied to me, made up this horrible scheme to murder you," here Koen directed his words at Minogan, "and even after he could see that you were a reasonable person, he still wanted to do it."

"Okay, understandable," June said, rocking her head from side to side as she weighed his words. "Now, hear me out. The reason I'm not upset with Minogan is that I understand why he did what he did." Koen opened his mouth to protest, but June held up her hand.

"You had your say, let me have mine," she said, and Koen gritted his teeth angrily, but remained silent.

"Where I come from we have a very old saying. An eye for an eye, a tooth for a tooth. Andrians have done more than enough to you to justify your doing something drastic to them."

"Yes, something," Koen interjected. "Not this!"

"Why does this upset you so much?" June asked, bewildered.

"Because it would have been murder! You didn't do anything to get things to the state they are! If it was somebody who'd done something, like Qu–" he stopped suddenly, face darkening to near indigo.

"Like Queen Morningstar," June said, quietly, after a moment of silence. "Like my mother." She shook her head and forced a smile. "You don't have to hold back as far as she's concerned. I never met the woman. She's nothing to me." *Liar,* June thought to herself.

"What I'm saying is that killing you would have been murder, because you're innocent. You didn't make things the way they are. You just got thrown in here, sink or swim."

June had to swallow hard and blink back the tears threatening to overwhelm her.

"Thank you, Koen," she said, drawing a shaky breath. She shook herself mentally, then continued. "Look, you were both working toward the same goal. You just had different ways of going about it. Minogan did, or planned to do, what he thought was right. But he realized it wasn't, he came clean, and nobody got hurt." *Not entirely true,* June thought, looking at Koen's face. "Now, do you think you guys can shake hands and we can move on?"

Minogan nudged his horse forward, hand outstretched, and waited. Koen eyed him warily, weighing his options, then took Minogan's hand and released it quickly, as though it were a poisonous snake. Obviously, things weren't quite kosher, but at least they had a temporary truce.

"Okay, then," June said, suddenly aware she was starving, "Let's grab some food and get going." Luckily, only one of the smaller bags had been lost as the horses had been wandering around in the forest, and most of their supplies remained intact. Taking some dried fruit and something similar to oatcake, they set out once more.

They'd all been hungry, obvious from the silence as everyone inhaled their food. June could hardly breathe for stuffing her face. After they'd had eaten, however, the silence of mouths full of food was replaced by a more uncomfortable silence, conversation suppressed by the look on Koen's face. Everyone seemed fascinated by their fingernails or their horse's mane. June cleared her throat.

"So," she said, "what exactly did Queen Morningstar do to cause what's going on now?" June looked from face to face, waiting for a response. Koen still looked on the verge of homicide, so finally, Minogan answered.

"More what she didn't do," he said, frowning slightly. "From what we heard–and obviously we don't get the news directly from the palace, so this is sketchy–she was a very, very powerful sorceress, but a very weak personality. Her mother, your grandmother, Queen Taharia, was the opposite; strong personality, weak magic skills. She kept things in line pretty well, but when she died..." Minogan shrugged in a 'well, you know' gesture.

"When did she die again?"

"About three years ago," Minogan said.

"So Taharia wasn't great at keeping things fair, either," June said. "Koen said your father died when you were ten."

"He did," Minogan said, clarifying. "Andrians still had to be careful then, because there were some laws protecting us. But when Queen Taharia died, all the greedy nobles in the countryside pushed the Sorcerer's Guild, which is like the queen's advisors, to revoke the laws, so they could take Valforte land, and they in turn pushed the queen, and..." He shrugged once more.

"I see." Something occurred to June then, something she couldn't believe she'd never thought to ask before. "Where was my father in all this?"

Minogan abruptly became very interested in his reins, and the group became very still, like rabbits avoiding a hawk in the high grass.

"I mean, there was a king or something, wasn't there?" June

asked.

Finally, it was Koen who raised his head to answer.

"Queen Morningstar never married," he said, looking slightly embarrassed.

"Ah," June said. "So I'm a bastard." All of the Valforte looked up at her then, eyes wide and shocked at her blasé tone.

"Relax, it doesn't bother me," she said, amidst horrified stares. "Happens all the time at home. One of the women I worked with had never been married and had four kids, all by different fathers. It's not a big deal there." By the expressions on the Valforte's faces, however, it would be a very big deal here.

June mulled over what she'd just heard. *Curiouser and curiouser,* she thought. A snort of laughter escaped her. The Valforte looked up at her once more, brows knitted.

"Sorry, I'm just thinking." She laughed again, more bitterly this time. "Is anything going to be easy on this stupid planet? First I have to travel all over the goddamn place to save it, and then once I save it, I have to actually make it fit to live in, which means trying to undo, if I'm getting this right, *centuries* of prejudice, mistrust and dislike." June looked up, a rueful expression on her face, head cocked to one side. "Does that about cover it?"

"You forgot finding a husband and producing suitable heirs to the throne," Errigal offered helpfully.

June managed to pull off a long-suffering sigh and a wilting glare simultaneously. "Anything else?" she asked, sweetly sarcastic.

Errigal dramatized a deeply thoughtful expression before shaking his head. "Nope, I think you got it," he said, unable to keep a slight smile from the corners of his mouth, and June rolled her eyes at him.

"Oh, good," she said. "I was starting to think that this might end up being *hard.*"

~10~

After several days of travel with no sign of the Eid Gomen, June and the Valforte allowed themselves to relax–a little. They stayed off the roads, which made for hard going. Tangled forests of shrubs often forced them to change direction for as much as half a day, and one had to be constantly alert, or run the risk of losing an eye to a branch.

Rosie, true to her mule heritage, was sure-footed and even-paced, but the horses stumbled constantly, and dumped their riders more than once. At least they could ride most of the time; June had left her boots by the lake, and walking on the prickly forest floor was murder on her feet.

With distractions such as these, and the colorful new curses she learned from the Valforte as they struggled with their mounts, June found there were days when she didn't think about Kyle, or her old life. The night was a different story. Despite her exhaustion, as she waited for sleep, memories flooded back unbidden, and she found herself staring at her engagement ring in the starlight, pondering the possibilities of a life not lived. They'd always planned on a family, two children, hopefully a boy and a girl, and those ghost children haunted her in her sleep, so many nights she woke with tears on her cheeks. Those nights became fewer and farther between, though, as June's old life grew sepia-toned, and her new life came into focus.

She could blame at least part of this change on Koen. Her little crush on him had been pushed to the side after Lumia, the revelations there requiring every bit of her concentration. Now, June was becoming aware of not only physical attraction, but an emotional attachment as well, a desire to be admired and respected by him. She sought his opinion above all others, and she checked his reaction first after she told a joke, or an interesting story.

There were *so* many emotions and questions wrapped up in this. Guilt, feeling like she should mourn longer for Kyle, even though he was surely dead by now at the end of what, from her short glimpse of him, seemed a full and happy life. Elation, bordering on giddiness, as the endorphins borne of attraction coursed through her veins. Self-consciousness, as she wondered whether Koen returned her feelings. And worry, for what if they got together, broke up, and she lost her only true friend here?

June knew eventually, someone would figure out how she felt, if not Koen. Her eyes followed him at every opportunity, admiring the lean muscles and effortless grace of his body. A week ago, when they'd found a clean stream, he'd taken his shirt off to bathe, and June, turning away quickly so no one would see her blush, walked into a tree, scraping a hell of a lot of skin off her forehead. The wound healed itself in seconds; the embarrassment continued for days.

So, June already had plenty to occupy her mind when it came time to make a decision. According to the map, (which they weren't even sure they could trust) they were nearing Prendawr City, the capitol of Prendawr. *Which makes it home for me,* June thought. The realization gave her the feeling of having swallowed a rock.

With concerns of a plot afoot, however, the group questioned if they should chance going into the city, or even be seen in the surrounding areas. If someone was in fact trying to prevent them from completing their quest, going to the city would be like walking into the proverbial lions' den. On the other hand, supplies ran dangerously low, and they all needed a full body bath, a hot meal they hadn't prepared arduously over a campfire, and at least one good night's sleep in a warm, clean bed.

An unsettling incident made their decision for them. They had continued to stay well away from the road since their escape from the Eid Gomen, since both their encounters with them had been on the road or just off it. As they came closer to the city, though, a number of small roads crossed their path, and it became impossible to avoid them. Until now they had been fortunate enough not to run into anyone (forget a plot; June didn't want to run into any Andrians and have to listen to their comments about her friends), but on this particular day, as they crossed a small road, someone found them.

"Can you help me?" the wizened old Andrian asked June, limping up to her, leaning heavily on a shillelagh. He pointed back the way he came, where an obviously disabled wagon sat by the side of the road, harnessed to two musk oxen-like animals with green moss growing in their thick, matted hair.

"My wheel is broken," he said, and stopped. He noticed the Valforte for the first time, and the sight of them seemed to draw him away from his words. His mouth opened slightly, and his eyes widened. The Valforte stared back at him, impassive. The man shut his mouth, shook himself, and turned back to June, his glance taking in her bare feet in the stirrups, scratched and dirty.

"My wheel is broken," he repeated. "I have another, in the

wagon, but–" he held up his hands, twisted and crippled with arthritis. June nodded in understanding.

She turned to the Valforte, eyebrows raised, questioning. *Would you mind?* Their eyes flicked back to the man, then they exchanged glances among themselves. Finally, Minogan nodded, and wordless, they dismounted and went to the wagon to begin their work. June and the Andrian followed slowly to accommodate the man's lameness.

"I'm June," she said, and the man bobbed his head.

"They call me Aiklan, Your–miss," he said, growing red in the face immediately. June gave no outward sign she had heard, but her mind spun in panic.

He knows who I am, she thought. *How does he know?* To buy herself time, she walked to the front of the wagon, to pat the oxen-creatures. Aiklan followed, eyes shifting suspiciously from the Valforte to her, his grip tightening on the shillelagh until his knuckles turned white as ivory.

"Is something wrong?" June asked, her voice conversational, unable to take the old man's ducking and twitching any longer. The man shrugged, smoothed the single wisp of white hair he still possessed back from a brow bleached light with age.

"In the city," he said, slowly, eyes cutting toward the Valforte, "they're looking for a group of Valforte. Four of them, from the west." The Valforte paused almost imperceptibly in their work, but continued, as though they hadn't heard. June swallowed hard.

"Oh? What do they want them for?" *Slow,* she thought. *Keep that panicky high note out of your voice.* Then, frightening proof of how much her world had changed, *He's one man, old and alone. If we need to, we can kill him.*

"Kidnap," he said. Out of the corner of her eye, June saw Koen glance up at her, eyes full of worry and warning. "Apparently, our queen had a sister, hidden on another planet, who returned to take the throne. And these–men, kidnapped her."

"Amazing," June said, frightened out of her wits, but determined not to show it. She'd get them out of this, somehow. As an ox-animal licked salt from her palm, she said, "I wonder if they have it wrong."

"Eh?" said Aiklan, brows knitting together in puzzlement.

"Well, what if these men were only trying to help her to get to a destination that was *very* important for her to get to, desperately important. And since it's such a confusing time for Prendawr, it could just be an unfortunate mistake."

Aiklan licked his lips nervously. "There's some who might not care about all that. There's a reward, a big one. People are hungry."

Oh no, he did not *just threaten me,* thought June, bristling. Drawing herself up, she looked Aiklan square in the eye. "Wouldn't it just be *terrible,*" she said, slowly, "if a man betrayed his future queen and his country for *any* sum of money."

Aiklan quailed under her gaze, shaken, and June felt a sudden surge of pity for him. He was just an old, frightened man, and judging by the state of his clothes and cart, he'd fallen on very hard times lately. June closed her eyes briefly, and blew out a deep breath. She seized her diamond and gold engagement ring and pulled it off her finger, ignoring the selfish little voice inside her that cried out for her to stop, and pressed it into his hand. It was just a thing, after all.

"I know times have been hard lately," June said, gently. "Perhaps this will help to ease things for you and your family." Aiklan opened his hand and gasped loudly when he saw the ring. His eyes met hers, and he nodded, mute.

The boys, in their usual seamless fashion, had already replaced the broken wheel and stood at the very back of the wagon, waiting, eyes locked on June. She nodded toward them.

"Your wheel is fixed," June said. "It was very nice meeting you, Aiklan." She stepped past him, but he caught her by the upper arm, pulling her back around by force of her own interrupted momentum. The Valforte's hands all clapped to their sword hilts, but June raised her other hand toward them in a steadying gesture, turning to Aiklan.

"Don't go near the city," he whispered, his own face close to hers, whispering as though afraid to be overheard. "They're looking for you, everywhere. You'll never get through."

June nodded, turning her face away slightly to avoid the worst of Aiklan's fetid breath.

"It was nice meeting you," she said again, and gently pulled her arm from his grip. She and the Valforte walked back to their horses without a backward glance, though June could feel Aiklan's eyes boring into the back of her head. Before he could call out to them again, they had mounted their horses and were gone.

Fifteen minutes later, Errigal was the first to speak.

"I don't know what you were worried about, June," he said, smiling. "You're a natural at this politics thing."

"What?" June said, turning to look at him.

"You explained the situation, bought him off, and got valuable information without admitting who we are or directly bribing him."

"Yeah, and I gave him a nice little piece of solid gold proof if he decides to take it to the authorities," she said, watching Errigal's face turn from amusement to dismay. "It was a gamble we had to take, though. I put my bet down that he was basically honest, just desperate and starving. If I'm right, we have nothing to worry about."

"And if you're wrong?" Minogan asked. June met his eyes and saw his thoughts there, plain as day. *You trusted an Andrian with our lives,* he was saying. *That's a hell of a long shot.*

"Then we have to make sure we keep the horses well-fed," June said, patting Rosie on the neck. "We do have another problem, though. This is bigger than the Sidhe, isn't it?" All four Valforte nodded. June smoothed a frizzy curl behind her ear before continuing.

"So, that means until we're done with what we have to do, we have to avoid people completely. If we see a village, we skirt around it. How many people could you easily take in a fight?" They exchanged glances.

"If they're professionals, probably three each. If not..." Koen shrugged. "Up to ten each, I would think."

"Okay," June said. "From now on, the rule is—twelve or less, attack. More than that, run." She paused for a moment, not wanting to say the next sentence out loud. "No prisoners, no mercy." *Just a few lives to save all of them,* she thought, trying to comfort herself. It didn't work.

All four nodded, but she noticed all of them looked rather bleakly at the supplies on the pack horses.

"Yeah, I know," June said. "No villages means no food."

"And no grain," Feoras said, patting his horse.

"How far are we from Fire Mountain, according to the map?" June asked.

Minogan sighed, glancing skyward. "Weeks," he said, shaking his head in despair. "Maybe more than a month."

June could feel a cloud of despair settling on her shoulders, but shrugged it off. "We'll make it," she said. "People can do amazing things when they don't have any other option." The Valforte nodded, but there was no heart behind the gesture. For the first time, June realized they actually might *not* make it. *We have to finish this,* June thought, fiercely. *I won't let everything I've given up be for nothing.*

They breathed a sigh of relief once they'd passed the city, and the web of criss-crossing roads and paths that increased their chances of running into someone dried up and disappeared. They were already used to living rough, as were the horses. In fact, if it weren't for the lack of food, life might actually have been pleasant, for everyone knew their places, what had to be done, and worked smoothly together in a comfortable routine. And, since Minogan had begun to trust June, the group grew closer, with the exception of Koen, who acted as though Minogan did not exist.

June's feelings for Koen grew, also, which added a level of stress to her life she could have done without, since a) she was still getting over losing Kyle, b) there was very little time for romance in her life, and, most importantly, c) she wasn't sure Koen returned her feelings. Yes, he was a friend, and a wonderful one, and he obviously cared for her. But most men she knew would have made their move by now, and he hadn't. Yet, at times she caught him looking at her in a way which wasn't at all brotherly. Or was that just wishful thinking?

So, between saving the world, mourning for her old life, and contemplating the possibilities of a new one, June had a fairly constant headache, and the starvation diet they now followed didn't help. One small meal in the morning and one at night, usually consisting of gathered vegetables or fruits, which held them for about five minutes before they got hungry again. The horses weren't doing much better, with rapidly depleting grain rations, and sparse forage between the tree roots.

Just when they thought things couldn't get bleaker, the forest ended, and the group stared in horror at what awaited them beyond. June dismounted, and walked, dreamlike, away from the trees.

A vast desert stretched before them, bare earth and rocks with a few tough scrubby shrubs, extending as far as the eye could see.

June dropped Rosie's reins and sat down hard on a nearby boulder, too tired and disconsolate even to cry. Fire Mountain was somewhere on the other side of this desert. The few supplies they had would never last. If they attempted it, they would most likely die.

Koen walked over to June, who didn't look up, but kept her eyes fixed on the distant horizon. He lifted her hand gently from her lap and poured a small amount of nuts and berries into it. Without looking at it, she lifted her hand and tipped about a quarter of the handful into her mouth, chewing slowly and sucking the juices from the crushed fruit. The food only provoked her appetite, and she winced as teeth seemed to gnaw her insides as her body screamed for more food than she could give it.

"We'll make it," Koen said, disagreeing with her unspoken comment.

"Oh, you think so?" June snapped. She immediately hung her head and sighed. "Sorry, that was rude."

"Ah, don't worry about it," he said, sitting down next to her on. "We're all a little testy lately. Hungry and tired and worried..."

"Thanks for the food," June said, lifting the handful to her mouth once more and taking another tiny bit. She looked critically at Koen for a moment, at the sharp angles showing through his shirt where once healthy flesh had been.

"You're getting enough, right?" He raised his eyebrows, a slight smile on his face, and she returned it, shaking her head. "I mean you're getting your share?"

Koen shrugged. "Yeah," he said, unconvincingly. June glanced guiltily down at the food in her hand.

"Here," she said, offering the bit she had left.

"No, no, you take it. I'm fine, really." His stomach chose this moment to emit a ferocious growl, and they both laughed.

"Split what's left with me? Please?"

Koen sighed, his eyes searching her face, then decided it wasn't worth the argument, so he held out his hand, and she tipped a little more than half of the food into it. He tossed it all back with one swift motion, closing his eyes as he chewed. June took the opportunity to admire his face, the balance between strong angles and boyish openness, and felt a warmth in her stomach and chest which had nothing to do with hunger.

Koen's eyes opened as he swallowed, and June quickly glanced past him to see what the others were doing. Minogan was busy setting the horses up with pitifully small nosebags, but Errigal and Feoras were nowhere to be seen.

"Where'd the twins go?" June asked.

"To scrounge up any food and water they can get, before we cross this." They sat silently, looking ahead at the slow death which awaited them, as June chewed the last bit of food Koen had given her.

"Do you really think we can make it?" June asked, half-whispering, looking down at her hands. There was a smear of berry juice on the base of her thumb, and she sucked it off slowly as she waited for Koen to answer. For a moment she didn't think he'd heard her. Finally he sighed.

"If we don't do this, we all die, right? Not just us, but everyone. So we don't have a choice."

"You do," June said, locking eyes with him. "You and the rest. You don't have to do this. This is a death sentence. Just–" she jumped up, walking away from him so he wouldn't see her face, "Just leave Rosie, a waterskin, some food, and go home. This isn't your fight."

"Oh, it isn't?" Koen said behind her. She didn't turn around, just stood with her back to him, arms crossed, staring at the ground.

"No, it's not," she said, unable to keep a slight catch from her voice, closing her eyes at the sound of it.

"I disagree. I live here too. It is my fight."

"You know what I mean," June said, fighting unsuccessfully to keep tears from spilling down her cheeks.

"I do." June heard him get to his feet behind her, and she stiffened, hoping he didn't come around to face her, but he stood by the rock. "Do you really think, after all we've been through, that we're just going to let you die out there alone?"

June snorted bitterly. "And dying in a crowd is better?"

"June, as impressed as I am with your skills, you go out there by yourself and you *will* die. With all of us together, there's a chance."

June raked her hands through her hair, frustrated and devastated. "I can't make you–" she began, but he cut her off.

"That's right, June," he said, voice gentle but firm. "You can't make us. You'd never make us. That's why you have our loyalty. Like it or not, we are not going to leave you."

June stood, eyes closed, hot tears squeezing out between her lids and running down her face. She felt like she might throw up her meager lunch.

"I don't want your deaths on my conscience," she said, voice shaking.

"And I don't want yours on mine," Koen said. "So go rest for a little and calm down, and then we're leaving. All of us. Together."

June barely managed to choke back a sob, hands over her face. She couldn't turn around, because she knew every emotion she felt was written on her face as plainly as a highway billboard. Finally, she heard the soft crunch of his feet on the dry ground as he retreated. Her legs gave out, and she sat down hard on her already bony rear end. *About to get bonier,* she thought miserably.

Arms wrapped tightly around herself, simultaneously nauseous and starving, head pounding with restrained tears, June sat alone with her thoughts.

Before this moment, the possibility of one of their deaths had been a terrifying shadow which occasionally swept across the front of June's brain, only to be swiftly pushed aside. Even after their close calls with the Eid Gomen, June hadn't accepted the reality that at least one of them probably wouldn't make it to the end of the quest.

Now, however, the truth stood before her, stark and undeniable as the bleak desert. If they made it, not just across this obstacle, but through the other unknown trials to come, it would be a miracle.

June thought of escaping, somehow evading the Valforte and completing the quest on her own, without endangering the lives of her friends any further. But Koen was right. She needed them. She didn't know the land, the customs, the creatures...and for a young woman raised in the luxury of 20th century America, a cross-country trek of this magnitude would be impossible. And if she failed...they'd all die, not just one or two of them. But who would those sacrifices be?

It felt as though drops of blood were being squeezed out of her heart as her vivid imagination called up images of her friends in various stages of pain and death. Minogan. Errigal. Feoras. Koen.

Koen. June's hands closed spasmodically, and she clenched her teeth against the moan which threatened to escape. Koen. Her one true friend, the man who always had one eye on her, making sure she was all right. The only person who made life on this godforsaken world worthwhile. The man she loved.

At last, sitting at what felt like the end of the world, wind whipping grains of the hard, barren earth up into her face, she admitted finally to herself that's who he was. The man she loved.

Exhausted, soul-sore, and heartsick, June lay on her side right out in the open and closed her eyes.

June woke disoriented from a syrupy-thick dreamless sleep. The sun was rising; she'd slept all the way through yesterday afternoon and last night. Confused, she rolled over to find Koen, Errigal, and Feoras wrapped in their blankets, beside a fire burned down to coals. Apparently, they'd decided to camp here for one last night.

Someone had covered her with her blanket during the night, and she sat up, pulling it around her shoulders against the damp morning chill. No one stirred at her movement, not even Minogan, propped up against a nearby rock, where he had most unusually fallen asleep on watch. Testament to their exhaustion. And they'd barely begun.

June turned to look across the desert, the indigo sky slowly giving way to vivid dark magenta, leaving her to imagine the blood-red sun which must have been rising on the other side of the trees. *Red sky at morning, sailor take warning.*

With a sigh, she began stoking the fire, and put water on for tea.

After breakfast, and a great deal of procrastination, strange for the Valforte, they started off across the bleak landscape. June's prediction about the morning sky had unfortunately been right.

Clouds soon began to gather, and within a few hours of them setting out, a steady rain with frequent, violent cloudbursts began to fall relentlessly.

The hard-baked earth of the desert soon turned to a sloppy thick mud which sucked at their feet and pulled at their boots. June didn't have to worry about boots, since she was already barefoot, and the Valforte soon removed their footwear as well. Even so, every step required at least twice as much energy than it should have, energy none of them had to spare.

The rain took care of their worries about water, but they didn't have much else to be thankful for. Their meager food supplies dried up a few days out, and they resorted to such desperate measures as cutting small slices of leather from the horses' saddles and chewing them, comforting their stomachs and mouths with a small amount of flavor and–juice? June wasn't sure what to call it. It was utterly foul-tasting, but it took great effort to restrain herself from swallowing the entire indigestible lump.

The horses were just as bad off as the people, forced to nibble inedible shrubs and drink only what had run down their noses into their mouths. June walked beside Rosie, to save the animal having to carry her. Everyone's ribs, people and animal, had been prominent before they left the forest–now they began to look like characters from a Halloween cartoon.

On the fifth day out, one of the pack horses stopped suddenly, pulling the line to a halt. It took deep, gasping breaths, head lowered almost as if in preparation to sneeze. Then, with a thud, it fell hard to its knees, paused for a moment, and rolled heavily to its side.

June stood, dumb with shock, and watched the animal's heaving side, the scarlet of its nostrils as they flared for breath. Errigal pulled a small knife from his belt and crouched beside the horse, murmuring soothingly.

"What are you doing?" June asked, her voice shrill.

"Just taking the pack off," he said calmly, slicing through the ropes. The lumps of luggage rolled off the animal's back, but it didn't stir, still laboring for breath. The other three men had approached, exchanging glances. Errigal peered closely at the animal's eyes and in its mouth, then looked up at Feoras and shook his head. With one swift movement, the knife was drawn across the animal's throat, and its hooves drummed feebly against the ground as its lifeblood poured out into the mud.

June must have made a small sound, her hands covering her

mouth, for they turned to her, shadows under and in their eyes.

"It was the kindest thing. Either that, or leave it to die slowly," Feoras said, and June nodded, eyes wide.

"We're not–you're not going to–" June said, staring at the bloodstained knife, still held at the ready in Errigal's hand.

"We have to," Minogan said. "We're going to die if we don't." June nodded, understanding, but nauseated at the way her stomach had begun growling furiously at the smell of the blood pouring from the animal's throat.

She turned away from the sight, and her eyes fell on Rosie. Suddenly, she really *saw* the animal, saw the dull coat, the hanging head, the dark eyes, peering at June like a prisoner condemned. June stroked the wet, cold neck, shaking her head in disgust at her ignorance.

With three quick movements, she released the girth, and the saddle fell off Rosie's other side with a wet splat, causing the mule to start slightly. June stroked her neck comfortingly as she undid the buckles of the bridle, pulling it off over the animal's face and dropping it on the ground. Rosie released the bit from her mouth gratefully, working her tongue and lips. June stepped in front of the animal, and Rosie lowered her head to June, allowing her to press her forehead into the mule's, hands on either side of the animal's face.

"I'm so sorry, girl," she said. "I didn't see. I'm so sorry." June left her head there for a moment more, stroking Rosie's face with her thumbs. Then, planting a kiss on the mule's forehead, she stepped back from her.

"Go on, get," June said, stepping forward to push at the mule's shoulder, directing her back the way she'd come. "Get going."

Rosie wouldn't budge, instead looking at her owner with a perplexed expression in her dark, intelligent eyes.

"Shoo," June said, louder, adding a clap which caused Rosie to toss her head in surprise, but still she didn't move. Senseless anger bubbled up inside June's chest.

"Get," June said, slapping the mule's rump harder than necessary. This earned a squeal and a slight jump backward, but the animal moved no further. Confusion and hurt was etched in every nuance of the animal's posture, from swishing tail to swiveling ears. *Why do you want to get rid of me?* Rosie seemed to say. *Have I done something wrong?*

The animal's distress propelled June into a rage. Fishing a rock out of the mud, she flung it at the animal's flank. It was a dead hit,

Rosie's skin flinching up around the area. She squealed again and shied back a few more steps, still looking hurt and confused.

"GO," June screamed, picking up another rock and stalking threateningly toward Rosie. Tears streamed down her face, but she hardly noticed. Rosie backed up a few more steps, head high in alarm, but would still not go. June flung the rock in her hand. "GO!" And this time Rosie did, wheeling and galloping off in the direction from which they'd come. June slumped onto a nearby rock to watch her go, until she disappeared behind the curtain of falling rain. She buried her face in her hands and rested her elbows on her knees, her whole body shaking with emotion and cold and misery.

The Valforte had watched this scene in silence, crouched beside the fallen horse. Now they, too, stood and released their own horses, cutting packs and saddles and letting them fall into the mud. June felt their thundering hooves as they fled, galloping in the direction they'd come. These horses needed no convincing. June heard the slight sucking sound of shoes in the mud approaching the boulder on which she sat. A moment later, she felt Koen's hand on her shoulder.

"Don't, please," June whispered. "Not now." The hand withdrew, but she could feel his presence, glowing next to her. June would have liked nothing more than to be folded into his arms and to cry her heart out, but she knew she'd lose control entirely if she did. There is nothing like the pity of the person you love to make you cry yourself out into an empty shell. June simply couldn't afford the luxury.

"She'll be fine now, June," Koen said quietly. "You did the right thing. We should have done it sooner." June lifted her face from her hands, and met Koen's sea-green eyes, looking sympathetically down into hers.

"It's not her I'm worried about," she said, and then dropped her eyes to the fallen horse, its open eyes filling with rainwater, body jerking grotesquely as Minogan, Errigal, and Feoras slit open its belly and tugged out the innards.

There was no possibility of lighting a fire; they had nothing to burn, and it would never stay lit in the rain, anyway, so Errigal sliced small pieces of meat from the inside of the animal, handing one to June and warning her to eat slowly, so she wouldn't throw up. She thought she might, anyway, since the dead horse's glazed eyes appeared to be staring at her as she chewed its flesh. Her body welcomed the food, though, even if her mind didn't, and warmth soon flowed through her limbs all the way to her fingers and toes. Her stomach had shrunk from constant starvation, however, and as soon as she had finished her small piece, she felt as though she'd just finished thirds at Thanksgiving dinner.

They took some small chunks of the meat and wrapped them carefully in bits of spare cloth, packing them down with the things they'd be taking with them, but most of it went to waste, since they could neither cure nor cook it.

Slowly, the pain of constant travel and misuse stabbing at every part of her body, she got up and rooted through her saddlebags. Her comb she wanted, but her soap had gotten wet, even through the leather, and had melted to a tiny, useless chip. June flung it away into the mud. She also left her sword in favor of the large dagger she'd gotten in the Eid Gomen dungeon. She set the map, her comb, her spare clothes and boots, empty water skin, eating utensils, blanket, and a few hair ribbons inside her saddlebag and shouldered it.

The men did the same, sorting through their things to find the essentials, for in their weakened condition, they couldn't afford to carry anything extra. A single cooking pot, in case they got lucky and actually *found* some food, each of their spare clothes, weapons, and a few personal items, and they started off once more.

The continuing rain dampened their spirits in more ways than one, not only keeping them in a constant state of discomfort, but obscuring their visibility, preventing them from seeing what little progress they made toward the mountain.

On top of everything, Feoras had come down with a wicked chest cold. June felt for him; she couldn't imagine this miserable trek with the added wretchedness of a leaking nose and sore throat.

"If it gets too bad, let me know," June said. "I can fix it, but..."

Feoras nodded in understanding. If she healed him now, she'd probably need to be carried the rest of the way. And nobody was in any condition to be carrying anyone. As they sat on some of the many boulders which dotted the stark landscape, June looked at her companions, shaking her head. Clothing hangers would have filled their shirts out more than they did, and greyish-brown hollows filled the areas beneath their cheeks and eyes.

June looked at the terrain in disgust, kicking her mud-covered feet at the sloppy ground.

"How the hell can it rain so much here without anything growing?" she asked.

Koen smiled wanly. "Taste the mud," he said. June looked at him, bemused. Koen scooped a bit of the grey mud onto his finger and popped it into his mouth. "Go on, taste it."

Hoping he had a reason, and this wasn't just dementia from prolonged hunger, June scooped a bit of mud and tentatively licked it, then spat and wiped her mouth vigorously.

"Bleagh, salt," she said, giving Koen a dirty look before tilting her head back and opening her mouth to the rain to rinse it.

"It's a salt desert," Koen said, still smiling.

"And you couldn't have said that, instead of making me put it in my mouth?" she asked, shooting daggers with her eyes in his direction.

"Makes a bigger impression," he said, eyes glinting mischievously. June shook her head in good-natured annoyance, slicking tendrils of her wet hair back. She was glad he felt well enough to joke. When the occasional ribbing that went on in the group stopped completely, June would be really worried.

Two days later, June woke without opening her eyes to the sound of Feoras's rheumy cough and the dull, constant hunger pains in her stomach. Even in the soft mud, her bony body had trouble finding a comfortable position. She was turning onto her back when suddenly she froze, body vibrating like a tuning fork. Something was different. Slowly, she cracked open her eyes–and was blinded by the sunlight.

With a triumphant crow, she leapt to her feet, startling the other Valforte, who also leapt to their feet, swords drawn, looking bewildered. June suddenly felt one-hundred percent energized; she whirled around, head tilted back so the warmth of the sunlight fell on her face. She stopped at the sight of an enormous mountain, Fire Mountain, a mere half-day's travel away. June fell to her knees.

"Thank you, thank you, thank you," she said, not knowing to whom she said it, but meaning it with all her heart. She rolled onto her backside so she sat on the ground, and faced the Valforte, who looked at the mountain with similar expressions of shock and relief on their faces.

"We made it," June said. "We–"

They all looked up as a dark shape passed over them. The faces of the Valforte, smiling and healthily blue with excitement, fell once more.

It was huge, at least sixty feet from nose to tail, and equal distance wingtip-to-wingtip. June took in the bullet-shaped head at the end of a serpentine neck, a hard-scaled underbelly, and a long, tapered tail as it soared overhead, straight toward Fire Mountain. They all watched, horrified, as it circled slowly around the peak, folded its wings and dropped down behind the mountain.

June whirled back around to face the Valforte, all of whom had now assumed attitudes of disbelief or hopelessness; hand over eyes, fingers entangled in hair, etc.

"What," June began, "was—"

"Dragon," Minogan answered, cutting her off, eyes still riveted on the mountain.

"A dragon," said June. "As in fire-breathing, scaly, sharp-toothed..." All four nodded, and June sighed. "God really does hate me," she said softly.

~11~

They saw another dragon as they crossed the short remaining distance to the mountain, but, like the other, it didn't bother them, merely soared overhead and dropped behind the mountain. June and the others were all thoroughly rattled by this latest development, but, unfortunately, turning around wasn't an option. So, scantily armed as they were, they continued forward, grateful at least for the sun.

In another welcome development, the salt desert ended at the base of the mountain, and soon they walked on green grass, growing thick between the trunks of small, birch-like trees.

Within minutes of leaving the desert, Koen and Errigal had each shot a small guinea pig-looking creature, and they hastily built a small cookfire. They couldn't even wait for the meat to be completely done, but kept prizing off bits of flesh as they cooked.

Soon, they sunk into a satiated torpor, sucking grease off their burnt fingers and staring into the flames of their fire. June sighed, adjusting herself against a tree trunk and leaning her head back, her dirty, peeling bare feet curling into the thick grass.

"God, that was sooo good," June groaned. "All I want now are some chocolate chip cookies."

"Some what?" Koen asked, and June looked at him curiously.

"Cookies," she said. "Chocolate chip cookies."

"I get the cookie part," he said, "but what's chocolate?"

June groaned again as she realized *chocolate* had come out in English, letting her head fall back hard on the trunk behind her.

"Are you freaking *kidding* me?" she asked. "You don't have chocolate here?" Four heads shook, and June, wide-eyed, looked from face to face.

"Well, what about peanut butter? Please tell me you have peanut butter." The blank looks she got gave her the answer. Sadly, she realized she'd eaten her final peanut butter cup about two months ago, not knowing it would be her last.

Errigal opened his mouth to ask more questions, but Feoras went into a coughing fit, and all eyes turned to him. He'd been getting paler and weaker by the day, and he hadn't been able to get much food down. June could easily see his poor condition, since Errigal, his twin, was right there for comparison. And thin as Errigal was, he looked like Mr. Universe compared to Feoras.

"Should I..." June began, but Minogan shook his head.

"No," he said, "you're still in no condition to be doing any magic. Let him be for a while, see what the food does for him."

June wanted to argue, but the looks on Koen and even Errigal's faces told her she wouldn't win this fight. Not yet, at least.

The group rested for the remainder of the afternoon and evening, napping, chatting, and eating in turns. June helped Errigal find some edible greens, including one that would make a nice hot tea, and the others managed to shoot four more of the guinea pig things. June was glad to find the tea, since it eased Feoras's cough quite a bit. Still, he had a ways to go, and they had to continue the next day. She considered healing him while the others slept, but had a feeling Feoras wouldn't allow it. So, she sat back and hoped nature would take over, ready to step in, in case it didn't.

Morning came, amid mixed emotions. Physically, everyone felt fantastic–even Feoras had improved during the night, thanks to food, rest, and relief from the elements.

On the other hand, trepidation over the next leg of their journey and the inhabitants of the mountain tempered their happiness. The Valforte didn't know much about dragons. They'd heard old legends of attacks on villages, but no more. For all they knew, dragons were vegetarians.

They decided to climb in a loose ascending spiral, since they didn't know exactly what they were looking for, or where it might be. June and the others couldn't see an obvious vent for the smoke which constantly ringed the mountain, either.

The mountain rose steeply from the ground, a very strange landmark, since it wasn't part of a range, nor was there even so much as a hill within miles of it. Just flat land and then, like a giraffe in a herd of goats, stood Fire Mountain. Coniferous trees and tangled underbrush covered the alp, making the going for the weakened travelers difficult. *I think I'd fall down and die of shock if things suddenly got easy,* June thought.

Koen and Minogan had taken the lead, June, as usual, in the middle, and Errigal and Feoras in the back, Feoras struggling hard to keep up. June kept discreetly tapping Koen and Minogan on the shoulder to get them to slow down and give Feoras a break, but they kept forgetting themselves, in a mix of excitement to complete the first part of their quest, and sheer exuberance at having energy again.

And then, suddenly, a break came.

Koen stopped, pointing about four hundred yards up the mountain. June never would have seen the small dark smudge through the trees, but Koen's trained eyes, from years of hunting in the forest, both saw the spot and what it was–a cave. An entrance into the mountain.

They were all out of breath by the time they reached the cave, and Feoras was coughing badly again; it was steeper and harder hiking straight up the mountain than the slow ascent they'd been making. But now they stood at the opening, peering into the shadows, wondering what came next. June finally broke the silence.

"Hey, wouldn't it really suck if we're getting all excited about this cave and it ends like twelve feet in?" she asked, and they all laughed as she led the way into the cave.

A few feet inside the entrance and June couldn't see her hand in front of her face, even if she held it up so close it touched her nose. The air chilled at least twenty-five degrees, and she shivered, hearing the slight gasps from the men as they felt it too. June edged forward, hands out in front of her, terrified of walking into a wall, or something more sinister. She turned slightly to talk to the Valforte.

"Guys, should we maybe go outside and make a tor–AAAAAAGGGGGHHH!" Suddenly, the floor was gone, and June slid feet-first on her back down a steep rock embankment, plummeting into the darkness, hands and feet splayed as she tried to find purchase to halt her terrifying descent.

Finally, with a bone-jarring *wham*, her feet slammed into solid rock, and she crumpled up like a ball as her body's momentum carried her into her legs. She flopped back and lay still for a moment, breath ragged, eyes closed, assessing the damage.

"Okay, *ow,*" June said, tears leaking out of the corner of her eyes as the pain caught up with her. She hadn't broken anything, but she'd torn herself up pretty good. Two of the fingernails on her right hand had been nearly ripped off as she'd clawed at the rock, trying to find a handhold. And her back–God, it felt like hamburger.

Eyes still closed, she reached back with her left hand, feeling slimy warm blood, bits of her shredded shirt, and bits of her shredded skin. Yup, it *was* hamburger. Already, though, she could feel her fingers and back healing themselves. Above her, she heard the Valforte yelling her name, fear in their voices.

"As I was saying, should we maybe go outside and get a torch?" June yelled up to them.

"Are you okay?"

June pushed herself into a sitting position and opened her eyes for the first time. "Yeah, I'm o–shit,"

Her feet still rested against the object which had broken her fall. Just above her toes, a huge, bright yellow eye, slitted like a cat's, had opened and was staring straight at her.

Silhouetted by a light source somewhere behind it, the dragon raised its massive head, on the end of a long, snake-like neck, and got to its feet, leaving June sitting on the ground twenty feet below it. It made no other movement, simply staring austerely down at her, silent, accusing. From far away, she heard the Valforte shouting for her, the fresh alarm in their voices making it clear they could see at least some of the action going on below them. June and the dragon stared at each other for what seemed like days, each waiting for the other to make a move.

"I–I'm sorry," June said, with no idea why she was talking to a giant winged lizard. "I didn't mean to–I fell..."

The dragon cocked its head at her, ruffling its wings.

"Who are you?" it asked, in a deep, booming voice. "What are you doing here?"

Well, knock me over with a feather, June thought. This made things a lot easier–or, it could make them harder. June got up slowly, dusted herself off a bit, and bowed. "I'm, um, Princess Ulfhilda," she said, nearly forgetting to call herself that horrible name. "And we're here looking for something."

"I thought the royal line was dead," the dragon said. June had to bite the inside of her cheek hard to contain a nervous giggle.

"That's what everyone thought," she said, and launched into a Reader's Digest version of the facts. The Valforte had gone silent, either listening carefully to the events unfolding, or possibly searching for larger weapons and a way down.

The dragon, meanwhile, sat back on its haunches, giving June its undivided attention as she told her tale. When she finished, it bowed its massive head in thought.

"I should take you to Tokesh," it said pensively. "He'd be interested to hear your story." He looked up at the top of the cliff June had fallen from. "There is a set of stairs carved from the rock to your left," he said, speaking now to the Valforte, and June could swear she heard amusement in his voice. "It may be an easier descent than your Princess's." June heard them shuffling quietly over to the stairs and walking slowly and cautiously down.

"Who is Tokesh?" June asked nervously.

"Our leader," the dragon said, and June's stomach cramped nervously.

"And your name is?" June asked, trying to keep the fear out of her voice.

"Rakoz," the dragon said. June nodded.

"Rakoz," she repeated. "Well, nice to meet you, Rakoz. I'm very sorry again for falling on you." Rakoz snorted, which, to June's alarm, caused some small sparks to fly from his nostrils.

"A small thing like you?" he asked. "If you hadn't fallen on my face, I probably wouldn't have noticed." Just then, the Valforte joined them, swords drawn.

"Rakoz, I'd like you to meet Minogan, Koen, Errigal, and Feoras, my friends." June desperately tried to signal to them to lower their weapons, as she could feel Rakoz bristling next to her, but they either didn't notice or didn't care.

"Follow me, please," said Rakoz, coolly, and they fell in behind the dragon, mindful of his swaying tail. He led them through an arched doorway into a hallway, lit by way of gutter-like trenches filled with fire on either side of the immensely wide walkway. It appeared the entire hallway had been carved completely from the stone of the mountain–June could see no seams at all.

As they entered the light, and June got a better look at Rakoz, it surprised her to see how stunningly beautiful he was, covered in iridescent black scales which glittered in the firelight.

She didn't dare to look at or speak to any of the guys. June was starkly terrified, but doing a pretty good job of holding it together. If, however, she looked at one of the others, saw the dread in their eyes, she thought she'd lose whatever now kept her from falling apart. She also tried not to examine too closely the fact that she was following a dragon deep into a dark, creepy mountain to meet still more dragons who were probably *not* vegetarians.

As they walked, June realized with a jolt the wounds she'd sustained during her fall had already healed. She flexed her hand in front of her face, marveling at how new fingernails had grown, to the same length as the others. She reached around under her shirt and ran her fingertips over her back. Other than the prominent knobs of her spine, her back was smooth and unbroken.

They approached an immense pair of stone doors, twice the height of Rakoz. He paused in front of them.

"Wait here, please," he said, and the doors swung open to admit him, closing behind him so quickly June couldn't see what was inside.

As soon as the doors slammed shut, however, the Valforte rounded on her in a volley of angry whispers.

"What are you–"

"–could have been *thinking*–"

"–completely trapped–"

"–dead–"

"Guys," June whispered, but they kept on. "Guys!" They stopped, looking at her mutinously. "Wanna tell me what our other options are, please? I don't know about you, but I'm not in any shape for a fight, and I don't think the five of us could take him," she gestured toward the door Rakoz had disappeared into, "much less more of him. Plus, this is Fire Mountain. The tablet piece is on Fire Mountain. They *live* on Fire Mountain. D'ya think they might maybe have a clue as to where it is?"

"June," Koen said, with an air of a mother trying to calmly explain to her child why we do not pull mommy's pants down in the middle of a department store, "Those are dragons. They are not going to help us. They are going to eat us."

"Well, Rakoz had a wonderful opportunity earlier, when I practically fell in his mouth, and he didn't. In fact, he's done nothing but treat us with respect. And do you actually know anyone who's been eaten by a dragon?"

Before anyone could respond, both doors opened, and a gravelly voice boomed, "Enter!"

Steeling herself for whatever lay ahead, June led the way inside, desperately hoping she was right.

They entered an enormous throne room of sorts, again carved entirely from the stone of the mountain. Fires burned in large stone pots scattered around the chamber, lending light to the space. At least fifteen dragons lined the walls on either side of the doors. And directly ahead of them, on a stone dais the size of a house, reclined an immense dragon, twice the size of Rakoz at least, and looking infinitely fiercer. Tokesh.

June bowed to him, and with a slight hand motion behind her back, gestured for the Valforte to do the same, which they did, grudgingly. They waited, heads bowed, for acknowledgment. Finally, Tokesh spoke.

"Rakoz has told me you are called Princess Ulfhilda, is that true?"

"It is, sir," June said, settling on sir, not knowing exactly what title would be appropriate.

"And you have come here on a quest to find one of three pieces of a missing tablet, is that also true?"

"Yes, sir," June said.

"And what will you do with these missing pieces of tablet, if you get them?" June noticed a slight emphasis on the word *if*. Hm.

"Um, save the world, sir," she said, wincing internally at the melodramatic sound of the sentence.

"Very well. But," *Ah, here's the 'but',* thought June, "how do I know you are who you say you are?"

"Have we given reason for you to think that we're not, sir?" June struggled again to keep her face blank and her voice steady, but she was having trouble. The fact that the dragons were very big, and she and the Valforte, very small, had begun to press on her.

Tokesh lifted one shoulder in a shrug, but did not answer. He stared at June, seeming to wait for her to say something, to explain herself, to throw herself prostrate at his feet and beg for mercy. *Show him you're strong,* a little voice inside her said. *All our lives depend on you showing him that you're royalty, that you're amenable, but not a pushover. Show him.* June took a deep breath, willing herself to hold eye contact, not to speak and show weakness.

Finally, Tokesh spoke, and June let her breath out in a small rush, the battle won.

"You are not the first of your kind to visit our mountain, you know," Tokesh said, an edge of aggression in his voice.

"Oh?" June asked, politely. She found it easier now to keep her voice steady–winning the non-verbal battle had given her some confidence.

"Nor the second, nor the third, nor the hundredth," he said. He shifted slightly on the dais before continuing. "Dragonslayers, they call themselves. Silly boys, barely men, with something to prove. Usually they do no harm, and we send them on their way, but a year ago..." Tokesh paused, and there was a slight rustling among the dragons lining the walls. "A year ago they somehow managed to get into the nursery. Destroyed hundreds of eggs and nestlings. So I ask you again, how do I know you are who you say you are?"

June took a shaky breath. "I am sorry for your loss, sir, I truly am, but I promise you, we're only here to see if we can find the tablet piece. We aren't in any condition for a fight." June heard Minogan hiss slightly behind her, in indignation at her professing their weakness. She knew, however, the only way to win this would be through honesty. "We nearly starved to death, on the way across the desert. We didn't even know you were here, until yesterday. We saw a dragon fly over us. That's when we knew, not before."

"All you have are words," Tokesh said. "You have no proof."

"You're right, I have no proof," June said, and the dragons rustled again. June was tired, sore from falling off a freaking cliff, and in no mood to get into a 'yes I am, no you're not' altercation with an overfed crocodile.

"We can go back and forth on this all day and all night, and I won't be able to satisfy you. That was a horrible thing those men did, and I hope you killed them for it, but I know even if you did, it's not enough. I also know that we didn't come here to harm you, we came here to do something that's going to benefit you too. I'm not going to be able to convince you of that with words, though. You're just going to have to make up your mind whether to trust us, throw us off the mountain, or kill us. I can't do anything about it."

Tokesh looked taken aback by this, but tried to conceal it as he considered her words. Finally, he spoke.

"I need time to think. Rakoz will take you to your chambers, where you will be fed and watered, and kept comfortable until I have made my decision." Rakoz came forward from the dragons on the wall, and beckoned them to follow. June bowed to Tokesh, motioning again for the others to do the same, and together, they went out the same way they had come in.

Rakoz led them down several side corridors to a smaller stone door, which opened before him into a wide room, its floor covered with clean straw, except for the center, in which a fire roared in a pit, a spit for cooking suspended above it. A neat stack of firewood leaned against the wall to their left. Beside the pit lay a freshly-killed sheep and a small pile of root vegetables. Torches lined the walls, and in the back was an archway, darkened so June couldn't see where it led.

"I hope you'll be comfortable here," Rakoz said. He sounded almost a little sorry for them.

"Oh, we're thankful just to be inside. This will be wonderful," June said.

"We apologize that we were unable to prepare your food, but..." he held up one massive, taloned paw, and June smiled.

"Understandable," June said. "Really, this is luxury. Please tell Tokesh we said thank you." Rakoz's eyes darkened in uncertainty, but he nodded and stepped back. June and the Valforte walked into the room, and the door swung shut behind them.

All four stood silent as they listened to the sound of Rakoz's nails clicking a retreat on the stone floor of the corridor. As the sound faded in the distance, Minogan pressed his shoulder carefully against the door and pushed, then tried to work his fingers into the crack where the door met the wall, pulling it inward. It didn't budge.

"Locked," he said, unnecessarily, glancing grimly back at the others. June waved a dismissive hand.

"Don't worry about it," she said. "If we need to, I'm pretty sure I can get us out."

"I don't like this," said Errigal, and the others nodded in agreement. "We're trapped in a stone dungeon by a bunch of monsters–" June held up a hand, cutting him off.

"Okay, first off, we are *not* trapped. If I can blow a lake up, I think I can take care of a teeny little door. Second, this is not a dungeon. Dungeons do not come with cooking pits, fresh food, comfortable bedding, and–" here June spoke on a hunch, pointing at the archway to the rear of the room, "restrooms. Prisoners are usually disarmed, too," she added, pointing to Feoras's sword. "And third," here June lowered her voice, "I would watch what you say, since I'm pretty sure we're being listened to."

The Valforte looked around wildly at the walls and ceiling, as though expecting to see a yellow eye peering down at them. Errigal pointed up, where the walls arched overhead, at some cleverly disguised ventilation holes. Also probably handy for eavesdropping. June nodded.

"Maybe, maybe not," she said, voice still lowered, "but no more monster talk, okay?" They all moved slowly out into the room.

It really was very comfortable, especially considering where they'd been sleeping for the past few weeks. The air was pleasantly warm, lightly scented with woodsmoke and fresh hay. The flickering light of the fire and torches cast a soothing, reddish glow on the walls and ceiling, reminding June of sleepovers with Ashleigh and Shannon, when they'd pitched a blanket tent in their rooms and held secret midnight meetings in the cozy caves.

June dropped her saddlebag in a corner and went to investigate the archway, to see if she'd been right about its purpose. Not only had she been right, but she found a pleasant surprise–indoor plumbing. A tiny waterfall cascaded from the ceiling into a hole in the floor. June put her hand into the refreshingly cold water and watched it run over her palm and down her fingers, smiling. No, this definitely wasn't a dungeon.

But it was a warning. June emerged from the archway and told the men of her discovery, smiling once more as they bolted to investigate for themselves. She could hear their exclamations of awe as she unpacked her eating utensils from her bag, then went to examine the vegetables which had been left for them. They seemed very potato-like, so June set to peeling and slicing them, thinking that tonight might be a good night to introduce the guys to shish-ka-bobs.

They emerged from the archway shortly thereafter, wiping their wet hands on their pants and still chattering excitedly about the water. Clearly, this wasn't common. June sighed silently. *I guess that's really the last time I'll be seeing running water,* she thought ruefully. Unexpected tears sprang to her eyes, and she tried to discreetly wipe them away, but she still got raised eyebrows from Koen. The man never missed a trick.

Errigal and Feoras began gutting and skinning the sheep-thing, and June asked Minogan and Koen to sharpen some of the smaller firewood sticks for the shish-ke-babs. The Valforte must have been exhausted, or they'd be raising holy hell about the amount of work she was doing. She could still see the shadows of fatigue on their faces.

June actually felt pretty good. They'd made it across the desert. Now everything rested in the hands of the dragons, and there was nothing to do but wait. For the first time in a long time, she hummed a little under her breath as she peeled and chopped vegetables.

"You sound happy," Koen said as he brought the sharpened, peeled sticks for the shish-ke-babs to her.

"Yeah, sorry," June said, eyeing him sidewise, knowing he and the rest of the guys weren't exactly at ease. Koen shook his head and smiled.

"Don't apologize," he said, amused. He paused, still looking at her, his eyes burning so intensely into her own that June had to drop her own eyes and swallow hard, trying to keep her shaky hands from betraying her.

Koen reached out and touched her shoulder gently, causing her to meet his eyes once more. June couldn't have felt more exposed if she were naked; everything she felt for Koen must have been shining from her eyes plain as a lighthouse beacon. He smiled at her, and it felt like a hot drop of liquid slid from her chest, down behind her navel, and between her thighs.

"It's just...nice, to see you look relaxed for once," he said. June thought Koen must be able to feel her pulse racing–her heart seemed to be moving her whole body as it pounded.

And then one of her shaking hands, the one holding the knife, gave a little jerk, and the blade slid across the vegetable she held, slicing the thumb on her left hand open and shocking June back to reality with the sharp pain, and the sensation of warm blood dripping over her hand. She jumped, dropping the knife and veggie and gripping the injured digit tightly in her other hand, the blood oozing out from between her fingers. Koen followed her gaze and started.

"Wow, you really cut yourself," he said, as June dropped the knife and vegetable and squeezed the injured thumb in the other hand, trying to staunch the flow. "Let me get a cloth..." Koen jumped up and hurried over to where the packs lay.

"No, don't bother, it'll close up on its own in a minute..." June said feebly, her face the same shade as the blood. *Wow, that was smooth, June. You are such an idiot.* Already she could feel the telltale tingle of her body healing itself. She looked up to see Koen rummaging through his pack for something. "It's fine..."

"At least something to clean up the blood–"

"I'll just rinse it under the water, really, thanks though," June said, standing quickly. As she did, she caught Errigal looking at her, quickly trying to hide a smirk as he caught her looking back. June gave him the dirtiest look she could muster before practically running off to the restroom.

She leaned her forehead against the wall next to the waterfall as the cold trickle rinsed the blood away from the already closed wound. She had never been so mortified in her life. Not only had she completely ruined a *perfect* moment with Koen, but apparently she was so obvious about her feelings even Errigal knew. Oh, God. Did Koen know? Well, if he didn't before, he probably did now. Oh *God....*

June was tempted to throw herself down the hole the waterfall fell into, but closer inspection told her she'd probably get stuck somewhere around her boobs, and visions of Koen trying to unjam her from the hole turned her off the idea pretty quick. She also considered staying in here forever, but eventually someone would either come looking for her or have to use the facilities.

So, with a sigh, and a final temperature check of her cheeks, she stepped out and walked back over to the fire in as dignified a fashion as possible.

Koen was finishing up the vegetables when he saw her coming, he looked up, concerned. "How's your thumb?" he asked, and June held her hand up to show him.

"See, it closes up on its own," she said, trying to put on a casual smile.

Koen took her hand in his to inspect it more closely, and she nearly gasped at the feel of his cool, callused skin on hers. *At least you don't have anything sharp in your hand this time,* she thought. *God, you're such a dork.*

"Amazing," he said, shaking his head and releasing her hand, to her mixed disappointment and relief. "I wouldn't mind being able to do that."

"Probably one of the few things about being a sorceress that I don't mind," June said, relaxing a bit. Either the incident a few moments earlier hadn't made him suspicious, or he hid it really well; either way, June didn't care. She was perfectly happy to play ostrich with this one. "In case you haven't noticed, I'm a bit of a klutz."

Koen shook his head. "If you only knew how many times I've cut myself on a knife, or stuck myself with an arrow, fallen off a horse...like I said, I wouldn't mind being able to do that."

He smiled at her once more, and June melted like butter in a saucepan. *You know, the starvation thing wasn't so bad,* June thought. *At least it kept me out of trouble.* Anxious to change the subject, she looked over at Feoras, cutting the meat into small chunks as she'd asked him to.

"How's your cold, by the way?" June asked, and Feoras cleared his throat slightly.

"It's okay," he said, but his voice had a nasty thick sound June didn't like.

"I'll take care of it after supper." June said. Feoras looked about to protest, but June cut him off. "I'll be perfectly fine to do it. I just need one good meal, promise."

"Well–okay, thanks," he said, and June was glad she'd mentioned it. He must be feeling really bad not to argue more.

They had a nice time roasting the shish-ka-bobs over the fire, laughing and joking. The guys seemed pleasantly surprised by the way they turned out.

"Wow, these are actually good," said Errigal through a mouthful of meat and vegetable.

"You know, I'm not sure I like the tone of amazement in your voice," June said, narrowing her eyes playfully. "Like you didn't think I could cook or something."

"I didn't," he said, and June threw a chunk of vegetable at him, which he deftly caught and popped in his mouth.

"Oh ye of little faith," June said. "You should see what I could have done with some tinfoil."

"Tinful?" Koen asked.

"No, tin-foil," June said, enunciating carefully. "It's like a cross between metal and paper. You can crumple it up like paper, but it stays where you crumple it, and it doesn't burn. So, we could have chopped all this stuff up, wrapped it in tinfoil, stuck it down in the coals, and just walked away for half an hour. And when we came back, it'd be done, and all the juices would be sealed inside, so it makes the meat really tender, and the potatoes don't get dry."

"Potatoes?" Feoras asked, voice thick with his cold.

"Like this," June said, holding up one of the root vegetables left stacked near the fire, "but a little different. God, you sound froggy. Let's get that cold taken care of." She stood, dusting straw off her rear, and walked around the fire to where Feoras sat.

"You really don't have to do this," Feoras said, eyeing her thin frame dubiously–out of everyone, he was the only one who understood what it took to work magic. "I'm–"

"Burning up, my God," June exclaimed, laying a hand on his chest and feeling the heat radiating from his shirt, then pressing the inside of her wrist to his forehead. It was moist with sweat, and they could have skipped the fire and cooked their food on his chest.

She looked into Feoras's face, for the first time seeing the fever-glaze in his eyes, her own wide with shock.

"Why didn't you say something? How long have you been like this?" Feoras cut his eyes downward, avoiding her gaze. June rounded on Errigal, who sat behind her. He flinched. "How long?" June asked Errigal, her voice low and dangerous.

Errigal shrugged, dropping his gaze uncomfortably. "Since a day before we left the desert," he said, and June made a noise somewhere between astonishment and disgust. She looked back and forth between the two of them, shaking her head.

"Three days?" June asked. Feoras nodded.

Annoyed, June pushed Feoras back a little more roughly than she intended, then placed one hand on his chest, and one on his forehead. The familiar tingling sensation coursed through her limbs as her power surged into him, until she could push no more. As she sat back, a slight wave of dizziness overcame her, uncomfortable, but nowhere near as bad as before.

June shook her head slightly to clear the last vestiges of faintness, then looked up at the four men. Feoras sat up, looking almost radiant, compared to how he'd been looking. June was angry with herself for not noticing how bad his condition had been, but more angry with Feoras and the others for concealing it.

June looked angrily from face to face.

"Never do that again," she said. "Any of you, ever. If you're sick, or you're hurt, you come to me, and we'll take care of it. Don't try to hide this crap from me anymore."

"You were too weak to do anything anyway, June," Koen said defensively. "We all agreed—"

"Yeah, I didn't want to be messing around with a *cold*. This was a possibly life-threatening fever. Do you realize how quick this could have turned? That he could have just dropped into a coma and not woken up? And why did you continue to wait, even after we had food?" June raked her fingers through her thick hair, sighing. "Look, just don't do that again."

"If we have to, we will," Minogan said. "We're not going to risk your life for—"

"Don't be ridiculous," June said, sharply, standing up. "You don't understand—"

"It's you who doesn't understand," Minogan said, drawing himself up almost imperceptibly, as in preparation for a fight. "Like it or not, you are the future of every living thing on this planet. We protect you until the last one of us falls, and we're certainly not going to put you in danger ourselves. You need to start standing aside and letting us do what we have to do. *You* still don't realize," here June tried to interject, but Minogan raised his voice, talking over her protestations, "that you have to live. That if it comes to one of us or you, it has to be us, because the world can go on without us. It can't without you." His gaze bored into hers, and she was only able to hold it for a moment before turning her head away angrily.

Of course, he was right. But June didn't care about logic at the moment. She only cared about preserving the four people she had left in the universe. The nameless, faceless masses—all could go hang, as long as these four stayed safe. One of them in particular, who currently looked at her with a mixed expression of sympathy and exasperation.

June looked at the ceiling, blinking back tears for what seemed like the umpteenth time this week. She could explain to them until she was as blue in the face as the Valforte, but none of them had been through what she had, and none of them would fully understand.

So, rather than stand and argue fruitlessly, she turned her back and marched over to her things, wrapped herself in her blanket, and lay facing the wall.

She heard the Valforte clearing the dinner things away, taking the utensils to be washed, and preparing for bed themselves. Finally, when she heard the soft crunch of the straw under their bodies, their breathing change to slow rhythmic sighs and soft snores, and saw the flickering firelight on the wall dim to a soft glow as the fire burned down to coals, only then did she allow herself to cry for the things not yet taken from her.

June woke, disoriented, not knowing what time it was, or even what day, entombed as they were in the belly of the mountain. Physically, she felt wonderful, so she couldn't understand for a moment why she felt so miserable–and then she remembered the argument from the day before.

Slowly, she sat up, rubbing her eyes and rolling her head to stretch her neck. Looking over at the fire pit, she saw all four Valforte sitting there, cups in their hands, talking quietly. June looked around the cavern with a sigh. Not a place you could easily avoid someone, or a group of someones. She briefly considered going to the restroom and hiding, but, as she'd concluded when she cut her finger yesterday, sooner or later, someone would need to use it.

When the Valforte saw her coming, they stopped talking, which didn't help June feel better. She sat down quietly in a space beside Errigal and accepted a cup of tea, made from the herb they'd found outside the mountain, and blew gently on the surface, watching the swirls of steam flicker wildly away.

Out of the corner of her eye, she saw Koen giving Minogan a very hard look. The two seemed to have reached an uneasy truce since Minogan's admission in the woods, but they still weren't back where they had been, not by a long shot. June wondered if her argument with Minogan yesterday had caused more tension between them.

"I'm sorry I shouted at you yesterday," Minogan said to her suddenly. As he spoke, Koen sat back in a satisfied manner, nodding slightly. June nodded without speaking or turning to face him, not trusting her voice to stay steady.

"It's just," Minogan continued, faltering slightly, "I mean, this is real for us, it's not a game–"

June's head snapped around to face him as he said this. She felt Errigal stiffen beside her, and Koen actually clapped his hand to his forehead, shaking his head in disbelief.

"I see," said June, her voice dangerously calm. "And you think that for me, this *is* a game."

Minogan's eyes grew wide as he saw the trap he'd set for himself. "No, I didn't–I didn't mean–what I meant–"

June shook her head, closing her eyes and sighing deeply. "If I were you, Minogan, I'd shut my mouth and quit while I was ahead." Still shaking her head, she turned away and stared into the fire. She saw Minogan open his mouth once more, but Koen smacked him hard with the back of his hand, giving him a *what-the-hell's-the-matter-with-you* look, and Minogan slumped back, looking defeated.

June took a steadying breath, trying with all her might to be patient and keep her emotions in check, then turned to face Minogan once more.

"I understand what you're trying to say, even if your communication skills need work," June said. Past Minogan, she saw Koen jerk his head in surprise, and Minogan himself raised his eyebrows, apparently aware of what a supremely asinine statement he'd made a moment before. "But I can't just stand by and–"

Minogan made a gesture of extreme frustration, throwing his arms up in the air and rolling his eyes, looking over June's shoulder and shaking his head in exasperation. "Why can't you just get this?" he said, annoyed and on the verge of anger, hands curled into fists. "You can't–"

"I get it, okay?" June snapped, her irritation with Minogan's single-mindedness finally getting the better of her. "What you don't get is that you four are all the family I have left, and it's a little hard to step aside and watch you get hurt!"

June watched Minogan's face as his expression turn from arrogance to dismay. His mouth opened and worked wordlessly for a moment. June felt an unexpected rush of sympathy for him.

"Relax, I'm not looking for a pity party. I want you to understand I'm not trying to be stupid or stubborn. You just...may need to remind me, now and then." Minogan nodded, face flushed dark blue, and lowered his head. Feoras and Errigal were now looking at her as though they hadn't really seen her before, and Koen watched her silently, his expression unreadable. June brought her cup to her lips as they sat in silence, eyes on the dancing flames, lost in thought.

~12~

A few hours and a large brunch later, they heard a scratching at the door. The Valforte sprang to their feet, hands on sword-hilts as the door opened, revealing Rakoz, who nodded to June. She nodded.

"Tokesh requests your presence, Princess," he said, his rumbling voice echoing in the chamber. June nodded and stepped forward, flanked by the Valforte.

Rakoz stiffened slightly. "Tokesh requests to see you *alone*, Princess," he said, shifting his weight between his front feet. "Without your escorts."

June turned to face the Valforte, knowing full well this would go over like a pay cut for union employees. All four were shaking their heads in protest, bodies rigid with tension. June shrugged and smiled, trying to be reassuring, but her heart thudded so fast in her chest there was barely a pause between beats.

"It's gotta get done, guys," she said softly, hoping that Rakoz couldn't hear her. "We can't risk making him mad."

"I don't like this, June," Koen whispered, and June was surprised to hear a tremor in his voice. "We can't get separated..."

"We don't have a choice," she said, and without giving them further chance to argue, she spun on her heel and followed Rakoz into the hall, not trusting herself with a backward glance.

June and Rakoz walked in uncomfortable silence, the only sound his talons clicking on the stone floor, worn smooth by centuries of rough dragon feet. In what seemed both an eternity and a millisecond, they arrived back at the throne room. The door swung open, but this time Rakoz hung back.

"Tokesh awaits you, Princess," he said, nodding. June bowed.

"Thank you, Rakoz," she said. "Maybe I'll see you a little later?" She hoped, if he knew she was about to be killed, her statement might force some kind of reaction. He merely nodded and stepped away, though, and squaring her shoulders, June stepped through the doors and into the chamber.

June never thought the absence of dragons could make a place creepier, but this seemed the rare exception. The two dozen or so dragons who had lined the walls yesterday were gone, leaving the chamber deserted, except for the enormous form of Tokesh, exactly as she'd seen him last, draped over the huge stone dais at the head of the room. His eyes glittered in the firelight as he watched her approach. June stopped at what she considered a respectful distance, bowed, and waited in silence.

Tokesh regarded her quietly for a moment, his expression inscrutable. Finally, after what felt like an eternity, he spoke.

"We have been watching you," he said, voice an even lower rumble than Rakoz's.

"I know, sir," June said. Tokesh jerked his head in surprise, grunting softly.

"You were very open, if this is true," he said, cocking his head to the side.

"I have nothing to hide," June answered. She did her level best not to fidget during another moment of uncomfortable silence.

"Are you always this thin?" Tokesh said suddenly.

June shook her head, smiling. "No. It was a difficult journey."

"And you came without horses?"

June inhaled deeply and swallowed to keep herself from faltering. "We had horses, but halfway across the salt desert, one died. We released the rest."

"How humane of you," Tokesh said, voice blank of emotion.

June shrugged, unable to think of a response.

"I am told," Tokesh said, rearranging his bulk on the dais, "that usually Andrians and Valforte do not get along. How is it that you travel together?"

"I didn't grow up here, so I don't feel the same as the Andrians," June replied. "They were hired by a sorcerer to protect me."

"And they hold no grudge against you?" Tokesh asked.

"They did at first, I think, but not anymore. At any rate, I gave them the opportunity to leave, several times, and they haven't, so I guess they don't mind me too much."

"They call you June."

"That's the name I grew up with," she said, trying to ignore a small pang in her heart as she thought of the people who'd given her that name. "I'm not really used to Ulfhilda."

Tokesh stared over her head for a few moments, lost in thought, and June took the opportunity to examine her own mind. She felt more hopeful than she had when she'd walked into the chamber. She doubted Tokesh would waste so much time questioning her if he planned to kill her at the end anyway.

"...queen?"

June just caught the end of his question as she emerged from her thoughts. "I'm sorry?" she said politely, hoping he wouldn't be angry she'd missed his question, but he repeated it patiently.

"I asked what you plan to do, once you become queen."

June frowned as she considered the question. "I haven't really thought about it, to be honest. I guess the first thing will be to fix the laws for the Valforte."

"Oh?" Tokesh said, in a *go on* tone of voice.

"They don't have any protection, to the point that their race is dying out. And I'd like to repay them for what they've done for me."

Tokesh took a huge breath and let it out, so even where she stood, June could feel the hot breeze blow her hair back.

"Do you know why I am questioning you this way?" he asked, and June nodded.

"I think so," she said. "I think you're trying to figure out what kind of person I am."

"Precisely," Tokesh said, nodding. "I'm wary of cooperating with an Andrian, much less helping one, especially considering what has happened to us recently." June nodded her head slightly, wondering if any of the 'nestlings' had been Tokesh's own offspring. "However, if what you say is true, my own people will die, if I do not cooperate with you." Tokesh looked to June for confirmation, and she nodded. "So, you understand my dilemma."

"I do," June said. "I don't blame you for not trusting me. But we need your help. You have the tablet here, and I need it. There's no way we can fight you for it, if you refuse–you'd kill us, and besides, I don't want to fight. If there's something you want in return, if it's mine to give, you'll have it, but please..." June swallowed hard. "Please," she finished lamely.

Tokesh looked at her, hard, for several minutes. Then, suddenly, he heaved his massive body off the dais, arched his back in a catlike stretch, and walked slowly over to her, till she practically stood between his front feet. He peered down at her severely.

"Will you keep your people away from mine?" he asked, and June could feel the vibration of his deep voice in the stone at her feet. "Will you make them leave us in peace?"

"I will," June said. "I swear it."

"Follow me," Tokesh said, and June's heart swooped in her chest. *This is it,* she thought.

Tokesh led her out another, smaller door, hidden in an alcove behind the dais. He had to duck his head as he passed through, and the ridged scales along his spine barely cleared the arch. More fire-filled trenches lit this passageway, but it had a disused air, as though no one had walked here for a long time. It curved and inclined, giving June the impression of walking a loose spiral *inside* the mountain, slowly climbing toward its peak.

Tokesh walked slowly, but she still had to jog to keep up. On and on they went, in increasingly oppressive silence.

Finally, the passageway ended at a people-sized stone door set in the far wall, which like the other doors in the mountain, had no handle on the front; it simply opened for you or didn't. As they reached the door, the dragon turned to her.

"This door has never been opened, in all the centuries the dragons have called this mountain home," Tokesh said. "However, the story was told that once, there was an Andrian temple within the mountain. The temple was abandoned, but a piece of a magical stone tablet was left within, and the dragons agreed to guard it, until a chosen individual came to retrieve it."

"Chosen individual?" June asked.

"Yes, it was foretold that someone would come to receive the stone piece. They were very detailed in their description of that someone." Tokesh chuckled slightly. "Unfortunately, not one among us can remember the description."

June smiled uncertainly. "So...I might not be the right person."

"True, but there is one way to find out," Tokesh said.

"Oh?"

"As I said, this door hasn't been opened since the Andrians left. It won't open for us. So, if you're the right one, it will open for you...or, if you're the wrong one, it won't."

Or it could have broken at some point in the past few centuries and won't open for anyone, June thought, thinking of the automatic doors at the supermarket which always seemed to be on the fritz. She looked up to find Tokesh watching her, and experienced an emotion akin to stage fright.

Oh God, what if it doesn't open, what if I try to blast it open and it doesn't work, oh God....

June was terrified to try the door, to try and fail. But she had to do something. Slowly, she raised her arm and touched her fingertips lightly to the stone.

The door swung open so quickly June snatched her hand back with a gasp. She'd psyched herself out so badly, she didn't believe the door would open. She looked up at Tokesh. He nodded respectfully.

"I leave you here, princess," he said, and turned to leave. June looked from the doorway, down into the narrow passageway beyond, to Tokesh's retreating form, and back again. Fear, horrible squeezing fear, enveloped her like thick, cold fog. He was leaving her alone.

"Tokesh," June called after him, and he paused, serpentine neck swinging his head over his shoulder to gaze inquisitively at her. June took a deep breath. "If–if something happens, if I don't come back–can–will you–"

Tokesh nodded gravely. "I will see that your friends are taken care of," he said, and June nodded grimly, lips pressed together.

"Thank you," she said softly, and Tokesh turned away and continued his retreat along the corridor. June watched until the last inch of his tail disappeared behind a bend, and the echo of his talons on the stone faded away.

She turned and faced the opening revealed by the door, black and forbidding, more so now with the combined factors of solitude and silence. *Standing here brooding about how scary it is won't get you there any faster,* June thought. *Get on with it.*

Heart in her throat, June stepped through the doorway and into the cold unknown.

She was only a few wobbly steps in when the door swung shut behind her, cutting off all light and scaring the bejesus out of her. She barely contained a scream, pressing herself up against the damp wall and clasping her hands to her chest. *If something happens in here, you're on your own,* June thought, shuddering.

She took a shaky breath and tried to block out images of creatures with sharp teeth and cruel beady eyes standing a few inches away in the blackness, coiling themselves to strike.

I need a light, June thought. At once, the passageway filled with a pearly luminescence, and June blinked, shocked, looking around wildly to find the source of the light.

It's me, she realized, holding a hand in front of her face and examining it. A gentle glow emanated from her body, strong enough to light about ten feet worth of corridor. She looked at the wall and waved her hand. *If it came from somewhere else, I'd be casting a shadow. But I am the light.* June shook her head, smiling, feeling blasphemous. *And June said, I need a light...and there was light.*

She and her aura moved slowly along the passageway. It continued in the same fashion as the one leading to the door; curving to the left, with a steady incline, just enough that, after about twenty minutes of walking, the muscles of her thighs burned.

June began to wonder whether she'd ever reach the end of the corridor. *Well, it has to end somewhere,* she thought. *The mountain has a top. I can't just climb into the sky.* Just as this thought went through her head, the passage opened in front of her, into a huge, conical chamber, the sides sloping upward and meeting in a point.

Her jaw dropped as she stepped into the room, her light illuminating the space with a hazy glow that made the room even creepier. Steps descended to a flat circle in the center ringed by twelve huge stone pillars, cut deep with strange runes. And in the center of this circle–

June's heart dropped into her stomach and bounced back up into her chest. A broken piece of stone tablet lay on the small pillar. Cautiously, she edged away from the wall and started down the steps, her soft footfalls echoing against the stone walls

"Greetings," said a voice on her right.

This time June did scream, and fell heavily on her side as she scrambled away from the voice. Looking up, heart pounding, she saw a short, balding man, dressed in a brown robe like a monk's. She leapt to her feet, backing away quickly.

"Where did you–how did you get in here?" she asked, voice shrill and feeble as she gasped for breath.

"I have always been here," the man said, face expressionless.

"Oh, really?" June said, trying to mask her fear. "And you've been living off what, pebble sandwiches?"

"I do not need food," the man replied. "I am a spirit, once a monk of the temples of Serhai, waiting to provide guidance to the person seeking this." With one hand, he indicated the stone piece.

June looked at the strange man standing in front of her, brow furrowed, mouth working as she tried to think of something to say. *Sorcerers, dragons, aliens, blue warriors...and now ghosts. The Easter bunny is sounding more plausible by the second.*

Edging forward, June stretched her hand out and brushed his arm. Or, meant to. Actually, her hand went right through him, and she jumped back with a squeak. The monk-guy still stood expressionless, blinking benignly.

"Okay, so...you're dead, then?" He nodded, without changing expression. "So, what guidance do you have to give me?"

"The three pieces of the tablet, the Tablet of Nuvyl, are hidden in three outlying areas of Prendawr." *Of course,* June thought, *we couldn't put them in a nice little clump somewhere. That would be simple.* "In order to procure each piece of the tablet, you must pass a test, which ensures that you have the will and dedication to possess the stones, and the power to wield them. Carved on the back of each piece is a map, which will direct you to the next piece, and finally to the place in which they must be assembled and activated."

June nodded for the monk to go on.

"Before you begin, I must ask you to consider carefully what you are about to do. The magic of the Tablet of Nuvyl is only to be used as a last resort."

"I don't think I'd be here if there were any other way," June said, and the monk nodded.

"Very well," he said, stepping back. "You may proceed." With that, he vanished, leaving her feeling as though she'd been conked on the head by a rubber mallet.

"But–hey, wait a minute," June shouted at the place where the monk had been. "What's the test? Wait! Hey, come on! You've got one job to do in how many centuries, and you don't even finish it!" She whirled in place, squinting into the gloom at the edges of her aura light, but he'd disappeared without a trace.

"Loser," June grumbled under her breath. She glanced down at the tablet, lying innocuously on its pillar. So, where was the test? Would something jump out at her when she got down there? Would it be multiple-choice?

Cautiously, June descended the remaining steps, until she stood just on the outside of the circle. Here, she paused, sensing the pillars formed a border of some kind, and once she crossed it, there was no telling what would happen. All eagerness gone, she stretched out a hand and grazed a pillar lightly with her fingertips.

As soon as the pads of her fingers touched the stone, everything inside the circle burst into flame, and June leapt back two or three stairs up. Even so, she could feel the heat of the flames. There was no fuel for them, no wood, only stone, and yet the fire burned hotter than anything she'd ever felt. And what she needed stood in the center of the smokeless inferno.

"A test," she said, softly, sitting down hard on the step, hands clasped between her knees. "Ha!"

June stared into the flames, her mind numbed by the sheer magnitude of her task. Somehow, she had to think of a way to use magic to walk through fire, but at the moment, she was hard-pressed to remember her name.

June moved closer to the fire, then narrowed her eyes,

concentrating, trying by force of will to put the flames out. Not a flicker, or a waver–they danced on, ignoring her efforts to quell them.

"Go out," she whispered, squeezing her eyes nearly shut. "Go out, go out." No effect.

"Okay," she said out loud. "What doesn't fire like? How about water? Water puts out fire." June stood up, closed her eyes, and concentrated, visualizing a huge mass of water, hanging above the fire in midair. It wasn't easy–her mind kept slipping, and she kept losing the image. Finally, though, she had it, a perfect unmoving portrait of what she wanted in her head.

Cracking her eyes open, she was more than a little surprised to see what she had conceived in her mind's eye had actually come into being. An enormous ball of water, the circumference of the pillar-lined circle, hung over the fire like a water balloon, minus the balloon. Stunned, her concentration wavered, and the fluid sphere shivered and expanded, showing alarming signs of loss of integrity.

This was no time to dwell on, *Hey, look what I can do!* She released her hold on the water, and with a whooshing splash, it crashed down onto the flames, splattering June. The chamber was immersed in dark silence as the fire went out.

"Huh," said June, out loud. "That was easy."

No sooner were the words out of her mouth than the flames sprung up again, twice as high as they'd been the first time. She let out an aggravated groan, clutching her head in anguish. Now what?

June sat down again, feeling a delayed wave of dizziness from the magic she'd just performed. She realized with a jolt of anxiety she didn't have too many shots at this. If she wasn't careful, she'd leave herself too weak to get back, and no one could reach her in here. She'd end up chilling with the monk for all eternity.

Chilling.

"Ice," she said thoughtfully. "Fire doesn't like ice." June stood up again, looking down at herself. She took a deep breath and blew it out between pursed lips. "Think cold," she whispered. "Cold, ice, freezing. Make yourself a suit of armor."

Suddenly, it felt as though she had just slipped on a refrigerated rubber suit. Her skin tried to shrink away from the cold, but, just like the light, she was the cold.

She walked to the ring and held her hand near the flames, then, emboldened by the lack of heat she felt, plunged it in up to the elbow. She felt something, all right, a sensation of warmth, but she wasn't burning, which was the important part. With a deep breath, reminding herself to concentrate, she moved forward.

Walking into the flames put June in sensory overload. The fire roared in her ears, making it hard to think, and the brightness seared her eyes even through closed lids, making them water in protest. She couldn't have opened her eyes if she wanted to; she'd have to go by feel alone. Unfortunately, this circle was about twenty feet across. If she missed her trajectory, she could be in here a long time.

June didn't have a long time, though. Already, she was sweating, and between the roaring in her ears and the sensation of being roasted to death inside an ice cube, she wasn't going to be able to keep this up for very long. Arms outstretched, she charged forward, sweeping her hands back and forth, desperately searching for the prize. She even shuffled her feet, hoping to catch the edge of the pillar and find the stone that way. Sweat trickled between her breasts and in small rivulets down her nose.

June stumbled, disoriented as the roaring abruptly ceased, and she could see again. She'd blundered straight through and out the other side.

"No! Dammit," June cursed, and turned around to face the fire once more. She blinked ferociously, trying to clear the reddish-orange haze burned into her retinas by the flames. June backed up a few steps, looking at the placement of the pillars, trying to figure out where the exact center would be. Clenching her fists in determination, she concentrated on clearing her mind and steadying her emotions. 'Ice suit' on once more, she plunged back into the fire for her final attempt.

As soon as she stepped in, she knew she was in trouble. The failure on her first attempt had weakened her and rattled her concentration. With a stab of panic, she realized she wasn't just hot–she was beginning to burn. Discomfort turned to pain, pain everywhere–her face, her arms, her chest, her legs, now burning with the intensity of being forced to hold a super-hot coffee cup, and getting worse.

Just when June thought she wasn't going to make it, her fingers brushed stone, and she lunged forward. As she did, her foot caught the edge of the podium, and she clutched the stone fragment to her chest as she fell to the ground.

Everything went dark and quiet. June lay on her side in the fetal position, fingers grasping the stone so tightly the rough edges cut into her fingers. Her skin seemed fine, a little red and sensitive to the touch, but she couldn't feel any blisters or sores. She smelled singed hair, and with one hand, reached up to her head to check the damage. Luckily, her hair had been soaked with sweat, and only about two or three inches had been burned off. Her ears ringing from the roar of the fire, June lay still on the ground next to the podium until the after-image of the flames faded from her retinas. Breath coming in ragged gasps, she got to her feet, stumbling and nearly dropping the stone as she did.

Even though her eyes had returned to normal, it didn't help much, for now she was surrounded by a dark so palpable she might reach out and tear away a handful of it. She didn't have the strength to light her luminescence, either—she could barely stand. Slowly, sliding her feet over the ground and holding her free hand out in front of her, she edged forward until her toe bumped the first step of the amphitheater stairs.

Bent over, using her fingertips to gauge where her feet should go, she made her way painstakingly up the steps, only falling to her knees once, clutching the tablet to her chest, terrified she'd drop it and either break it or not be able to find it again in the dark. Finally, she reached the top of the stairs, and set out slowly across the distance between the edge of the amphitheater and the wall of the temple.

As she shuffled across, eyes straining, an overwhelming fear settled over June, and she froze. She could feel a presence, could feel herself being watched.

"Who's there?" she asked, unable to keep a quaver from her voice. "Mr. Monk? Who's there?" Silence. "Who's there?" June persisted, but she heard only the slight echo of her voice. She suddenly became very aware of the open space surrounding her, the lack of a wall to press herself against.

The black began to close in from all sides. Once more, her imagination called up a circle of monsters, slimy beasts with glittering eyes, crouched in the dark just beyond her reach. June's bladder constricted in response, and she pressed her thighs together, fighting her body's response to terror. The panic felt like a caged animal in her chest, throwing itself against the bars...it was only a matter of time before it broke free.

June squeezed her eyes shut, her closed lids somehow more comforting than the unknown element tormenting her, and tried to steady herself. *It's okay,* she told herself, as if trying to soothe a child. *This is all in your mind. You're getting freaked for no–*

Just then, June heard a small *pop* behind her. Probably nothing more than a pebble her foot had moved, or even the contraction of the rock cooling from the fire. But it was enough to release the panic in her chest and send her sprinting for the wall, hand outstretched, no longer mindful of tripping over or running into anything. All coherent thought fled, leaving a white noise whistling meaninglessly between June's ears.

Her hand smacked into the stone of the wall, her body a moment later, carried by momentum. The impact jarred her, but she recovered quickly, singularly focused on getting out. She ran along the wall, hand dragging along the stone, until at last, the stone vanished, and her palm floated above emptiness.

June was well on her way down the passage, her sprint now slowed to a frantically fast walk, before it occurred to her this might *not* be the way out. She hadn't seen another way in, but that didn't mean there *wasn't* one, especially since she'd only had eyes for the stone piece in the center of the room.

It was too late now, though...she'd been in here for about five minutes already, and she had no desire to go back into the temple and explore the possibilities of another exit. The idea of being in the wrong passageway fueled the dying fire of her fear, though; what if she came out somewhere else in the mountain and couldn't find her way back?

A moment later, June hit something solid, then stumbled out into a lit corridor as the something revealed itself to be a door. She fell to her knees, blinking, glad to be back in the light. As her eyes adjusted to the brightness, she examined the corridor she'd entered. It looked the same as the one she'd come by, but she couldn't be sure. June pushed slowly to her feet and began to walk.

Fear had been the only thing spurring her on before; now the adrenaline was fading, and she had to rely on sheer stubbornness.

She was so tired. All she could think of were beds, of every shape, size, and type. The king-sized bed she and Kyle had slept in at a Vermont B & B on a ski trip. Her childhood daybed, with soft Bambi-print flannel sheets. The bed which awaited her now, a pile of straw and a torn blanket. Anything. Any place to lay her head down.

Suddenly, Rakoz stood before her, blocking the way. June stopped, trying to keep from swaying as she stood.

He lowered his head toward her, looking concerned. "You look unwell."

"Just tired," June said, weakly.

"I'll take you back to your chambers," he said, and June stumbled into a side corridor after him. "Did you get what you came for?"

"Yes, thank God," she answered, struggling to raise her voice above a whisper. She couldn't even lift her head, just watched her bare feet slapping clumsily against the floor.

Rakoz stopped before a door, and June saw with relief it was the door to her and the Valforte's room. Without even pausing to thank Rakoz, she stumbled inside.

"June," Koen exclaimed, running forward to meet her, flanked by the others. "Where have you been? You were gone for hours!" He stopped short, looking wide-eyed at the stone she still clutched tight to her chest.

"Is that it?" he asked, voice filled with awe. Smiling wanly, June held the tablet piece out to him, and he took it, reverently, handling it as though it were a sleeping infant. The other Valforte crowded close to examine it.

They were so engrossed in the piece of stone, the fruit of their endeavors, that none of them managed to catch June as she fell face first into the straw in a dead faint.

~13~

Before June opened her eyes, she felt pangs from her empty stomach. She found herself on a soft heap of hay near the wall, covered with a blanket. She rolled onto her side and pushed up on one elbow, rubbing her face sleepily. Facing the fire pit, she saw the Valforte talking quietly. Errigal caught her eye and nudged the others, who turned to look at her. June raised her hand and waved.

The men got up and came to her, Koen with a cup of tea, which she accepted gratefully, sitting up. They looked at her with expressions mixed with curiosity, anxiety, and awe. June smiled.

"Hey, guys," she said, trying to inject some joviality into her tone. "How's it going?"

Errigal snorted, and the others just shook their heads. Koen looked at her like cauliflowers had just sprouted from her nose.

"How's it going?" he asked. "How's it going? You come back after being gone for hours, with your clothing singed and half your hair burned off, you pass out, and we can't wake you for *a full day*– June, what the hell happened to you?"

"Wow, no wonder I'm hungry," June said, with a smile no one returned. She cleared her throat uncomfortably and launched into a summary of events, from after she had left them to meet Tokesh until the point of her return. When she'd finished, they all stared at her, agog. June shrugged, trying to suppress a self-satisfied grin.

"Wow," said Feoras. "That's a hell of a story."

"Yeah, I'm thinking I'll be able to put together a kick-ass mini-series when this is over." Four sets of brows furrowed in confusion, and June shook her head dismissively.

"Never mind," she said. "Where's the tablet?"

Minogan trotted over to where they kept their things against the wall and carefully extricated a cloth-wrapped package, bringing it back to June and depositing it gently in her lap. She ran her fingertips over the cloth in amazement.

"I didn't even get to look at it," she said, unwrapping the stone.

It looked very Ten Commandments-ish, a brown, flat, triangular piece of stone, the front covered entirely with runes. June got a strange sensation, similar to when she'd first been getting used to speaking a new language. She didn't understand what the runes said, but she knew how to pronounce them, could hear herself speaking them in her mind. At the same time, she understood it would be a very bad idea to read them out loud. She shuddered slightly, sensing the awesome power of the tablet.

"Can you read it?" Koen asked, and she nodded.

"Don't know what it says, but I can read it, yeah," she said. "Can you?"

Koen shook his head. "Doesn't look like anything I've ever seen."

"Yeah, well, don't try, any of you. This is—it's dangerous, I can feel it."

June remembered what the monk said, about the map, and flipped the tablet over. A crude map, with no names, merely large dots and curving lines. She turned it from side to side, trying to make sense of it. Suddenly, she groaned loudly.

"What is it?" Minogan asked, leaning forward with the others.

June sighed, raking her hand through her hair. "The monk said there was a map on the other side of the tablet, to show us where the next piece is hidden. And unless I'm wrong here, the other piece is clear on the other side of the kingdom. Again." She passed the piece to Minogan, then scooted over beside him to point it out.

"See, here's Fire Mountain, I think, the way they made it a triangle makes it look like a mountain, and this big dot has to be Prendawr City. Down here's where I think it says the other piece is, it looks like it's near the ocean, see the waves? Is there a coastline over here somewhere?"

The Valforte nodded.

"So we have to go from here—" June put her finger on the mountain-triangle—"all the way to here." June slid her finger southeast down the map, farther south than where she thought Lumia would be, even, until her finger rested on a large X in the exact opposite corner from Fire Mountain.

The Valforte studied the map closely. Then Feoras sat back with a deep, windy sigh.

"I'm right, aren't I?" June said, as they all sat back in various positions of resignation—heads alternately bowed or faces turned up as in supplication. "Aren't I?"

Minogan nodded slowly, looking up at June with eyes which suddenly seemed ten years older.

"You're right," he said, softly.

June made an aggravated noise and stood up, hands entangled in her hair as though she was about to pull it out.

"Are we ever going to catch a break?" she asked, pacing back and forth. "Now we have to try and make it across the entire kingdom, on foot, with no horses or supplies, without being seen or captured." She stopped pacing and bowed her head, hands on hips. "How much more of this are we supposed to take?" she asked, softly. "We can't...we're skin and bones. We're weak and we're tired...and I don't think we're going to be able to make this."

"Do we have a choice?" Koen asked, and June sighed.

"No," she said.

"Actually, you may," said a deep voice, and they all whirled around, leaping to their feet, weapons drawn. Rakoz stood watching them. "I'm sorry I startled you. We've been listening to your conversation," here Minogan's eyes narrowed slightly in distrust, "and Tokesh sent me to make you an offer of help."

June didn't dare to hope for what he was about to offer. "We may be able to carry you in the air to your destination," he said. "What would take you about two months on foot–"

"Would take about a day in the air," June finished, smiling widely. "We accept your offer, with gratitude."

"June," Minogan whispered harshly, and she turned to him.

"What?" she asked between her teeth.

"What happened to democracy?" he hissed, and she looked at him in disbelief.

"Are you guys honestly going to vote that we walk for two, maybe even three or four months, and kill ourselves rather than accept their offer to fly us there, which would take one day?" She looked at each of the Valforte in turn as they exchanged glances.

"No," Minogan said, finally.

"Then what is the problem?" she asked. He merely shook his head and looked at his feet.

June turned back to Rakoz and smiled. "Thank you, thank you so much," she said. "You have no idea what this will mean for us. Thank you."

Rakoz nodded. "I will pass your thanks on to Tokesh. We leave at first light," he said, then turned and left.

June turned back to the Valforte, her face radiant with joy. "Did you hear that?" she asked. "One day. One! Isn't that wonderful?" Errigal, Koen, and Feoras all looked as happy as she felt, but Minogan just shrugged and went to the fire to pour himself more tea. "What's his problem?" June asked, lowering her voice, and Errigal gave his patented mischievous grin.

"Oh, him," he said, looking over his shoulder to make sure Minogan wasn't listening. "He's afraid of heights."

They spent the rest of the day packing their things carefully, fitting as much food as they could manage into their bags. They left most of the meat behind, since unfortunately they had no salt to cure it with, but the root vegetables would last as long as they kept them dry and unbruised. June sang as she worked, skipping from bundle to bundle, happier than she'd been in months. The first part of her task had been completed, and the second part had just gotten vastly easier. Finally, things had begun to go their way.

At last, after a small supper and a cup of tea, they went to bed. June lay awake for some time, aware from the uneven breathing and soft sound the straw made as someone turned over, that she wasn't the only one chasing sleep.

For the first time, she actually felt excited about the quest. *It's not impossible,* she thought. *It's happening. A third of it is already done.* Smiling to herself, she wiggled down further into the straw and drifted off.

It seemed as though she'd just closed her eyes when Errigal shook her awake. June sat up, rubbing her face and yawning. *God, how do they do that without alarm clocks?* she wondered, watching as the Valforte wandered around the chamber, getting their tea and taking care of their morning toilet. June took a few moments in the rear chamber before joining the others.

June was still finishing her tea as the others began clearing up. Watching them work, she noticed Minogan and Koen still avoided one another carefully as they packed the breakfast things. She frowned thoughtfully as Koen walked over to the fire.

"Done with the kettle?" he asked, and she nodded.

"Koen, wait," she said, as he picked up the kettle and turned to go. He turned back to face her, his brows raised expectantly, a slight smile on his face. June suppressed a little shiver as his sea-green eyes met her own.

"When are you going to make up with Minogan?"

Koen's smile faltered a bit, and his eyes darkened as if a veil had dropped behind them. "Why do you ask?" he said.

"Because," June pressed her lips together, considering her words carefully, "this is no pleasure hike we're on here. This is dangerous. And if something happens, to either of you," June swallowed hard at the thought, "I think you're going to regret it. Not making up, I mean."

Koen nodded. "I'll keep that in mind, thank you," he said, with a diplomatic little smile, and turned away.

He said that in the exact same tone Kyle used to use when he told me he'd take care of the laundry, she thought. *Ah well. Worth a shot.*

Just as June packed her utensils away, Rakoz scratched on the door, then let himself in. "Ah, you're ready. Excellent," he said.

June had to force herself to take a shaky breath. Leaving this room, which had felt more like home to her than anywhere they'd been so far on their journey, would mean once again leaping off into the unknown. Only it was worse now, because she had a taste of what she could expect, and she doubted the next 'test' was going to be easier.

Yeah, but we'll be over halfway done then, once we've got the second piece, June thought, with a backward glance as the door swung shut behind them. *And that could be by nightfall.*

They followed the dragon down a different set of passageways, each looking the same as the others. June wondered how on earth they navigated these—there were no markings at all, as far as she could see. *Well, I suppose if you grow up here, it's probably second nature,* she thought. *And it's a great defense strategy. There's no way a stranger would be able to find their way in and out. Too bad it didn't work for their babies.*

"I don't mean to upset you by bringing this up, Rakoz," June said, slowly, "but I was just wondering—it doesn't seem like it would be easy for someone to find anything in here, much less be able to find your nursery."

Rakoz nodded gravely. "You're right, the mountain is designed to confuse enemies," he said. "We don't think they actually meant to target the nestlings and the eggs, but somehow, they stumbled onto the right passage. Unfortunately for them," here he drew his lips back in a grim smile, "they were unable to find their way back out."

"Forgot their bread crumbs, huh?" June murmured. Everyone turned to look at her curiously. "It's a story, from where I come from. There's these two kids, Hansel and Gretel, and they have this mean...never mind," as she saw the looks on their faces as she began to ramble. "It's relevant, I swear." Koen hid a smile behind his hand, and June gave him a dirty look.

The passageway began to change; the lit trenches on either side ended, and the floor and sides looked more like a natural cave than a carved structure. As they moved further in, it grew darker and colder, fading to total blackness ahead.

"Put one of your hands on my side, please, each of you," Rakoz said.

"Oh, we can make our way, don't worry," Minogan said.

"Yes, but I'd prefer not to step on one of you by accident," Rakoz said, a smile in his voice. "This way, you don't inadvertently walk under my feet."

Silence followed this statement, during which June thought Minogan probably put his hand on Rakoz's side. She herself touched the dragon gingerly. The feel of his hide startled her. Just one of the scales was about the size of her whole hand, fingers spread, and the scales were smooth as glass and solid as iron, but warm, and alive. It was very odd to feel something which felt like it belonged on an armored vehicle on a breathing, *speaking* creature.

June was glad for his presence a moment later, when the last grey shadow retreated into the gloom. It amazed her how quickly her other senses picked up the slack; June could acutely feel the air on her skin, raising goosebumps with its chill, and hear the breathing of her companions and the quickened thump of her own heart.

June became aware of the slow lightening of the passageway only when she scratched her nose, and saw the dim, blurry outline of her hand before her face. They were approaching an opening.

Ten minutes later, they stepped blinking out into the sunlight. Despite the comfort of their lodgings, June turned her face toward the sun and inhaled clean, fresh outdoor air, which none of them had breathed in days.

They joined three other dragons outside; Tokesh, and two smaller dragons. She looked at the dragons in amazement. She'd only ever seen the dragons flying high above them, or in the dim firelight of the catacombs. June had thought them beautiful then, but out here, they were *magnificent*. The sunlight caught their smooth scales, reflecting shimmering, shifting blues, reds, and greens. June caught similar looks of astonishment and appreciation from the Valforte.

Shaking herself slightly, June bowed to Tokesh, who nodded in acknowledgement. "This is Eklos and Barm," he said, and the two dragons inclined their heads deeply to June. "They will be helping to carry you and your friends." He stepped aside, motioning with his huge head for June to follow him. He lowered his massive head to hers as he spoke, bathing her in warm but not unpleasant breath.

"You won't forget your promise?" he said, quietly, and June

shook her head vehemently.

"If I'm not back within eight or nine months, assume I'm dead," she said. "I swear, I'll come back. Start thinking about where you want your boundaries." June paused. "I'm not going to forget this."

Tokesh nodded, apparently satisfied. "I wish you success on your journey," he said. "Farewell."

With that, he turned and disappeared back into the passageway.

June watched him for a moment before turning back to face the dragons. She hadn't taken much notice of their surroundings, but now she looked over the spectacular vista stretching out before them.

They stood on a flat shelf jutting out from the mountain, about halfway up its side; a handy little landing pad. Below them, the mountain's green oasis, more startling from up here, gave way to the salt desert which even now gave June chills to look at.

The Valforte stood around looking like kids waiting for the school bus, so June pulled herself back to the task at hand. "Is there a seating arrangement?" she asked.

"Two each on Barm and Eklos, and one on me," Rakoz said. "I'll be flying lead and cutting the wind for the others, so it'll be a bumpier ride."

June looked dubiously at the Valforte. They all looked nervous, Minogan as though he might pass out. *I've flown on an airplane, at least,* June thought. "I'll go with you, in the lead." For once, the Valforte didn't object to her offer to go ahead of them.

"Of course," Rakoz said. The dragons began picking up the traveler's baggage in their front claws. "All ready?"

June looked at the guys, who nodded weakly back. "All ready," she said. Rakoz, Barm, and Ecklos stretched their necks out flat on the ground. By first standing on the front leg of the dragon, then clambering up on the neck, they could climb onto the dragons' shoulders. June noticed Errigal and Koen went on Barm, and Minogan and Feoras on Ecklos. *So much for patching things up.* She settled herself as comfortably as possible where Rakoz's neck met his shoulders, between two of the ridges running along his spine.

"Are there any sensitive areas I shouldn't tug on?" June asked, bending forward, and Rakoz laughed, sending alarming vibrations through his body and June's.

"No, on the contrary," he said. "Make sure and scream loudly if you happen to fall off. I don't believe I'll notice otherwise." A sidelong glance told June that Minogan was in real danger of fainting now. When Minogan wasn't looking, she mouthed, *'hold on to him,'* urgently to Feoras, who nodded vigorously, although he wasn't looking too confident himself.

"Everyone holding on?" Rakoz asked, and June looked at her companions. Everyone had a death grip on one of the back scales of the dragons.

"Ready whenever you are, Rakoz."

"Where are we going?" he asked, and June giggled nervously.

"Oh, yeah, that'd be good, wouldn't it?" she asked. "Take us southwest, if you don't mind. I have a map, if you need it." Errigal had modified her old saddlebag into a messenger bag, so she could keep the tablet close to her, and refer to it if necessary. Also, she was terrified of dropping it in flight. The bag made her feel safer.

"We'll see if we need it, once we get closer," he said, and then suddenly stretched his wings out, startling June. They looked like enormous bat's wings, thin, leathery skin stretched over a bony frame, with a small talon on the center joint.

"Hold on," Rakoz said, and June did, squeezing tight with her legs and gripping the ridged scale in front of her. A few turbulent, wind-whipping wing flaps later, and they were airborne. Rakoz wheeled to the right, toward the sun, flapping hard until they gained altitude, then simply rode the updrafts in a gliding soar.

June looked around, open-mouthed, relaxing and straightening up. Flying in a plane felt like watching a movie compared to dragon flight. This was a full sensory experience. The air was crisp and cold on her skin, too far up to smell like anything but itself, an ozony tang with a touch of frost she could taste when she opened her mouth. The wind rushed by her ears and lifted her hair, tugging playfully at her clothes.

They flew through a low cloud, and June slowly raised both hands off Rakoz's neck and stretched her arms out to either side, spreading her fingers and watching them cut through the cloud like sharks' fins through the water. She closed her eyes, reveling in the dizzying sensation, feeling the wind trying to pull her from her seat.

Putting her hands back down on Rakoz's neck, she turned to see how the guys were doing. Errigal, Koen, and Feoras appeared to be over their fear and peered about curiously. Minogan, on the other hand, was deathly pale, clutching the dragon's scales as though his life depended on it. Seeing Minogan's misery tempered June's own euphoria, until she caught Koen's eye and he flashed her a brilliant smile which just about knocked her off Rakoz's back with its intensity...and the resulting emotion.

"How do you like it?" Rakoz called over his shoulder, and she turned back to face front.

"It's–God, it's the most wonderful thing I've ever done," June shouted back, as the wind tried to rip her words away. "How can you stand to be on the ground?"

"I can't, usually," Rakoz shouted back, and they both laughed. "Just so you know, I'm taking a bit of a serpentine route, so we can avoid flying over any Andrian-populated areas," he said, trying to project his words over the roar of the wind. "It's not like they can do anything to us up here, but we don't like to remind them we exist, otherwise, we get visitors at the mountain."

"Your call," June shouted. "You seem to have done this a few times before."

"I must say, I never thought I'd be flying with an Andrian on my back," Rakoz said, after a moment's silence. "Especially after what happened."

"The babies?" June asked, and Rakoz nodded, flapping once lightly to maintain altitude. "Well, hopefully I can make sure something like that never happens again," she said, stretching out on his neck and resting her chin on her hands.

"You've really got plans, haven't you?" Rakoz asked.

"Well, yeah. Would *you* leave Prendawr the way it is, if you were king?" Rakoz was silent for a moment.

"And what happens if you fail?"

June shrugged, tracing the edges of his neck scales with her fingers. The thought had kept her awake more than one night. What if the people refused to accept the changes she implemented? Were too close-minded to even consider them? Absolute monarchy or no, there was such a thing as a rebellion.

"Then I step down," June said. "I'm not going to be my mother and bend to everyone's will. If they don't like it, they can deal with their country themselves. I'll find somewhere else to live."

Rakoz twisted his head around to look at her, and she lifted her own from where it rested on his neck to meet his eye. They looked at one another for a moment, then Rakoz nodded and turned back. There had been a lot of appraisal in his look, and skepticism, but June thought just before Rakoz turned away, there had been credence.

She certainly hoped so. She really respected the dragons, found them honest and generous. By rights, given their history with outsiders, Tokesh should have killed them on sight. Instead, they'd been given lodging, provisions, and transport to the other side of the country. She looked forward to having them as allies.

They traveled over miles of beautiful green forests, sparkling lakes and rivers, and plains of rippling grass. At first, June thought she could travel like this for days. Then a few hours later, her hips and knees began to stiffen, succumbing to outward pressure from straddling Rakoz's thick neck. The fresh briskness of the air left her face chapped and raw, and she could no longer feel her fingers or toes. Looking back at the others, June noted she wasn't the only one experiencing difficulties. *Thank God I peed after I had that cup of tea,* June thought. She had to go, but it wasn't urgent. At least not at the moment.

As the sun dipped low in the sky over their left shoulders, however, it had become urgent. Very urgent. *Well, if I do lose it, at least he probably won't feel it, with all his scales*, June thought. Then, just when she thought she couldn't hold it any longer–

"You see that, in the distance there?" Rakoz asked, and June stretched up, looking over his head, to see a glittering strip under the dusky western sky.

"What is it?" she asked, squinting.

"The ocean," he said. "We're here."

"Oh thank God," June murmured, as she watched the strip widen, until finally she saw the cliffs overlooking the sea.

Rakoz swung his head from side to side, flapping his wings to gain altitude, searching for something. Then he called out to June again. "Do you think that's it?" he asked. "Over there?" With his nose, he indicated what appeared to be some sort of archway carved into the stone, right on the edge of the seacliff.

"Yup, probably," June said, not really caring much, just wanting to get off so she could find a nice private rock.

Rakoz folded his wings and began his descent, gliding gracefully toward the archway. As they came closer, June saw what she'd first mistaken for a huge stone in front of the archway was actually a set of carved stairs, round and set in levels to create a platform. *That's it, all right,* she thought. It felt like recognizing the same song from two different notes.

Rakoz landed on the ground as though he weighed no more than a sparrow, stretching out his neck so June could dismount, which she did with great difficulty, her legs having now decided that they wanted to stay in the position they'd been in for the past eight hours or so.

"Excuse me, I have to..." June gestured helplessly toward a large nearby rock, then made a dash for it, her legs screaming their dissent the whole way. Safely out of the others' sight, she jerked her pants down and squatted. For one panicky moment, nothing happened, and she thought her whole apparatus had just shut down, but then–"Oh, jesus christ," she said under her breath. Nearby, she heard Errigal moan loudly in relief, and giggled a little to herself.

After what seemed like an hour, her bladder had emptied, and she fixed her pants and stepped out from behind the rocks, walking over to Rakoz. "Sorry," she said, "but we usually have to go every few hours. That was a really long time for us."

"Nature calls," Rakoz said mildly, and June smiled.

"You bet," she said, then looked at the dragon curiously. "Don't you have to, um..."

"Not nearly so often as you, perhaps once a day," he said.

"Wow," June said. "I'm impressed." She turned to look at the Valforte, who were emerging from behind the rocks, Minogan looking as though he'd like to fall to his knees and kiss the ground.

"So," she said, turning back to Rakoz, "Will you stay here tonight, or go back to the mountain?"

"We'll go back," he said. "Flying at night is even more enjoyable than flying during the day."

"Maybe you can take me for a midnight ride, when I see you again," June said, smiling.

"It's a bargain," he said, dipping his head.

"Seriously, though, thank you so much. I can't even imagine having to cover all that distance on foot, it would have taken us months. I don't even know that we would have made it. Thank you all," she included Barm and Ecklos in her gaze, and they nodded, "and thank Tokesh for me, for us, once again."

"I'll do that. I wish you luck on your quest, and I hope to see you soon." Rakoz unfurled his wings and lifted himself gracefully in the air. Barm and Ecklos followed suit, and they were gone, swallowed up by the growing darkness. June watched the spot where they had disappeared for a moment, aware of the sound of waves crashing against the sea cliffs.

"Never again," Minogan said, breaking the quiet. "I will never, ever, do that again."

"You were very brave, Minogan," June said, turning to look at him, trying to smile sweetly, and not mockingly. "Thank you for making the sacrifice for all of us." Minogan merely mumbled something unintelligible, then walked stiffly off in search of firewood. Errigal, Feoras, and June looked at each other, trying to hide snorts of laughter so he wouldn't hear. Koen merely ignored Minogan, however, and began scraping aside the grass for a firepit.

"Do you want to go over and look at it now?" Feoras said finally, as they all got themselves under control, pointing to the archway, looking grim and forbidding, standing as it was on the edge of the cliff, an inky purple glow from the twilight casting strange shadows on its surface.

"No," June said. "I think I need to rest first. Let's get a fire going and eat, and I'll worry about it in the morning." No one posed any objections, so June lit the fire magically with the wood Minogan had gathered, a talent she'd only recently discovered. They had a large but starchy dinner, several cups of tea, and then fell asleep, the stars casting silvery light on them, the gentle rush of seawater lulling them into a deep, relaxing slumber.

~14~

"Oh...my...GOD," June said the next morning, before she even opened her eyes. "I have never been this sore in my entire *life*."

Her companions had similar problems from their prolonged dragon ride the previous day. It took June three tries to get up, and when she finally did, she wanted to sit back down. Everyone ate breakfast standing or walking around, trying to work the kinks out of their sore muscles.

Their gazes kept drifting to the archway, eyes anxious. The Valforte seemed to be more nervous than June; they understood fighting, but an unseen enemy such as this, one whose moves could not be anticipated–at least June had some idea what was coming, if only the vaguest one.

Finally, when they finished breakfast and could no longer put it off, they approached the archway. A feeling like molten lead, heavy and sickening, filled June's stomach. She'd been nervous last time, but this was more than nerves. Something was about to go terribly, horribly wrong, but she had no choice but to go forward and do the best she could.

"Guys, I want you to promise me something," she said, and they all turned to her. "Promise me, if anything happens, you won't wait too long. Go right to Lumia, and tell Queen Mab. Don't waste time trying to be heroes."

"June..." Koen started, eyes narrowed.

"Promise."

"Okay, fine." He looked around at the others, who nodded reluctantly. "We promise."

"Good," she said. "Let's go."

"Do you want us up there too?" Minogan asked. June paused uncertainly. She'd just assumed they'd come with her, but they might not want to, after all.

"It's up to you," she said, and began walking toward the archway, not waiting to see if they'd follow her.

The archway and platform stood on top of a small but steep hill. As June got closer, she noticed the rocks littering the ground around the platform were in fact crumbled pieces of pillar, like the ones at Fire Mountain. *And I bet if I wanted to count them, there'd be twelve,* she thought, nudging the base of a pillar with her foot.

Finally, she stood at the base of the platform. She turned her head slightly and saw the Valforte out of the corner of her eye, waiting uncertainly about ten steps behind her. Their presence fortified her and gave her the confidence to overcome the increasing dread in her stomach and climb the stairs to the top of the platform.

She was about two steps from the top when the monk appeared. Even though she'd been expecting him, she jumped, and heard one of the Valforte cry out in surprise.

This one was slightly taller, thinner, and had more hair than the first monk. He had the same expression on his face, though, benign and otherworldly. *Well, I guess he would be otherworldly,* June thought. *Since he's a freaking ghost.*

"Greetings," he said, bowing slightly.

June returned the bow. "Ditto," she said, almost hoping for annoyance on his part. She got no such satisfaction, just the same calm blinking expression.

"You have come for the second piece of the tablet," he said, and June nodded. "What you seek," the monk turned away from her, toward the archway, and pointed, "lies there."

Through the archway, June saw the foamy white caps of the waves as they wrestled with each other between rocky outcroppings jutting out of the water below.

"In the ocean?" June asked with a steadying breath, and the monk nodded. "So, just, like, anywhere, or at least in this general area?"

"If you are the right one, you will find it," the monk said. "Farewell." And with that, he faded from sight, despite June's protests.

"Hey, wait, you can't...*arggh*!" She stamped her foot and turned to the Valforte, who stood staring at her, slack jawed. "Could he have been any more vague?"

None of the men responded; just continued looking as though they'd just seen Rakoz in a top hat, cane and shoes doing a tap routine. June turned away from them and stomped down the other side of the platform.

"*What you seek is in there,*" she said mockingly, as she peered through the archway. It came right to the edge of the cliff, and June put a hand on the stone for support.

The cliff gave way to a drop of at least a hundred feet. The rock face fell smoothly to the sea, with no ledges to walk on, no knobs of stone for a handhold. June's annoyance melted away, replaced by the reality of what she had to do.

The Valforte had joined June at the archway, Minogan staying well back from the cliff.

"Wow," said Errigal, taking hold of the other side of the stone and actually hanging out over the edge. "That's a long drop."

"Yup," June murmured, as Errigal stepped back to let Feoras and Koen take a peek. She felt cold all over, a combination of premonition and fear.

"How are we going to get you down there?" Koen asked as he stepped back from the arch and glanced up and down the cliffline. "I didn't see any paths, did you?"

"No, I didn't," she said, quietly, unable to take her eyes away from the roiling sea. Something in her voice made Koen glance over at her, and one look at her face drained the color from his.

"June, no," he said.

She turned and smiled weakly at him, at all of them. "I don't think there's any other way," she said.

And turning her back on them, June leapt from the cliff.

"No!" Koen's shout was the last sound she heard before the rushing wind filled her ears. She held her hand over her nose, pinching it shut in preparation for the impact. The descent seemed to take ages, long enough for her to take in the little details–her shirt fluttering up around her face, a seabird flying near the cliffs on her right.

She hit the water with the impact of a detonating bomb. The cold water attacked her mercilessly, and the shock of it nearly made her lose her lungful of air, and paralyzed her limbs. Then her body spasmed, and she paddled ferociously toward the surface.

As soon as she felt air on her face, she took a huge breath–a mistake, since just as she opened her mouth, a wave closed over her head, causing her to swallow a large amount of seawater and pulling her under. She struggled to the surface once more, spluttering and wheezing, close to panic.

No, she thought. *You have not come this far to drown, for chrissake. Pull yourself together!* She waited for the next wave to hit, then immediately took in a large breath of air in its wake. Looking up, June saw all four Valforte hanging out from the archway, and waved to show she was all right. Her body now seemed to be performing the magic necessary to keep her warm–the water just felt cold now, whereas when she'd first hit the water, it had been shock-inducing.

She looked up at the Valforte once more. She could hear their voices from far away, but the wind and waves drowned out their words. Suddenly, she had a powerful urge to see Koen again, just one more time, just his face, so powerful she nearly began to cry. *A teardrop in the ocean*, June thought, a little incoherently.

With a final glance upward, she wrenched herself away from the Valforte and struck out toward the open ocean. Watching for the rhythm of the waves, she dove under a large one, then bobbed up in its wake. Taking a deep breath, willing herself to clear her mind, she slipped under the black water.

She swam straight down, aware of the oppressive silence surrounding her as she got further away from the turbulent surface. She opened her eyes and found the water didn't sting them at all. Of course, there wasn't anything to see.

Like the inside of a cow, June mused. How was she going to find anything down here? *Oh, yeah, duh*, she thought, as she resurrected the whole body luminescence she'd used in the passageway to the first temple.

Another issue quickly took the place of not being able to see; not being able to *breathe*. Her lungs cramped against themselves as she struggled for a few more minutes below the surface. And she hadn't even reached the bottom yet. Was this how she had to do this? Dive down, search the bottom–if she could find it–swim back up, take a breath, go back down? Impossible!

I need AIR, she thought desperately, and immediately, her lungs filled with sweet, fresh oxygen. June stopped swimming for a moment in her shock.

Now that was neat, she thought, smiling, her lips feeling strange as they pulled taut against the cold water. *I could have used this when I rescued Koen. Guess I didn't say the 'magic words'.*

She renewed her descent, relieved this wasn't going to take ten million trips back and forth, and continued swimming, her body illuminating tiny particles, and the occasional silvery flash of a fish attracted to the light, but nothing more. Until–

June had been swimming so hard she nearly slammed face-first into the sandy bottom. She pulled up sharply and looked around, pedaling her arms to keep herself from floating up. She caught sight of a good-sized rock, about the size of her head, and swam toward it, picking it up and cradling it in her arms, its weight drawing her toward the bottom. Now, she could walk along the sea floor without having to expend all that energy to keep herself down.

Air, she thought to herself, filling her complaining lungs once more. She closed her eyes, trying to center herself. *Which way is it?* she thought. *Which way is the tablet?*

At once, she felt drawn to her left, and she turned and began to walk, watching as her footsteps displaced tiny clouds of silt. *This is weird*, she thought. *Taking a stroll along the ocean floor. Who'd have thunk it?*

June's overinflated ego was taken down a few notches a moment later when she walked face-first into a giant stone pillar rising from the sea bottom. *What idiot left this here?*, June thought wryly to herself as she rubbed her nose and forehead.

She stroked the pillar in wonderment, tracing the tiny grooves with her fingers. *Amazing*, she thought, and walked past it, into an amphitheater similar to the first temple, in Fire Mountain. Steps led down into a round area at the bottom, which contained a podium, where the second piece of the tablet rested.

June descended the steps slowly, cautiously, squinting through the murky water. *I'd better not have to do anything else for this stupid thing*, she thought, waiting for something to jump out at her. But nothing did. Ten seconds later, she had the tablet piece safe in her hand. Grinning like a fool, she dropped her weight-rock and headed for the surface.

At once, panic seized her, twisting her insides mercilessly. June stopped her ascent and held her depth, looking around wildly for the threat she knew was there. *They're coming, they're coming*, her terrified mind repeated. But who? Who was coming?

A split second later, June saw a flash of something large, swimming just at the edge of her light, and she recoiled, whimpering deep in her throat. Another one, on her left this time. Then right in front of her, this time close enough for her to clearly see its grey skin and large, black, soulless eyes.

The Eid Gomen.

Don't panic, don't panic, don't panic, June thought, but she only managed to create an endless litany of *don't panic*'s in her head. She shook herself, looking inwardly at her arsenal. Nothing so far had prepared her for this.

Already, though, her body had primed a weapon for her. June felt a ball of heat throb just behind her navel, growing until it encompassed her entire body.

Now! something in her cried, and she pushed the heat out of her, and felt it spread like a ripple in a pond. June could feel three or four impacts as it hit objects, large objects, and a second later she saw a limp grey foot float into her vision, its owner apparently knocked unconscious. Not dead, though. She'd only bought herself some time.

June swam for the surface, not knowing what the hell she was going to do when she got there, since until now, she hadn't thought about how she would get back *up* the cliff.

Her head broke water, and June looked wildly around for the archway. There, on her left. June began swimming toward it, screaming her head off.

"Koen," she yelled, crying out the first name that came to mind. "GUYS! GUYS! ANYBODY! QUICK!"

They can't hear you, a panicky voice in her head moaned. *It's over. You're going to die down here.*

"KOEN," June screamed with every bit of breath in her body, her voice cracking with the strain. "PLEASE!" At last, heads poked out through the archway, and June nearly sobbed with relief, especially since she was pretty sure her little alien friends had woken up and were after her once more.

June wracked her brain, trying to think of a way to get herself up there, but she had nothing. She'd done so much magic in the past hour, and was so weak, it was a miracle she could swim at all, much less carry around a big stone–

The tablet. She looked down at it just before another wave hit and drove her under. She might not be able to get herself up, but a five-pound tablet she could probably manage.

With the last of her strength, she raised her arms holding the tablet up into the air, and, kicking her legs like mad to keep herself above water, she threw it. She watched as the tablet caught on the wind like a leaf, and flew slowly up toward the top of the cliff.

"Catch," said June, weakly, barely able to keep her head above water, every paddle and kick a negotiation with her spent muscles.

The last thing June saw as cold hands closed on her ankles and dragged her underwater was a blue arm reaching out a hundred feet above her to pluck a piece of stone from the air.

June's consciousness swirled and throbbed, flashes of awareness coming like pulses of a strobe light in the dark. She felt herself being pulled through the water, then a shock as cold air hit her soaking wet skin as someone dragged her by the arms along the ground. The horrible, clicking voices of the Eid Gomen, the dripping sound of water, another human voice. It felt like an insane, disjointed slide show, images and sounds striking against her in her confusion, making her want to stay unconscious.

Then she was dropped roughly so the back of her head cracked sickeningly against rock. Something pointy prodded her side, hard. June moaned softly and squirmed away.

"Wake up," clicked one of the Eid Gomen's voices, as the prodding continued, increasing in intensity. *Go away,* June whined in her head. *Go away. Just let me sleep, or die, or whatever it is my body's trying to do right now. Go away.*

"Up," the voice said, louder, this time paired with a hard kick to her ribs. Hot, red pain exploded behind her closed eyelids, and she rolled over on her stomach and vomited seawater, coughing weakly. Hands grasped her by the upper arms and roughly pulled her up on her knees, her head lolling, too weak to lift it.

"Look at me," the horrible voice clicked again. A wiry hand grasped her hair at the roots and pulled her head up.

Through slitted, blurry eyes, June saw an Eid Gomen standing before her, in the center of a torch-lit stone room, not much more than a cave. This Eid Gomen, however, was dressed, in grey robes the same color as its skin, and gave off an impression of power. *Take me to your leader,* June thought.

"Do you know where you are?" it said, oily black eyes fixed expressionless on her face.

June coughed weakly, spitting a mix of salt water and snot on the floor in front of her.

"How many guesses do I get?" she asked, her voice hoarse from stomach acid. The Eid Gomen's lipless mouth curled in a sneer, showing rows of small, pointed teeth, making its already horrifying face nearly unbearable to look at.

"You are in one of our many fortresses," it said, pacing slowly in front of her, pressing the tips of its eight long fingers together. "*Many* fortresses. We are everywhere, princess. There is not a corner of this kingdom we have not infiltrated. We outnumber your people three to one." It stopped pacing and stood facing her, expectant.

"I'm sorry," said June, biting the inside of her cheek hard, using the pain to keep from passing out again, "did you have a point, or are we just feeling proud of ourselves today?" The Eid Gomen snarled angrily, and someone poked her hard in the kidney with the same pointy stick they'd been using earlier, causing her to arch her back and grunt in pain.

"My *point,*" the Eid Gomen said, resuming its pacing, "is you haven't got a chance of completing this quest, not one single chance. Even if you were to escape from us now, which," it looked her up and down, "looks terribly unlikely, we would still stop you. Failure, for you, is inevitable. So, we'd like to offer you a deal. A bargain, if you like. Help us, and we'll help you."

"Help you do what?" June asked, more to buy time to think than anything else. Her mind slowly cleared, and she tried to look for a way out of her situation. Past the Eid Gomen in front of her was a passageway, but a glance over her shoulder revealed three guards, two holding her up and one brandishing the base of his spear at her. She could also feel something blocking her magic. It seemed hopeless.

"Help us destroy the people of this world, and we'll rebuild yours," the Eid Gomen said, stopping directly in front of her and tucking his four-fingered hands into his wide sleeves.

"What do you mean?" she asked, suspiciously.

"If you help us, we'll put everything back the way it was, before the sorcerer came and snatched you from your world," he said, lowering his voice to a horrible, confidential hiss. "You won't even remember this. You'll never think of this world again. It will be as though it never existed. We can do things beyond your wildest dreams. Ask, and whatever you desire is yours."

June closed her eyes for a moment, picturing herself back in her own apartment, waking up on a Sunday morning beside Kyle, between clean sheets, smelling the sweet fragrances of soap and shampooed hair and laundry detergent. Of paying the bills, getting married, having a family, never again having to worry about starvation or magic or Armageddon.

And then she chased the vision away, for the last time. What was done, was done, and even though it seemed she'd lost everything for a world which seemed to deserve destruction, there were four people here, good, honest, true people worth saving. One in particular who June realized she loved more than anything in her old life.

"Just one question," June said slowly.

"Yes?"

"If you're so sure I'm going to fail, then why are you trying to buy me off?"

The Eid Gomen's lip curled again.

"You just threw away your only chance," it said, sounding almost pleased. "Enjoy eternity–in hell."

The Eid Gomen waved a hand at the doorway behind it, and the guards dragged June away on her knees, down passage after passage. She didn't bother to struggle; she knew she didn't have a prayer. And a tiny, exhausted voice at the back of her head kept saying, *Maybe it's better this way.*

Finally, they stopped before a stone door. The bolt was drawn back with a groaning complaint, and the guards tossed June unceremoniously on her stomach into a room, bare except for a small pile of straw in one corner. She turned just as the door slammed, and heard the same lamenting groan from the bolt as they locked it.

She lay on the floor for a few moments, heart pounding, shivering uncontrollably. Her clothes were still soaked, and it would have been generous to call the air in here chilly. Slowly, she got to her feet and went to the door. The light from the hallway torches streamed weakly through a small opening the base of the door, through which June supposed food and toilet buckets would be passed. Otherwise, the cell was dark.

June began to pace the cell by the door, briskly rubbing her arms and stamping her feet to warm herself, trying not to think about how much trouble she was in. Aside from having been imprisoned by the enemy in a fortress God only knew where, she was soaking wet, freezing cold, hungry, and dehydrated. And she couldn't even do any magic. June thought if something didn't change in an hour or so, she'd go into hypothermia. And she highly doubted the Eid Gomen would be standing by with heating pads and hot tea.

Just then, a rustling in the rear of the cell made her whirl around, squinting to see in the dark. With a soft *flump*, a blanket sailed from the dark corner and landed at her feet.

June bent slowly to pick it up, keeping her eyes riveted on the corner. Her eyes were beginning to get accustomed to the darkness, and she thought she could make out a silhouette, sitting hunched on the other side of the room.

"Thank you," June said, straightening up and wrapping the blanket, which smelled like an old dog, around her shoulders. Cautiously, she took two steps toward the corner and the hunched figure, which sat almost abnormally still against the wall. "I'm June, by the way. What's your name?"

A voice crackly as static electricity cackled from the corner.

"Name, name," it said, in a strange sing-song. "What does name tell you? Not where I'm from, not what I'll do."

"No," June said, more intrigued than frightened, "but it's a good start to a conversation."

The voice snapped in delighted laughter, reminding June of a Halloween cartoon hag.

"Canny, canny creature," it cooed. "Tamsik is what I am called. But I thought you were called by a different name, that's what I thought."

June cocked her head, all physical discomfort forgotten in her curiosity.

"What did you think I was called?" she asked.

"Hmmm, let's see, let's see," the voice said, playfully, but without malice. "Thought maybe...Ulfhilda?"

June felt her face blanch in shock, followed by a strong resurgence of shivering. "How did you know that?" she whispered.

"Been waiting for you, long, long time," it said, then cackled. "'Bout time you showed up, you."

"You've been waiting for *me*?" June asked, brows furrowed. "Why? For how long, exactly?"

The thing in the corner, for June was no longer sure it was human, or Andrian, or whatever, giggled delightedly, like a child sharing a delicious secret.

"For ages, ages, hundreds of years."

"Hundreds of years?" June asked, her excitement turning to skepticism. "I hate to break it to you, but I was only born a few months ago," She snorted, shaking her head. "Weird as that sounds."

"Not the first time you were thought of, though," Tamsik said slyly.

"So...what, was there like a prophecy or something?" June asked, and Tamsik's shape bounced excitedly in the corner.

"Prophecy! Good word, that! Yes, prophecy," it said, cackling again.

"So what did the prophecy say?"

"Can't tell," Tamsik whispered, and June raked her fingers through her wet hair, exasperated.

"You can't tell me." The shadowy figure in the corner shook its head vehemently, and June rolled her eyes. "So you've been waiting a hundred years to...to tease me?"

"Oh, no," Tamsik said, its voice suddenly hushed and reverent. "Waiting to give you a present."

"A present." June sat on the floor, too tired to stand anymore, and rested her elbow on her knee, chin in hand. "What kind of present?"

"Later, later," it said, and June buried her face in her hands.

"Okay, later," she said, her voice muffled through her fingers. She straightened up and pulled the blanket tighter around her shoulders, already feeling warmer and better. "So..." June said, casting about for conversation. "What are you in for?"

Tamsik giggled again.

"Safer," she said, (June now felt sure it was female) and June could see her shrug one shoulder in a mock-innocent gesture.

"Safer for you, or for them?" June asked, and once more Tamsik collapsed in delighted giggles.

"Both," she answered finally.

That clarifying statement pretty well killed the conversation, so June propped herself up against the wall by the door and dozed for a while, chin on chest, wading thickly through disjointed dreams of water and wind and huge oily black eyes.

She awoke with a start to a scraping sound beside her. Looking down, she saw two wooden bowls of thin broth had been pushed inside, each with a lump of sodden bread floating in the middle. It looked fairly unappetizing, but still, her stomach growled at the sight of it.

June heard a rustling sound behind her, where Tamsik had been sitting, and turned to face her as she approached. As she stepped into the light, however, June's jaw dropped, and she looked with horror at the creature standing before her.

Tamsik's skin was the exact shade of brown chicken eggshells, covered in sparse hair of the same shade from head to toe. Her knobby-kneed legs bowed outward, and her hands, with two fingers, like thin lobster claws, hung pretty well even with her knees. Her wrinkled midsection was partially covered by a dirty rag only slightly more decent than a loincloth, and partially by her flat, pendulous breasts, which hung bare to the tops of her thighs. Her face looked like a chimpanzee's, lightly furred and hourglass shaped, with a small nose disappearing into her upper lip, and protruding ears. Long, matted, scraggly hair floated down from the crown of her head.

Tamsik laughed and pointed at the horrified look on June's face.

"Ugly, yes," she cackled as she leaned forward to take one of the bowls (June flinched backward to avoid being smacked in the face by one of the hanging breasts). June smiled weakly, with no idea how to respond to this. And really, there was no arguing.

June shook herself forcefully, dragging her eyes downward to the bowl of broth.

"Um, is this safe to eat, do you think?" she asked. Receiving no answer, she reluctantly looked back up at Tamsik.

Tamsik paid June no attention–rather, she sat facing the door, listening intently. Then, with no warning, she turned her head to the side, stuck one of her four fingers down her throat, and vomited.

"Oh, wow," June said, taken completely off guard. "Hey, are you all right?" Still Tamsik paid her no attention. Instead, she now sifted through her sick-up, searching for something. June pressed her hand over her mouth, unable to take her eyes away, despite her nausea.

Tamsik suddenly picked something up in her two claw-like fingers and crowed triumphantly.

"Ha," she said, and held it out to June as though expecting her to take it. June squinted at the proffered object.

"Um, very nice," she said hesitantly.

"Take it, take it," Tamsik whispered urgently. "It's yours!"

"No, really, thank you, I'm fine, you keep it," June said, both hands up in a polite warding-off gesture.

"Take it," Tamsik hissed, still more urgently. "Meant for you! You must!"

"You mean this is the thing you were telling me about?" June asked, and Tamsik nodded excitedly.

"Go on," she said, and June gingerly took the object from her between thumb and forefinger.

It was like a combination of glass and stone, smooth and crystal clear, about the size of a bottle cap, but perfectly round, and filled with some sort of clear liquid, which June could tell only by the small air bubble inside which bounced from side to side as she shook it.

"Hurry up," Tamsik said, looking nervously at the door. "Swallow!"

"Swal–no, oh no," June said, looking down at the stone in her hand. "It's too big, and I don't really–"

"You must," Tamsik said, as June continued to regard the object lying in her palm. "If they get it..."

"Look, I'm sorry, but I'm not swallowing something when I don't even know what it is!"

"Trust me?" Tamsik asked suddenly, making June look sharply up and meet her eyes. Strangely, she *did* trust Tamsik, for no reason at all. After another moment of searching Tamsik's eyes, June dropped her gaze, shaking her head.

"I don't believe I'm doing this," she muttered, pulling out a corner of her shirt to wipe the bits of throw-up off of the stone before she swallowed it.

"Don't wipe it," Tamsik whispered nervously, glancing up at the door again. "Goes down easier slippery!"

"Oh, my God, you are *so* not helping," June moaned. Then, without thinking, she popped the stone in her mouth and swallowed hard. She had a panicky moment where she thought it had gotten stuck in her throat, but it slowly eased its way down, landing in her stomach with a sickening *plop* she could feel. June put her hand on her stomach, her attention turned inward.

"Okay..." she said cautiously, patting her belly lightly.

Then the pain hit. Horrible, cramping pain which sent June toppling over on her side to curl up in the fetal position, limbs shaking in shock. She clutched her midsection with both hands, fingers curling into her flesh as though to rip it out from the outside.

"Hurts, does it?" Tamsik asked cheerfully. "Only a moment, now. Has to settle itself a bit."

June screamed through clenched teeth, rolling and writhing on the floor, tears streaming down the sides of her face, unable to think or speak coherently through the pain spreading from her belly like a hot knife.

Then, abruptly, the pain stopped, leaving June gasping for breath and sniffling on the floor. She pushed her hair back from her sweat-soaked brow and rolled on her back, still panting, eyes staring blankly at the dark ceiling.

"What the hell did you do to me?" she asked finally, pushing herself up on her elbows to look at Tamsik, who returned her look with an unsettlingly ape-like grin.

"Not me, the stone," Tamsik said, still apparently unconcerned at what June had gone through a moment before. "Has to settle itself in. Only hurts a moment."

"You could have warned me!"

Tamsik shrugged good-naturedly, and June shook her head.

"Whatever. Now that I swallowed this thing, you want to tell me what it does?"

Tamsik shrugged again.

"Don't know," she said, and June sat bolt upright, clutching her stomach again.

"You don't *know?* You made me eat it and you don't *know?"*

"You do," Tamsik said. "You will. It will tell you what and when. Carry it till it calls you."

"Once," June said, "just once, I would like to ask someone in this godforsaken country a question and get a straight answer."

Tamsik didn't acknowledge this, merely pulled her bowl over in front of her and began to eat.

"Isn't this going to—aren't I going to—hmm?" June waved her hand at the lower half of her body. Tamsik cackled again.

"Won't come out till you need it," she said, between sloppy mouthfuls of sodden bread. Sighing, aware she wasn't going to get any more useful information, June pulled her bowl in front of her and began to eat.

June woke hours later another scraping sound. Two bowls and a jug of water had been pushed through the space at the bottom, as well as a fresh potty bucket. She got up and stretched, then collected the full bucket and pushed it through the slot, careful to keep it from slopping over the sides. She took a large gulp from the jug, then took her bowl over to the corner and began to eat.

"Tamsik, food's here," June called, but there was no response from the corner. "Dinnar ees sarved," she called, in a horrible French accent. Still, Tamsik didn't move, simply lay on her side in her dark corner. A terrible, cold feeling began to creep over June, like the premonition she'd had before approaching the archway. June set her bowl down at her side.

"Tamsik," she said again. Silence.

She stood up, peering through the gloom to where Tamsik lay, her back to the room, still as stone. Slowly, she walked over to her, then knelt down, pausing for a moment before stretching out a hand and grasping Tamsik's shoulder. That simple touch, the feel of Tamsik's cold, stiff flesh under her hand, confirmed what June already knew. Tamsik was dead.

June recoiled, wiping her hand on her pants.

"Oh, God," she whispered. "Oh God, oh God, oh God." Before she even realized it, June had reached the door and begun pounding on it with her fists.

"Someone, please," she cried, dropping to her knees and sticking her head out the opening at the bottom. "Someone's dead in here! Help! Anybody!"

Fifteen minutes later, June slumped in the corner behind the door, dead-eyed, throat and hands sore from screaming and pounding. No one had come. Either they didn't hear her, or they didn't care.

I'll just wait till they come around with the next meal, June thought. *That's all. When they come, I'll tell them, and they'll—they'll take her away, or something. Whatever they do when this happens. It'll be okay.*

June briefly considered covering Tamsik up with her blanket, but practicality won out over sentimentality. It was freezing, and June knew she would sorely regret giving up the blanket. Tamsik, on the other hand, had transcended regrets and earthly desires. As she stared at the body, she wondered if Tamsik had been holding on to life just long enough to pass the stone on to June.

I don't blame her, June thought. *If I spent the last hundred years in here, I'd be pretty happy to knock off as soon as I could, too.*

June's head had dropped to her chest when the scrape of food being pushed under the door woke her.

"Hey," she shouted, pushing the objects roughly away from the door so she could get her head through the slot. "Hey! Someone died in here! Hey! Wait!" Head through the door, she watched as two thin, grey legs strode away from her, not pausing once in their stride.

June pulled her head back inside the door and began to pace the room. *Maybe he just went to get someone, to help him carry her. That's probably it, he just went for help. He'll be back.* She strode back and forth, comforting herself with these thoughts. Then, suddenly, her eyes fell on the objects which had been pushed through the door, and her blood froze.

One empty bucket. One jug of water. And only one bowl of broth.

They already knew Tamsik was dead. They just didn't care. And they were leaving June in here with her corpse.

"No!" June launched herself at the door. She pounded the rough stone until her hands bled, shouting incoherently until finally she collapsed in a sobbing heap at the base of the door. The truths of her situation hit her one after another, like breakers on the hull of a ship. She'd been captured by the enemy. No one knew where she was. No one was going to rescue her. She was alone, save for a soon-to-be-rotting corpse, and would be alone for all eternity, the silence of her cold, dark existence broken three times a day by the scraping sound of a bucket, a jug of water, and a bowl of broth pushed under the door.

~15~

June woke with another start–she had apparently cried herself to sleep, propped up in the corner by the door. This time, it wasn't the sound of her meal being pushed through the slot that awakened her, but a rustling sound, in the corner where Tamsik's body lay.

Slowly, she pushed herself up the wall into a standing position, peering into the corner. A flicker of movement caught her eye, and she jumped, pressing herself harder against the wall. Her heart pounded, and she felt beads of sweat breaking out on her skin, despite the chill air. She picked up the still-empty bucket, held it cocked as a weapon, and began to edge slowly forward, toward Tamsik's body and the rustling sound. As she moved closer, she saw what had been making the noise, and with a horrified scream, began to beat the straw with the bucket.

Rats. At least a dozen rats which had swarmed over Tamsik's corpse now fled in every direction, hopping and squeaking in terror. Whimpering, she chased every one of them into cracks in the walls or out the food slot, until silence fell once more.

Unable to stop herself, June returned to Tamsik's body to see what the damage had been. As she caught sight of the body, she turned away with a cry of horror, sinking to her knees under a wave of dizziness, hand pressed to her mouth, eyes squeezed shut to try and block out what she'd seen.

Tamsik's face had been eaten away, as had the skin on her belly. It looked as though the little bastards had made themselves a tunnel into her abdomen, as a sticky-looking dark stain trickled down into the straw from the gaping hole.

They'll be back, too, a voice in June's head told her. *They won't be gone for good until she is, one way or another, whether they finish her off or the Eid Gomen finally come to cart her away...*

"SHUT UP," June screamed, clutching her head. "SHUT UP SHUT UP, SHUT UP!" Claustrophobia's cold fingers closed around her neck, and she lurched to her feet, wheeling around the room. With a tormented, primal scream, she scooped up her food and hurled it across the room, splattering the contents and splitting the wooden bowl so it fell in two halves on the floor. Reeling, she fainted.

Scrape, scrape. June woke to the sound of her food being pushed through the door. She sat up, feeling wobbly and disjointed, and glanced across the room apprehensively. Sure enough, her new friends were busily devouring her old one, rustling and squeaking contentedly. She squeezed her eyes shut and took a steadying breath.

Don't you get it? said a logical voice in her head. *The Eid Gomen are trying to drive you crazy, and shame on you, you're letting them. Don't you dare lose it. If you do, the opportunity may come and go, and you'll be too busy sniveling in a corner of your mind to take advantage of it.*

Opportunity for what? she asked. *Escape? They don't even open the goddam door, ever. How am I going to get out of here?*

Never you mind that, said Miss Sensible, primly. *Just keep yourself sane and the rest will fall in place.*

Hmmph, thought June, but Miss Sensible was right. They *were* probably trying to drive her crazy. So, escape or no, June intended to stay sane on sheer principle.

June lost count of the meals, her only way of keeping track of the days, and so let all concept of time slip away, a factor which did not help her quest to keep her sanity. She hung on by a thread, mainly by sleeping as much as possible, and by maintaining a shaky truce with the rats. They stayed at the other end of the room with the body, and June and her food stayed on this side.

When she couldn't sleep, she tried to burn energy as quickly as possible, to tire herself out so she could sleep again, mainly by doing pushups, sit-ups, and jumping jacks, singing every song she'd ever heard, including show tunes, nursery songs, and commercial jingles, and reenacting her favorite scenes from movies.

Hygiene proved to be a challenge, though. Each time she woke up, and before she lay down to sleep, she scrubbed the surfaces of her teeth with a corner of her shirt, just to get some of the yuck off. Unfortunately, the Eid Gomen barely provided her with enough water to drink, much less wash in, and so June had to rotate between the parts of her body which needed the most attention, namely face, armpits, hands, and privates. Everything else just had to go hang. After a few days, it didn't matter. Tamsik's body, despite the cold and the attentions of the rats, began to decompose, and the resulting miasma of decay drowned out every other scent possible, including June's own body odor.

It was a good thing June was such a hand at denial; otherwise, she never would have made it. For the most part, she could overlook the hard truths of the situation, and the developing probability she would never see another face again, Andrian, Valforte, or even Eid Gomen, never speak to another person, never see another sunrise or even change her clothes.

Every so often, as she lay down to sleep after another vigorous bout of physical and mental exercise, thoughts like these would creep in, but June resolutely quashed them. If she did let them in, she'd lose it for sure, even though somewhere deep inside, she'd given up all hope of escape or rescue.

So it was a great shock when June woke one (morning? afternoon? night?) to a grinding squeak outside the door. Before she could react, the door swung open, and a figure holding a torch stepped inside.

June raised her arm in front of her face, shielding it from the torch, which to her dark-accustomed eyes felt like direct sunlight, and pushed herself into a sitting position, knees pulled up and feet firmly on the ground, ready to leap up and fight, if necessary.

"My God," said a familiar voice, one which lit a candle in her soul, and June burst into tears.

Koen pushed past Minogan and knelt in front of her, taking her by the arms and looking closely at her face.

"My God," he said again, face pale even in the flickering torchlight, "are you all right? Are you hurt?" June simply shook her head, unable to speak.

Over his shoulder, she could see Errigal and Feoras edge into the room behind Minogan. The smell seemed to hit all of them at once.

"What *is* that?" Minogan groaned, his voice muffled through the hand clapped over his nose and mouth. "It smells like something–" He cut himself off abruptly as he raised the torch and saw Tamsik's body in the corner.

The rats had scattered when the Valforte entered, all except for one particularly cheeky one which perched on the partially exposed bone of Tamsik's upper arm, eyes gleaming in the torchlight as it sniffed the air, perhaps trying to figure out if the men were good to eat as well. Minogan swung back to face June, eyes wide with shock.

"What the hell..." Errigal said softly. Koen looked from the corpse to June, jaw clenched and lips pressed tight together.

"Come on," he said gently, helping June to her feet. "Can you walk?" June nodded in response, still borderline hysterical, unable to speak. Koen put a supportive arm around her waist and she sagged gratefully into him, crying even harder as she realized she'd never expected to feel the touch of another person, ever again, much less the one she wanted to touch her most of all.

"*Shh*, it's okay, it's okay," Koen said, his tone soothing. "You have to calm down. You can cry all you want later, but if we're going to get out, we have to be quiet. All right?"

June took several deep, gulping breaths, forcing herself to breathe slowly, and wiped her face.

"Okay," she whispered, swallowing hard. She met Koen's eyes and he nodded encouragingly.

"Let's go," he said, turning to the others, and they quickly filed out of the cell, Koen still holding her tightly around the waist. June took one last look at the room she thought she'd be spending the rest of her life in, and the corpse which would lie forgotten within.

The body of an Eid Gomen lay outside the cell, its neck broken. Feoras rolled it into the cell and shut and bolted the door.

"More food for the rats," he said, then looked quickly at June to see if she'd heard.

June wasn't in fact hearing much of anything. All the what-if's she'd suppressed for so long had caught up with her now. She couldn't get rid of a vision of two skeletons in the cell, Tamsik's in one corner, her own in the other, long hair, turned to grey in death, flowing from her skull down over her bones. Forgotten.

They led her quickly and quietly down a maze of corridors, stopping occasionally to listen for approaching footfalls, then darting forward once again. June could feel Koen's eyes on her face every now and then, trying to gauge her condition, but she simply stared at the floor in front of her feet, unable to lift her head, only capable of moving her legs enough to keep up. Numbness packed her mind in thick dark wool, keeping her from thinking or speaking.

They turned into a corridor which rose steeply to an opening draped in ivy, and Errigal darted outside while the others waited in silence. At his signal, a warbling bird call, they rushed into the sunlight, picking up packs hidden behind bushes near the entrance.

The combination of the light and the fresh sea air, not fouled by rotting flesh, gave June a feeling of being immersed in ice water, and she gasped and staggered, nearly falling to her knees.

"Whoa, you okay?" Koen said, deftly catching her before she hit the ground.

June swallowed and looked around, blinking, feeling as though she'd been woken suddenly from a deep sleep. "Yeah," she said, meeting his concerned eyes. "Yeah, I'm okay." She got to her feet, and they broke into a slow jog to keep up.

They ran for at least an hour, north along the coastline Finally, they found a stream and followed it inland until they reached a copse of pine trees and stopped, panting and spent.

"I think we'll be safe here for a few hours, at least," Minogan said. "We'll have to move out after that, though."

June flared her nostrils as she forced herself to breathe through her nose to stop panting, feeling the burn of her tired calves and thighs. "Do I have time to take a bath?" she asked.

"I think so," Minogan said. "Just don't wander off too far, in case we have to run."

"Is there any soap?"

"I'll take care of it," Errigal said, and began searching around the bases of the trees, kicking aside pine needles and clumps of moss.

"June, what–" Koen began, but she cut him off.

"Not yet. I'll tell you everything, I promise, but...just give me a few minutes." Koen looked as though he were going to say something else, then nodded, shoving his hands in his pockets and walking off down the stream.

"Where's the tablet?" June asked, with a sudden jolt. Feoras held up the saddlebag she'd carried the first piece in, and she took it from him, relieved to find two pieces of stone inside. She sat down on the ground and pulled out both pieces, which seemed to form the two outer pieces of the complete tablet. She flipped the new piece over to look at the map.

"As far as we could see, the map says to go north, so that's why we ran this way," Minogan said. "Rather than trying to backtrack later."

"Good thinking," June murmured, tracing her fingers over the tablet, laying it down next to the first piece again. *All this trouble for these hunks of stone,* she thought. *It had better be worth it.*

Errigal emerged from the woods a few moments later, carrying two familiar plants with him. One was a root that, when mashed in water, produced a clean-smelling suds they'd used before to preserve what little lye soap they had. The other was a plant June had always called toothbrush tree, with minty-tasting leaves and twigs. The leaves could be chewed as a poor substitute for gum, but the frayed ends of the twigs made tiny primitive toothbrushes.

June slipped the tablets reverently back into the saddlebag. "Thanks," she said, taking the plants from him and standing up. "I'm just going to go down here a little ways, not too far," she said, pointing to a slight bend in the stream conveniently hidden by a small screen of trees. Without waiting for a response, she walked off.

Before she did anything, she chewed up the mint twigs and scrubbed her teeth and tongue vigorously, several times, going through four twigs in all. She stuffed several of the leaves in her mouth, relishing the fresh taste, as she peeled her filthy clothes from her body and dropped them on the bank. Looking down at herself, she shook her head in amazement. Her hipbones jutted out above her formerly full-muscled thighs, now reduced to shadows of their former selves. *Looks like I just got back from a spa trip to Daschau.*

She broke half the soaproot off and waded into the icy stream water. She shivered, then closed her eyes and concentrated briefly, feeling warmth spread from her midsection to her cold extremities.

June moved to the center of the stream and sat down, so the shallow water came up to just below her sternum. Digging a stone out of the stream bed, she mashed up the root and slowly, thoroughly washed herself from head to toe three times, scrubbing the stink from her skin. At one point, she realized the smell was actually still in her nostrils, and she blew her nose repeatedly into her hand until it bled.

Once satisfied with her body's cleanliness, she used the other half of the soaproot on her ragged clothes, then dried them magically.

Wow, she thought. *I've actually gotten so used to magic now, I missed it when I couldn't use it.*

Clean and scrubbed, June spat the mouthful of mint leaves out, rinsed her mouth with stream water, and walked back to the Valforte, feeling close to herself again. Already, her experience in the Eid Gomen dungeon seemed far away, like a bad dream.

June rejoined the men, who sat or lay on the ground resting, and sat down herself, fluffing her damp hair.

"Better?" asked Koen.

"*Much,*" she said, leaning back on her hands with a sigh and crossing her ankles in front of her. "Thanks for the stuff, Errigal."

"Not a problem," he said, then rummaged in a sack next to him and tossed her a pear-like fruit. "We can't risk a fire right now, but–"

June took a bite of the fruit, wiping her mouth as the juice ran out of the corners, sucking the sweetness from the meat.

"This is fabulous," she said, around another bite. "I don't think I've ever tasted anything so good." She practically inhaled the rest of the fruit, and tossed the core into the stream, watching as it bobbed away. "You guys need a few more minutes, or are we ready to go?"

Everyone stared at her in surprise. "You sure you're ready to go,

June?" Koen said doubtfully. "We could probably wait, if you need to take a short nap..."

June stood up and stretched. "I don't know if I'll ever need to sleep again," she said, thinking of the hours she'd spent sleeping or dozing in her cell. "If you guys need more time, take it, otherwise let's put some more distance between them and us."

"If you're sure," Minogan said, standing up and putting on his makeshift pack.

"I'm sure," she said. "We'll talk along the way." June shouldered the saddlebag containing the tablet pieces, argued briefly with the men over who should carry her other things (they flatly refused to allow her to carry anything more than the saddlebag), and off they went.

"So, what the hell happened to you?" Koen asked, as they headed for the coastline once more.

"Why don't you guys tell me your version, then I'll tell you mine," she said, wanting to postpone reliving her nightmare as long as possible. Koen narrowed his eyes at her, but their attention turned to Minogan, who had begun speaking.

"We couldn't figure out what happened to you, when you threw the tablet up to us," he said. "We thought you'd been injured, or you drowned. But then we kept thinking, if you were hurt, you wouldn't have had the strength to get the tablet up to us. So we looked around a little, and we started seeing Eid Gomen tracks. It took us almost four days to find the fortress, and another four to find the entrance we used and stake it out, to make sure it wasn't a well used one.

"It was hard, because the Eid Gomen do patrols above ground, and honestly, I don't know how we managed not getting captured or killed ourselves, we had so many close calls. But we found the entrance, and got in. We found a guard underground, and," Minogan smiled almost nostalgically, "*convinced* him to take us down to where prisoners were kept. And once he had, we snapped his neck."

"We didn't want to make a mess," Errigal said, grinning.

June stayed quiet for a moment as she absorbed this. "Was that how long I was in there for?" she almost whispered. "Eight days?"

"Actually, we went in on the ninth," Feoras said.

"Oh," June said, feeling a little sick. Only nine days, and she had nearly lost her mind.

"Your turn," Koen said. June took a deep breath, tilting her face upward as though in supplication for strength, and began.

She hadn't meant to be so detailed, had only planned to give a brief outline of events, but her mind seemed determined to purge itself, and every moment of pain, terror, and near-insanity came tumbling out. When she finished, there was no sound but their soft footfalls on the sandy soil and the squawking of seabirds. She'd kept her eyes down while talking, but now raised her head cautiously to gauge the reaction of the others. Their faces ran the gamut from respect and admiration to absolute horror, guilt, and sympathy.

"So, they just threw you in there, never opened the door, never spoke to you again?" Errigal said, and June smiled grimly. "Never came to take that poor dead woman away?"

"I would have lost my mind by the third day," Minogan said, shaking his head in disbelief.

"It was close," June admitted.

Koen looked like he wanted to throw up. Looking at his face, remembering how he'd been when they found her in the cell, June wondered (not for the first time) if he felt something for her like what she felt for him, but dismissed the thought. *He's just a kind, empathetic person,* she scolded herself. *Get over it.*

"It's over now," June said, acknowledging their sympathy but not wanting to talk about it anymore. "I'm okay, everybody's okay, we got the second piece of the tablet, so as far as I'm concerned, we came out ahead."

"What do you think that stone was?" Feoras asked. "The one what's-her-name made you swallow."

June's hand went to her stomach automatically. "I really have no idea," she said, looking thoughtful. "I know it's important, though."

"Was that really a good idea? Swallowing something, without knowing what it was, or anything about who gave it to you?" Koen's nauseated expression was gone, but he still looked disturbed.

June sighed. "No, actually, it wasn't a good idea," she said. "But—I don't know, something just told me it was the right thing to do." The group lapsed into silence, lost in their own thoughts.

They made camp at dusk a few hours later, eating a meager dinner of fruit and nuts they'd gathered along the way, the vegetables they'd brought from the dragons having been consumed in the last week, while she'd been imprisoned. As they finished, Minogan cleared his throat uncomfortably, and June looked at him curiously.

"We were wondering..." Minogan began slowly, "You see, our village is kind of between here and the next place on the map. It would be about two days travel off of our course, but..."

"Oh, cool," June interjected. "You want to stop and see your families? That's a great idea!" Minogan's face split in a relieved smile. "Errigal and Feoras can see their wives..."

"Minogan can see his *girlfriend...*" Errigal said teasingly, and Minogan threw a stick across the fire at him. June smiled, venturing a quick sidelong glance at Koen. No mention of a girlfriend for Koen. Hmm...

Girl, you are an insatiable horn dog, a scolding voice in her head told her, and she lowered her head so no one would see her blush. Insatiable? Definitely, when it came to Koen.

Speaking of Koen—by the way he was looking at Minogan, or rather, not looking at him, it didn't seem as though he'd yet taken her advice on patching things up. Koen looked up at that very moment, and saw her glancing from Minogan to him and back again. Her thoughts must have read plain in her face as he caught her eye, for he shook his head and breathed a long-suffering sigh.

Slowly, he got up and walked over to Minogan, who stood up as well, eyeing Koen warily. Koen stepped right in front of him and stopped, looking Minogan over from head to toe as if sizing him up—and then punched him square in the face, knocking him to the ground.

"Koen!" June leapt to her feet, shocked. Errigal and Feoras stayed sitting, expressions of mild interest and amusement on their faces, as Minogan stared up at Koen, stunned, holding his sleeve to his gushing nose. Koen merely stood over him, hands on hips, face stony. Then, finally, he held out his hand to Minogan, whose face split into a grin as he took it and was helped to his feet. Both clapped each other on the back, sat down once more, and began chatting as though nothing had happened.

As Minogan talked, Koen's eyes cut to June, who was still on her feet, mouth open, shaking her head. He raised his eyebrows and nodded in her direction. *Happy now?* June sat down. *I could live to be a hundred,* she thought, *and I'd still never understand men.*

June woke up about an hour before dawn, the sky lightening from black to a deep vibrant indigo. She rubbed her eyes, turned over on her back, and laced her fingers behind her head. She couldn't remember exactly what she'd dreamed, only that it had been cold and dark, and she'd been alone.

Gee, wonder where I was, she thought sarcastically. She tilted her head back and looked behind her, where Minogan sat propped up against a tree, sword across his lap, looking like a raccoon with his two black eyes. She waggled her fingers at him in a slight wave, and he nodded to her, not exactly smiling, but with a softening of his normally severe features.

Slowly, her body began to relax again, the peaceful silence of the morning punctuated by the soft snores of her companions. She could feel the gentle thump of her blood coursing through her veins, and pressed one hand to her stomach to feel the strong pulse of her aorta.

She found herself sifting through all the events of the past few months, not trying to evaluate it, but as casually as one would look at a photo album, stopping occasionally to examine a detail, but not trying to make sense of things, just–looking. And in the midst of it, she found hope.

Her life had been nearly perfect, and she'd been snatched from it and thrust into a world of uncertainty, dropped into the pool and forced to sink or swim. But, just as quickly, it could change again. Happiness had been taken from her, but the possibility of happiness remained.

As the sun began to peek above the horizon, the Valforte stirred, and Minogan got up and sheathed his sword. June rose too, for the first time in Prendawr truly, deep down inside, believing things might work out.

~16~

Fifteen minutes later, June and the Valforte were hiking along the beautiful but seemingly endless coastline. They fell easily into the rhythm of traveling again, waking with the dawn and stopping four times a day; a break before and after lunch, lunch itself, and dinner, when they set up camp at night.

Even when they had little or nothing to eat, they adhered to the schedule, taking comfort in its predictability. And the food situation wasn't *so* bad; Errigal, with his extensive botanical knowledge, was able to keep them supplied with fresh greens, and occasionally one of the guys brought down a small mammal or bird, even an occasional snake. They steered clear of large game animals, for they'd have to leave any meat they didn't immediately consume, without horses to carry it, and this would have conflicted with everything their fathers had taught them about hunting, not to mention leaving a clear trail for those who might be following.

Even though they left each meal a little hungry, and woke each morning still tired, their spirits were high. They had essentially completed over half their quest, and the Valforte would soon be meeting their friends and family, whom they hadn't seen in months. June felt better, day by day, had even gained a little weight despite the meager portions, and the nightmares stemming from her imprisonment were losing their teeth. Fresh air and warm sunshine rounded everything out.

Looking back later, June realized what a mistake they'd made, letting themselves be lulled into complacency.

At breakfast, the morning of the third day out from the Eid Gomen fortress, June woke up feeling nauseated and uneasy. After packing her things up, she quietly walked a little ways away from the Valforte and sat Indian style on the ground, pushing her mind out to search the surrounding area. She couldn't find any reason for the way she felt, but this didn't make her feel any better.

"Hey, guys," she said as she rejoined them. "This is going to sound really stupid, but I have a weird feeling this morning."

"Like?" Minogan asked, pausing as he extinguished the fire, the first one they'd dared to light since escaping the fortress.

June shrugged. "I don't know," she said, feeling silly. "Just–

hinky, kind of."

"Hin-kee?" Feoras asked, and June realized that had come out in English.

"Umm...paranoid, I guess you'd call it."

"Did you do your search thing?" Koen asked, and June nodded.

"I couldn't find anything, but still..." Now June felt even stupider. *You probably ate too many of those pear-things last night, and all you're feeling is your stomach gearing up to be sick later.* She forced a laugh, shaking her head. "Never mind." The others resumed their work, and ten minutes later, they set off.

Since leaving the Eid Gomen fortress, the landscape had been pretty well the same–high, windy sea-cliffs, covered in knee-high purplish grass. Now, it began to change, sloping down and flattening into a black sand beach, the few stunted pine trees which had been scattered along the way straightening up and drawing together to form a slowly thickening forest, into which Minogan said they'd begin traveling tomorrow, changing their direction inland to reach the Valforte village.

Looking forward to that, June thought grumpily, her thigh and calf muscles burning from pulling her bare feet out of the sand with each step. They'd only been walking for an hour, and she couldn't wait for the midmorning break.

When the attack came, it came from the sea.

June stood stunned for a moment, watching the Eid Gomen's heads break the surface of the incoming waves as they charged up onto the beach, reminding her of footage she'd seen of Normandy.

"Back! June, get back," Koen shouted, as the others dropped their packs on the sand and drew their swords. June, weaponless, ran back about twenty feet, but stopped, unwilling to leave her friends but unsure of what to do.

There were about twenty-five Eid Gomen in total, all carrying their horrible weapons, both slashing and stabbing at the Valforte.

Despite the surprise of the attack and the number of attackers, her companions held their own, drawing swords and knives and slashing two-handed against three, four, and five Eid Gomen at once. The silence of the battle disturbed June–she was used to movie battles, men shouting and screaming, but only the sounds of iron against iron and the occasional grunt could be heard. June stood, unable to move.

Then, one of the Eid Gomen pushed past Minogan and ran straight for June, who gasped and backed up. Suddenly, everything seemed to move in slow motion. June saw Minogan turn to pursue her would-be attacker, face flecked with the blood of his enemies.

He'd only made it a few steps when another Eid Gomen rushed him from the side and drew the sharp edge of his spear under Minogan's chin. His hands flew to his throat, eyes bulging as blood poured out from between his fingers.

Minogan's eyes, full of gruesome surprise, met June's. She heard her own heart beating in her ears, louder than the clanging metal around them. Three heartbeats. *Bump. Bump. Bump.*

Then his knees buckled, and he fell face-first into the sand.

June had just drawn breath to scream when the Eid Gomen who had been running for her hit her, slamming her into the sand. Even as they struggled, June's mind raced, replaying what she'd just seen over and over again. *Dead. Minogan's dead. Dead. Dead...*

A wave of anger washed over her, hot as lava. The Eid Gomen pulled back, mouth open in shock (the look of horror on its face nauseating, such human emotion displayed on such an unnatural face) and burst into flame, falling off into the sand. The Eid Gomen who'd killed Minogan had been charging her also, spear raised, but stopped when it saw what had happened to its comrade. It had no time to retreat, however, before it too burst into flame at the instant June's eyes fell on it.

June half-ran, half-crawled to where Minogan lay face-down in the sand, hands still clutching his throat. She pulled him over on his back, oblivious to the battle, now in its final stages, going on behind her. He was still alive.

"Let me see, let me see," June said, struggling to pry his blood-slippery fingers from his throat. "It's okay, let me see..." She got his hands away and pressed her own to the gaping wound, concentrating fiercely, trying to fix the damage before it was too late. Minogan gasped for air, his hitching breaths bubbling wetly as blood ran into his severed windpipe, the look of panic on his face twisting June's heart into a knot.

Then, his body stiffened, his rigid muscles arching his back off the sand. The terrified expression on his face froze as his mouth opened in a gasp, and then his eyes seemed to catch sight of something calming in the sky over June's shoulder. Slowly, he relaxed, and his hands fell away from his throat. He didn't take another breath.

"No," June whispered. "No. You can't...no." She shut her eyes and concentrated even harder, the exertion making her dizzy. "Come on, come on..." she hissed through gritted teeth.

Even as she pushed, she knew she had at last found magic's limit. She could heal wounds, light fires, protect her friends, kill her enemies. But she could not raise the dead.

June looked into Minogan's eyes, still fixed on a faraway point, his pupils dilated. Slowly, she released his throat and sat back, watching dully as blood, still trickling from his wound, soaked wetly into the black sand. She felt something warm on her cheek and swiped at it with her hand, mixing Minogan's blood with the tears running freely down her face.

"Oh, God," said a voice behind her, and someone fell with a thump to their knees. She turned to find Errigal, face nearly grey, staring at Minogan's body in the sand. Feoras stood just behind him, his face drained of all blood as well, mouth open in shock. June reached back and grasped Errigal's hand, at the same time looking for Koen.

The beach was littered with the bodies of the Eid Gomen. Koen had been walking about five hundred yards away, apparently looking for June and the others. When he caught sight of June, her face smeared with blue blood, the color drained from his face as he ran toward them and skidded to a halt near Minogan's feet.

June looked away, unable to watch, Koen's pain more devastating than her own. She heard him grunt, as though someone had punched him hard in the stomach, listened to his breathing grow hard and ragged. Then she heard a *chink* noise, and his footsteps retreating. June's shoulders shook with silent sobs, her whole body trembling.

When she dared to look up again, she found Koen's sword stuck in the sand, its owner nowhere to be seen.

June, Errigal, and Feoras stayed silently by Minogan's body for the better part of an hour, no one able to bring themselves to move or speak. Finally, June wiped her eyes once more, got up, and walked to the water. For a moment, she hesitated, afraid the Eid Gomen might come leaping out of the ocean again, but she could feel the danger had passed. If only she'd listened to her intuition earlier.

June spent a few minutes rinsing Minogan's blood from her face and hands, impervious to the cold of the seawater; she was already numb. When she thought she'd gotten the last of the gore from her skin, she returned to Errigal and Feoras.

"What do you do, when someone dies?" she asked softly.

Errigal made no move to respond, but Feoras shook himself as he turned to her, blinking his eyes to bring them into focus.

"The body is cleansed and dressed, and we—we burn them on a pyre," he said, the word *burn* seeming to catch in his throat.

"Okay," June said, more than a little nauseated at the thought of putting Minogan's still-warm flesh into a fire. "Do you think you two can get the wood? I'll..." June gulped, dreading what came next, but knowing it needed to be done, "I'll clean him up."

Feoras nodded, looking relieved—although whether at June's offer to prepare Minogan's body, or just to have something to do, she wasn't sure.

"We can do that," he said. "But—is it safe to leave you now?"

June nodded. "I just wish I'd listened to myself, earlier," she said, and Feoras shook his head.

"We were the ones who made you doubt yourself," he said, still shaking his head. "What's done is done." His voice broke as he spoke those last words, and he turned away, pulling his brother gently to his feet as they walked toward the forest.

"Feoras," June called after him, and he turned, wiping his face on his sleeve. "See if you can find Koen, will you? Don't make him come back if he's not ready, just...make sure he's all right." Feoras nodded, and he and Errigal walked off into the trees.

June left Minogan and walked over to where they'd dropped the packs, carrying them over near his body. In Minogan's, she found two shirts, one stained, the other spotless, and a clean pair of pants. *He was probably saving the clean ones, for when he saw his family and his girlfriend,* she thought, and she began to cry again. With Minogan's knife, laying in the sand by his side, she cut the stained shirt into rags, leaving one long piece, like a scarf, off to the side. June dug out his waterskin, nearly empty, and filled it with seawater, pouring some into a bowl and setting the skin to the side. With a deep breath, she took the knife and began cutting Minogan's blood-soaked clothes away from him. Dipping one of the rags she'd cut from his shirt, she began carefully washing his body.

It took nearly an hour—she had to stop, several times, too overcome with emotion to continue. It hadn't been like this when her parents died. She'd been led into a white room, shining with stainless steel tables and instruments, smelling of bleach and chemicals. A white sheet had been drawn back from each of their faces, both of them looking as though they had fallen asleep, except for a small bruise on her father's left temple. It had all been so clean, so sterile, and she'd had time to prepare herself.

This was different. Minogan's life had been taken before her eyes, he'd died in her hands, messy and raw. Terrifying. And her fault.

June wiped the last bit of blood and dirt from Minogan's face, then took the scarf-like piece of shirt she'd cut earlier and wrapped it tightly around his neck, tying the ends together and neatly tucking them in. As she did so, she felt someone watching her, and turned to find Koen looking at her with a strange expression on his face. At first, she thought he might be upset, with Minogan lying naked in front of her, his clothes cut and thrown off to the side. They looked at each other for a moment, then Koen dropped his eyes.

"Need help?" he asked, and June nodded.

"If you're up for it," she said, holding up the clean clothes and inclining her head toward Minogan's body. Koen knelt down beside her and together, with great care, they dressed their friend for his last journey. June got her comb and pulled it gently through his hair, sprinkling a little clean water into it to get it right. When she glanced back up, Koen looked at her with the same expression on his face as earlier. June cocked her head questioningly, and he dropped his eyes again.

"I should have been the one to do this," he said, regretfully.

"It's okay," June said, throat tight with emotion. She'd give anything to make it okay for him, anything at all.

"No, it's not," he said, miserably, his eyes traveling the length of his friend's body. June felt her eyes burning with tears. If this had been Ashleigh or Shannon...how would she feel?

"Do you want me to give you a minute with him?" There was no response from Koen–he merely bent his head lower.

"I'll–I'll go help Feoras and Errigal." She stumbled to her feet, suddenly desperate to get away. Seeing the pain on Koen's face, so clear and sharp and fresh, it felt like being gutted with a dull knife. And she could do nothing but leave him alone.

It was nearly sunset when June, Feoras, and Errigal returned to Minogan's body, where Koen still sat, exactly where June had left him. He jerked his head up as they approached, like someone awakened suddenly from a deep sleep.

June spread Minogan's blanket out next to him, and Koen and Feoras lifted Minogan onto the cloth. Each of them took a corner, and together they walked off down the beach, slowly, reverently.

As the sun was setting, they laid him carefully in the center of the pyre, on a soft bed of pine boughs Errigal had gathered, and laid his sword on his chest, clasping his hands over the hilt.

Each picked up one of four unlit torches lying on the ground nearby. June touched a finger to hers, and it immediately burst into flame. The others crowded around her, lighting their torches, then spread out to make a circle around Minogan. They stood in silence, in the growing gloom, staring at Minogan's face, his eyes closed for the last time. Twenty-six, never to marry, never to have children, to kiss another woman, to dance or shoot another arrow. The last page in the book of Minogan's life.

June stood like this for what could have been hours or minutes, replaying the day's events, watching herself stand and do nothing while her friends fought for their lives, and one lost the battle. If she'd done something with magic, maybe...

A quarter of the people I love in this world are now dead.

Without warning, Koen began to sing in another language, his voice clear and strong, and Errigal and Feoras joined him. June didn't understand the words, but they were beautiful, mournful and uplifting all at once. The song went on for several minutes, and then with one last, lingering note, the Valforte lapsed into silence.

Koen threw his torch onto the pyre, and June, Errigal, and Feoras followed suit. There had been no rain for a week, and the dry wood of the pyre soon became a wind-whipped inferno. The last glimpse June caught of Minogan was his hand, resting on the hilt of his sword, before the flames swallowed him up forever.

As Minogan's pyre burned down, they filed slowly away, lying or sitting down on the sand nearby, wrapping themselves in blankets, their eyes reflecting the flames burning in honor of their friend.

June had no memory of falling asleep, but when she opened her eyes, night had fallen, and the pyre was now just a bed of coals burning in the sand, flickering as the breeze from the sea blew over them. She sat up and looked around. Errigal and Feoras were fast asleep, wrapped in their thin blankets, but where was Koen?

She caught sight of him when a breeze stirred the glow of the coals, showing him on the opposite side of the pyre, sitting with his blanket wrapped around his shoulders, staring into the charred remains.

June got up and went to him. She paused briefly as she got close; he didn't look up, didn't acknowledge her visually, but she felt a vibe from him, an appreciation of her presence. She lowered herself to the ground beside him, glancing at his face, skin drawn tight across his cheekbones and around his mouth.

Without thinking about it, she reached out and grasped his hand where it rested on his knee, interlacing her fingers into his. Koen squeezed his eyes shut and clenched his jaw, taking her hand and pressing it tightly between both of his, but still he didn't look at her, just stared into the coals. They sat this way, supporting each other without speaking, until the sun came up over the water.

Later that morning, the subdued party awkwardly rearranged their traveling formation, since the five were now four. Koen finally took the lead, June in the middle, Feoras and Errigal bringing up the rear.

They had changed course now, moving inland, back into the forest. June shared a theory with the others; between the attack from the sea which had claimed Minogan's life, her underwater capture, and the subterranean city under the lake, June thought the Eid Gomen were amphibian. She also believed they were somehow using the water to confuse her senses, as the only times she'd ever had trouble sensing them was near a large body of water. They agreed to steer clear of anything larger than a good-sized stream.

The journey now became tiring and tedious, oppressively silent, everyone lost in their thoughts and unable to bring themselves to casually chat. In the silence, June wrestled with guilt.

She blamed herself for Minogan's death, knowing she should have pushed harder to convince them of imminent danger, should have done something other than stand dumb at the sight of her friends being attacked. Every time she closed her eyes, she saw Minogan's eyes widen as the spear was drawn across his neck, the panic on his face as he lay on the ground, struggling to breathe, drowning in his own blood. Her nightmares returned with a vengeance.

Four days later, as they trudged wearily through the trees, June felt a prickle on the back of her neck, as though they were being watched. She stopped dead in her tracks, catching Errigal unawares so he plowed into the back of her. June barely noticed, though–she merely stood where she'd stopped, watchful as a deer. All three stared as she turned slowly, eyes straining to see between the trunks of the trees.

"What is it?" Feoras whispered.

"I'm not sure," June said softly. "I could swear..." She broke off as, between the trees behind them, she saw a bright flash of green and purple. A memory came flooding back, something she'd forgotten, a familiar voice pushing through the black as she'd been dragged semi-conscious through the tunnels of the Eid Gomen fortress.

"Bastard," June whispered. Anger rose inside her like a flooding stream, finally breaking over its spillway. With an inhuman cry of rage, she pulled Errigal's sword from the scabbard at his side and charged after the streak of color she'd seen.

"Hey," she heard Errigal exclaim, and heard the others call after her, but she was in a place where no one could touch her as her feet pounded against the forest floor, sword raised in front of her.

She caught up with Halryan in a small clearing about four hundred yards away, attempting frantically to cast some kind of protective spell. June waved her arm as though pushing a door roughly shut, and Halryan was lifted off his feet and slammed into a tree. She thrust the sword against his neck, his eyes dazed, a small trickle of blood running from his left nostril down into his black mustache.

"What are you doing here?" June growled, cold fury in every syllable. Halryan's eyes cleared, startlement and confusion replaced with fear.

"I–I–my lady, it is so good to see you, I was on my way–"

June heard the guys run up behind her and their exclamations of disbelief, but didn't turn her attention from Halryan.

"Let's try this again," she said, voice still low and dangerous. "I already have a pretty good idea of what you're doing here. I want to hear it from your mouth."

Halryan tittered nervously, looking around the clearing as though for help. "My lady, I was merely returning home to collect some things before I left the kingdom for good. I do apologize, but I met with–"

"*I heard you in there,*" June bellowed into Halryan's face, and his expression turned from fear to terror. "A *human* voice! *Your* voice!"

"I–I–my lady, I don't..." He trailed off, unable to come up with a suitable explanation.

"How long have you been working for them?" June asked. "Before Lumia, or after?"

Halryan's mouth worked and he blinked rapidly as he tried to think of some excuse, some way of denying the accusation. Finally his shoulders slumped in defeat.

"After," he said, and June heard the Valforte gasp behind her.

"How long have you been following us?" she demanded through clenched teeth.

"Since you left the fortress," he said.

"So it was you who told them where we were, on the beach."

Halryan turned his head away and nodded, unable to meet her eyes. "Your magic protects you from being found by sorcery," he said. "They sent search parties, but I was the first to find you, and they instructed me to continue following."

"Do you know what you've done? Do you?" June pressed the sword blade closer to his neck, and a thin line of blood welled up around the blade.

Halryan began to weep, which only made June angrier. "I am so sorry, my lady, I had no idea..."

"Don't you dare give me that line," June growled. "The only thing the Eid Gomen want is to destroy this planet. So don't give me this crap that you had no idea, when you knew damn well that to help them succeed is to kill us all!" She lowered her head slightly, unable to look at his face any longer, breathing hard. Finally, she looked back up at him.

"Where I come from," she said, slowly, "we kill traitors." June stepped back and lowered the sword, releasing the pressure of the blade on Halryan's neck, and his hand went shakily to the cut it left there. June turned to Koen solemnly.

"Minogan was your best friend," she said, softly. "Would you like to do the honors?"

"Gladly," Koen said, drawing his sword, murder in his eyes. June turned back to Halryan, whose eyes frantically searched for an escape route.

"Don't even try it," she said. "I'd have you down before you moved three steps, and you know it."

Halryan's eyes grew even larger, and sweat trickled from his brow down the bridge of his nose as he watched Koen's slow approach. He stopped in front of the sorcerer, grasped his sword firmly with both hands, and prepared to swing.

Halryan squeezed his eyes shut, tears now running down his face. "Please, no, wait, I can tell you–I can tell you–" He pressed himself against the tree, cringing, his nails digging into the bark of the. "Wait, please..."

Koen brought the sword down in a sweeping, graceful arc, blade shining in the greenish sunlight filtering through the trees.

"*I'M YOUR FATHER,*" Halryan screamed.

The blade stopped a mere hair's breadth from Halryan's neck, and he let out a whistling sob of relief. Koen looked to June, eyes wide and questioning. June, however, looked at Halryan, confusion bending her brow.

"What did you say?" she asked, cocking her ear toward him, certain she hadn't heard him right. Halryan continued to sob weakly, head turned so his face pressed into the tree trunk.

"What did you say?" she repeated, taking a step toward him.

Halryan took a gasping breath and swallowed. "I'm your father," he said, opening his eyes and looking at her.

June pulled herself up to her full height and stepped into Koen's place in front of Halryan, directly in front of the sorcerer, raising Errigal's sword so that the tip pointed at his belly, causing him to visibly suck his stomach in.

"What do you mean, you're my father?"

"Precisely what I said, June," he said, voice shaky, and she realized with a jolt that he'd used her name. "I'm your father."

June looked at the others for help, but they merely stared glassy-eyed in utter disbelief. She closed her eyes, trying to get her head to stop buzzing so she could get a semi-clear train of thought going.

"So, you and my mother were dating, or what?" she said, pulling her hair away from her face in a gesture of exasperated confusion.

"I–well, no, not exactly–you see, there was a potion..."

It took a moment for comprehension to sink in.

"Oh, God." she whispered. "You sick bastard." Halryan merely looked at the ground without responding, a solid yes for June.

"I–I–it's complicated, you understand?" Halryan grinned at her feebly, as June merely shook her head in disbelief.

"No, I don't understand," she said.

Halryan dropped his eyes to the ground once more and took several deep breaths. June was about to poke him with the sword when he spoke.

"I was paid," he said.

"Oh, this just keeps getting better!" June raised her swordless arm and let it fall to her side, feeling like she'd just dropped down the rabbit hole in Alice in Wonderland, where nothing made any sense anymore. Not that anything had been making a whole lot of sense the rest of the time. "Who paid you?"

"I don't know."

"You don't know," June said, nodding, mouth pursed in a sarcastic smile. "How did you get the money, then? Who approached you about it to begin with?"

"There were a series of at least three messengers between myself and the person who paid me, specifically so I couldn't identify my employer."

"Your employer," June laughed bitterly. "Well, they must have known you pretty well, not to trust you with that information. Considering what a reliable, stand-up guy you are." She paused, thinking. "Didn't my mother, like, fire you, after you drugged and raped her?"

Halryan was quiet for a long time. "She had no memory of the incident," he said finally, and for the first time, June saw something like true emotion, not put on for her benefit, on his face. "She went to her childbed, still believing she was a virgin, unable to understand how such a thing had happened."

June stared at Halryan, hatred burning in her belly. "You're pure evil, you know that?" she asked.

Halryan burst into fresh sobs.

"Forgive me, my daughter," he said, covering his face with his hands. "Forgive your poor father his sins. Give me another chance, I beg you."

June thrust Errigal's sword so hard into Halryan's solar plexus that she not only felt the crunch of his spinal cord, but felt the blade pass through several inches of wood, nailing him to the tree. His hands fell away from his face, and his blue eyes sprang open wide in surprise, light blue eyes, so much like her own. Hot, thick blood ran down the sword onto her hand, and she recoiled as though burned, horror at what she'd just done overcoming the fury which had caused her to do it. She stared down at her hand, watching blood–her blood, really–drip from her fingertips onto the pine needles.

"Whoa," Errigal said, his voice awed. She whirled around to find all three Valforte staring at her, eyes wide and mouths agog. Behind her, Halryan gave a dying twitch, and June whirled again, backing up so quickly she slipped and fell on her butt. She looked up just in time to see Halryan–her father–stiffen one last time, then slump over the sword pinning him to the tree.

June leapt to her feet and ran. Later, she'd have no memory of the low branches that whipped her face and tore at her clothes, or of sobbing the whole way. She only really came back to herself when she found a small stream and flung herself into it, scrubbing the blood off her hands with sand until the blood on them really was her own, then flinging herself onto the bank, and crying until every muscle in her body ached, finally lying spent, mind shocked into silence.

She wasn't sure how much time had passed before she heard

someone walking slowly through the woods behind her. June sat up and turned around, wiping the dirt off her cheek, to find Koen looking down at her sympathetically.

"Hey," he said, softly.

June raked her fingers through her hair.

"Hey," she answered, voice froggy from crying.

"You okay?" he asked, and June laughed, a cold, hollow sound.

"Oh, yeah," she answered. "Peachy keen."

"Anything I can do?" He took a few steps closer and cocked his head to one side, hands in his pockets.

"Yeah, there is." June sniffed and shifted around so she faced Koen, sitting Indian style. "You can tell Errigal and Feoras they can go ahead and go home, for good. You too. I've had it with this bullshit. I'm out."

"You mean you quit?" Koen raised his eyebrows, but otherwise showed no sign of surprise. "You're not going to finish the quest?"

"No, I'm not," she said, petulance creeping into her voice. Koen sighed, then walked over and sat down in front of June, facing her.

"And what happens to you?" he asked.

"I'll figure something out."

"You'll figure something out. Well, comforting to know you have a plan." June didn't respond to his bait, merely picked at a spot of pine sap on her pants which had dried to a glaze. Koen sighed, and leaned forward, elbows on his knees.

"Why now? After all you've been through, why did that push you over the edge?"

"What, you want a list?" Koen shrugged, and June began to enumerate on her fingers. "One, Halryan, of all the foul, disgusting men on this planet, is my father. Was my father. Two, I wasn't born from love, or passion, or a night of drunken shenanigans. I was *bought*. Bought and paid for. And for what, I don't know. And three..." June's hand, outstretched, began to shake, and she clenched it tightly into a fist. "I just killed a man. I'm a murderer."

Koen pulled back and snorted. "You are *not* a murderer, June," he said, shaking his head.

"I killed him. My hands pushed that sword into him and ended his life. How am I not a murderer?"

"Because we would have killed him anyway! He deserved to die! He was a traitor, was responsible for Minogan's death..."

"That's not the point," June yelled, pounding her fists into her knees. "It doesn't matter that he was any of those things, or that he would have died anyway. What matters is *why* I killed him." June pressed the heels of her hands to her eyes, which were beginning to burn again with tears.

"Why did you kill him?"

June looked away toward the stream for a long time before she answered. "Because I hated him," she whispered. "Nothing more. And God help me, if he was here now, I'd do it again."

They were both silent for a moment before June spoke once more. "The old June would never have done that."

"I don't think that the old June ever dealt with anything like what you've had to go through here," Koen said, then leaned forward once more and grasped her by the shoulders. "Listen to me. We are at war. There are casualties in war, not to mention that the man was a worm and he *deserved to die*, no matter how it happened. You shouldn't feel bad that it happened to be you who got the honors."

June leapt to her feet, pulling away from Koen, and began to pace, unable to stand still. "You're still not getting it," she said, feeling blood rushing to her face as her emotions rose. "I know you would have plugged him the minute I stepped back. I know that. But I killed Halryan in cold blood, without a moment's hesitation. This place," she waved her hands widely at the trees, the sky, the ground, "is changing who and what I am. The person who put a sword into Halryan's guts is not the same one that her parents raised. And that is the person that I want to be. Not–" June stopped, her voice breaking. "Not this."

"You say it like you're a monster," Koen said softly. He had gotten to his feet during June's speech and stood about six feet away, watching her quietly, arms crossed over his chest. "You're not a monster, June. You're just a person who's been driven way, way past the edge."

June stood silent, head turned aside, blinking furiously to try and stem the flow of tears threatening to overspill her lids. Through a watery blur, she saw Koen walk slowly over to her, so close that she could feel the warmth of his body on her bare arms, which she wrapped around herself in a protective gesture. Once more, Koen took her by the arms and began to speak.

"You think you're turning hard, or cold, or maybe you even think you're going crazy. But you *are* the same person, the same person who threatened us with a bone club that first day, the same person who fought with the barmaid, the same person who negotiated with dragons. You're the strongest person I've ever met, and I think that for the first time in your life you're discovering how strong you really are. But you *haven't changed*, June. You're tough, but you're still sweet and loving and beautiful, all at the same time, just like you were at the beginning. And that's why I–"

Koen stopped, and June, who had been listening to this with her head turned away, turned to look at his face, his gorgeous sea-green eyes glowing with a strange light as they looked down at her. His hands came up, skimming over her shoulders and up her neck, cupping her face gently. And before June's mind could wrap itself around what was happening, his lips covered hers, and her heart, so shriveled and empty moments before, exploded in jubilant ecstasy.

Koen broke away suddenly, stumbling back a step, his eyes wide with shock. "God," he said, running a visibly shaking hand through his hair. "God, I–I'm sorry, I don't– I didn't mean–" He closed his eyes briefly and swallowed hard, Adam's apple bobbing. "I shouldn't have done that. I apologize."

June, experiencing a beautiful kind of head-spinning drunkenness, was a little slow to catch up.

"Shouldn't have done what?" she asked, her hands on her lips, wishing she could wrap the kiss up in a little scrap of cloth and keep it in her pocket forever.

Koen blinked at her. "I let the way I feel–I'm–look, I'll accompany you to our village, and then I'll stay behind, so you won't have to feel uncomfortable being around me every day." Koen was backing up, slowly, his hands out in a placating gesture, as a sense of growing horror crept over June.

"Koen," June said, and he paused in his retreat, his face so pale it reminded her of when she'd pulled him out of the river. "Stop for a minute, please." Koen stopped, barely; he looked ready to bolt any minute.

"I don't want you to leave," June said. "And I'm not going to be uncomfortable around you. In fact," she paused, swallowing hard, "I'm in love with you, and I've been waiting and hoping and praying for a long time for you to do what you just did." June held her breath and watched Koen's face as it went through its transformation from mortification to cautious hope, from cautious hope to relief and happiness as he came to her once more and wrapped his arms around her.

And as his lips left hers and traveled over her cheek, her neck, she heard his own whispered confessions of love, and fell blindly forward into the arms of fate.

~17~

An hour later, they lay naked on the forest floor, June's head pillowed on Koen's chest, their skin covered with a sheen of sweat. She closed her eyes and pressed her cheek close to his chest, sighing deeply, inhaling his scent. His hand came up and stroked her hair.

"I have to be dreaming," he said, sounding dazed. June smiled, then opened her eyes and turned her head up to see his face. He was looking down at her, head pillowed on his opposite arm, shaking his head slowly. "This can't be..."

She understood completely. An hour ago, her little lean-to shack of a world collapsed on itself, leaving her with a pile of rubble and no strength to rebuild. Now, someone had built her a palace.

June pinched him just above his left nipple. "Ow," he said, pulling his arm out from under his head to massage the spot.

"See, not dreaming," she said, and he smiled and closed his eyes, pulling her tight to his side and kissing the top of her head. God, it felt so good to be with him it almost hurt. This kind of pain, though, she could live with.

"So, how long have you been in love with me?" June asked, laying her head back down and throwing her arm over his midsection, admiring the way her dark skin contrasted with his blue.

He laughed softly, and took a deep contented breath. "Pretty well from the first moment," he said, almost dreamily.

"What, at that stupid 'This is your life,' meeting with Halryan?" she asked. "When I was playing hysterical female?"

"No, before that," he said. "When you passed out in the field, and we came down to carry you up, right when you first got here. Looking at you lying there–I don't know, I just thought to myself, 'Koen, you're going to get yourself in a lot of trouble.'"

"I had no idea...."

"Well, I didn't know about you, either," Koen said.

"Oh, please," June scoffed, raising her head to look at him. "I could barely walk without falling over anytime I got near you. I kept dropping stuff, breaking things, cutting myself with knives."

Koen laughed again. "I remember that," he said. "God, I thought you cut your finger off."

"Yeah, I just about drowned myself in the bathroom from

embarrassment." June shook her head and laid it back down, smiling. "Funny how things work out," she said, tracing the taut muscles of his abdomen with her finger.

Koen sighed, looking up at the canopy of trees above them. "You know, that was the real reason I was mad at Minogan," he said, and June looked sharply up at him again. "He knew how I felt about you, I told him just a few days after we started on the quest. When I found out he'd planned to kill you all along..."

June dropped her eyes, embarrassed. "I'm sorry," she said.

Koen looked at her. "You have nothing to be sorry about. If it wasn't for you, we never would have made up before...well..."

Just then, they heard someone coming through the woods, from direction Koen had come. There was no time to get dressed; Koen merely grabbed his shirt and threw it over June and himself, hastily arranging it to cover the most important areas.

"Ah." Feoras was standing a few feet away, looking as though he'd just swallowed a frog. "I was just–you'd been gone–we were–I was–ah..." Stricken, he turned on his heel and marched quickly back the way he'd came.

June managed to wait until the sound of his footsteps had receded before bursting into helpless giggles, burying her face in Koen's side. Koen, meantime, just groaned, his hand over his eyes.

"Of all the..." he trailed off, groaning again.

June, regaining control of herself, wiped her eyes and looked up at Koen. "Well, at least this saves us the awkward announcement."

"What announcement?" he asked, nudging her gently aside and sitting up to put his shirt on.

"The 'we're together,' announcement," June said, locating her makeshift bra a few feet away and arranging her assets into it.

Koen looked up, shocked. "You were planning on telling everyone?" he asked, eyebrows raised.

June felt a cold little stone drop into her stomach. "Why not?" she said, her tone cautious. "Are you embarrassed or something?"

"Embar–oh, June, no," Koen said, realization dawning as he leaned over and grabbed her hands. "No, it's just..." he sighed, "what we're doing here is not exactly legal," he said.

"What?"

Koen flexed his jaw, pulling his lips into a bitter smile. "'Relations' between Valforte and Andrians are strictly forbidden."

"You're kidding," June said, horrified.

"I wish." He shook his head ruefully. "But it's an actual law, signed into effect by none other than your mother, Queen Morningstar."

June, who had been sitting with her legs drawn up and her arms lying across her knees, dropped her head down between her arms.

"That's why you backed off so quickly," she whispered, remembering his horrified reaction when he'd kissed her. "God, my parents were nightmares. I don't think they did one good thing in all their lives, the both of them."

"They made you."

June looked up to find Koen smiling at her in a way that made her insides squirm pleasantly. "You're very sweet," she said, standing up to pull her pants on, pausing on the way up to kiss him. "Well, that'll be the first law to go, then."

Koen said nothing, merely stood up alongside her and stepped into his pants. "Ready?" he asked, a somewhat grim expression on his face as he offered June his arm. She cocked her head curiously at him, and he shrugged.

"I just have a feeling 'Congratulations' won't be the first words out of their mouth."

They weren't. Errigal and Feoras both waited by the tree where Halryan had met his end. The body had been pulled down and disposed of somehow, but quite a bit of blood still stained the trunk and the ground, and June shuddered. No matter what Koen, or anyone else, said, she'd taken another person's life in anger. Her own father's. And yes, he'd been about thirty seconds from dying anyway, but it neither excused nor erased the fact that she had taken it upon herself to end Halryan's life. But she couldn't take it back, no matter how much she wanted to. It was just another thing she'd have to live with.

Both Errigal and Feoras looked up as they approached, looking very uneasy–and disapproving? June wasn't sure, but their scrutinizing gazes made her want to drop Koen's arm guiltily.

They stood staring at each other in the clearing, June shifting uncomfortably from foot to foot, an expression of challenge on Koen's face, daring someone to say something.

Feoras cleared his throat. "What are we doing now?" he asked.

Koen looked at June expectantly. She remembered that nearly two hours ago, she'd quit the quest. She gave him a rueful smile.

"I don't know," she said. "Do you think we can manage another few hours, or should we just camp for the night?" All three men squinted upward through the trees.

"We might just want to camp," Feoras said. "I don't think we're going to get enough distance to make it worthwhile." They began to set their things down, and June stiffened.

"Um, do you think we could find another place to camp?" she asked, glancing at the bloodstained tree at the edge of the clearing. Errigal and Feoras followed her gaze, and nodded in understanding.

They walked back down to the stream, deliberately taking a slight angle to the left, to avoid the exact place they had 'expressed' their feelings for each other, smiling secretively as they walked. An uncomfortable silence settled over the group as they gathered firewood, punctuated only by the clearing of throats and the snapping of branches being broken down for the fire.

June, spying a nice big branch lying at the base of a tree, wandered over and began breaking it into a manageable armload of wood. She felt someone come up behind her, and turning quickly, found Errigal regarding her with a strange look on his face.

"Hi," she said, a little unnerved by his expression.

Errigal looked over his shoulder before speaking. "Do you know what you're doing here?" he asked quietly, eyes searching her face.

June took a deep breath and put one hand on her hip. "Why don't you just tell me what's on your mind, Errigal?"

"If the Andrians catch a Valforte with one of their women, June– they'll kill him."

June's head snapped back in shock, her eyes immediately searching out Koen, filling the kettle in the stream.

Well, what did you think, when he said it was illegal, she thought to herself. *That they'd write him a ticket?*

June looked at the ground. "I didn't realize," she said.

Errigal nodded. "I didn't think you did," he said. "Just something to keep in mind."

Without another word, he took the branches June had been breaking up and carried them to the camp. June looked at Koen, now apparently involved in serious conversation with Feoras.

Probably getting the same treatment I just got, she thought. Then–*God, why can't anything be easy? Why can't I just have something nice, something good, something* mine?

Slowly, she made her way back to the camp, sitting down next to Koen, who beamed at her as she approached. She could barely return his smile, and certainly not at the wattage he'd put out. He put his arm around her, and unable to resist, she leaned into his embrace, felt the tingle all the way to her toes as he kissed the top of her head.

June stayed silent all the way through their veggie-only meal, as did everyone else. Not until Errigal and Feoras went to clean the pots and pans did Koen finally say something. "You got quiet."

June squeezed her eyes shut and sighed, trying not to lose control of her emotions. "Koen, I don't know if we should be doing this," she said, with a tremor in her voice, though it felt like an earthquake was building up inside her.

Koen sighed and rolled his eyes. "Talking to Errigal, I gather?" June nodded dully. "Yeah, I got the same treatment from Feoras." He paused, turning himself so he faced her directly. "Listen to me. I know the risks. I've gone over it over and over again, ever since the beginning. And you know what I came up with? You're worth it."

June shook her head and dropped her eyes, but Koen grasped her gently by the chin, lifting her head to look in her eyes. "My father always said that if it's worth having, you have to work for it. And you...you're the most amazing person I've ever met. I couldn't have dreamed you up before I met you; you're beyond imagining. I understand why you're scared, the consequences of this could—*could*—be serious. But if you leave me now, or ever..." he closed his eyes, then opened them again, "well, put it this way—I'd rather die with a heart than live without one."

June's eyes had slowly been filling up with tears as Koen spoke. Now they spilled over and flowed down her cheeks.

"You're an idiot," she sniffled, laughing. "A very nice, romantic idiot, but still an idiot." Koen looked at her, still waiting for a more definitive response.

"God, I love you," she whispered.

And Koen took it for the answer it was, pulling her into his lap and kissing her until they were both breathless.

They slept on opposite sides of the fire that night by unspoken agreement. June had already gleaned from previous conversations, notably when she'd found out about her illegitimacy, how people here felt about sex before marriage. She looked across the fire at Koen, wondering if he was feeling guilty. He gave her quite the lascivious grin, which she returned. *Well, if he thinks he's going to hell, he's pretty darn cheerful about it.*

June rolled over on her back, sighing contentedly. After only a few hours, she felt like she'd been with him forever. There was something so familiar there, a feeling of home. Thinking about him, his face, his smile, his touch, she could easily forget everything she'd lost, and everything she still stood to lose. She recognized Koen for what he was—the greatest gift she'd ever been given. And a reason to fight for her future.

Two days later, they were still in the woods, making their way toward the village. Actually, Koen and June didn't so much walk as float, drunk on each other, much to the annoyance of Errigal and Feoras. But today, even the brothers were in good spirits, as they'd begun to recognize the forest around them, and estimated they'd probably arrive at the village today.

Suddenly Koen stopped walking and looked at the sky, his face paling. Errigal and Feoras, following his gaze, soon had similar expressions on their faces, and June squinted through the branches to see what had caused their distress.

Black smoke, and a lot of it, hovering hazily just over the tops of the trees. If they'd been walking in the open, they would have seen it miles away, but the trees had obscured their view until now.

"Stay here, June," Koen said, and he, Errigal and Feoras took off running toward the smoke.

"Wai–Koen!"

"Wait here," he shouted over his shoulder, and was gone.

June paced back and forth for about thirty seconds before losing patience. "Oh, screw this," she muttered, and sprinted in the direction the men had taken.

Ten minutes later, she caught up with them and stopped dead in her tracks, horrified by what she saw. Koen, Errigal, and Feoras stood with dazed expressions on their faces in the center of the smoking ruin of a small village. Stone foundations and a few charred beams were the only things left to show where buildings had stood.

June stepped out of the trees and walked straight into Koen's arms, pressing herself against his chest. His whole body shook, whether in anger or shock, or a combination of both, June couldn't tell. She stepped back from him, one arm still around his waist, looking at the damage.

"Who did this?" she whispered, and Koen's jaw tightened.

"Andrians," said Feoras, behind her.

"Why?"

"Pick your reason. Greed, hatred...boredom," Errigal said, prodding the remains of one building with his sword, face clouded with emotion. June shook her head, momentarily speechless.

"The people–God, they're not..."

"No, they all got away, from what we can see," Koen said, speaking for the first time. "This isn't the first Valforte village this has happened to, or the second, or the tenth. We keep ourselves pretty well prepared, just in case."

"But–" June stuttered, unable to comprehend what her eyes and ears were telling her. "Don't you fight?"

"They won't fight, June," Koen snapped, and she recoiled. He closed his eyes and took a breath, regaining control of himself. "They know they can't beat us in a fair battle. So they poison our water, burn our crops, kill our livestock. They rape our women, they kidnap our children and force them into indenture. There are several thousand Andrians in Prendawr. There are only a few hundred of us left. And since we refuse to stoop to their levels, because we won't kill women and children, in a few more years we'll probably be gone."

June swallowed hard, trying to imagine for a moment what Koen, Errigal, and Feoras's lives must be like. She had a feeling she'd never even begin to understand.

"Is there a rendezvous point? Do you know where they are?"

"There are a few places they might have gone," Errigal said. "One's that way," he pointed north, "and one's that way," he swung his arm southeast, "and there's another about ten miles that way."

June gently disentangled her arm from Koen and sat down on the ground, closing her eyes and centering herself, then flew out of her body to search.

She found them about five miles northwest. "I think if we hurry, we can get there by nightfall," she said, noting with a satisfaction she hadn't even gotten dizzy from her search. She was getting stronger, or at least her control of magic was.

"Could you tell how many there were?" Errigal asked anxiously. June shook her head.

"It doesn't work like that, no," she said. "At least not on higher beings. I only know there was a group of them, that way. And that they were Valforte."

"So you couldn't see them at all, for like, a rough head count?" Errigal persisted, and June shook her head.

"Come on, let's walk and talk," she said, and they began moving toward the villagers. "It's hard to explain. It's not so much seeing as feeling. All three of you have kind of a signature vibe, and the people I found have it too. Andrians feel different, and so do Eid Gomen."

"You called that draek, though," Koen said, and June nodded.

"Yeah, animals are much easier," she said. "It's kind of like people forgot the most basic language, the one we all started out with. I could try and communicate with a Valforte or an Andrian all day long with my mind, they'd never even know I was there. Animals usually know I'm there before I'm even aware of them." June snorted. "Weird," she said. "I didn't even know I knew all that."

They hauled ass through the woods, stopping occasionally so June could make sure they were on the right track. She frequently glanced up at Koen, and he shot her quick smiles and reached out to squeeze her hand in response, but otherwise remained gravely focused on making as much time as possible.

Her legs ached, and her stomach growled, but she wouldn't have dreamed of complaining. After all they'd done for her, the least she could do was make sure they got to their families as soon as possible.

At last, as the sun approached the horizon, June estimated they had about three miles to go. Suddenly, Koen stopped and looked at her, as if seeing her for the first time.

"June, do me a favor," he said, setting his pack down and shaking out his blanket. "Wrap this over your head, like a hood, and keep your arms inside. Just for now, okay?"

At first, June looked at Koen, perplexed, but then realization dawned on her as she looked down at her dark arms. So soon after the village's destruction, if someone saw her, an Andrian, before things had been properly explained, she could excite a panic. So she wrapped her head and shoulders in the blanket so only her eyes showed, and looked to Koen for approval.

"Better?" she asked, and he nodded.

"Yeah." Then, more quietly, "I'm sorry."

"Don't be," June said, without hesitation, as they began walking again. "But–Koen, is this going to be okay, my coming with you? Do you want me to, like, stay outside the village or something?"

Koen looked at her with something like exasperation. "Don't be silly," he said. "Do you think I'd let that happen?"

"Well, I don't want to force myself on them, if it makes them uncomfortable."

"Just leave it to me, okay? It'll be fine, I promise." He gave her a comforting smile, and June lapsed into silence, not convinced.

Fifteen minutes later, Koen stopped abruptly and held up his hand for silence. Pursing his lips, he gave a short, staccato whistle, a perfect imitation of a bird. They waited in silence. Koen repeated the call and waited once more, but the woods remained still.

Just as he prepared to call again, an echoing whistle came from up ahead. Koen turned to Errigal and Feoras, who grinned widely. June, however, was sweating under her makeshift berka, unsure of the reception she could expect.

A few moments later, a figure with reddish hair and blue skin, armed with bow and sword, stepped in front of them. He had bits of branches and other trees stuck into his clothing as camouflage. When he caught sight of the Valforte, his face broke into a delighted smile.

"Koen," he said, stepping forward and embracing him. "Errigal! Feoras! God, it's good to see you! But you're so thin! And where's–" he broke off, seeing Koen's eyes darken at the unspoken question.

"Bad luck," the man said softly, closing his eyes. Shaking himself slightly, he opened his eyes, which fell on June's cloaked form. "Who is this, though?" he asked.

June glanced at Koen, ready to follow his lead.

"A friend, Onic," he said. Onic's eyes narrowed slightly in suspicion, but he nodded and turned, beckoning them to follow.

"We've got a temporary camp set up," he said as they followed him, "until we find somewhere to settle. Trouble is finding someplace with soil rich enough to farm, but poor enough the Andrians won't want it. Not like the last land we had was so great, though."

Errigal groaned. "I have nightmares about plowing the east field," he said, laughing. "You could turn that ground a hundred times a year, and still come up with rocks the size of your head every time. Even when we were children, our father used to make us follow the plow and pick up all the rocks. God, I hated that!"

"When did the attack come?" Koen asked, and Onic turned to look at him. "Yesterday," he said. "We had about half a day's warning, though, so we were able to get a decent amount of supplies out. We wondered, actually, whether it had anything to do with you, whether you'd failed in the quest or something. What did you do with the Andrian bitch, anyway? Dumped her off a cliff, I hope," he said, chuckling to himself. June again glanced up at Koen, whose teeth were clenched–Errigal and Feoras maintained an uncomfortable silence behind them.

Ahead, the trees parted to reveal a number of large, chimney-like stone formations, the tallest of these being perhaps fifteen feet. The Valforte had set up camp among the bases of these. There were perhaps forty men, women, and children, sitting around cookfires, popping in and out of small tents or shaky shelters of pine boughs. As Onic led them forward, some of the Valforte looked up, and their eyes widened in amazement and delight.

Out of nowhere, two blonde streaks flashed by June, and Mara and Sara threw themselves on their husbands, squealing in delight. June watched misty-eyed as they broke apart, feasting on the sight of each other's faces and chattering excitedly. Soon, a large group of Valforte had gathered, pressing in close and asking excited questions. June's heart began to pound, standing off to the side and out of the way. What would they do when they found out who she was?

A middle-aged woman and man, the woman dark-haired, the father with lighter hair like Koen's, pushed through the crowd to embrace him.

"My son," the woman said softly, lovingly, and June felt as though she'd just been doused in ice water. Koen's mother and father? All this, and she had to meet the parents, too? Just as she was seriously considering slipping back off into the forest, Koen's mother turned her eyes to June.

"Who is this?" she asked, and Koen pulled himself upright, and walked over to June. Gently, he pushed the blanket off her head, then came to stand beside her, arm around her waist, in a protective, but possessive, gesture.

"This is June," he announced, "also known as Princess Ulfhilda." He smiled warmly at the crowd, but defiance shone in his eyes, almost daring someone to speak against her.

The silence was deafening. Onic looked as though he'd swallowed a chipmunk, and Mara and Sara's wide eyes darted between Errigal and Feoras to June and back again. Koen's mother tried to hide her shock, but her son's arm around an Andrian woman's waist seemed to be overwhelming her. June merely concentrated on smiling, and not puking.

Finally, Koen's father, eyes veiled, bowed deeply. "Your Highness," he said, and the others followed his lead. June stiffened.

"Please don't," she said. "You don't have to do that. Just call me June."

Koen's father nodded. "June, then," he said, but the veil behind his eyes lifted. June already felt closer to him than any of these other strangers—his was Koen's face, weathered and shaped by time, but familiar.

Beside her, June felt Koen let out a deep breath he'd apparently been holding. *Ha ha, not so calm and collected as you looked, huh?* she thought, smiling wryly up at him.

"Well," said Koen's mother, finally. "This is cause for celebration, your homecoming! Let's get you some food." The crowd dispersed, all but two women, one the age of Koen's mother, and the other a bit younger than June, and beautiful, with dark eyes and raven's wing hair. Both looked anxiously around, as though searching for someone. Koen looked at them and swallowed hard.

"Wait here," he said, and walked slowly over to the two, like a child approaching a spanking.

June watched as Koen spoke softly to them, and saw the young woman's face crumple into an expression of utmost sorrow. The older woman took the younger to her breast and held her as she sobbed, face hard and nearly expressionless. This was a woman who had known pain. *Yeah, well, takes one to know one,* June thought, at the same time hoping she'd never get *that* hard.

A soft touch on her shoulder made June whirl around in surprise. At the same time, she realized tears had been running down her own face, and she hastily swiped at her cheeks.

It was Koen's mother, who seemed taken aback at June's tears, but quickly recovered her composure. "Will you come to our fire...June? You must be tired, and thirsty."

June glanced over her shoulder at Koen—it seemed as though he'd be a while yet, and the camp was small, he'd have no trouble finding them. And Errigal and Feoras had already disappeared.

"I'd love to, thank you," she said, and followed the older woman down a small pathway between the neat rows of tents, stopping at one, where Koen's father sat on an animal skin on the ground next to their cookfire.

He got to his feet as June approached, waiting to sit again until she'd been seated on opposite side of the fire. She smiled as confidently as she could manage, and he returned the smile, with a bit of wry amusement at (June thought) her attempt at nonchalance. Yup, she knew this face, all right.

Koen's mother poured June a cup of tea from the kettle hanging over the fire, and she accepted gratefully, inhaling the steam.

"Mmm, thank you," she said. "It's been so long since we've had real tea. Months, probably."

"What have you been drinking, then?" Koen's mother asked.

"Something Errigal gathered in the woods—it's better than nothing, but it's not the same."

"Lut weed?" Koen's mother shook her head. "Poor things. You're all so thin, too," she said, eyeing June, who laughed.

"I know," she said. "I haven't weighed this little since I was a kid." June took a careful sip of the tea, closing her eyes in bliss at the bitter, but *real*, taste.

"Koen told me he had sisters," June said, after a few moments of silence. "Are they here?"

"No, all grown and married, living in other villages," Koen's father said, his eyes softening as his gaze seemed to turn inward. It was obvious this family loved each other deeply, which reminded June of her family.

Koen's mother sat beside his father, watching June closely.

"Is Minogan—was he killed?" she asked finally. June sighed, wrapping her hands tightly around the cup for the warmth.

"About a week ago," she said, briefly meeting Koen's parents' eyes. "We were attacked by the Eid Gomen." June looked into her cup, unable to think of anything else to say.

"Koen must have been devastated," his mother whispered, her eyes filled with tears.

June nodded, still looking into her cup, suddenly remembering Minogan would have been this woman's nephew.

"He was," she said. "We all were, but him especially." Koen saved them from more awkward silences by arriving and sitting next to June, looking a bit grey and drawn. Their eyes met for a moment, and Koen reached over and squeezed June's hand reassuringly. *I'm okay.*

Koen's mother beamed as her son joined them. "Tea?" she asked, jumping up, and without waiting for a response, poured a cup and handed it across the fire to Koen, who took it, smiling.

Just then, another man, around Koen's father's age, approached. At first, he stared at June, seeming to lose his train of thought, then he snapped out of it and turned to the Valforte.

"We're planning a dance tonight, in honor of our travelers' return," he said. "At moonrise."

"Over the hill?" Koen's father asked, and the man nodded. "We'll be there." With a final glance at June, the man walked to the next campfire, presumably to inform them.

"Hungry?" Koen's mother asked, and pulled a loaf of bread from a basket nearby and began slicing it. As she handed them each plates with two slices of bread and a small puddle of honey on the side, June had to restrain herself from stuffing both pieces in her mouth at once, and Koen appeared to be having the same difficulties.

"Thank you so much," said June, speaking quickly so she could hurry and eat the bread. "We haven't had bread, either, since—"

"Lumia," Koen said thickly, through a mouthful of bread. June reached out and wiped a droplet of honey from the corner of his mouth, shaking her head in mock disapproval. Turning back, she noticed Koen's father had been watching this byplay with great interest–and, possibly, growing approval.

"Are you home for good?" he asked.

Koen shook his head, swallowing the last piece of his bread. "No, the next part of our journey took us by here, so we thought we'd stop home and see everyone." He shook his head. "Didn't expect what we found, though."

"Homes can be rebuilt. We're just thankful we all made it."

It occurred to June that Koen and his parents might need a little time to catch up in private. Leaning over to Koen's mother confidentially, she asked, "Is there an area the women use for..."

"Ah," she said, pointing. "Just behind the large rock there is a clump of trees. That's the women's area." Thanking her, June stood up, squeezed Koen's shoulder, and walked off.

Finished with her business, she stepped out of the bushes and encountered one of the twins' wives. She smiled shyly at June, as though she'd like to say something, but didn't know what.

"Are you Mara or Sara?" June asked, and she giggled, tossing her blonde hair back.

"Sara," she said, "married to Errigal. Are you coming to the dance tonight?"

"As far as I know," June said, and Sara smiled.

"We haven't had a dance in forever," she said, "and we certainly weren't expecting to have one here." Her smile faltered a bit, but she quickly recovered. "You'll love it. We tell stories, and sing, and obviously dance," she said, blushing blue. "And the food!"

"You have me with the food," June said, and Sara laughed, a pleasant tinkling sound.

"We'll have you fat as anything before we let you go again, don't worry." She looked over her shoulder, then at the bushes again. "Well, I have a lot to do before tonight. I'll see you there!" June waved and made her way back to the camp.

June had a hard time finding the right campsite again; twilight had almost faded, and all the faces looked strange in the firelight. June finally spotted Koen, bent forward, talking to his parents, who looked very serious. A few feet away, she faked a small coughing fit to alert them to her presence, and they all straightened up and smiled at her.

A few hours of small talk and furious cooking by Necia, Koen's mother, and they made their way over a hill alongside the camp into a wide, flat field. A large area in the middle had the grass pulled up by the roots, and in the center burned a huge bonfire, around which most of the Valforte had already congregated.

It was chaos, warm, wonderful, friendly chaos–at least for the Valforte. June got a bit of the cold shoulder, but she understood; she'd been half-expecting to be stoned to death, so being ignored wasn't too disappointing. As Koen was squired away, with an apologetic glance over his shoulder, June waved to him with a reassuring smile and sat on the ground in an unoccupied area near the fire.

To her surprise, however, a young man came and sat beside her with two cups of steaming liquid, and handed one to her.

"I'm Lartel," he said, smiling. "Welcome to our makeshift home."

"June," she said, nodding to him, since shaking hands wasn't the custom here. "As I'm sure you already knew." Lartel smiled and nodded vigorously, while June investigated the beverage he'd brought her; a kind of hot wine, with a sharp, bitter taste. She didn't really like it, but took a large gulp anyway, to be polite, and to try to warm up in the cool night air.

"Quite an adventure you've had, I hear," he said.

June nodded, taking another sip of her drink. "That's an understatement," she said, and he laughed.

"Perhaps you'll regale us with the story tonight."

June smiled and shrugged. "I'm not really sure," she said. "I've never been to one of these before, so I don't know what the custom is."

"Oh, I'm sure everyone will want to know all about you," Lartel said. "I know I'm interested to hear the story."

"Well, maybe you'll get the chance, then," June said, forcing herself to take the last sip of the wine (thank God it was a small cup!) and setting it beside her on the ground. Just then, Koen appeared, looking down at her and smiling, face flushed dark with excitement.

"They're about to start," he said, helping her up from the ground. "We'll sit over there with Errigal and Feoras, if that's okay."

"Sure," she said, smiling at him, happy and confident in his element. She looked over at Lartel, who had also gotten up.

"It was very nice to meet you, Lartel," she said, and he nodded as Koen took her arm and led her away.

"Is that water or something?" she asked, once they were clear of Lartel, pointing to a cup in his other hand. "It's not that hot wine stuff, is it?"

Koen looked at her curiously. "No, it's mead," he said. "Why, do you want some?"

"Just a sip." June took at mouthful and handed the cup back, swishing her mouth before swallowing. "God, Lartel gave me that wine, and I just couldn't get the taste out of my mouth. Thanks."

"You mean you had ryn?" he asked, and June shrugged.

"I don't know," she said. "Whatever it was, it was gross." Koen raised his eyebrows in surprise, but said nothing further.

They sat down on a log with Errigal and Feoras and their wives. Sara (or at least she assumed it was Sara) gave her a warm smile as she sat down, which June returned.

Apparently, they were the guests of honor, even though everyone but June lived here, since as soon as they sat down, they received heaping plates, full of the choicest bits of meat, bread, fruit, and vegetables. All four of the travelers looked at each other with huge grins before digging in–this was more food than they usually ate in a week.

When they'd finished, Koen groaned and leaned back, setting his plate down between his feet.

"I don't understand it," he said. "I could have had three plates full of that before. Now I spend all my time starving to death, and when I finally get to eat, I can't even stuff myself properly."

June, also very full, stacked her plate on top of Koen's, sucking meat juices off her fingers.

"Your stomach shrinks, when you starve," she said, and Koen looked at her skeptically.

"Really?" he asked.

"Really, it's a proven fact. Doctors where I come from like to cut dead people up and prove this stuff to themselves."

Koen looked disgusted. "If you say so," he said, and June laughed, turning to look into the fire.

Suddenly, music struck up behind her, making her jump. She turned to see the musicians, who she'd overlooked before, playing a mix of different sized skin drums, and a few wind instruments that brought to mind piccolos and pan pipes.

Everyone got up to dance, even the children, in the space around the fire, their dancing a mix between Irish folk and some sort of strange wild polka. Errigal and Feoras led their wives out, and Koen turned to her.

"Do you want to dance?" he asked, and June looked past him at the exuberant dancers.

"Um, I think I'll just watch for now, thanks."

"Do you mind if I..." June shook her head.

"You go right ahead, Koen," she said, smiling. "You wait around for me, you'll be waiting all night." He kissed her swiftly on the mouth, and with that, he was gone, lost in the swirl of bodies dancing with abandonment around the fire.

June watched them contentedly, happy just to watch people being happy, when she noticed a little girl, maybe around six, staring at her solemnly.

"Hi there," June said. "What's your name?"

"Anke," said the little girl.

"That's a very pretty name," June said. "Why aren't you dancing?"

"My foot," said Anke, pointing down at her right leg, sticking out from under her dress, and June barely restrained herself from gasping. The little girl's foot was twisted and misshapen, so she had to walk on the side of it, rather than flat, like a normal person.

"I see," said June, trying to keep her face blank. "Would you like to sit with me and watch the dance?" Anke nodded and climbed up on the log next to June. She didn't watch the dancers, though, merely continued to stare at June.

June, who didn't have too much experience with small children and wasn't sure what to do, pretended to watch the dancing, while keeping a subtle eye on Anke.

Finally, the little girl reached out and touched June's arm lightly with her finger. "You're brown," she said, and June smiled.

"Yeah, I guess I am," she said, looking down at her skin.

"Papa said that the dark people like you are bad. They're the ones that burned our house down."

June bit her lip and sighed. "Your papa's right, kind of," she said. "People who look like me do bad things sometimes."

"Why?"

"Well... " *Good lord, here we go,* June thought. "Probably because they're scared of you."

"But we didn't do anything to them!"

"I know, sweetie," June said. "But people think really silly things sometimes, and they just get sillier if no one proves them wrong. I'll tell you a secret, though," June said, and Anke leaned in, eyes wide, enchanted as any child at the idea of a secret.

"What?" she whispered.

"I'm going to be a queen, hopefully soon," June said, "and I'm going to try and make my people be nice to your people, and stop burning their houses down. Maybe everyone will be friends, even."

Anke's face broke into a big smile. "I hope so," she said. "I miss my bed."

June heard a shuffling noise behind her, and turned to find Lartel standing a few feet away, staring at her with a strange expression on his face, half fearful, half...regret? She smiled uncertainly at him, but just then Koen came running up, laughing and out of breath.

"You sat over here long enough," he said. "Come on, let's dance."

June rolled her eyes. "Koen, please, I—whoops!" Koen had grabbed her arms and pulled her into the churning mass of bodies. June tried in vain to follow the steps, but only succeeded in looking like an octopus having a seizure. She laughed till her sides hurt, though, something she hadn't done in a long time.

Finally, the music died down, and people returned to their seats, chattering animatedly. June flopped gratefully down on the log, and Koen fell down beside her. "You know something?" he asked.

"What's that?" June panted, kneading a stitch in her side with the ball of her thumb.

"You're a horrible dancer," he said, grinning evilly, and June punched him in the shoulder as he cackled. Her witty comeback was diverted, however, by Koen's father, who stood between them and the fire, addressing the crowd.

"As you all know, usually, we have a number of different storytellers regale us at these events. Tonight, however, we thought it would be appropriate—and interesting—if our esteemed guest the Princess would tell us the tale of her return to Prendawr, and subsequent adventures." The crowd applauded politely, and Koen's father bowed to June. She looked wildly at Koen, who nudged her firmly toward the fire.

"Go ahead, you'll be fine," he said, and suddenly she was staring at around a hundred blue faces, all staring expectantly back at her. Some of the faces smiled encouragingly, some stared with disapproval or even hate, but everyone obviously wanted the story.

So June cleared her throat, and told it.

Her audience was captivated from the first, her kidnap from the world she'd grown up on, seeing her true face for the first time, and learning of her weighty destiny as sorceress and princess. And if she'd been paying attention, she'd have noticed after her description of the discovery of Halryan's deception at Lumia, most of the faces which had been hardened toward her began to soften, and sympathy shone from many eyes. Her recount of the dragon ride brought wonder, her experience in the Eid Gomen fortress, compassion. And most were in tears as she told of Minogan's dramatic death on the beach.

June, however, had difficulty telling the story. As she began, she started to feel a bit off in her stomach, but put it off to so much rich food after hardly anything at all over the last few weeks. As she continued, however, she began to feel a slight tingling sensation in her fingers and toes, which intensified into numbness and swept slowly inward, up her arms and legs. By the time she finished her story, and accepted the congratulations and thanks of those who had listened, both arms and legs were numb, and she'd lost feeling in her torso as well.

June stumbled away from the crowd, smiling and nodding her thanks to everyone, trying to get away from the people. She knew she was going to collapse, but more than anything, she didn't want to make a scene.

Finally, moving her deadened arms and legs with a supreme effort, she found a quiet spot outside the firelight and sat down heavily, trying not to panic, to calm her mind and heal herself, as she'd done with numerous cuts and scratches along the way. Try as she might, though, the numbness kept advancing, and now tiny red spots flashed before her eyes.

Then Koen was crouching in front of her. "Good job on the story, June," he said enthusiastically. "If they weren't on your side before, they sure are now." He paused, pulling back to look at her. "What's wrong?"

"I think I'm sick," June said, maneuvering her numb tongue and lips with difficulty. Koen's face immediately darkened with concern.

"What's the matter?" he asked. "Was it the food?"

With gargantuan effort, June shook her head, but couldn't answer him, only managing to stay upright by some miracle of muscle memory. She had a high-pitched ringing in her ears now, gaining in volume and threatening to drown out all sound. Koen reached out and grasped her hand, and his eyes widened in shock.

"You're freezing," he said. Then his eyes widened still further, and he licked his lips. "Oh, God, June," he said. "The wine, the ryn that Lartel gave you? Was it bitter? June, was it bitter?"

June had lost her battle, though—the red spots now completely obscured her vision with a flashing scarlet screen, and the roaring in her ears now sounded like a jet engine. She was barely aware of slumping over into Koen's arms, of his frantic yells for help, or of her final quiet slip into the black.

~18~

June opened her eyes, and immediately closed them again, wincing as the light hit her retinas, causing a sharp pain to worsen what was already the worst headache she'd ever had. Slowly, trying not to move her head, she reached up and felt her forehead, and the back of her skull. No physical explanation presented itself–her head wasn't swollen or misshapen, and she couldn't find any gaping holes.

Slowly, she opened her eyes again, raising her lids a little at a time to acclimate to the light. She lay on a small cot, inside a tiny tent, really nothing more than a few hides stitched together and thrown over some sticks. June tried to recall how she'd gotten here, but the last thing she remembered was arriving at the Valforte dance last night. June groaned as a thought hit her. *Please, God, tell me this is not a hangover, and please tell me I did not make an ass of myself in front of Koen's family and friends.*

Speaking of Koen–turning her head, she found him, curled up asleep on the floor beside her cot. Something about this struck her as odd, but seeing him comforted her, and she actually forget her headache (for a very, very short moment) as she watched him sleep. Gently, she reached out and brushed his shoulder with her fingertips.

He leapt up as though she'd electrocuted him, and June pulled back, jostling her head and causing fresh, nauseatingly sharp pains to shoot up inside her brain and dance merrily. He whirled around, trying to see who had wakened him, completely disoriented. Then his gaze landed on June, and his face paled alarmingly.

"My God," he said, dropping to his knees beside her and pulling her hand to his chest, looking at her as though she was the Second Coming. "My God."

June had a great deal of difficulty trying to figure out what was going on while also trying to tame the lion sharpening its claws on the inside of her skull.

"Say something," Koen whispered, and June smiled, nonplused.

"Um, she sells sea shells by the sea shore?"

Koen abruptly released her hand and leaned over, grasping her right foot. "Can you feel my hand?" he asked.

"Yes," said June, not wanting to nod her head.

"Move your foot," he said, and she wiggled her toes in his hand.

He let go of the right foot and grabbed the left. "This one?" he asked, and she moved the toes on that foot, too. "You can feel all the parts of your body?"

"Koen, tell me what the hell is going on," June snapped, finally losing patience. Her head throbbed from the volume of her voice echoing within, and from restraining unexpected tears. Koen leaned over, gently kissing her forehead, and taking her hand again.

"I'm sorry," he said. "It's just—okay, what do you remember?"

"Apparently not the important stuff," she said petulantly.

"Do you remember taking a cup of something from Lartel?" Koen asked, and a fuzzy memory swirled to the surface.

"I think s—yeah, yeah, I do," June said.

"Well, in that cup was a very large amount of a poison we call crebul," Koen said, and June's eyes widened in shock.

"He *poisoned* me?" she asked, pausing just long enough to be thankful she hadn't gotten drunk and done something stupid. "Why?"

"Same reason as Minogan, we think," Koen said, "although Lartel wasn't aware of the reason for the quest, so he wouldn't know that killing you beforehand would be a really stupid idea. Or killing you at all, for that matter."

June paused, letting all this information sink in. "You said, you think," she asked finally. "Where is he now?"

"Dead," said Koen, looking grimly satisfied, and June's eyes widened still further, this time in horror.

"You didn't," she said, scandalized. "Koen, tell me you—"

"I didn't," he said, looking mildly regretful. "Only because the bastard beat me to the job."

"Beat you to...he killed himself?"

"Yeah," Koen said. "Left a short note, saying he'd just destroyed his people's only chance at survival, couldn't stand the guilt, and then took the same poison he'd given you."

"And he died, when he took the poison?"

Koen looked up at the roof of the tent, shaking his head.

"*Anyone* would have died if they'd taken that poison," he said, looking back down at her. "Anyone but you."

June made a small scoffing noise. "He probably just didn't give me enough, Koen," she said, and he actually laughed out loud.

"Are you starting to remember things now?" he asked, and she nodded. "Remember how, right after you drank the poison, you had a sip from my cup to rinse your mouth? That was one of the ways I realized what had happened. Just from that little, tiny bit that was still on your lips, and stayed on the cup, my fingers and toes went all tingly. I thought it was from dancing, then sitting down by the fire, but when I saw you, I realized what happened."

He smiled ruefully. "See, it's a poison we use occasionally, when we have predators after our livestock. But because it's so dangerous, when we're children, they give us a watered-down drop, so we can recognize the taste of it instantly, just in case. Lartel knew you'd probably never had ryn before, so he thought you'd just think that was how the drink tasted. And he was right."

"How much did he give me?" June asked, and Koen's eyes changed slightly.

"We found the cup," he said, softly. "Far as we could tell from the odor, it was half ryn, half crebul."

And just a little drop had messed Koen up. "Half a cup?" June said, shocked, and Koen nodded. "Well, then, how—how am I alive?"

Koen closed his eyes and pressed his lips to June's knuckles. He stayed like this a while before answering.

"We didn't think you *were* going to live," he said, finally. "All this happened three days ago."

"*What?*" Even as her exclamation of disbelief came out, she saw the truth in his face for the first time. He looked haggard and unshaven, *very* unlike him—he'd always been meticulous about his personal habits and cleanliness. But here was a man who had eaten little, slept less, and worried constantly for three straight days.

"There was a time when—" Koen swallowed hard and turned his head away, "when we thought you were—gone. The healer kept saying that even if you lived, you might never wake up again, or be able to walk or move, or that you might not be able to—think, anymore."

"Oh, Koen." June forgot her own pain as she imagined what he'd been through in the past few days. What she would have gone through, if he'd been lying in this bed, and she'd been pacing anxiously beside it.

Just then, the tent flap was pushed aside, and Necia walked in, carrying a tray with a cup of tea, some bread and meat on a plate, and a bowl of broth. She froze as she saw June, nearly dropping the tray.

"You're alive," Necia said, face pale.

"That's the general consensus," June said, smiling. Necia laid down the tray just inside the tent. "I'll go get another cup of tea, then," she said, looking poleaxed, backing out of the tent.

Koen still stared at June as though unable to convince himself of her reality. June reached up with one hand and brushed the hair off his forehead, then took the back of his neck and pulled him down to her. He offered no resistance, but slid his arms under her, wrapping her in an embrace that nearly took her breath away and pushed his face against her skin, where her neck met her shoulder.

"A few months ago, I never even knew you existed," he said, his voice muffled against her skin. "Why is it that now I can't even bear the thought of living without you?"

June couldn't think of anything to say, merely pulled him tighter to her and breathed deeply of his comforting scent, feeling the tension in his body slowly melt away.

Necia re-entered the tent, and Koen pulled away, rubbing his hands briskly over his face. When he looked at June again, his eyes were slightly red, and she smiled sympathetically.

"Go get some sleep," she said, squeezing his hand.

"No, no, I can just sleep here on the floor, it's okay."

"No, it's not okay," June said, her voice firming up. "Go sleep someplace where you're not going to wake up every time I scratch my nose. You're exhausted, you've been through hell, and you need some real rest." Koen opened his mouth to protest, but June cut him off.

"I'm not going anywhere," she said, whispering. "I promise."

Koen closed his eyes and breathed deeply, then nodded. He bent over and kissed her. "I'll see you later," he said reluctantly.

June nodded, and he turned and stepped out of the tent.

Necia still stood by the door, looking at June as though she'd suddenly turned into a platypus. June pulled her blanket back and slowly pushed herself up into a sitting position, amazed at how weak she was. Necia pulled herself from her reverie and rushed over to help June sit Indian style on the cot, then brought the tray and set it down beside her, taking a seat on a stool beside the cot.

"I don't think you should have the meat, all you've had in the past few days is broth, but we'll try you on the bread and the tea," she said, and June agreed enthusiastically, her headache having receded, and the lion having now taken up residence in her stomach.

June couldn't eat much, though, since her stomach had shrunk even more as the result of a liquid diet, and for the most part she just sat and sipped her tea. Necia looked at her with a peculiar expression, and June cocked her head to the side inquiringly.

"I'm sorry for what happened here," Necia said finally. "That– that's not the impression we wanted you to have."

June nodded. "I'm not mad. I just wish Lartel would have thought things through. I mean, did he honestly think Koen would be with me if I was like the Andrians who burned your village?"

Necia sighed, and a small rueful smile touched her lips. "To be honest, we didn't have the slightest idea what was going on when you arrived, and Koen..." she trailed off, shaking her head at the memory. "I really thought he'd lost his mind. An *Andrian...*"

"I can't blame you," June said, shaking her head.

"Koen's father said we should wait, though, that maybe there was more to the picture than we were seeing." Necia smiled. "And he was right. Unfortunately, word didn't get around quickly enough."

"Apparently," said June, carefully bending over to set her cup on the ground, then lowering herself back down on the cot, keeping herself propped up on one elbow to listen to Necia. Just a few minutes of sitting up to talk and eat had exhausted her. God, when would she be able to get back on the road to continue the quest?

"So, everybody hated me when I got here?"

Necia nodded. "I think we all had an unfair image of you in our minds, some spoiled little royal who needed escorting around her empire for who knew what reason. I actually had a picture in my mind of my son at a corner of your litter, and some Andrian walking alongside, cracking his whip."

They both laughed at this, although June had a very pleasant, but fleeting mental image of Koen in a loincloth, muscles straining from the weight of the litter, skin glistening with sweat. *And you're, what, an hour out of a coma, practically? Good God, woman,* she thought, trying to restrain herself from blushing in front of Necia, considering it was her son June was having improper thoughts about.

"Did you say you didn't know why we were on the quest?" June said suddenly, replaying Necia's words in her head to distract herself.

"Oh, I would have thought Koen told you," Necia said, slightly surprised. "One of the conditions of the quest was that none of them reveal the reason for it. It was explained that you were the princess, but that was all anyone knew."

"Hmm," June said. "Well, that explains why Lartel poisoned me, then." Necia looked at her curiously, and June leaned over toward her, lowering her voice confidentially.

"I don't want to start a panic or anything, so keep this between you and your husband, but...if we don't complete this quest, the Eid Gomen will destroy the world. Or, rather, we're trying to repair the damage they've already done, that's going to cause the world to end."

Necia's face paled, and she swallowed hard. "So, if he had succeeded on killing you..."

"He would have destroyed everything," June finished for her. Necia looked at June with a touch of awe.

"Your life is complicated, isn't it?" she asked. June laughed so hard her elbow slipped and her head landed with a *flump* on the pillow.

"You could say that," she said, gasping for breath, wiping at the tears streaming down her cheeks. "You could definitely say that."

Someone suddenly spoke outside the tent, making June jump. "May I enter?" said the male voice.

"Yes, please," Necia said. "This is the healer, Yabcis," she said in a low voice to June, as a white-bearded man, skin pale blue and wrinkled, pushed aside the tent flap and stepped inside. He froze as he caught sight of June.

"If I hadn't seen it, I'd never believe it," he whispered, eyes wide. Necia had vacated the stool and stood respectfully off to the side, but the man ignored the stool and knelt beside the cot, amazingly agile for such an old-looking man. He peered intently into her eyes, and took one of her hands in his cool, dry ones. "May I examine you?" Yabcis asked, and June nodded.

He proceeded to squeeze her fingers one at a time, making sure she had feeling in each of them, then her toes. He asked her to solve several simple math problems, then stood at the other end of the tent and held up combinations of fingers to check her eyesight. Finally, he and Necia helped her out of bed and made her walk up and down the center of the small tent twice. Her legs shook, but they went where she told them to.

After the surprisingly thorough and precise examination, she was pronounced healthy, but in need of rest and food.

"When will I be able to leave?" June asked laying back down.

"Two weeks," Yabcis said, and June sat straight up again.

"Two *weeks*?" she exclaimed, and Yabcis hurriedly tried to make her lay back down. "You don't understand, we can't spare two weeks," she said. "Maybe one, of which I've already slept away three days, but definitely not two weeks from today!"

"If you wish to regain your full strength, you must not travel for the full two weeks," Yabcis replied firmly. "I will return tomorrow, to check your progress. Good day."

June flopped back on her pillow with an aggravated groan, then turned to look at Necia, who glanced uncomfortably between the flap through which the healer had just left and June. June shook her head at her. "We can't afford two weeks, Necia."

Necia cocked her head. "I think you're going to have to, my dear. Yabcis is old, but he's not to be trifled with. And the way Koen dotes on you, I doubt he's going to go against the healer's advice."

"Nobody has to tell him," June began, just as the sounds of Koen and Yabcis conversing outside the tent reached them. Necia chuckled as June made an aggravated growling noise in the back of her throat.

"I hope that cot is comfortable, June," she said, turning to leave. "Looks like you're going to be there for a while."

June woke up slowly, pleasantly, to the sound of laughter outside the tent. Opening her eyes, she found the tent empty, but Koen's voice, sounding happy and relaxed, was easily recognizable coming from outside.

She slowly got to her feet, noting happily her legs were already stronger and steadier than they had been the previous day. Unable to find her clothes, she wrapped the blanket over her nightgown for modesty, and smoothing her hair, walked outside.

The sun was bright enough to make her blink, but pleasantly warm and healthy-feeling. Koen, his parents, and Errigal and Feoras, both with their wives, sat outside the tent. As soon as Koen spotted her he leapt to his feet.

"Hey," he said with a smile, "you shouldn't be out of bed."

"I'm fine, really. Besides, sunlight is good for sick people. Even though I'm not sick anymore." Koen led her by the arm to an animal skin beside the fire and pushed his own cup of tea into her hands.

"Hungry?" he asked her.

"Starved," she said, and her stomach gave a convincing roar. They all laughed as Koen's mother handed her a plate of bread and cheese, which June fell upon, sighing with pleasure between bites.

Koen watched her eat, amused. "Easy, now, we just got you better, don't choke to death."

June was tempted to ask him if he wanted some 'seefood', but with his parents there, she decided she'd better not.

Full to the brim, she forced a few more mouthfuls down, just because it tasted good, and set the plate down with a barely stifled belch. Almost immediately, she began to feel the effects of her full belly; a wave of pleasant sleepiness washed over her, and her eyes began to droop.

Koen chuckled softly. "Okay, time to go back to bed, I think."

June shook her head and tried to act alert, difficult because she couldn't seem to get her eyes to focus on his face. "No, no, I'm fine, really."

"No, no, you're not, really." He got to his feet and hauled her up by her armpits, ignoring her whine of protest. With a weak wave to everyone, she was led back inside the tent and back onto her cot.

"I can't stay in here forever," she moaned. "I'm all *antsy.* I want to get *up*..."

Koen laughed as he arranged the blanket over her. "You are a horrible sick person," he said. "The longer you fight it, the longer you're going to stay sick. So lay down, for heaven's sake, and do what your body tells you to. Go to *sleep*." He kissed her on the forehead and gave her a long, warm look which caused a tingling sensation in certain areas of her anatomy.

"Koen?"

"Yes?"

June shot a look at the tent opening and dropped her voice. "Do you think you could come back later tonight? When everyone's asleep?"

Koen looked at her with a mingled look of astonishment and merriment. "You cannot be serious," he said. "You can't even sit up for five minutes!"

"I don't have to *sit up*," June said, mixing her best little-lost-puppy and come-and-get-me-big-boy looks to what appeared to be great effect. Koen actually had to shake himself bodily to pull his eyes away from hers.

"No, no way," he said, smiling. "Get some sleep." He turned toward the tent flap.

"Kooo-eeeen," June whined, and he turned to look at her again. "Please," she said, making her eyes as big as she could. "I just–I need to be close to you."

Koen took a deep bracing breath through his nose, flaring his nostrils as he struggled with himself. "We'll see," he said softly, then turned and left the tent.

Satisfied, June closed her eyes and slept.

Several hours later, June woke up in darkness, the sound of soft breathing coming from the foot of the bed. June sat up and groped in that direction, her hand landing on a knee. Her hand was grasped by another and squeezed tightly.

"Hey," said June.

"Hey," Koen answered quietly.

"Why didn't you wake me?"

"You were snoring so peacefully, I just couldn't bring myself to do it," he said, a smile in his voice. June smacked him on the leg with her other hand, then leaned backward, pulling on his hand.

"You're cold," she said. "Come in here and warm up."

Love tonight was everything June needed it to be, soft and sweet and honest and gentle, warm and close and reassuring. Her fatigue lent a pleasant dreamlike quality to every sensation and lowered her self-awareness, allowing her to give over completely to Koen. It amazed her to think they'd been together for such a short time– already, she knew every inch of his body as well as her own, and he apparently had similar information regarding her own anatomy.

This is home, June thought later, nestled comfortably against his side, her head on his heart, swinging contentedly between awake and asleep, her fingers running absently over the rippled muscles of his abdomen. Koen himself breathed so deeply she thought he had fallen asleep until he spoke.

"You okay?" he whispered, and June giggled foolishly.

"Mmm-hmm," she said, pressing even closer to him (any closer and she'd be on the other side of him). He sighed and kissed the top of her head.

"You okay?" June whispered back, and he sighed again.

"Yeah," he said. "That was–needed." June nodded into his chest, feeling his breathing grow more uneven, and she turned her head toward his face.

"I had my hand on your chest," he said, finally. "You weren't breathing, and your heart was going like this." He tapped an irregular beat on her bare back with his fingers. "And then it stopped. And Yabcis stepped back and opened his mouth–I swear, he was going to say you were dead–and then all of a sudden you took this huge gasping breath, and your heart started going like you'd just sprinted a mile." June shuddered, the reality of what had happened hitting her afresh.

"It's over, though," she said, trying to sound strong, lacing her fingers into his hand, and squeezing. "I'm not going anywhere."

"What happens next time, though?" he asked. "When they get lucky, instead of us? Lartel wasn't the only person in this kingdom who wants you dead."

June sighed. "Not to sound corny," she said slowly, "but the key to this whole thing, I think, is to enjoy what you have, while you have it. If you spend all your time worrying that you're going to lose it, when you finally do lose it you realize that you wasted all your time being scared, rather than making the most of it."

"I can't help it," Koen said, his voice sounding thick all of a sudden. "You're my heart, June. I can't live without my heart."

She took a deep, shuddery breath before responding, a hot rush of tears pressing against her tightly closed lids. "Koen..." June gulped, trying to steady her voice. "Before I realized how I felt about you, all I could think about was how much I lost, or how much had been stolen from me. My whole life, just ripped right out of my hands. But when everything happened, the day that Halryan...well, all of a sudden, I could see how all of those horrible things had led me to you. I mean, I had to come clear across the universe for us to find each other. And now I have this feeling like, I'm home for the first time, with you. I just can't imagine that God would bring me so far, rearrange so much to bring us together, just to separate us again."

Koen sighed, lowering his mouth to hers. "I hope you're right," he said, as he set his head back on the pillow. "God, I hope you're right."

June would gladly have pushed herself to move on if left to her own devices. Here, with Koen's family and friends, she had a glimpse of the kind of normal life she could lead when all this was over. Yes, she'd probably be living in Prendawr City, but at least she'd have time to set down roots, rather than bouncing all over the kingdom looking for pieces of rock. And setting down roots with Koen was a very attractive idea.

But for now, she lay trapped in bed, completely surrounded by a number of increasingly overbearing mother hens, including Necia, Sara and Mara, Koen, and even little Anke, who brought her a corn dolly she'd made herself. Still, June had to grudgingly admit she felt better, her prominent bones receding inside a layer of healthy flesh and her mind sharpening with the loss of fatigue. And annoying as the clucking and fussing got sometimes, it was nice to be able to sit back and be taken care of completely.

So, after two weeks of constant care, feeding, and sleep, Yabcis declared June fit for travel once more. The looks on Sara and Mara's faces dampened June's excitement, and both women exited the tent quickly, along with the healer, which left Koen and June alone.

June sighed, twisting her dark hair absentmindedly into a coil at the back of her neck. Koen raised his eyebrows inquiringly. "What's the matter?" he asked, and she dropped the coil, letting her hair fall down her back.

"I'm wondering if we shouldn't just let Errigal and Feoras stay here," she said. "They're newlyweds, for heaven's sake. They should be here starting their families, not running around risking their lives."

Koen shook his head slowly as he looked at her.

"You have asked them, and me, at least half a dozen times I can think of if we want to leave the quest. And we have answered the same number of times that we do *not* want to leave the quest. They see helping you to power as an investment in the future of the Valforte. Yes, they want families, but they also want a safe future for their wives and their children."

"Still," June said, "should we ask them again? Maybe they feel differently, now that they're here with Mara and Sara. Maybe..." she trailed off as she saw Koen's gaze harden. "What?"

Koen shook his head, getting up from where he sat on the cot next to June. He came to stand in front of her, arms crossed.

"Stop trying to clear your conscience," he said.

June's mouth dropped open in shock. "Wha—I'm not—that's just..." she sputtered. He stared steadily at her, and it took a supreme effort not to drop her eyes. "That was rude," she said, hurt, unable to keep a slight waver from her voice.

"It's the truth." Koen backed up a step, running his hands through his hair. "You're trying to absolve yourself of responsibility for them, for us, and it's not going to work. You're going to have to get used to this. You are going to be the Queen, and the responsibility of every man, woman and child's life will be in *your* hands."

"How is that different from now?" June asked hotly. "Or did you forget the whole reason for the quest?"

"It is different," said Koen, grabbing the stool and dragging it between his legs so he could sit facing her, elbows on knees. "There's no choice involved in this. But when you're the Queen, every day you're going to make decisions that affect people's lives—and possibly end them. And you have to learn to accept that as a matter of course."

June looked at the tent wall over Koen's shoulder, mouth tight with anger. As a matter of fact, the thought had occurred to her already, many times; it woke her up in a cold sweat in the middle of the night. And she didn't like being reminded of it.

"We are vested in this," Koen continued, "all of us. And as much as you hate it, the time will come when people will have to lay down their lives for you...and you have to let them."

"Someone already did, in case you forgot," June spat.

Koen shook his head again, but more gently. "And you would have exchanged places with him, if you could," he said.

June stood up and turned her back on Koen, angrily fluffing the pillow on her cot and turning back the blanket.

"I'm going to bed," she said, reaching for her comb and her cup with the chewed teeth-twig.

"June..." Koen said from behind her, but she ignored him, continuing to angrily rearrange her things. He got up then, and put his arms around her from behind. She struggled briefly against his embrace, but she was still weak from her illness, and besides, her heart wasn't in it. She let her head fall back against his shoulder, and he lowered his lips to her cheek.

"I don't like saying this, and I like even less that it's true," he whispered. "But I need to know that your friendship with Errigal and Feoras, and your love for me," he swallowed hard, "isn't going to interfere with the quest. I need you to promise me that if I fall..."

"Oh, Koen, please don't do this to me," June said in a half whisper, half moan.

"If I fall," he continued, "or any of the others do, that you're not going to endanger the world on our behalf."

"That's not fair," June said, pulling away and turning to face him. "It's not fair. Everyone else gets to run around and save each other, and I just have to stand there like an idiot and watch you die? I already stood by and watched someone die for me, and I won't do it again!"

"I never said you got the easy part," Koen said, his eyes sad, "but it's the part you have to fulfill. You have to promise me—"

"I just told you I—"

"You have to promise me," he said firmly, over her protests, "or we can't continue like this."

June rocked back on her heels, shocked. "Are you giving me an ultimatum?" she asked, incredulous. "Are you *seriously* giving me an ultimatum?"

Koen shoved his hands in his pockets and avoided her eyes. "Yeah, I guess I am."

They stood for a moment in silence, Koen looking miserable, June trying to decide between crying and taking a swing at him.

"I love you more than there are trees in this world," he said, "and giving you up would probably kill me outright, but there are things bigger than us going on here, and nothing gives us the right to disregard the lives of thousands and thousands of people to indulge in our own selfish happiness."

A little selfish happiness would make a nice change, June

thought, as her eyes filled with tears which spilled over and ran down her cheeks and chin, making dark spots on the front of her simple brown cottony dress. She looked at Koen blackly.

"So I'm damned if I do and damned if I don't," she said, voice shaking with barely suppressed emotion. He said nothing, merely turned his head away.

"Well, you certainly have me backed into a cozy little corner, don't you," she continued. "Either I promise you that I'm going to let you die if that time comes, or I give up my own personal happiness with the knowledge that I can save your life, if the opportunity presents itself. Nice, Koen. Real freaking nice."

"I wouldn't do it if I didn't have to, you know that. And you know I'm right."

In a fit of temper, June kicked the stool that Koen had vacated, so it bounced off the wall of the tent and onto the ground, legs up in the air like a dead bug.

"Fine," she shouted, making Koen flinch. "Fine! Go ahead and die, you self-righteous bastard! Get killed by the Eid Gomen or the Andrians or whoever the hell else decides they want to kill us this week! I *promise* I'll stand by, meek as a mouse, and watch–" a sudden vision of Minogan's death filled her mind's eye, but it was Koen's face contorted in pain and terror, and Koen's sea-green eyes bulging as he struggled for breath. The wind went out of her like someone had kicked her in the stomach, and she sat down hard on the cot, covering her face with her hands. She felt the cot move as Koen sat down beside her quietly.

"June, I..." he began.

"I know," she snapped, then took a ragged breath. "I know," she said again, softly, miserably. "I know you're doing your best. I know this isn't your fault. I just–" she took her head out of her hands and tilted her head back, eyes closed. "I want to know when the universe is going to stop trying to take everything good away from me. I want to know when I can start living instead of just surviving. And I was stupid, relaxing now, thinking because I have you, everything's going to be all right. Because that's not true." June sniffled and kicked miserably at the floor, then pulled herself straight and wiped her face.

"We should get some sleep," she said. "We're starting pretty early tomorrow."

Koen looked at her suspiciously, and she shook her head.

"I can't deal with this anymore tonight. We talked, you got what you wanted–" Koen looked at her with an *oh-come-on* expression on his face, and she shrugged. "I need to go to sleep," she said.

Koen looked for a moment as though he wasn't going to leave, but something in June's expression must have changed his mind, for he leaned over and gave her a soft, lingering kiss goodnight, then disappeared through the tent opening without another word.

Sleep didn't come easy for June, nestled on her side in the blankets, staring blindly into the darkness. Over and over the argument with Koen replayed in her head, liberally punctuated with daymares in which he died in various messy, horror-show ways.

Her mind whirled, trying to figure out a way to protect her friends and Koen without breaking her promise. The protection spells at night, of course, and frequent 'reconnaissance checks' as she'd come to think of her out-of-body scouting patrols. But there wasn't anything else she could do.

Except leave on her own. Sneak out of the tent tonight and just go. She had the tablet pieces, could figure out how to get to the next temple, and she'd watched Errigal enough so she was sure she could find food for herself. And, when it was all over, come back here, and pray that Koen could forgive her. And even if he couldn't, she thought she'd rather live without him, knowing he was alive and safe, than live with his death—or the deaths of the others—on her conscience. Already, Minogan haunted her dreams, his presence vaguely accusatory, and his memory always in the back of her mind.

Flipping over on her back, June laughed a little. As if Koen wouldn't have her tracked down inside an hour. Unless—could she cover her tracks by magic?

With a groan of annoyance at her restless mind, she kicked the blanket off and sprang to her feet, smoothing her hair. God, she wanted a cigarette. All she could have, though, was a cup of tea, and she hoped there were enough coals left in the fire to boil water. Wrapping her blanket around her, she strode out the front of the tent.

Koen sat by the already-stoked fire, pouring boiling water into a cup. He didn't even seem surprised to see her, just handed her the cup he had poured and made himself another as June sat down.

"Can't sleep?" he asked, keeping his voice low so as not to disturb those in the tents around them. June shook her head, glancing briefly at him before returning her gaze to the fire.

"Me neither," he said, his eyes searching her face. "So what's keeping you up?" he asked, and June shrugged.

"Lots of stuff," she said, rubbing her thumb over a scratch in the horn cup.

"Like?"

June lowered her head, then raised it again to look Koen in the eyes. *Might as well be honest,* she thought. "Like taking off," she said. "Leaving you behind, finishing the quest on my own."

Rather than recoiling in shock, Koen nodded, his eyes steady on her own. "That doesn't surprise you, though," June half-questioned, half-stated.

Koen smiled ruefully and nodded. "Why do you think I'm here?" he asked, and June raised her eyebrows. "I expected you to come out packed and ready to go." He rubbed at his neck muscles with one hand, a thoughtful expression on his face as June watched him expectantly.

"Look," he said, setting his cup down on the ground and turning to face June. "I'm sorry if I'm coming off like I'm preaching to you, but even you have to admit that everything I've said is true–"

"Yes, Koen, it's true," June said, impatience creeping into her voice. "But turn the tables for a second. Now it's you who has to live, and me who has to protect you with my life, no matter what. Now the Eid Gomen are killing me, tearing me apart while I scream–but to step in would endanger your life." June paused for a moment to let this sink in before continuing.

"Now ask yourself," she said, leaning forward and locking his eyes like two battling deer would lock antlers, "Could you stand there and do nothing? Leave me to die and walk away, for the good of the 'noble cause'?"

Koen tried to hold her gaze, but June could almost see the images her words had conjured in his mind, and he had to tear his eyes away and look toward the fire once more.

"That's what you're asking me to promise," June said. "Do you think it's fair? To expect of me what you know damn well you couldn't do yourself?" Koen stared into the fire still, hands clenched tightly into fists, shaking his head almost imperceptibly. He inhaled sharply and turned back to June, his answer written plainly on his face.

June leaned forward and clasped his hands. "Hopefully, we'll never have to worry about this," she said. "But if something happens, if it comes to..." she trailed off, swallowing hard. "I'm going to have to use my own judgment, not stick to a promise that could end up killing you or Errigal or Feoras. I can't promise anything, other than I'll do my best to do the right thing."

Koen shrugged in surrender. "I guess that'll have to do."

~19~

They managed to catch a few hours sleep before waking an hour pre-dawn, and when they did wake up, they hit the ground running. The whole camp hummed with activity, everyone running around to make sure they had all the basics, new clothing, knapsacks, blankets, plenty of food, and new waterskins. They had so many supplies, June began to worry for the donkey, which she'd dubbed Elmer. Elmer was slowly disappearing under a growing mountain of sacks and rope, and his furry ears sagged in resignation. He perked up, however, when June slipped him a small piece of honeycomb.

Looking around at the tents and lean-tos, June couldn't help but wonder if the Valforte could afford to give all them all these supplies. They couldn't refuse, though, and she prayed they had plenty of food cached up somewhere else.

At last, after the supply list had been checked probably by every single man and woman in the village, they were ready to go. Koen, Errigal, and Feoras wove through the crowd, saying their farewells. June hung back, still unsure of her position with the Valforte, but a tug on her shirt made her look down to see Anke.

"Hey," said June, crouching down beside her. "Thanks for coming to say goodbye to me."

At this, Anke burst into tears, which caused June's stomach to spasm with guilt. "Oh, no," she said, pulling the little girl into her arms. "Don't cry, sweetie. I'll come back to visit, I promise. And you have to come visit me in the city, too." She held the little girl back from her slightly, wiping her tears with her sleeve. "See, here," June said, digging in her new satchel, which held the two tablet pieces, her personal care items, and the corn dolly Anke had given her. "Look," she said, pulling out the doll. "I carry this with me everywhere. I won't forget you, I promise."

Anke looked slightly mollified, and hiccupping, gave June one last hug before hurrying off to her father, who waited a few feet away. June and Anke's father met eyes, and he gave her a smile, which she returned.

"Good luck," he said, and led Anke away, leaving June to ponder the impression she'd made on the Valforte. Here was a man who had hated Andrians, with good reason, and yet brought his daughter to see her, and wished her luck.

Necia and Koen, Sr. walked up just then, and June stood up from where she'd been squatting on the ground.

"Good luck," Necia said, her eyes warm.

"Good luck," Koen's father echoed. "It's been a great pleasure meeting you."

"Likewise," June said, looking at them both. "And thank you, for everything. You've been...kinder than you should have, under the circumstances." Both Necia and Koen Sr. made gestures of dismissal, but June shook her head.

"You have," she said firmly. "I'm an Andrian, and–" June gestured at the neat rows of tents clustered around the base of the rock formations. "I didn't deserve your kindness."

Koen Sr. looked at her with a warm smile. "Take it on account, then," he said. "Fix this kingdom as it should have been long ago."

"Deal," June said, and Necia hugged her tightly, then moved off to the side as Mara and Sara approached, with brave faces.

"I appreciate the loan of your husbands," June said, attempting levity. Then, more seriously, "I swear, I'll do my best to bring them back to you intact."

"Take care of yourself, too," Mara said, and the three of them hugged, before the twin women ran off to their husbands once more, to more embraces and whispered assurances of the future.

A hand slipped around her waist.

"Ready?" Koen asked, unable to keep himself from glancing a little sadly at the crowd of his friends and relatives.

June nodded. "You?" she asked, and he returned the nod, as Errigal and Feoras gave their wives one last embrace and came to stand beside them.

"All set," Feoras said, a little thickly.

"Here we go," June said, and with waves and shouted goodbyes, they and Elmer walked off into the forest, the sounds of the crowd dying down behind them as the trees swallowed them up.

The morning passed silently, Errigal and Feoras thinking about what they had left behind, and June and Koen thinking of what lay ahead. The last piece of the tablet, and then what? *Hopefully, an instruction manual,* June thought, considering the fact she had no idea how to use the damn things.

They didn't make much ground that day; it seemed as though they needed to find their rhythm, and June realized she'd lost muscle strength during her illness. Her legs burned and her lower back ached by early afternoon, and when Feoras suggested a small clearing as a campsite about an hour before sunset, she nearly kissed him.

Exhausted as she was, Koen's meaningful glance after dinner stirred something almost feral inside her, and they slipped off down a nearby stream with muttered excuses. Errigal and Feoras barely glanced up; they'd gotten used to this behavior before their stay with the Valforte, and didn't seem to mind, and Koen and June were careful to be discreet. After all, the brothers had left their wives at home—no need to rub their noses in it.

Physical and mental fatigue made lovemaking quick, but no less satisfying. Afterward, June lay on Koen's shirt and watched as he bathed naked in the stream, his back to her.

"Looking good there, babe," she said, eyeing his backside appreciatively, and he turned to look at her, perplexed, droplets of water running down his chest. June suppressed a shudder of renewed lust. "You gained some weight," she said. "It looks good on you."

Koen looked down at himself, patting his well-muscled middle. "Goes down a lot easier when you don't have to find it, kill it or cook it yourself," he said, grinning, and she returned his smile.

"Yeah, and when it actually exists," June said, and Koen laughed as he stepped out of the stream toward her.

"Yeah, that helps, too," he said, as she rolled over onto her own shirt to make room for him to sit. He looked down at her critically. "Not so bad yourself, but you could still stand to gain fifteen or twenty pounds."

June looked down at herself, her jaw dropping. Yes, she was still a little thin, but five, maybe ten should do it. "Twenty?" she asked, astonished. "My God, man, what are you trying to do to me?"

"What?" he asked, smiling, his brow furrowed. "I like a little something to grab on to."

June pushed his icy hand away and smiled. "Well, nice to know I don't have to go on a diet around you. Still, though..." she looked down at her stomach and thighs, trying to imagine an additional fifteen pounds distributed between them.

"Or better yet," Koen reached out and drew an large, invisible balloon over her abdomen, from just beneath her breasts down to her pelvis, letting his hand rest just below her navel.

"Ah ha, I see," June said. "Barefoot and pregnant, that's how you want me, huh?" Koen smiled, but the smile was tinged with sadness.

"What's that look for?" she asked, and he turned his head away.

"It'll never happen, that's what," he said, bitterness in his voice, and June sat up.

"What do you mean, it'll never happen?" she asked.

Koen looked down uncomfortably. "Well, we can't get married."

June looked at him, bemused. "Well, first of all, marriage and pregnancy are not mutually exclusive states," she said, earning her a look of horror from Koen. "Yeah, hon," she said, shaking her head in amusement. "Just how did you think babies were made, anyway?"

"Well, I–I just–I didn't–oh, be quiet, you," he said, face turning dark blue, visible even in the dim light, as June collapsed into giggles. "I just wasn't thinking, okay?"

"Whatever you say, my love," June said, struggling to straighten her face. "Moving on–why can't we get married?"

Koen was silent for a moment, then stood up and began to dress. "It's against the law, for one thing," he said, shaking the bits of dried leaves out of his shirt and pulling it over his head.

"Uh huh," June said. "And who makes the laws?"

Koen frowned and shook his head, dismissing her meaningful look. "The law is one thing," he said. "What people will tolerate from their queen is another. And they're going to expect you to make a respectable match."

"A respectable match?"

"An *Andrian* noble, June. Not a Valforte peasant."

June made a disbelieving noise, eyes narrowed at Koen. "Are you telling me that all this time, you expected that I was going to marry some other guy? And what the hell were you going to do? Kiss me goodbye when we got to Prendawr City. 'Have a nice life, June.'"

"Of course not," Koen said, lips pursed in an angry pout that would have been cute had June not been ready to take his head off. "I thought–I had figured..."

June shook her head, incredulous. "So, what? You were going to hang around and be my boy toy, my dirty little secret?" Koen's refusal to meet her eyes gave her all the answer she needed. "Koen," she said angrily, kicking him. "You can't be serious!"

Koen rubbed his shin, still avoiding her eyes and refusing to speak. "Aside from the fact that we would have had a lot of explaining to do when I kept popping out *blue* kids," she said, "what makes you think I would agree to that?"

"June, as much as we keep telling you, you just don't get how it is here," Koen said, rounding on her and causing her to flinch. Furiously, he shook out his pants and began to put them on rather violently. "These things are *not* done! And no, I didn't mention it, because I thought that maybe, once you got to the capitol and actually saw what it's like there, you'd agree, considering that it's the only way that you and I would get to hold onto each other!"

June sat solemnly and regarded Koen, his face dark with anger as he fumbled with the buttons on his pants.

"Koen, look at me," she said, and he glanced down at her grudgingly. "I have been through hell, trying to save this goddamn place." June said, "I want one reward for this, one. And I don't care what anyone else says, I *will* have it."

Koen sighed and looked heavenward before meeting her eyes once more. "You are the most stubborn woman I've ever met," he half-groaned. "Do you have any idea–?"

"Koen, it's only 'not done', until someone does it. Besides," she said, standing up, still naked, and wrapping her arms around his neck, "what better way to lead the people than by example?"

Koen shook his head disapprovingly, but offered a smile, albeit a small one. "Am I ever going to win an argument with you?" he asked.

June kissed him playfully. "Absolutely not," she said, releasing him and bending down to pick up her clothes. "Come on, it's really dark now, we're going to fall on our faces trying to get back."

"Wait a second," he said, and June straightened up from putting her pants on to face him. "I'm not saying these things because I'm worried for me. I'm worried for you. If you go through with this, flaunt us in front of people who think my people are worse than animals, they're going to tear you apart. If you want your life to be easy after this is over, I'm telling you right now, this is not the way."

June took a deep breath and closed her eyes. "The easy way is generally not the right way," she said, opening her eyes. "I've compromised on a lot of things, Koen. But not on you. I love you. I want *you.* And I won't belittle you, or the way I feel about you, by pretending for one minute that you are not the love of my life."

Koen pulled her tightly against him in a nearly bone-crushing embrace. "God, I love you," he said, his voice muffled in her hair. June closed her eyes and rested her head on his shoulder, holding him as tightly as he was holding her. He released her and stepped back, looking at her as though for the first time. "So, does this mean that you want to marry me?" he asked.

"Ye-es," said June, a wry smile on her face.

Koen smiled a little nervously, clearing his throat. "Will you marry me?" he asked, and June's face split into a very wide grin.

"I thought you'd never ask," she said.

Koen kissed her, hard enough to take her breath away, apparently too overcome with emotion to speak. Then, wordlessly, they practically floated back to camp.

By unspoken assent, they didn't tell Errigal and Feoras the news; they already knew what their reaction would be, and they wanted nothing to dampen their own happiness, especially not a dose of reality from the others. So they contented themselves with secretive smiles and furtive glances as they cleared up the dinner things and June drew the protective circle around them and Elmer, and happily optimistic visions of the future lulled them to sleep as they lay staring at each other in the darkness, across the dying coals of the fire.

Koen and June's happiness seeming to grease Time, causing it to slide by effortlessly as they journeyed steadily northwest toward the third and final tablet piece. Only one thing dampened June's spirits; renewed thoughts of the mystery surrounding her birth. She'd been too distracted directly after Halryan's death, with things like Koen and her poisoning and stay in the Valforte camp, but since life was settling down once more, her thoughts returned to the puzzle.

"What I still don't understand is," June said to the others, for maybe the fiftieth time in three days, "is why bother getting my mother pregnant at all? I mean, if the point was to kill her, wouldn't it have been easier to engineer some kind of accident, rather than wait nine months for me to pop out? And it's not like they had any guarantee that I would be born, anyway. You don't get pregnant every time you do it." Feoras cleared his throat, his face darkening in embarrassment, and June gave him an exasperated look. "Come on, Feoras, we all know how babies are made here," she said.

"True, but we don't need to discuss it in polite company," he grumbled.

"Oh, since when is this polite company?" June retorted playfully, thinking of the melodious symphony she'd been treated to last night, after Errigal had found some wild cabbage to supplement their diet. Thank God for the open air.

"Anyway," she said, continuing. "If the point was to kill her, that's a hell of a roundabout way to do it."

"Maybe they weren't trying to kill her, maybe they were trying to drive her crazy," Errigal said. "If I were a girl, and I turned up pregnant all of a sudden with no explanation, I think that would mess with my head a little."

"But it all boils down to someone trying to get her off the throne," June said, "and if that's the case, then what the hell is the point in doing it by creating a ready-made heir?"

"You're operating on a lot of assumptions here. What if they didn't mean to kill her?" Feoras said, but June cut him off.

"I don't see the point otherwise," she said, tripping over a tree root and startling Elmer, who she was leading–Koen put out a hand to steady her, but otherwise remained silent. "Whoops. Thanks, hon. But there's no reason to just make her have a baby."

"You're assuming that whoever wanted your mother pregnant was the same one who killed her," Feoras said, and June frowned.

"That kind of goes back to the point I just made, which is that there is no reason to just get her pregnant. It makes even less sense that way." June shook her head. "The only thing I keep coming back to is that someone wanted a new heir to the throne, but I don't understand why. I mean, if you want the Queen out of power, why not just go in and take over yourself?"

She sighed, for the moment defeated. "I hope someone has an explanation for this when everything with the tablets is over with. I'd like these loose ends tied up." June looked over at Koen, who wore a grave expression. "You're quiet," she said, and he looked up at her, worry in his eyes.

"This gives me a really funny feeling," he said, shaking his head thoughtfully. "It just seems like there's so much more going on here than what we're seeing."

"Yeah, me too," June said. "I hate mysteries. I can't even read mystery novels without flipping to the last page."

The trees broke ahead of them, onto a large clearing, and they cautiously approached. The coast seemed clear, and they stepped out into the field, covered with reddish grass onto which a clear, bright sun shone. The grass crushed beneath their feet and sent up waves of lovely, warm scent June could only think of as the smell of life as she inhaled it deeply.

The field was so vast, by the time they'd gotten halfway across, they had just begun to see the tops of the trees on the other side. These trees reminded June of redwoods, except they had broad, flat leaves rather than needles.

"Whoa," she said, pointing at one tree as they drew closer. "Either my eyes are getting bad, or that's one hell of a nest something built up there. Two nests. Oh, hey, there's a whole bunch of them!"

"Where?" Errigal said, and June edged closer, positioning her shoulder under his chin for him to look down her arm, like a gunsight.

"There," she said, "just under that big cloud–what?" she said, for he had stopped walking, and his eyes grew wide, then squinted to slits as he looked closer. Koen and Feoras crowded close to Errigal as he pointed the nests out to them.

June felt slightly disconcerted by this, but a black flying object off to her left distracted her.

"Hey, guys, I think that's Momma Bird now," she said, pointing. "My God, what the hell kind of bird is that? It's huge!"

"Not a bird," Feoras said, and the flat tone of his voice made her turn and look at him. All three men stared with wide, wary eyes at the enormous flying creature, soaring toward the nests.

Elmer's ears had perked up during this exchange, and his nostrils had been flaring, but no one had paid much attention to him. Now, however, he lurched backward, nearly jerking June's arm out of its socket, and gave a series of earsplitting, panicky brays.

"Elmer, stop," June said, clamping her hand over the animal's muzzle as he continued to struggle against the rope, realizing from the Valforte's actions this wasn't the time they wanted to be making any noise–but too late. The enormous flying creature had wheeled toward them, approaching at an unnerving pace.

"Damn," Koen said, and, grabbing June's hand, pulled her along with the rest of the Valforte as Elmer bolted off to the left. A horrible screech sounded from behind them, like twenty discordant voices screaming all at once, and June ventured a glance over her shoulder.

It was a Pegasus. A giant, black horse, with enormous leathery wings, its fangs (yes, fangs, didn't remember that part from the storybooks) bared aggressively, cold fury burning in its emerald green eyes as it bore down on them, wings folded like a diving falcon.

"Down," yelled Koen, and threw himself on top of June, forcing her down with him face-first into the grass, and Errigal and Feoras did the same, just as the creature skimmed over them with another screech. As soon as it passed over them, the Valforte leapt to their feet, Koen dragging June up with him and drawing his sword.

"What the *hell?*" June said, almost angrily, as she watched the Pegasus climb and wheel, presumably for another go.

"Pegasus," Koen said breathlessly. "Don't let it spit on you."

"Don't let–what?"

The men looked wildly around the clearing. "That way's closest," Koen said, pointing in the direction they had been going, and grabbed June's hand to pull her with him once more. "Come on."

But June's eyes had focused once more on the sky, so wide with horror they clearly reflected the terrible scene before her.

"Oh, no," she said, with a tone of defeat in her voice which made the men turn and look.

Apparently, the screech of the Pegasus had been some sort of war rally, for the sky was now peppered with winged, black, angry horses, diving toward them in an enraged swarm.

"Can you stop them?" Koen asked urgently. "Communicate with them, or something?"

June shook her head, unable to take her eyes off the approaching cloud of avian equines. "No, there's too many," she said. "And I don't think I can stop–" She was cut off as Koen pulled her bodily toward the forest, making it to the shelter of the trees just as the–herd? flock?–reached them.

Unfortunately, trees weren't much of a deterrent, as with a thundering of hooves which shook the ground, the Pegasi landed and galloped into the forest after them. June could hear by the nearness of their furious snorts they were gaining swiftly.

Realizing that there were no options, June yanked her hand from Koen's and turned to face the stampeding herd, both hands out in front of her in a *stop* gesture, focusing intently.

At once, a wall of flame sprang up between them and the animals. June heard screams of pain as a few of the leaders, unable to stop in time, ran into the fire. She pushed with her hands, and the wall advanced on the horses, without burning the trees or the dead leaves blanketing the ground. At last, she heard the thunder of hooves as the animals retreated, and dropping her hands, let the fiery barrier go out.

"Phew," June said, wiping sweat-damp tendrils of hair off her forehead. "That was–"

"On your left," Koen yelled, and June turned just in time to see one last coal-black Pegasus charging her, lips pulled back to reveal its pointed yellow teeth. Before she could react, Koen leapt between the creature and herself, grabbing her and throwing her to the ground once more, her face pressed up against his chest so she couldn't see. She heard a sharp exhalation from the Pegasus, almost like someone shooting a blowgun, and a wet *splat* sound, followed immediately by a grunt of pain from Koen.

June squirmed around so her upper body was free of Koen's, and she could face the creature. As made eye contact and raised her hand, the animal burst into flame, falling to the earth as a pile of ashes in a matter of seconds.

Koen gave another grunt of pain, more like a moan this time, and June pulled herself out from under him–and froze.

"Oh my God," she gasped.

Koen's shirt was entirely burned away in the back, and his skin blistered and peeled away before her eyes with a sizzling sound. A nauseating smell emanated from the developing wound; a combination of chemistry lab and burned hamburger.

Quickly, June pulled her waterskin from her satchel and poured it over his back, then ripped her own shirt off to blot away the saliva of the Pegasus as he writhed in sheer agony, reciting an endless litany of curses and groans of pain under his breath. She became aware of Errigal and Feoras standing nearby, watching anxiously.

"Give me your water," she said, and both handed their waterskins over. June dumped one over Koen's back, saving the other in case she needed to give it to him by mouth. After dabbing the water away, careful not to tear what little skin remained, she peeked gingerly under the cloth to see if the burning had stopped progressing.

It had, but a great deal of damage had already been done. His back was a raw, bloody piece of meat, glistening wetly between the curled-up edges of what remained of his skin. Errigal made a small sound of disgust and turned away, and Feoras put his hand to his mouth. Koen lay very still on his stomach, barely breathing (no wonder—the expansion of his back as he inhaled must have been excruciating), eyes squeezed tightly shut.

June drew breath sharply through her teeth with a hissing sound of sympathy as she viewed the damage, laying her ruined shirt aside and rubbing her hands together briskly. She paused only long enough for a brief prayer to whoever might be listening, then closed her eyes, and laid her palms on his raw flesh.

The energy flowed out of her in a nauseatingly intense rush, and continued for several minutes. Just when June was beginning to worry that she'd pass out, the drain on her resources slowed to a trickle, then stopped completely. Taking a deep breath, she peeked through slitted lids, then opened her eyes wide with astonishment as she ran a finger along his smooth, unbroken skin. The only sign of damage was a slight patchy scar about the size of an orange in the center of his back.

Slowly, Koen unclenched, removing his fist from his mouth (a small trickle of blood ran down the side of his index finger and thumb, where his teeth had cut in) and reaching around to touch his back. June gently took his hand, guiding it over the spot where he'd been burned, so he could feel for himself. As he felt the unblemished tissue, he laughed nervously, a ragged, shaky sound, and turned over to face June. He passed his hand over his face, and she noticed it shook badly.

"Wow," he said. "That really, really hurt."

June laughed and shook her head slightly, worried that more pronounced movement would worsen the dizziness she now felt. "That has got to be, like, the understatement of the year," she said. "You're okay now, though? Doesn't hurt anymore?"

"No, it's fine," he said. "Not that you could do anything about it even if it wasn't. You're going to fall over any second. God, you're white." Koen looked up at Errigal and Feoras, who, strangely, were looking everywhere else but at them.

"Borrow a shirt, guys?" he asked, and Errigal immediately pulled his over his head and handed it to Koen, eyes averted, and Koen handed the shirt to her. *Oh, yeah,* June thought, as she realized she sat there in only the cloth sash she used as a makeshift bra. She fumbled with the shirt as her eyes slid in and out of focus, and Koen gently took it back from her.

"Arms up," he said, and June complied gratefully as he slid the shirt over her head. He picked up the remaining waterskin and helped her hold it to her lips for a few gulps, then took a drink himself. "Better?"

"Yeah," June gasped, wiping a few droplets from her mouth. "Little hungry, though." Koen frowned, then stiffened, as they all did, at the sound of slow, approaching hoofbeats.

"Ah, thank you," Feoras said, relaxing, as he strode forward to take Elmer's trailing lead rope. The donkey looked a little ashamed, as though he felt guilty for running off and leaving them, but all June cared about was that he had returned with his entire load, askew, but intact.

Koen got to his feet, tearing away the remains of his ruined shirt, and began rummaging through the pockets and sacks the animal carried, finally coming up with an earthen jar covered with leather.

"Sweet is best, right?" he said, and June nodded, glad he'd remembered the little first-aid lecture she'd given them. He unwrapped the jar and frowned. "I could have sworn we had more honeycomb than this."

"Elmer likes it," June said weakly, and Koen shook his head in exasperation. "Elmer also likes grass, hon," he said.

"But he *really* likes honeycomb," she protested.

"So do the rest of us," Koen said, sitting down beside her. June opened her mouth to protest, but Koen crammed a good-sized piece of the sweet honeycomb into it, cutting off her argument.

"Can't be feeling that badly if you've got the energy to argue," he grumbled good-naturedly, breaking off a small piece of comb for himself. June, already perking up from the taste of the natural sugar, shot him a skeptical look, and he nodded in acquiescence.

"Never mind, point taken," he said, handing the container to Errigal and Feoras. Elmer, meantime, had perked up his ears at the sight of the well-known package, stretching his neck out and flaring his nostrils hopefully, and Koen shot him and June both a dirty look.

"Why did the Pegasus attack us?" June asked, and all three men turned to look at her in disbelief.

"What do you mean, *why*?" Feoras asked.

"Well, they're not usually vicious–I mean...okay, I guess not," June trailed off, cramming another piece of honeycomb into her mouth in annoyance as the three Valforte tried–and failed–to disguise their amusement.

"Okay, first of all, they're not exactly *real* where I come from. They're pretend, like a story you tell kids. As a matter of fact, I had a toy Pegasus when I was a kid. It was purple and had these pretty feathery wings and...oh, *shut up*!" Koen had fallen over on his side, no longer trying to hide his merriment, clutching his stomach, and June pegged him with a handy pinecone before getting to her feet. Errigal and Feoras had also doubled up with laughter.

"I guess we'll just leave you to deal with them when they come back, then," June said, scowling, as she took Elmer's lead rope and started to walk away, aware of how shaky her legs still were, and the way the world wobbled when she moved her head too fast. "Come on, Elmer."

That sobered the men up, and they scrambled after her.

"Sorry," said Koen, unable to hide a residual grin. "Pegasus are very territorial, especially when it comes to their nesting grounds. And they're not real friendly outside of their territory, either." He peered at her face, head cocked to one side. "You okay?"

"Yeah, I'm fine," June said, flashing what she hoped was a convincing smile. "I wasn't really mad, I was just kidding."

"That wasn't what I was talking about."

"I'm a little woozy, but I'm fine." June turned her head away, pretending to glance at Elmer, but used the opportunity to blink her eyes rapidly in an attempt to focus them. She stumbled, and Koen caught her elbow, then pulled her in closer and put his arm around her waist.

"Just a little further, till we're away from the Pegasus, and then we'll camp for the night," he said, and June abandoned pretense and leaned against him for support. He kissed her on the temple, then motioned for Errigal to take Elmer's rope, steering her back near the animal's flank. "Thanks for fixing my back, by the way."

"Thanks for taking the hit; I didn't even see it coming." She slid her hand up his back, as he was still shirtless, grateful for the newly-healed skin. "Now I get the whole, 'Don't let it spit on you,' thing."

Koen chuckled softly. "Yeah, they're mean bastards, all right." He laughed again. "Sorry, that was just so funny. 'It was purple, and had pretty feathery wings...'"

"It had a real hair mane and tail, too, and a little pink brush to comb them with. At least, till I got a hold of my mom's matches the one day." June giggled. "Actually, that's the only similarity between the toy and the real thing. I burned both of them up."

Koen laughed, pulling her close affectionately and kissing her again. "We're going to make it, you know," he said, answering June's unspoken question, and she turned to look at him.

"You think?" she asked. "Sooner or later our luck's going to run out."

"We'll make it," Koen said, and for the moment, June was more than happy to trust him.

The next few weeks passed uneventfully, which made a nice change. The only item of interest was the weather, slowly growing colder, with a brisk, damp bite in the air, making them huddle close around the fire. And one morning, June opened her eyes to find herself damper and colder than usual, surrounded by a sparkling blanket of frost.

"How bad does it get in the winter here?" she asked, and Errigal frowned dismally.

"Pretty cold," he said, "with a lot of snow, usually."

June made a sound of annoyance, looking at her boots, already wearing thin from travel. Aside from herself and Koen, who'd ruined their shirts in the Pegasi encounter and were now wearing their spares, everyone had one change of clothes, one pair of moccasin-boots, and one blanket, which doubled as a cloak in bad weather. Errigal and Feoras could wear both sets of clothes, and June and Koen could double up their pants. But sleeping on the wet ground in a blanket, then wearing the covering all day as a cloak—they'd done it, both in the forest between Meckle and Lumia and crossing the salt desert, and June had no desire to do it again, considering it had nearly killed them. And the temperatures hadn't even been freezing then.

"I hope we find the last piece soon, then," she said. "Be nice to get this over with before winter."

"Well, it's usually a month after the frost before we get any real snow," Errigal said. "But there's no telling."

On that positive note, they set off once more, June grateful to get moving, for even now the rays of the sun were weakening, losing their warming power, especially amid the shade of the trees. Only an hour after starting, though, they came across another clearing, and all of them stopped as they got a look at what lay ahead.

A large hill rose abruptly from the surrounding trees, bare of all plant life, a barren brown mini-peak. And at the top of this, the same color as the ground, so June almost missed it, an enormous manmade structure. A temple.

"Whoop, there it is," she murmured, and Koen turned to look at her curiously. "Huh?" he said.

June shook her head and smiled. "Nothing, just a blast from the past," she said. The four of them continued to stare at the imposing sight, June with a growing sense of apprehension. She hadn't allowed her imagination rein on what the next test would be, but now it broke loose and ran wild, cantering through her thoughts, and tramping painfully on her confidence.

A few hours later, they ascended the small but steep mount, all quietly lost in their own apprehensions. They were all out of breath when they reached the top, and Elmer was getting balky and bad-tempered.

The huge temple reminded June of the Roman senate building, but in brown. Twelve pillars supported the overhang shadowing the entrance, which looked tiny in contrast, and an indeterminate number of steps ran the width of the temple and served to compliment its overall authoritative feeling.

June stared, having forgotten her hands halfway through raking her hair back, so she now appeared to be trying to hold her head on. After a few moments, she realized everyone was staring at her, and she attempted a smile which turned out more like a grimace.

"So, what now?" Koen asked gently, the tone of one trying not to upset a mental patient. "Do you just want to go in, or...do you want a cup of tea, first?"

"Yeah, tea would be good," June said, feeling a need to center herself before entering that tiny black mouth of a doorway. "Oh, God," she whispered, too softly for anyone else to hear. "Help me, please."

Generally, by the time they'd gotten the fire hot enough to boil water, at least an hour had passed, but it seemed on this day only five minutes had gone by the time Koen handed her a cup.

"Do you want something to eat?" he asked, and June gave him a half-pleading, half-withering look. "Yeah, me neither," Koen said, flopping down beside her with a sigh. "Sympathy nausea."

June snorted into her tea despite herself. "Do me a favor and puke for me a couple of times while I'm in there, okay?" she said.

They all fell silent, June staring at the fire until with a sigh, she set her cup down and stood.

"Well, no time like the present," she said shakily, and Koen stood up beside her and took her hand.

"Should I–should we come in with you?" he asked, and June shook her head, smiling wanly.

"I don't think this is anything that swords or big muscles can protect me from," she said. "And besides, I'm going to have enough to think about without performance anxiety." She turned and nodded to Errigal and Feoras. "Wish me luck," said June, and they did, in unison. She fluttered her fingers in a wave goodbye, then pulled Koen away from the others a few steps, noting as she did the brothers lowered their eyes and busied themselves with breaking up sticks for the fire, to give June and Koen privacy.

June faced Koen, swallowing hard, a burning, prickling sensation starting at the corners of her eyes, causing her to blink hard. Koen reached out and touched her face, his eyes soft, and June turned her face into his hand and closed her eyes.

"Don't," he said, softly. "You'll be fine. You're more than capable of handling whatever is in there. You've got nothing to worry about."

"Yeah," June said, straightening up in a show of fortitude she didn't feel. "Just in case, though," she stepped into his arms and kissed him. "I love you."

"Stop that, you're making me nervous now," Koen said, forcing a smile. "You'll be fine, and I'll be here when you come out."

"Okay," she said, stepping back with a deep breath. "See you later, then." She turned to go, struggling to keep her knees from buckling at the sight of the temple looming before her.

"June," Koen said, and she turned. "I love you, too."

June gulped and smiled, then turned and climbed the steps, entering the doorway into the unknown.

~20~

As June stepped inside the temple, the torches, set in simple iron brackets lining the walls, burst into flame, making her stumble. Re-gathering her courage, she moved down the passageway.

After several hundred feet, the corridor emptied into an amphitheater, similar to the one at Fire Mountain, with shallow steps leading down to an area encircled by twelve pillars. Torches, like those in the corridor, lit the room, and tall candleholders, June's height at least, lined a path down the stairs to the pillars.

"Here we go," she whispered, and descended the steps.

As she slowly walked down to the center of the gallery, she could make out a podium, set off-center in the circle, with a slim wooden box on top, and a large, flat stone, sticking up about a foot from the ground, in the center of the circle.

June paused as she reached the closest pillar, waiting for it to burst into flame or something similarly spectacular, but nothing happened, and so she stepped inside the circle, shoulders hunched, expecting something to fall on her head. No monk, no nothing. Holding her breath, she edged toward the podium to examine the box.

"Welcome," said the voice behind her, and June started with a scream, turning furiously on the spectral monk standing behind her.

"Was that really necessary?" she hissed angrily.

"You have come for the final piece of the Tablet of Nuvyl," said the monk, ignoring her. "This time, however, we will not require a demonstration of your magical ability, but proof of your determination to stay the course you have chosen." June opened her mouth, frowning, to ask a question, but the monk continued.

He glided to the stone and gestured with his hand. "From earth, are we risen, and so to earth do we return," he said. "If you want the tablet, however, you must return a piece earlier than planned."

"I–huh?"

The monk lifted his right hand and extended his index finger, not in a pointing gesture, but as a display. "A piece of you, for a piece of the earth," he said meaningfully, and a wave of nausea hit June as realization washed over her.

"Oh, ew," she said, closing her eyes briefly. "Come on, guys. This is taking things a bit too far."

When she opened her eyes again, the monk had gone, but the lid of the box resting on the podium had opened to reveal a glittering silver knife. As if in a dream, June reached out and picked up the knife, turning it in the torchlight. The dagger flashed with a sinister cold light, as though it knew its purpose, embraced it.

June switched the knife to her left hand and held her right up to her face, pointing her index finger and examining it closely. She'd never really thought about her fingers, other than to paint her nails once a week back in the old days, and she flexed the sacrificial finger slowly, wondering at all it could do. Pick up a coin, dial a telephone, pick her nose, for Christ's sake. And now she had to give it up.

God damn it, why was it always her? She'd had her entire life taken away from her, her face, her identity– and now they wanted parts of her *body?*

"Why don't I just chop my head off for you, while I'm at it?" she yelled at the echoing silence of the amphitheater. "It'll save me a lot of trouble!" She paced back and forth within the circle made by the pillars, trying desperately to calm herself.

"Okay," she said. "Okay okay okay okay. You can do this. You've been through stuff that probably hurt a lot worse than this will. And it'll be over really, really quick, as long as you get your nerve up and just do it. Like a Band-Aid. Just like a Band-Aid."

June turned on her heel and purposefully strode over to the stone, kneeling down beside it and laying her hand on its cold surface. With the knife in her left hand, she looked at her finger with a critical eye, trying to decide where to make the cut, and how. She knew amputees had limbs severed at the next available joint, as a rule.

She stuck the knife between her teeth and palpated the first joint of her finger, where it met the hand, between her left forefinger and thumb, trying to recall her skeletal anatomy lessons from college. In order to cut properly, she'd have to hit the slim layer of cartilage between finger and hand with force, since she didn't think she'd have the personal fortitude to simply push the blade through. However, she could only discern the precise point of separation between hand and finger by probing painfully hard. It wasn't exactly an easy target.

"Okay," June said, falsely buoyant. "Let's give it a try." First, though, she ripped a wide swath off the bottom of her shirt, preparing it for use as a bandage. If she waited till after, she'd be fumbling around with nine fingers, spurting blood, which probably wouldn't work so well.

"Here we go," she breathed, laying the cloth strip within easy reach. She pulled her middle, ring and little fingers back out of the way until her skin stretched uncomfortably, then locked them in by folding her thumb over top, laying her hand down on the stone palm-up. Once more, she felt for the joint, then took the blade in her left hand and brandished it at about eye level.

"Ready...set...*shit!*" She dropped the knife on the stone with a loud clatter, banging her fists into the hard surface, overcome with terror at the thought of what she was about to do. Tears ran down her face, and she leaned onto the stone and put her head in her arms.

"I can't do this," she cried to herself. "I can't do this! Why do I have to do this? Why is it always..." her throat constricted as her sobs intensified, and she gulped for air. "Why is it always me?"

If you don't do this, everyone on the face of this world dies, said her internal voice of reason. *Koen, Errigal, Feoras, all the Valforte people who took care of you...everyone.*

June swiped at her eyes angrily. "Okay, fine," she shouted. "Fine!" She slammed her hand back down on the stone, pulling her other fingers out of the way as before. She raised the knife.

"One... two... shit, here we go... THREE!"

The knife fell, and pain shot from June's finger all the way up her arm, causing her to scream out, but the pain was nothing compared to what she felt when she looked down.

"No, oh no," she moaned.

She had missed her mark. Missed it by the amputation equivalent of a mile. Rather than chopping her finger neatly off at the joint, the knife had hit higher, between her hand and the middle knuckle, cutting through skin—and burying itself only halfway through the bone. She gave a squeaking sort of whimper, blood flowing freely from the injured digit.

June now had to make a choice. She could now saw—for she'd proven her aim was crap—the rest of the way through the bone, and hope it would be enough for the sacrifice. Or, she could press the point of the blade through the joint, where she'd originally intended to cut, and be sure of enough flesh for the offering.

She decided on plan B, joint separation. The small part of her mind not screaming *ow, ow, ow* said a) better to only do it twice, in case three-quarters of a finger wasn't enough, and b) if she cut it at the joint, it would heal better. For already she'd noticed something disturbing—her cut wasn't healing, unlike every other injury she'd had here. Apparently, pain and suffering was part of the bargain.

Shuddering from cold, probably the early stages of shock, June sat up on her knees, positioned the point of the knife on the skin above the joint...and leaned forward. This time, the knife slid through with ease, and a new jolt of pain shot up her arm, accompanied by a thicker flow of blood. The stone on the other side stopped the blade, however, leaving skin holding her finger on either side of the dagger. With an almost drunken decisiveness, she pressed the blade firmly down and jerked her right hand away, tearing the skin and leaving her finger to twitch forlornly on the stone.

With a laughing moan of relief and pain, she dropped the knife again, fumbling for the strip of cloth she'd prepared and wadding it up against her wounded hand. Movement from the stone, however, momentarily distracted her.

The surface seemed to liquefy around her separated finger, turning to quicksand and swallowing up both dagger and digit. The sand settled, then began to roil again, and from the sediment emerged a solid chunk. The final piece of the tablet.

With her trembling left hand, June snatched the tablet, terrified the stone would swallow it up once more and she'd have to cut off another finger. As she did, the stone solidified as though it had never been anything else, save for copious amounts of June's blood smeared over its surface. She stuck the tablet into the top of her pants, to leave her hands free to stop the bleeding.

June was now shaking badly, and shivering with cold, even though beads of sweat stood out on her forehead, running into her eyes and down the bridge of her nose. Blood loss and stress combined to send her on a swiftly accelerating downward spiral into shock.

You'd better get out of here, or you're staying for good, she thought, and lurched up the stairs, stopping once to vomit, falling as she did and nearly cracking her head on the stone steps. *You can do it, come on,* June told herself firmly, wiping her mouth with her good hand, the injured one wrapped in her makeshift bandage and pressed tightly just under her breasts. *Just get to Koen.*

June struggled up the remaining stairs and out the passageway, her vision narrowing rapidly. Half running and half stumbling, she burst out of the temple entrance into the blinding sunlight.

Later, June could only guess how her dramatic appearance must have looked, white as a ghost, covered in blood, and staggering. It must have spurred Koen forward, because she hadn't taken two breaths before he was at her side, flanked by Errigal and Feoras.

"Holy sh–June, what happened?" He grabbed her hand, rough in his excitement, causing her to cry out in pain as he pulled the bandage away from her un-finger. "Who did this?" he asked, vengeful anger fighting with concern for room in his face. "Who–"

"I did," June said, and Koen recoiled as if burned.

"You did?"

June held up her hand, trying to glare at him, but not quite able to pull it off. "I need to lie down, please," she said, her voice shaking slightly, and without another word Koen replaced the bandage, then carefully led her down by the fire. They had unpacked Elmer while she'd been inside, and now the three of them rummaged through the baggage, returning with June's and Koen's blankets, the last of the honeycomb, and some spare rags. While Koen covered her with the blankets, Feoras pressed a fresh rag to her hand and raised it high in the air, and Errigal propped her feet above chest level with a few makeshift pillows.

"Wow, it's like having a team of paramedics," June said, before Koen crammed a piece of honeycomb in her mouth. "*Mmph, mmm mmph*," she said, plucking the enormous piece out of her mouth with her good hand, then biting off a smaller piece and tucking it into her cheek, to suck on it slowly.

"Bleeding's slowing down, I think," Feoras said, peeking under the pile of rags. "We need to clean it, though, before we bandage it, don't we?" June nodded. "Just boiled water, that should be clean enough," she said, and he gently lowered her arm before he left to get the kettle.

"Feeling better?" Koen asked, sweetly, but something in his eyes put up a red flag in June's head, and she pushed herself up on her elbows. "Yeah, pretty much," she said. "Hand hurts like a son-of-a-bitch, though."

"Head clear?"

"Perfectly."

"Then would you mind telling me why you cut your goddamn finger off?"

June pressed her lips together and tried not to laugh. Koen rarely used foul language, and something about the novelty of it struck her as amusing.

"I didn't realize that question was so funny."

June looked up at Koen, and the half-furious, half-scared look on his face killed the laughter bubbling inside her chest.

"I'm sorry," June said. "I wasn't laughing–look, it's been a hell of a day, you're going to have to cut me a little slack here." She launched into an explanation of what had occurred inside the temple, glossing over the gory details of the actual amputation. When she was finished, all three men were a little grey in the face.

"These guys are *sick*," Errigal said, shaking his head in disgust. "You'd think they'd make it a little easier to save the world, but no. You have to walk through fire and swim to the bottom of the ocean and cut off part of your hand..."

"An important part, too," Koen said, looking at his own hand and flexing his fingers. "That's probably the finger you use the most."

"At least it wasn't my thumb," June said. "That could have killed me, it's got an artery in it. Plus it's bigger." June sat up completely, then gently peeled back the wad of rags on her hand, grimacing in disgust. "God, I made a mess."

She really had. A few bits of yellowish-white cartilage stuck out of a mass of mangled tissue, mainly the torn and uneven edges of skin from where she'd ripped her hand away from the knife.

June sighed. "It's no good," she said, looking sadly at the place where her finger had been. "I'm going to have to stitch this. How the hell I'm going to do it with one hand, my left at that..."

"I'll do it," Koen said. "Just tell me what to do."

"Are you sure?" June asked, dubious. "This is probably going to get pretty messy."

"I'll do it."

The washing of the wound turned out to be the most painful, especially since she had to pick the crushed bits of cartilage and bone out of the wound, and some of them were still a bit...stuck. Koen boiled some long hairs from Elmer's tail and ran the needle through a flame as per June's instruction, then deftly stitched the skin together over the exposed joint with hardly any direction from her at all.

"Why didn't this heal, I wonder?" Koen asked as he worked. "Everything else on you does."

"I don't know," June said. "I think it was the knife. The first cut I made didn't heal either."

Koen looked up at her, frowning. "You cut twice?" he asked.

"I missed."

He winced in sympathy. Koen looked up suddenly as he finished the last knot. "You don't suppose..." he said, brow furrowed, pointing the needle down at her neatly stitched wound. June looked back at him quizzically.

"Don't suppose what?"

"That...that maybe your power..."

June couldn't stifle the giggle quickly enough. "What, that this was my 'magic finger?' I don't think so, but..." She picked up a leaf lying beside her foot and balanced it in the center of her left palm. With the smallest amount of concentration, she levitated it about four inches above her palm before incinerating it, the ashes sprinkling down onto her hand like snow. She turned away and blew them off, wiping her hand on her pants.

"Nope, we're good." Koen nodded sheepishly, and June couldn't resist ribbing him. "'Magic finger,' huh?"

"Well, it's not like I know how these things work," he said defensively, reaching over for a bit of boiled cloth to use as a dressing. It was still wet, but June reached over and touched it gently with the tip of one finger, instantly drying it, and Koen began carefully wrapping it around her hand.

"I shouldn't laugh, actually," she said. "For all I know, it could have been. It's not like I'm an expert with this magic stuff."

Koen tore the ends of the strip of cloth long-ways, like a snake's forked tongue, then pulled the pieces twice around her wrist in opposite directions before tying them together, securing the bandage.

"Thanks, hon," she said, leaning forward to kiss him, and he smiled. "Oh, hey," she said, the tablet piece poking her in the stomach as she bent, "let's have a look at this." She pulled the blood-smeared piece of stone out, the final triangular piece of the tablet, with a deep, reverent breath.

"Something on the back again," Koen said, as she held it up before her, examining the runic words on the front, and she flipped it over to look. After staring for a few minutes, she shook her head in despair. "You've got to be kidding," she said, and Koen came to sit beside her.

"What?" he asked, and she practically tossed the piece into his lap.

"Does that or does that not tell us we have to go to Prendawr City?"

Koen's eyes flew over the carving, a line running southeast from a crudely drawn hill to an equally simple carving of a castle. Koen studied it carefully, then pressed his lips into a thin line, looking even unhappier than her. "Mm," he said.

"So, straight into the lion's den. Because as far as we know, they're still looking for us."

"Mm."

June chuckled, leaning over to kiss him on the cheek. "One of the things I love about you, hon," she said. "You're so *articulate*."

"Mm."

They spent the night camped outside the temple, for even though the building creeped them all out, it would have been silly to pack everything up and move to the base of the hill.

When June woke the following morning, her hand had swollen to the size of a softball in the night, throbbing painfully and shooting agonizing bolts of lightning up her arm every time she jostled it the slightest bit. And the morning was even colder, the frost visibly thicker on the ground.

Koen noticed the discomfort in her hand (could it have been the constant litany of profanity muttered under her breath, punctuated by a spectacular crescendo when she bumped into something?) and fashioned her a sling from what remained of their ruined shirts, to her murmured thanks. Errigal and Feoras had also caught on to her venomous mood, and everyone steered pretty well clear of her as they left the temple, June walking slightly apart from everyone else, feeling the need for a private pity party.

Vision of the next few weeks stretched out before her. They somehow had to make their way back down to Prendawr City (hopefully before it snowed) get *inside* the city without anyone noticing their motley crew, and then figure out where the hell they were supposed to go.

Plus, she had weeks ahead of her filled with pain from her healing wound with no painkillers, plus trying to get used to life with only four fingers on her right hand, which she could already tell was going to be interesting. All just when she had begun to think things were going to be okay.

She was still in a funk when they camped for lunch, and sat away from the others, hunching her body over her hand and staring into space. Koen came to her with a plate, and something in his other hand.

"Bothering you a lot?" he asked, and she nodded miserably. "I had Errigal see if he could find this for you," Koen said, showing her what he'd been holding in his other hand, a thin, brown root.

"Oh, Koen," June said, her shoulders slumping, "*please* tell me that's what I think it is."

"Craef," he said. "Painkiller." June made a swinging grab for it, but Koen pulled it back out of her reach. "Listen," he said, "you have to be careful with this. It's serious stuff." He pulled out his knife and sliced a thin cross-section off the end, about the size and thickness of a quarter, then cut the quarter-sized piece in half. "This is all you need for today," he said, holding up one half, "and this you can take right before you go to bed. Don't swallow it–stick it in your cheek and suck on it for about ten minutes, then spit." He handed the two wafer-thin halves to June, and she popped one in her mouth. Almost instantly, she felt a slight tingling in her cheek, and smiled at Koen.

"Thanks, babe," she said, and he kissed her on the forehead. "Thanks, Errigal," she shouted over Koen's shoulder, and he waved and nodded, mouth full of food.

Koen looked at her with a wry smile. "In the mood for company now?" he asked, and she smiled.

"Sorry. Yeah, I'll come over." Koen stuck the root in his pocket, picked up her plate, and led her to the fire. As he turned his back, June pretended to clear her throat, and popped the other piece of the craef root in her mouth. She appreciated the warning, but Koen just didn't understand how much this hurt.

Forty-five minutes later, as they set off once more, June's eyes were glassy, and anything that moved, be it Elmer's ears flicking or tree branches waving in the breeze, left multicolored trails as it traveled across her vision. Something seemed wrong with her internal equilibrium, too; she kept listing to port as she walked. Kind of surreal, like she'd fallen asleep watching a movie and now dreamt she was in it.

Koen put a hand up to Errigal and Feoras, who halted, and turned to June with an expression of long-suffering patience on his face. "June, are you all right?" he asked.

"What?" she asked, trying to concentrate on his words, but getting distracted by his eyebrows. She'd never really looked closely at them before. They were fantastic, especially for a guy, perfectly shaped without being fem–

"Are you okay?" Koen repeated.

June bobbed her head exaggeratedly. "Ah, yeah, sure, good."

"Where's the other piece of craef I gave you?"

"The other–what, sorry?" A bird had flown by, trailing a glittering rainbow of blue and green, and June had turned completely away from Koen to follow its progress amongst the trees.

Koen sighed. "Never mind, I think I know the answer to that question." He turned to exchange an annoyed-yet-amused look with Errigal and Feoras, who waited by the donkey, shaking their heads in disbelief. "Guess I get to carry you again." He scooped her up in his arms, eliciting a whoop of delight from June. "Can't have you wandering off on us, now, can we?"

"*Nooo...*" June said softly, concentrating on rolling and unrolling her tongue.

Koen laughed as they set off once more. "Good thing I kept the rest of the root," he said.

Thanks to the craef, now carefully rationed by Koen, despite June's protestations she'd learned her lesson, and her body's quick adjustment to the increasingly colder temperatures, the weeks passed much more comfortably than June had anticipated. They'd taken her stitches out, leaving a jagged pink line of scar tissue where her index finger used to be. It still jolted her occasionally, looking down at her hand, expecting five fingers and seeing only four.

Koen found her one morning spacing out beside a pool which had leaked off of the small stream she'd been washing in. It made a perfect mirror, and June had been sitting, lost in thought, staring at her face and her hand in turn.

"You okay?" he asked, startling her. "Oh, sorry."

"Yeah, I'm fine," June said. "Just...thinking. About how much things have changed. How much I've changed."

"We've had this conversation before, I think," Koen said, sitting down beside her.

June nodded grudgingly. "Just looking at it from a physical standpoint, then. I don't look...did you see me, before I looked like this?"

"Nope, since the moment you arrived, you looked like that."

June nodded thoughtfully. "It wasn't–I wasn't pretty, before, like I am now. But I miss the old me." She shrugged. "Once we get to the castle, and I'm looking in a mirror every day, maybe it'll help me forget."

"You still miss it?" he asked, and she nodded, laughing.

"Every time I have to squat in a cold stream to bathe, or lay down to sleep in a blanket on the freezing ground, or even just think that this would have been over in *a week* if I had my car...yeah, I miss it."

Koen nodded, looking at the ground. "Do you–do you miss *him*?" he asked, without looking up at her, and she smiled sympathetically.

"Like an old friend," she said. "Not like what he was to me then."

He nodded, looking up at her finally, and it seemed to June like a great deal of worry had left his face.

"They're probably going to want to get going," Koen said. "We should head back."

"Not even a few minutes to spare?" June asked, a suggestive purr in her voice, and Koen looked over his shoulder.

"Well, maybe a few," he said, grinning, as he lay her down in the moss.

They were both halfway undressed when an alarm bell went off in June's head, and she stiffened in Koen's arms. "What's the matter?" he asked, and June shushed him.

"Something's wrong," she whispered, looking nervously at the stream behind them, even though she knew the danger wasn't from the water this time. "Get dressed, quick. And quiet," she said, unnecessarily.

As they crept silently through the woods, they heard voices coming from their campsite, strange, loud voices. June and Koen exchanged glances briefly, and continued forward.

Four Andrian men, dressed in leather studded armor that reminded June of the Romans again, threateningly interrogated Errigal and Feoras, as the two Valforte sat on the ground, answering their questions with blank stares. A fifth rummaged through Elmer's pack, tugging roughly at the ropes, causing the poor animal to let out an occasional painful protest.

June looked questioningly at Koen, who closed his eyes and shook his head. "Royal Guard," he mouthed. "Your guys."

June gazed thoughtfully at the men, who were threatening Errigal and Feoras more strongly now, before turning to Koen again.

"Stay here," she whispered, and Koen's eyes widened as his grip on her hand intensified. He shook his head vigorously, then snatched his hand back as though he'd been burned. In fact, he had, a bit.

"Stay *here,*" June whispered, fiercely.

June stepped into the camp like a golfer into the clubhouse. "Is there a problem, gentlemen?" she asked airily, and all five wheeled on her, swords pointed menacingly.

The huskiest of them, one of those who had been interrogating the Valforte, laughed when he saw her and lowered his sword.

"Well, boys, look who's come to breakfast," he said, eyeing June hungrily. "A little sweet treat. In boy's clothes, no less."

June eyed him coldly, pursing her lips distastefully. "You might want to change your tone when speaking to your future queen," she said, icily, and Husky's jaw dropped, as did the jaws of the other four men. He turned to look at the Valforte, then at June again.

"Princess?" he asked, his voice hoarse, and June nodded, hoping she looked condescending. Behind the Andrians, both Errigal and Feoras covered their mouths to hide smirks at her play-acting, and June looked quickly away to keep from collapsing in nervous giggles.

Husky straightened up, covering his heart with his right hand and bowing deeply. "I am Captain Edad, Your Highness," he said. "At your service."

June said nothing, merely stared him down until he cleared his throat and looked nervously away. "Where are the rest of them, Your Highness?"

"The rest of what, Captain?" *That's it, keep up the bitchy cheerleader act till you find out what you need to know. You have the upper hand right now, don't drop it.*

"The rest of your escort, Your Highness. We were told you were traveling with four Valforte."

June flicked her eyes to Errigal and Feoras, then back to Edad before answering. "We lost two men," she said. "It's been a dangerous journey. Now, if that's all..." June raised her eyebrows, and Captain Edad cleared his throat.

"I'm afraid not, Your Highness," he said. "My orders are to take you to the capitol."

"Orders from whom?"

"From my lieutenant, Your Highness."

"And where do his orders come from?" June struggled with herself, trying not to fumble or cross her arms, but merely to stand straight, arms at her side, giving no reason to question her authority.

"I'm not privy to such official details, Your Highness," Edad said, uncomfortably, "but my orders are to take you in, by force if necessary."

June looked away for a moment, then returned her gaze to the Captain's, dropping all pretenses. "I'm going to offer you a deal," she said, taking a step closer to him. He rocked back on his heels slightly, but held his ground, and in that instant she knew her words would be futile.

"Walk away now, forget everything you saw and heard–and you leave with your lives. Try to fulfill your orders, though...you won't be so lucky. I'm the Princess. My orders supersede anyone else's, you don't have to feel guilty about disobeying your lieutenant. Walk away, and keep your mouths shut."

"I can't do that, Your Highness," he said, stiffening, and started to turn toward the Valforte, still sitting on the ground, surrounded by soldiers. "I have my orders, and I must follow them."

June met Errigal and Feoras's eyes, and they confirmed what she already knew had to be done. "Please," she said, appealing once more to Edad. "Don't make me do this."

"Orders are orders, Your Highness," he said, just before he burst into flame, along with the rest of his soldiers, their bodies flaring like flashbulbs before crumbling to ash and falling to the ground in sooty piles. Errigal and Feoras, caught in a veritable ring of fire, covered their heads, and pulled their legs in tight to their chests.

June barely noticed this, though–her eyes were on the smoldering remains of Captain Edad and his men. Five men she'd just killed. Five. Probably with wives at home, children, pets, for God's sake. Gone, because they stood in her way. What kind of monster was she becoming?

Koen came jogging out of the woods, staring, like June, at where soldiers had stood moments ago. Feoras and Errigal cautiously unfolded themselves, peeking at the smoky remains before standing up.

"Wow," said Errigal. "Remind me never to tick you off."

June closed her eyes and clenched her jaw, biting back mild hysteria. Koen shot Errigal a dirty look, then turned to June. "Are you–"

"Fine, I'm fine," June said, a little too quickly and too high-pitched. "Just dump the ashes in the river, and bury the weapons." She pointed to the soldiers' swords and knives, lumps of blackened, twisted metal. "Someone's going to come looking for them. I don't want them to find anything, especially not anything that points to magic."

Errigal and Feoras immediately set to the tasks she'd given them, and June turned to Elmer, re-balancing his load and straightening the straps twisted by the soldier's tugging, still awkward with her missing finger. She felt Koen come up behind her, but pretended she hadn't, focusing on donkey and hemp and burlap.

"June," he said softly, and she gritted her teeth without answering, lowering her head as she smoothed Elmer's hair out under a strap.

"June," Koen said again, louder this time, and she took a deep breath.

"I really, really don't want to talk about this right now, okay?" said June, her back still turned to him.

"You can't blame yourself," he said, and June laughed bitterly. "It was the only thing you could have done. If you'd let even one of them go, they'd have run straight to the city and spread the alarm. And they might have stopped us before we finished. You had no choice."

June, having straightened Elmer's load, now rested her forehead on the donkey's neck, inhaling his clean animal smell, trying desperately not to think about the past ten minutes. Just then, Errigal and Feoras re-entered the campsite, and she turned to them.

"Hidden good?" she asked, and they nodded.

"Found a nice big animal den back there, deserted," Feoras said. "We shoved the weapons in there and covered it up. And the ashes went in the water."

"Good. Everyone ready to go?" They nodded, Koen's eyes fixed solemnly on her face. "Let's get out of here, before their friends show up."

They left the area, agreeing to walk straight through until sundown, skipping lunch and foregoing an evening fire. The soldiers had been a seriously bad bit of luck, because with their disappearance, alerts would be raised, making it harder for June and her companions to slip into the city without being spotted.

Koen walked with June a short way behind Elmer, Feoras having taken the animal's lead rope, and Errigal searching for berries to snack on along the way. They were both silent, June stonily so, Koen frequently casting anxious glances her way.

"Are you angry with me?" he asked finally, and June snorted.

"Why would I be angry with you?" she asked, turning to look at him for the first time. He shrugged.

"Because I wasn't there," he said, and June shook her head, exasperated.

"You weren't there because you did what I told you to," she said. "You couldn't have done anything, anyway. Errigal and Feoras were unarmed and surrounded, and if you fought hand-to-hand, someone could have gotten hurt in the meantime."

"So you admit that it had to be done," Koen said, leaping on this tidbit. "You had to kill them."

June's mouth tightened, and she turned away from Koen, looking straight ahead. "I never said it didn't have to be done."

"Then why are you upset?"

She shook her head, crossing her arms over her chest. "I already told you I don't want to talk about this right now."

"When are you going to want to talk about it?" June rolled her eyes without answering, and Koen sprang in front of her and grasped her by the shoulders. Feoras glanced back briefly, then continued to walk the donkey about two hundred yards to give them some privacy.

"June, listen," Koen said, forcing her to look him in the eye, which she did grudgingly. "You have a huge burden to carry, the weight of the entire world on your shoulders. And what's almost as bad is watching you try to carry it on your own, loving you, and wishing to God that I could take it from you and give you a break for once. I can't do magic, I can't rule the country, and I can't put those stupid tablet pieces together to save the world, no matter how much I wish I could. All I can do is be here for you, but I can't even do that if you won't talk to me." He brushed her hair away from her reddening eyes. "This I can carry for you," he said. "If you give it to me."

June made a gulping sound as her throat, constricted from emotion, tried to swallow. "It's complicated," she sniffled, and Koen smiled, pointing at the sun, which hadn't reached its noontime apex.

"We've got time," he said, slipping an arm around her and pulling her close to his side as they began to walk once more. Feoras clucked softly to Elmer to get him moving again.

June took a deep breath, then began. "Okay, first of all, I feel like crap because I just killed five men who someone loved. And the only thing they did wrong was do their jobs."

"And second?" Koen asked, tone deliberately neutral.

June sighed again. "We have a saying where I come from. 'Power corrupts, absolute power corrupts absolutely.' Do you have anything like that here?"

"No, but I understand."

"I'm scared for my soul, Koen." Her voice trembled as she said it, and Koen squeezed her bracingly, his arm still comfortingly tight around her. "This is going to sound stupid when I say it, but I'm really powerful. I'm just starting to get how powerful, and the fact that I haven't scratched the surface of what I can really do, and once I get trained properly...Koen, there isn't going to be anyone who can stand up to me. I'll be invincible."

"Ah." Koen nodded. "So you're afraid–"

"Right now, it's okay, because I can still feel guilty when I do stuff. I mean, I have killed *six* men. *Six.* And I haven't had to answer for any of it. And I'm not going to have to, am I?" June glanced up at Koen, who shook his head. "So, what happens when the last little bit of the old me disappears, and it finally soaks through all my layers that I can do anything–*anything*–and not have to face any kind of consequences? And if someone tries to make me..." June shrugged helplessly.

"Hmm." Koen pursed his lips thoughtfully. "You want my opinion?"

"Please." June watched Koen's face anxiously as he strung his thoughts into words.

"I think the fact that you're so terrified it's going to happen is going to keep it from happening. You're too self-aware to have something like that sneak up on you. And I know you think you're changing, but you're not, believe me. You've adapted, you've grown, but you haven't *changed.*"

"What happens when I *grow* into a person who does what she wants, no matter who gets in the way?" June's expression was skeptical, and Koen nodded thoughtfully.

"You won't," he said. "And I'm sorry; I don't have a neat little answer for you explaining the whys. But my heart knows your heart, and it's telling me that a person like that could never take root inside you."

June leaned over and kissed him gratefully. As they broke apart, June noticed Feoras had pulled Elmer to a halt, and he and Errigal waited for them to catch up.

"What's wrong?" Koen asked, and Feoras pointed.

"Looks like we're getting close," he said, pointing ahead of them and down the hill at a deeply rutted treeless strip wending its way through the forest. A road.

As soon as she saw it, June's insides turned to ice, and she gasped audibly, causing everyone, even Elmer, to turn and look at her.

"Find a place to hide," she said. "Quick." Feoras turned the donkey away from the ridge on which they now stood, trotting back into the woods with him. Errigal scaled a nearby tree, and June and Koen dove under a leafy bush, close enough to see what was going on. They waited in silence.

Minutes passed, and June, her own eyes fixed immovably on the road, could feel Koen glancing frequently over her way, questioning her silently. He reached over and touched her wrist gently, but June just shook her head, pressing her left index finger to her lips.

"*Shh*, watch," she said.

At last, they came, marching four abreast, spears glinting cruelly in the sunlight, their expressionless, oil slick eyes blankly fixed on the road ahead, eerily quiet, especially since their shoeless feet made no noise on the dirt road. The Eid Gomen. Koen stiffened beside her, hand over his mouth, but for June this was only the confirmation of what she already knew. The time for the final confrontation had come. And everything they'd already done was child's play compared to what lay ahead.

It took twenty minutes for the column to pass, and five minutes later, June crawled out from under the bush, followed closely by Koen. Errigal dropped out of the branches in a shower of twigs, leaves, and other assorted tree-dirt, and Feoras, sighting them from his hiding place, led Elmer toward them.

Feoras hadn't been able to see the Eid Gomen from where he stood, and had no idea what had happened.

"That was the Eid Gomen," June said. "About–how many would you say?"

"I've never seen so many of anything before, but–thousands." Koen's head shook rhythmically back and forth; June got the feeling that if she grabbed his ears to still it, his body would continue moving.

"Heading toward the city," June said. "And there's more, heading to Meckle, and all the other villages and towns in Prendawr. Probably even Valforte villages as well."

"How do you know?" Feoras eyed her with polite skepticism.

"I could feel their intent," June said, pointing with the remaining fingers of her right hand in the direction the Eid Gomen had disappeared, "and something's–something's in the air. It's all stirred up, like sharks before a feeding frenzy. It's time."

It was almost comical, the way all three men took a deep breath at once. June wasn't in much of a giggly mood, though. "I don't think we're that far, now," she said. "If we keep going through the night, we should be able to make it by noon tomorrow."

"Almost full moons tonight, at least," Koen said. "Shouldn't be a problem, even in the trees, without torches."

Errigal looked at the others with dawning horror. "They're planning on surrounding the city?" he asked, and June nodded somberly. "So, this means we have to get through their lines and sneak into and through the city without being detected?"

"Yep," she said. "Come on, Errigal. If you thought any of this was going to be easy, after all we've been through, you're the single most naive person I know." He nodded grudgingly, kicking at the ground.

"Time's a-wastin'," June said, after another few moments of silence. "Let's go."

~21~

They didn't even have to wait for noon to arrive at Prendawr City. They traveled all day, skittish as rabbits, jumping at the smallest sounds, and through the blessedly cloudless night. Just before dawn, they stood at the edge of the forest, looking out at a farmer's fields–and up at the walled, hilly fortress of Prendawr City.

"Okay, we need to strategize here," June said, turning to the others in a whisper, though there wasn't a soul in sight. "Have any of you ever been to the city?" All of them shook their heads no.

"Damn," she said, disappointed. "Okay, we can work with that. The main thing is we have to find the back gate, and get you guys in and through the city without anyone noticing..." June broke off, touching her face reflectively, and Koen cocked his head suspiciously at her. "What?" he asked, and she looked at him excitedly.

"Do you remember what Halryan said, about my face, and my skin?" she asked. "He said it was an easy spell, one that an apprentice should be able to manage. Except on Earth, of course."

"So..." Koen was still looking at her as though concerned for her mental health.

"*So,* I should be able to turn you three into Andrians." The Valforte looked at each other uncomfortably, and June rolled her eyes. "Yes, I know, icky yucky Andrians. Get over it."

"Well, it's not just that," Koen said, shifting from foot to foot. "First of all, is it–will it be permanent?"

"I doubt it," June said. "Mine wasn't."

"Well, what if we're in a crowd and it just...falls off?"

June laughed. "Ooh, somebody doesn't trust me," she said, smiling, and Koen immediately began to protest.

"I don't mean–"

"Relax," June said, still smiling. "I don't think it'll 'fall off', and if it does, I'll just flame the closest few people and we'll run for it."

Her expression turned serious, and she shrugged. "If you have any other suggestions, please, let me know. But this is the best I've got. They're looking for an Andrian woman traveling with Valforte men. And even if that doesn't red-flag us...well, I can't be taking any time for bar brawls." All of them smiled at this faraway memory, then exchanged meaningful glances.

"You're right," Koen said finally.

"I mean, unless you want to stay here..." Koen shot her a withering look.

"Oh, sure, we'll just let you go in there on your own," he said.

"All right, then. Who's first?" Koen stepped forward, facing her with a slight smile. "Remember, you screw it up, you have to live with it," he said.

"Oh, ha ha, very funny, as if I wasn't nervous enough. Thank you." June took a deep breath and closed her eyes, placing her hands on top of his head. "Ready?" Koen's head bobbed under her hand, and with that, she began to concentrate.

Opening her eyes a second later, she was so shocked that she actually stepped back a pace. "Oh, wow," she said. "Oh, *wow*."

Koen held his now dark bronze hands and arms up in front of his face in wonderment, and Errigal and Feoras stared goggle-eyed at him.

"Did it hurt?" Errigal asked, peering at Koen's face. There was a slight ethnic cast around his eyes and lips, but if someone wasn't specifically looking for it, they'd never know the difference. His hair had even darkened, from its usual sandy brown to something closer to black.

"No," Koen said, sounding a little shaken, and June looked at him sympathetically. Yeah, she knew how *that* felt.

"Let me get these guys fixed up, then we'll go, okay?" June said to Koen, reaching out to squeeze his hand, and he nodded, stepping off to the side. Errigal and Feoras's transformations were just as simple, and soon all three Valfortes were examining their tawny skin in the morning light.

"I don't mean to break up the party, but what about Elmer?" June asked, stroking the animal's neck. "Do we just unpack him and turn him loose? I mean, we're not going to need our stuff anymore."

A loaded statement, if ever there was one. If June managed to do what she had to do, she'd be in power, and the meager supplies remaining on the donkey would be unnecessary. And if she didn't...well, they wouldn't need supplies then, either.

"That's probably best." Koen shook himself free of his reverie and came over to help her untie the few supplies left on Elmer's back, setting them down at the base of a tree. "He'll wander over to that farmer's place, mix in with the other animals."

June moved to the donkey's head, slipping the simple rope halter off and kissing him on the nose.

"Wish us luck, boy," she said, and they left him grazing peacefully at the edge of the trees and set off toward the city.

"Let's get our stories straight here," June said, as she checked for the third time that all the tablet pieces were still in her satchel as they walked across the recently harvested field. "You're my husband," she squeezed Koen's hand, "and you two are his brothers. We were on our way to visit family members and we were robbed, that's why we have no money, and I'm wearing men's' clothing. We stopped here to see if anyone could help us."

"Why not say we're visiting family here?" Feoras asked.

"Because you know darn well someone's going to ask us who we're visiting, and we'll make up a name, and someone will say, 'Oh, so-and-so? That's my neighbor; I'm just on my way home now. I'll take you right there.' This way, we don't have to be worried about getting caught in a lie."

Koen looked at her suspiciously. "You're way too good at this," he said, and June flashed him a sunny smile.

"Growing up as an American teenager has given me the ability to concoct a completely unshakable alibi in seconds, my love," she said. "So if we get stopped, I'll do the talking."

The ground began to slope into a valley then rose sharply upward in an enormous, two-tiered hill on which Prendawr City sat. The first tier appeared to be the main portion of the city, and a large, imposing stone castle perched on the top of the second hill. However, they could now see that the valley, the only remaining obstacle between them and the city, was filled with Eid Gomen, squatting around fires and strolling about with weapons in hand.

The four of them lay on their bellies and watched the scene before them, June resting her chin on the back of her hand and staring downhill.

"Maybe I should have turned us all into Eid Gomen first," she whispered, then shook her head. "I don't think I could have played it *that* cool."

"So, what now?" Feoras whispered.

"See, the trick is somehow to get through the lines, making enough of a disturbance to distract them, but not enough to get the guards inside the castle looking and pointing before we get there. Covert is our watchword here."

"So, you're changing the definition of covert to mean impossible?" Errigal said.

June reached over Koen's back to smack him. "A negative

attitude is *not* going to help us here, you know," she said primly, before returning to her meditations. "Three ways," she said softly. "Over, under, or through. And not using enough magic to make me weak." Endlessly she stared at the masses of Eid Gomen, pushing her mind to the limits of her imagination, but came up with nothing feasible.

June clasped her hands together, aware of the Valforte staring at her, Koen especially. Lowering her forehead to her hands, she closed her eyes.

Please, God, she prayed. *I think we can both agree you've lumped quite a bit of crap on me here, and I haven't asked for too much in return. I'm asking now. I need a miracle. We need a miracle. The whole world–*

A screaming whistle, followed by a sudden *whump*, interrupted June's prayer. Her eyes flew open, and she watched in astonishment as a series of fiery cannonballs arced up and over the city walls from within, falling amid the rapidly scattering Eid Gomen.

"Thank you," June said to the sky, then grabbed Koen's hand. "Come on," she shouted, and without hesitation ran full-speed down the hill toward the enemy, currently too distracted by the fireballs raining from the sky to pay much attention to four disheveled travelers dashing through their midst.

The valley quickly filled with smoke, and Eid Gomen ran back and forth. The group's reflexes were tested more than once to avoid collisions with scurrying grey bodies. All of the Valforte had their swords drawn, but only for defense–attacking would draw attention, which was the last thing they wanted.

In what felt like both an hour and a second, they were through, pressed against the stone of the wall, panting and coughing, their eyes burning from the smoke.

"Come on," June gasped.

They began searching the base of the thirty-foot wall, looking for an entrance, June knowing the soldiers would never open the big gate just for them.

Just when she had nearly given up hope, Koen's voice rang out.

"Door," he said, stopping in front of an arched, solid metal gate. June looked at them all, pale under their now-dark faces, and shook her head. *Do not adjust your television set,* she thought.

"Okay, are we straight?" she whispered, and they nodded. "No one cut themselves?" A quick check revealed all skin intact, with no telltale drops of blue blood in sight. "Okay then," she said, then turned and began to pound on the door.

"Help," she shouted fearfully (not too hard to fake–she was actually terrified). "Please, let us in! Help us!"

The door swung open, and June fell inside, followed by her companions. An Andrian soldier, his face greyish, slammed it shut behind them. "How'd you get through?" he asked, eyes wide with shock.

June gulped, clutching her chest and feigning shock to give herself a moment. *It's on now, girl,* she thought to herself. *Screw this up, and you're done.*

"Oh thank you," she said. "The attack...we just ran through, hoping they wouldn't notice us. And they didn't. Oh thank you so much."

The soldier eyed June curiously, dressed as she was in men's clothing. "Where are you from?" he asked suspiciously.

"Up north," June said, her words tumbling out. "We were on our way to visit my uncle's farm, down near Meckle, we planned to settle there, and we were robbed on the road, that's why I'm dressed like this, they took all my gowns–this is my husband Koen, and his brothers, Errigal and Feoras."

"Strange names. Never heard them before." The guard looked suspicious, and June gave him a smile. "Didn't their mother just have the most *unique* taste in names? They're only three of thirteen, you know. You should hear some of the others."

"And why the hell did you decide to charge through a thousand Eid Gomen to get in here?"

"We haven't had anything to eat for two days, sir, we're starving. And we've no way of getting any food, and Meckle is so far away. We were hoping for some charity..."

The guard looked for a moment as though he was going to continue his questioning, then changed his mind and waved them away. "Perhaps someone here can help you, but you need to move away from the wall."

"Oh, thank you, sir, I do thank you for your kindness, we won't forget," June said as they backed down an alley leading onto small side street. As soon as they rounded the corner, June leaned against the wall and closed her eyes, thanking God she hadn't screwed up.

"You have to be the best liar I've ever met," Koen said.

June opened her eyes and smiled at him, strange as he looked with his bronze skin. "Yeah, I know," she said, standing upright. "That's what everyone tells me." She smoothed her hair back and rebraided it, looking down at her clothes as she did so. "This is going to attract attention," she said, sticking one leg out and looking at her pants. "I'm going to have to find a dress somewhere."

"I hate to break it to you, but we don't have any money, June." Koen said, eyebrows raised. June, however, wasn't looking at him. She was looking to her left, over a low stone wall, into a small yard behind someone's house, where a clothing line hung, weighted down by a full load of laundry. Pants, underwear, stockings–and dresses. Looked just about her size, too.

June took off the satchel and handed it to Koen. "Guard this *with your life,*" she said. "And get ready to run, all of you."

Without another word, she had hopped over the low wall, crouching as she landed, glancing to the left and right before dashing over to the line. She found a blue dress which looked about right, simple linen, and tugged it down. As she did so, she caught movement out of the corner of her eye, turned–and froze.

A woman about her age had come out of the house and picked up an empty laundry basket sitting beside the door. Panic washed over June. She stood out in the open, right where this woman was headed, with one of her dresses in her hand.

The woman straightened up and headed straight for June. But something was–off. There was no way she could have missed seeing June by now, she was standing in the middle of the yard staring right at her. And yet the woman simply put the basket down and began taking down the laundry, folding it, and putting it into the basket, humming to herself as she did so.

June risked a glance at the wall from which she came, where the Valforte stood, eyes wide with shared panic at her plight. *What do I do?* June mouthed to them. They shook their heads helplessly, then ducked below the wall as the woman turned around. She *still* hadn't seen June, despite standing five feet away from her with a clear line of vision.

Finally, June ventured a step backward, then another one, then another one. Her movement confirmed it. The woman simply couldn't see her. Slowly, careful not to make a sound or knock anything over, June edged toward the wall, dress clutched tightly to her chest.

The woman had reached the spot where June had been standing, and her hand rested on the empty span of rope where the dress had been. "I could have sworn..." the woman murmured to herself.

June vaulted over the wall and, with the Valforte, ran down the small side street into another alley where June once again flopped against a wall, wiping beads of cold sweat from her brow.

"Why couldn't you have done that when we were trying to get through the Eid Gomen?" Errigal said, his voice mildly accusatory.

"First of all," June said, licking her lips. "I wasn't aware until just now that I *could* do that. And second of all, *you* could still see me. It was only her that was affected. Which means I wasn't actually invisible. Just invisible to her. So I would have had to mess with the minds of a few thousand Eid Gomen, not to mention all the soldiers standing guard on the ramparts. Not real feasible." She shook the dress out and pulled it over her head, then tucked her arms inside to take off the pants and shirt.

"Okay?" she asked, smoothing the dress over her hips, and Koen nodded, his eyes full of sudden desire.

"It's been a while since I've seen you dressed like a woman," he said softly, in a tone that caused both Errigal and Feoras to find other places to look.

June smiled, flattered. "Down, boy," she said, taking the satchel back from him. "We've got work to do."

They made their way casually onto one of the main streets, blending seamlessly with the few people out and about. Those who were around scurried between houses and vendors carts, talking in low, excited tones, their faces worried. *And why wouldn't they be?* June thought. *They're under siege.*

Koen, who had her arm tightly clamped under his, leaned over and whispered, "This is really, really strange."

"What's that?" she murmured back.

"No one is looking at us."

June turned to look at him curiously. "Well, why should—oh, I see." She looked him up and down, then smiled. "You want me to leave you like that?"

To her surprise, Koen actually seemed to consider it. "God, it would make life so much easier. Not just walking down the street, but just...living. And with you, of course." He sighed. "I couldn't live with myself, though."

June pulled closer to him. "I know," she said. "Besides, I like you better in your natural state." He looked at her in surprise, but they weren't really any place they could discuss it freely, and he let it drop.

They carefully wended their way toward the center of the city, to the hill atop which the castle rested, trying to appear nonchalant, so as not to arouse suspicion. When they arrived, however, their hearts sank.

Soldiers stood at twenty-foot intervals all around the base of the hill, guarding the castle, and none of them looked as though they were about to wander off for a smoke break. Once more, June felt a sinking feeling in the pit of her stomach as she surveyed the scene.

"Damn it," she said under her breath. "Why can't anything be easy?"

They turned away and began to walk again, before someone caught them staring and arrested them on suspicion.

"And you're sure that's where we have to get," Koen asked quietly. "Nowhere else in the city, maybe?"

"No, that's it," she said. "Let's find somewhere to chill out, and we'll come back at sunset, when there are less people."

They found a safe, quiet alley, relatively clean, and huddled down. One of the Valforte stayed on guard, while the rest slept, or tried to. June managed to get a few hours of shut-eye, but horrible dreams and stomach cramps kept waking her up, and she spent most of the day in a semi-conscious doze, neither sleeping nor awake. And whenever she opened her eyes, she could see she wasn't the only one having trouble sleeping. Everyone knew the culmination of their work over the past several months, and the fate of the entire world, rested on the events of the next twenty-four hours.

June was shaken awake by Koen, on whose shoulder she'd been sleeping (and drooling, she noticed, wiping her mouth). "Hungry?" he asked, passing her a good-sized chunk of bread.

"Thanks," she said, ripping off a piece and stuffing it in her mouth. "Where did this come from?"

Errigal smiled. "Took my cue from you and 'borrowed' it."

June smiled. "I see," she said. "Glad to know I'm such a good influence on all of you." She stretched, then paused, looking at the long shadows stretching from the buildings and the pinkish tint of the light.

"That time, huh?" she asked, and Koen nodded. June swallowed another hunk of bread with difficulty, knowing she should eat, but too nauseous to have much of an appetite. She handed the bread to Errigal and stood, dusting off her dress. "How're the streets? Crowded?" she asked, and Errigal shook his head.

"There's *nobody* out there," he said, and June frowned.

"That's a good thing and a bad thing," she said. "Bad because there's nobody but us to notice, but good because there's nobody to notice us." The men blinked, and she smiled. "Did you get that?"

"Not really, no," Feoras said, and June shook her head

dismissively.

"Let's just go," she said. "Try to be as invisible as possible."

As they walked through the deserted streets, June wondered if they shouldn't just go to the soldiers, explain what had to be done, and hope for the best. After all, this whole thing was really probably just a misunderstanding, bred by whoever lay behind the conspiracy, but when she ran this past Koen and the others, they responded with a vehement negative.

"As of right now, you don't know who's a good guy and who's not. We can't trust anyone, not yet," Koen said, and Errigal and Feoras agreed.

"How am I supposed to take power though, not even knowing who's the enemy and who's not?"

Koen laughed bitterly. "Welcome to politics," he said. "You'll probably never know. But can we please wait until there's less at stake than the entire world?" June nodded, and they continued to walk on in the growing gloom.

At last, they crouched at the edge of a building at the base of the castle's hill, watching the stick-straight soldiers as they stared out into the darkness, each one with a small torch behind him in a bracket stuck into the ground. A perfect line, impenetrable.

"Damn it, damn it, *damn it,"* June hissed, as she moved back further behind the building, amid soft warnings from the others to keep her voice down.

"Can't you do that thing you did earlier, with the woman in her backyard?" Errigal asked, and June shrugged angrily.

"I don't know," she said. "It was an accident to begin with. And for all four of us? Against—how many soldiers are in view of us? Fifteen, at least?" She sighed, rubbing her hands over her face. "I probably *could* do it, but it would take a lot out of me, and I'm really afraid to do that, since I don't know what the hell I'm up against here." She patted the satchel at her side then pounded her fists into her thighs.

"God, I don't know what to *do!"* Tears sprang to her eyes, and she swiped them away angrily. "We are so close, so *frigging* close, and here we sit, fifteen people between us and the end of it! Here we *frigging* sit!"

"Hey, *shh,"* Koen said, pulling her into his chest and rocking her like a colicky baby. "We're going to get in there, don't worry. No matter what happened, we always thought of something. We'll get through." He pulled back to look at her, cradling her face in his hands.

"Try and clear your mind," he said. "Relax, and maybe you'll...feel something, like you usually do."

June sniffled pathetically then straightened up. "Okay, let's try that." For several minutes she kept her eyes closed, concentrating, letting her imagination float where it would, before giving up. "I can't," she said. "I don't know whether I'm just stressed, or if there's really no solution but–I've got nothing."

For the first time, June saw real fear in their eyes, and she felt almost ashamed, as if she'd let them down. Her magic usually came in at the 11th hour to save the day. But their figurehead had failed them. And she'd failed herself. And possibly the world.

They sat in silence for hours, the black of the sky fading to indigo and pink, until a disturbance at the gates caught their attention.

"The gate's been breached! The gate's been breached!" June glanced at the soldiers as their eyes widened and their faces paled. They looked at each other helplessly, uncertain of what to do.

"Enough of this crap," June muttered, and before anyone could stop her, she stepped out of their hiding place and walked purposefully up to the nearest soldier, who seemed even more unnerved by her sudden approach than by the announcement of the invasion.

"Hi, excuse me, I'm really sorry, but I need to get up there." June pointed up the hill behind him. "Do you mind?"

The soldier looked completely poleaxed, turning to look behind him at the castle and back at June. "Up–up there?" he asked, and June nodded pertly, a polite smile on her face. "I–I'm sorry, miss," he stammered, "but I–I'm not supposed to–to let anyone up there." He laughed nervously, almost giggling, but cut off abruptly as Koen, Errigal, and Feoras stepped out to stand behind June.

"I appreciate your dedication to duty," June said, still smiling, "but I need you to listen to me, real closely." The soldier's eyes flickered to his comrades on either side of him, who also seemed flummoxed by her sudden appearance and demands. *Note to self,* June thought, struggling to maintain a seamless facade. *Invest in better military training.*

"Do you know who I am?" The soldier shook his head, without taking his eyes from her face. "I'm the Princess." His eyes widened still further, and he started abruptly.

"We've been looking for you everywhere," he said. "For months and–" June cut him off with a finger to her lips.

"I know that," she said, "and I'm here. That's why I have to get up to the castle. Now."

"Look, maybe I should call my captain..." he said, looking around for help, and June only barely managed to keep her hands from clenching spasmodically. Behind her, she could hear shouts, and the faint, distant clang of metal meeting metal. The battle had begun.

"There's no time," June said, turning and gesturing to the area of the gate, where the fighting was fast approaching a fever pitch. "There's something I have to do, now, before the Eid Gomen get up here to stop me. And if I don't get up there to do it, the consequences are going to be devastating."

The soldier shifted uncomfortably from foot to foot, the panic of sudden responsibility overwhelming him. "I–I don't know..."

Losing patience, June grasped the unfortunate soldier by the back of the neck and pushed him forward, so he could clearly see the fighting.

"Do you see that? See it?" she asked, pointing with her left hand to the grey tide steadily washing over the town below. "There are *thousands* of them. In a few minutes, protocols and chains of command are not going to matter anymore. Unless you let me up to the castle so I can fix it!"

The soldier's hairless upper lip was now covered in beads of sweat, which he licked away nervously. "Go," he said, stepping aside, and June, Koen, Errigal, and Feoras rushed up the hill past him.

Climbing the steep hill had all their thighs burning in a matter of minutes. "Where are we going?" Koen gasped. "Inside the castle?"

June shook her head uncertainly, heart pounding, both from physical exertion and anticipation. "I'm not sure," she said. "Maybe we should try to find a back entrance, like we did with the gate."

They reached the top, where the walls of the castle met the bare rock it was built on. "Spread out," June said. The four began to jog slowly around the walls, eyes scanning anxiously for any sign of a hidden opening. Then Errigal called out.

"What's this?" he asked, beckoning June to come over and pointing to an area of the rock in front of him. As she approached, she noticed a small nick at eye level, a dark smudge in the stone's surface. When she got closer, though, she saw it was a carving. A tiny carving of a pillar, like the ones at the Serhai temples.

June rubbed her thumb over the carving then ran her hands over the face of the rock, looking for some kind of latch or secret trigger. Not finding one, she stepped back from the rock and rolled up the sleeves of her dress. "Back up, guys," she said, and they darted back behind her as she closed her eyes in concentration.

Crack! A small explosion from just in front of them sent up a cloud of brown dust, obscuring their vision. When it cleared, a small pile of rubble was left–and the dark entrance to a tunnel, leading deep underground.

June gave a small laugh of relief, letting her chin fall forward onto her chest momentarily. "Thank *God,*" she said, running a hand over her hair. "Come on guys, let's go." She turned to step over the rocks and into the tunnel, but stopped when she realized she wasn't being followed.

The three men stood looking down from their spectacular vantage point at the advancing Eid Gomen army, looking like a flood of grey water as they poured through the streets, advancing on the center. A more terrifying sight June had never seen in all her life.

"Holy shit," she said, swallowing hard. "Come on, we've gotta get out of here."

Koen bowed his head, his back still to June, then turned to Feoras and Errigal. "What are we thinking, guys?" he asked softly, and Feoras turned to look at the archway of the tunnel, stepping inside and past June, who eyed him with confusion. The entrance of the tunnel was short, so even June and the Valforte had to duck to get in, but opened up once inside to a height of about six feet.

Feoras stretched out his arms, trying to estimate the width of the opening. He cleared his throat, and June noticed he wouldn't meet her eyes.

"We should be able to hold it for about twenty minutes, I think, the three of us," Feoras said, his voice sounding strained. June looked from Koen to Feoras and back again, perplexed. Then, as Koen at last met her eyes, the reality of what they were discussing hit her.

"No," she said, feeling the blood drain from her face. "No way."

Koen dropped his eyes again and turned to look over his shoulder at the invasion, then down at the thirty or so soldiers in total who surrounded the castle's hill. He didn't answer, and June charged away from the tunnel opening and grabbed his arm.

"This is *not* an option, Koen, so all of you can just put it right the hell out of your heads!" She pointed down at the advancing Eid Gomen, turning to look at her three companions. "There are *thousands* of them, Koen. The three of you...that's suicide."

"We don't have any other options, June," Koen said quietly. "We have to buy you time, so you can do what you have to do."

"Don't give me that crap! You can come down into the tunnel, there's another option!"

"Strategically, this is the best place for a fight. They're all going to be bottlenecked as they come in, but further down, they'll be neatly lined up, and they'll take us out in minutes, seconds even. Here..." Koen licked his lips, "Up here we can buy you a good amount of time." An ear-piercing scream rang out above the others from below, and Koen turned to look. June's eyes never left his face, though.

"Strategy be damned," she said. "I am not letting you do this, any of you. Come on, let's go." She tugged at his arm, but he gently eased it out of her grip, giving her a look full of both love and sorrow.

"What happened to democracy?" he asked softly, and she narrowed her eyes at him.

"It's with your sanity, probably, wherever the hell that is!" June flared her nostrils as she glanced between the three of them. "I'm pulling rank, okay? I'm–I'm commanding you to come with me now!"

Koen snorted and shook his head sadly. "And what are you going to do if we disobey? Have us executed?" He grasped June by the shoulders, looking deep into her eyes. "You think I want to do this? That Errigal or Feoras do? We don't have another choice. You have to go in and stop this, and we have to stay out here and help you do it. I'm sorry, but nothing you say is going to change our decision."

June looked miserably back at him for a moment then turned away, her eyes filling with tears. "So much for a happy ending, huh?" she said softly. "I should have known better." She looked back up at him, eyes so full of pain Koen couldn't stand to look into them, but lowered his head. "You realize that if you do this, you leave me with nothing. Everything I've had or loved will be gone."

Koen shook his head, his jaw clenched, and his eyes reddening. "You'll make it," he said. "You'll make it. You're the strongest person I've ever met, the smartest, the bravest. You'll make it."

June snorted bitterly, tears running freely down her face. "So you say," she whispered, and turned away from him, walking over to Errigal and Feoras, who were grimly watching the enemy advance.

"I'm so sorry, guys," she said. "I wanted to bring you home safe." She swiped at her face, smearing the tears up her cheeks and into her hair. "I'll make sure Mara and Sara are taken care of, I swear."

"We never questioned that, June," Feoras said. "That's why we stayed with you till the end." He stepped forward and gave her a hug, surprising her. "Knowing what you'll be makes the sacrifice worthwhile," he whispered in her ear before stepping back.

Errigal stepped forward and embraced her as well. "Good luck," he said, and joined his brother. "Can I ask a favor?"

"Anything," she said.

"Can you..." Errigal gestured to his face, still golden-bronze, to mimic the Andrians, and June clenched her teeth. They wanted to die as themselves. She stepped forward, placing a hand on each of their heads, and a moment later, they were Valforte once more, in all their blue glory. Both nodded their thanks, and June turned with trepidation to say goodbye to Koen.

He had stepped over to the entrance of the tunnel while she spoke to Errigal and Feoras, hands in his pockets, eyes downcast. Without asking, she removed the glamour spell, as she had for the twins, and he looked with relief down at his blue skin.

"Thanks," he said, holding his hands up.

"Not a problem," June said, her voice thick, and he raised his eyes and reached out to touch her face.

"You have no idea what you've meant to me," he said. "I never–"

"Don't," June whispered. "Please don't. Don't make this harder than it already is. Please."

Koen smiled ruefully. "You're mad at me, aren't you?" he asked, and June shrugged.

"Yeah, I am, I think," she said. "But I have a lifetime to get over it." She threw herself into his arms, burying her face in his neck. "I love you," she said in a near-sob, and he tightened his arms around her.

"I love you," he whispered back. "Don't forget that."

June laughed bitterly as she pulled away, wiping her face. "Like I could," she said.

And with one last, lingering kiss, she went off into the black, leaving the others to their own destinies.

∼22∼

Torches once more flared to life, destroying the flimsy barrier holding her emotions in check, and she lapsed into hysterical sobs which echoed off the stone, surrounding her in misery. Everything was gone. Did this world mean to leave her with anything?

If you don't get your ass moving, their sacrifice is going to be for nothing, Miss Sensible offered, and June took several deep, hitching breaths, forcing her body under control. Hand on the satchel carrying the three tablet pieces, step by step she forced herself to continue downward, ever deeper under the castle.

Ten minutes later, she nearly missed the entrance, a very small doorway on her right, just under a torch. She'd been expecting the corridor to lead *to* what she was searching for, not past it. June stopped, running her fingertips over the edge of the doorway, before ducking inside.

No one had been in here in hundreds, possibly thousands of years. That had probably been true of the temples as well, but here cobwebs and thick dust left a grey blanket of decrepitude on the walls and floor. As she entered, four candles, each on a corner of a stone altar in the center of the room, flared to life, igniting the cobwebs covering them and causing a small conflagration, startling her.

It was a small, bare room, not at all what she'd been expecting. Actually, June didn't know what she'd been expecting. The room itself was circular, its only feature the rectangular solid stone altar in the center of the room, with a candle at each corner. Slowly, she walked to the altar and looked at its surface. In the center was a square depression, a carving of a pillar in the center, and the square looked like the exact size of the assembled tablet pieces.

June squatted on the floor and took off the satchel, carefully extracting each cloth-wrapped piece, unwrapping them, and setting them on the top of the altar.

This is it, she said, taking a deep breath. *The moment, the reason you've had everything taken from you. It'd better be worth it.*

Carefully, she fitted the pieces into the depression, like a child's simple wooden puzzle. As she set the last piece in, the cracks where the tablet had broken blazed brightly, making June shield her eyes. When she looked again, the tablet was whole and unblemished, and

June ran her hand over it in wonderment.

"Welcome," said a voice behind her, and June jumped, realizing halfway through her tiny scream who it was.

"You people do delight in scaring the shit out of me, don't you?" she said, turning viciously on the ghostly monk, who looked benignly at her. "I'm really not in the mood to screw around right now, so unless you have something to add to the proceedings..."

"Before you continue, I must ask you one final time...are you truly committed to this course of action?"

June looked at him, eyes narrowed, giving the spectral figure a look bordering on pure hatred. "After all I've been through, after everything *you* sadistic bastards have put me through, you actually have the nerve to ask me if I'm really 'committed to this course of action'? God, you are *so* lucky you're already dead, 'cause I could come up with some real creative ways to kill you right now!"

Her outburst had no effect on the monk, who nodded politely. "I understand your frustration. However, I loved this world when I was in it, and I would hate to see it destroyed, if there was any other way."

June had turned halfway back to the altar when he said this, and stopped, a roaring sound in her ears, her blood turned to icy seawater. Slowly, she turned back around to face the monk.

"What did you say?" she half-whispered, struggling to breath around the iron bands constricting her lungs.

"I said I would hate to see this world destroyed, if there was another way."

June opened and closed her mouth like a fish out of water. Pointing at the tablet with a shaking hand, she asked the question, though she already knew the answer, to her horror and heartache. "What happens if I read the words on this tablet?" she asked.

The monk blinked in mild surprise. "It destroys the world, of course," he said matter-of-factly, just as she imagined he would say, 'Why, of course I'd like a cup of tea!'

From somewhere far away, nauseating sharp pains shot up her legs as her knees hit the dusty stone floor. June struggled for breath as her mind whipped this revelation around her skull. *It was all for nothing,* her mind screamed. *It was all for NOTHING!*

She moaned, falling forward slightly on her hands, her head hanging between her arms, her breath coming in ragged sobs. Koen was up there dying, with Errigal and Feoras, and Minogan had already given his life. For a lie. And she'd nearly done it. She'd nearly read the words, nearly–

"Oh, you had to go and spoil our party. Shoo!"

June looked up at Queen Mab, standing inside the doorway, staring down at her, and her jaw dropped.

"You," she gasped, flopping over onto her hip, barely catching herself from falling completely over. "What are you doing here?"

"I thought it would be obvious, by now," said the Queen. "I've come to see my little project to fruition."

June's head spun, and the now-familiar red lights flashed in her vision. She shook her head to clear it, swallowing hard against the nausea overwhelming her.

"But—but you live here," June said. "Why would you want to destroy Thallafrith?" The Queen's face hardened.

"No, my dear, my home is Earth, which you thought was your home for so long. So I arranged a trade with our little grey friends. I'd help them destroy this world, long considered impossible to crack by the Eid Gomen, and in exchange they'd clear Earth of humans." Mab gave a tinkling laugh, and shook her head indulgently, seeing June's uncomprehending expression.

"It's very simple, my dear. We were on Earth long, long before humans. They were amusing creatures, and we played with them, made pets of them. But it seemed like we'd turned our backs for a moment when they'd multiplied like rabbits, and created that horrible, horrible electricity, almost entirely blocking our magic. Our prissy pets, weak, small things that probably wouldn't have survived without us, pushed us out, and we were forced to take asylum here. But we would take Earth back, no matter how long it took.

"Once we got here, we befriended the royal family, and we've been trusted confidantes for centuries. A few years back, your dear young mother told us a story she'd just heard from her mother, about some magical tablet pieces that, when put together and read by a member of the royal family—by her own free will, that's the important part—would destroy the world.

"We had an opening now, you see, but a dilemma just the same. Your grandmother and mother both knew what the tablets could do—they couldn't be forced, and besides, your grandmother died a short time later. So we waited, and at last, a pompous, arrogant new member of the Sorcerer's Guild came to the castle, inept and brainless. So we used him, bought him, twisted him—and he performed better than we could have hoped. A little blood-thinning potion during the birth, and there you were, orphaned and helpless and innocent—and completely unaware of the tablets. We didn't even have to suggest sending you away; it was another advisor, frightened by the sudden multiplication of the Eid Gomen. But it worked perfectly. And here we are." Queen Mab smiled sweetly, but there was venom in her smile, and June nearly shuddered.

"But–they captured me, tried to kill me. They killed Minogan. It's not–" June was cut off by the Queen's laughter.

"A convincing ruse, no?" she asked, still giggling. "And we had to kill *someone;* otherwise you'd have begun to get suspicious."

The Queen cocked her head to one side, shaking it, almost sympathetically. "Don't you find it odd that the Eid Gomen were such powerful sorcerers, but never used a bit of magic against you, except to keep you from doing magic? And the number of times you were allowed to escape? Of course," she continued, "that one escape of yours, under the lake, they weren't expecting you to do anything like that. You killed several hundred of them, nearly *ruined* the bargain."

Minogan died for a game, June thought, feeling sicker than ever. *A trick. Nothing was ever real. All the times they put themselves in danger for me–and they didn't even have to.* "Why did you need Halryan to follow us, then? If the Eid Gomen are so powerful?"

Mab threw her head back and laughed, showing two rows of perfect white, sparkling teeth, menacing in the candlelight. "Oh, as if we needed that sniveling, talentless thing! Another ruse, my dear. Another backtrack to throw you off the main trail. No, we knew where you were at every moment, with no help from slimy little impostor sorcerers."

For a brief flash of a moment, June actually felt sorry for Halryan, a man whose life was as futile as his death.

"That's all well and good," June said, "but you have one small hitch in your plan, don't you?"

"And what's that?" Mab asked, her voice like nails on a chalkboard suddenly, but June smiled anyway.

"I'm not going to read your goddamn tablet," she said. "So all your hard work was for nothing."

"Yes, well, I didn't know *he* was going to be there," the Queen said with a frown, gesturing to where the monk, now vanished, had stood. She shook herself, and gave June another saccharin smile. "But isn't it true that everyone has their price?" The Queen bent toward June conspiratorially. "Name it, and it's yours."

"Why didn't you just buy my mother like that? She didn't exactly have the strongest character, from what I hear."

"The only offer I could really make her would be a new life on another world. She'd never lived on another planet; she would have been terrified to even consider it, the mousy little thing. I'd have had to kill her if she refused, ending the royal line, and all hopes of using the Tablet of Nuvyl. But you–you have a price. So tell me...what will it take for you to read the tablet?"

June swallowed another rush of stomach acid that surged up her throat and into her sinuses, nearly causing her to gag. "There is nothing you have that I want," June said, her voice low and dangerous. "There is nothing you can do to make me read that thing."

"But is there anything I can *un*do?" the Queen said, and June's heart skipped a beat. "The Eid Gomen can control time, you know. We can go back to Earth, find your fiancé, then take you to a world where you can begin a new life together. Even save your dear friends up there, your *lover*, their families, anyone you want. All for just a few spoken words. You've been through the universe, dear. What's one planet, when there are millions out there?"

June closed her eyes, trying unsuccessfully to block the possibilities from her mind. She and Koen, Errigal and Feoras too, even Minogan, brought from a time before his death, taken somewhere else, somewhere new, allowed to live in peace.

To live with the lives of thousands and thousands of innocent people on all your consciences, a voice inside her said. *Do you want to live like that? Do you even think Koen would still want you, knowing you'd sold out?*

June opened her eyes and met the Queen's. "Go to hell," she said. "You've taken everything from me. You're not getting another damn thing from me."

The Queen flared her delicate nostrils, but composed herself quickly. "All right, then," she said. "Another bargain. You read the tablet; your lover boy dies quickly, at the hands of the Eid Gomen. Refuse, and you get to watch me kill him slowly. *Very slowly.*"

June lost her temper and sent a surge of anger at the Queen, its force enough to make the air around them waver. Unfortunately, the Queen was both skilled and prepared for the attack, and batted it off to the side, laughing as she did so.

"Ah, child," she said. "You can't defeat me that way. Now decide. Read the tablet now, or die with the sound of your love's intestines hitting the floor ringing in your ears."

That pushed June's stomach right over the edge, and she turned away and vomited on the floor behind her.

"Oh, poor thing," Mab said, her voice full of cruel mockery.

"Made you a little sick, that last part? It'll be nothing compared to seeing it. And smelling it."

June didn't hear this last part, though. She was on her hands and knees, staring stupidly at her pile of sick, specifically at the something which glittered in the midst of it. As she peered at it, she remembered. Tamsik. *It will tell you what to do with it, and when,* Tamsik had said. *All you must do is carry it until it calls you.*

Well, it hadn't exactly called her, but here it was, and since she'd been sick a few times since swallowing it, and it hadn't appeared before now, she had to assume...slowly, she reached out and picked it up out of the mess. Its texture surprised her; rather than hard and smooth, as it had been, it felt rubbery and fragile, like a water balloon. And like a water balloon, it was also filled with liquid.

June still had her back turned on the Queen, who shifted anxiously behind her. "What are you doing?" she asked suspiciously, and June's heart contracted in fear. She didn't want Mab to see this.

"Just give me a minute, okay? I'm thinking," June said, hoping that she'd managed to put just enough impatience in her voice to be convincing. She clutched the hand holding the former stone to her chest, closing her eyes. *What do I do with you?* she asked, concentrating. *What do I do?*

Drink it, said a voice, from deep inside her, and June was reminded absurdly of Alice in Wonderland. June peered down at the object in her hand. As she looked, it appeared to spring a leak in the top, and clear fluid coursed down the sides, trickling into her palm.

What have you got to lose? June thought, then popped the whole orb in her mouth, using her tongue to crush the thing on the roof of her mouth, squirting the tasteless fluid down her throat, then spitting the empty sac on the floor, coughing a little so the Queen would just think she was being sick again.

A ball of heat began burning in her belly, spreading slowly outward to her limbs and head, so intense it was uncomfortable. "Hoo," she said softly, as the heat began to intensify and grow stronger, increasing in power.

Power.

June stood up slowly, turning to face the Queen. "Were you still on Earth when people started making movies?" she asked. "Cartoons?"

The Queen shook her head, curiously. "I don't believe so, no."

June walked back over to stand beside the altar, resting her elbow as casually as she could on the edge, considering she expected herself to burst into flame any minute, so intense was the flood of hot power coursing through her body. The hairs on her arms and legs stood on end, and if her hair hadn't been braided back, she would have had an afro for sure. And all this power strained to burst forth.

"My favorites were the kids' movies. There was always a princess, always a prince, and always a bad guy...or an evil queen. Those movies taught me a lot, though." *Almost ready, almost....* "You know the most important thing I learned from them?"

"What's that?" asked the Queen, sounding mildly amused, as though sure June had lost her mind.

"The bad guy never wins."

June laid both hands down on the tablet and opened the dam she'd been holding closed. The tablet began to glow with an eerie light, the runic letters burning bright blue, and the stone grew warmer, scorching her hands. Then something grabbed hold from within, and using it as a conduit, sent waves of energy undulating through her chest, thumping worse than the biggest bass speaker ever made. Her mouth had opened, spouting words she'd never spoken before, words she didn't understand, the meaning of the runes carved into the tablet.

At the same time, the strength she'd gotten from Tamsik's stone fought for position in her body, against the tablet's strength in a deadly struggle. Panicking at first, June struggled against both for possession of her body, then, coming to her senses, she joined forces with the power of Tamsik's stone, and slowly, she was able to bend the Tablet of Nuvyl to her will.

The power of the tablet was destructive, of that there was no doubt. But rather than allowing those forces free rein to destroy the world, June was directing them–toward the Eid Gomen and the Sidhe.

The ground shook with amazing force, and small rocks and clouds of dust tumbled from the stone ceiling of the underground room, pelting June on the head and shoulders.

The Queen, who had been watching with an evil smile, suddenly realized something was wrong.

"What are you doing?" she cried, then rushed forward, meaning to take June by the arm. As soon as her fingers brushed June's arm, however, a bolt of blue electricity arced out of June's body and into the Queen's, sending the Sidhe flying across the room, where she hit a wall and fell crumpled and motionless on the floor.

June continued to use every bit of strength available to control the devastation. The ground lurched under her feet while bigger pieces of the ceiling and walls crumbled to the floor, and smoke rose from her hands where they touched the tablet.

A bit more, she said, her voice growing strained as she continued pushing with all her might. *Just a bit more....*

A flash of light, an explosion from the tablet, and June was blown back, completely airborne, as the ceiling collapsed, blanketing the cavern in rock–and silence.

June didn't know how long she'd been unconscious, but her throat felt as though she'd swallowed half-dozen nail files, and her body felt broken in fifty different places.

She opened her eyes to darkness, total and complete. With a grunt, she lit herself up, as she'd done at the bottom of the ocean, and looked around in astonishment.

June lay under a huge slab of stone which had fallen from the ceiling, luckily catching on the wall and creating a handy roof, protecting her from other falling debris. She reached up and brushed her fingertips across it, astonished at her luck, but wincing at her still-burned hands, sore from contact with the tablet.

Then the other events of the day came back to her in a rush, and she quickly wormed her way out from under the stone.

The room was in ruins, rubble covering the altar at the center. She approached it cautiously, moving a few chunks of stone covering the center, where the tablet had lain.

It was still there, looking as it had after June had pieced it together a few hours ago, but crumbled into dust at her touch. Smiling grimly, June took a huge breath and blew the dust away, scattering it. No one would use it again, for good or for evil.

June turned, and as she did, caught sight of a swatch of gold and white silk, sticking out from under a large boulder. Queen Mab. Unarmed, she picked up a hunk of stone and slowly walked over to investigate.

"Ew," June said out loud. The Queen hadn't been as lucky as June. The boulder had fallen squarely on her, several tons of solid rock. She'd never had a chance. With an effort, June worked up a small amount of saliva and spat. "Bitch."

With a last look around the ruined room, June turned toward the exit, which had remained clear, and took a deep breath. She was afraid to go out there, afraid to learn Koen and the others had been killed, for, once she knew, she couldn't return the knowledge. With a deep breath, she stepped into the hall and went back out the way she'd come.

About halfway out, June reached a dead end; a portion of the ceiling had collapsed, blocking the passageway completely. She thought about blasting through, but feared injuring the Valforte, if they were still alive and on the other side. Then she remembered the passageway had continued on past the temple room. Maybe there was another way out.

June jogged along the passageway, her speed increasing as her head cleared and her anxiety for the Valforte–and to find out just what the hell she'd ended up doing–grew. She finally came to a plain, wooden door, which opened outward when she tugged on the iron ring which served as a doorknob.

June stood in an anteroom, between the wooden door and some kind of curtain. Taking a deep breath, she pushed through it....

And was greeted by the terrified screams of a young woman and the blinding light of day. She'd stepped into a huge, marble hallway, lined by portraits and tapestries. The screams came from a maid in a blue gown with a crisp white apron and hat, her arms full of fluffy soft towels. In other words, she was in the castle.

The maid's continued screams shook June from her reverie. "Hey, it's okay, *shh*..." June said. The woman didn't let up, and unfortunately for her, June was running short on patience.

A moment later, the maid stared at June in shocked silence, a red hand print, minus one finger, on her left cheek.

"I'm Princess Ulfhilda. How do I get out of here?"

"Oh, Princess," the maid said, bobbing anxiously. "Everyone's been looking for you, we've been so–"

"Not what I asked you," June snapped. "How-do-I-get-out-side?"

"Oh, um..." the maid said, flummoxed. "Well, here, follow me." The maid turned on her heel and began to walk sedately ahead.

June growled in annoyance. "Look, this is kind of urgent," she said, and the maid glanced over her shoulder at June and began to walk faster, rear end swaying pertly.

"Nope," said June, running up alongside the maid, ripping the towels from her arms and throwing them off to the side. "We run. Now."

The maid complied, and soon they ran down a set of gold and marble stairs leading into a huge foyer. Straight ahead were an enormous set of ornate carved doors, at least three times June's height, and a number of bearded gentlemen in familiar outfits anxiously pacing back and forth. June's stomach clenched at the sight of their puffy purple hats, reminding her of Halryan.

"It's the Princess," the maid shouted to them happily as they ran up, as though she'd found June under a chair, rather than screaming like an idiot at her appearance.

"Your Highness!" One of them swept the obscene hat from his head and bowed deeply, and the others followed. "You are the very picture of your mother—we've been looking—"

"Get out of the way," June snapped, and they stepped aside, wide-eyed. As she swept past them, the doors swung outward ahead of her, and she sprinted through at full speed. She pulled up short, trying to decide which direction to go in to get to the tunnel entrance more quickly, finally choosing the left. The only thing on her mind was to find Koen, and no possible obstacle could have stopped her at this point.

The body of an Eid Gomen was her first clue she'd chosen correctly, the first in a trail of broken corpses leading to a pile which, save for about a foot at the top, completely obscured the tunnel opening into which June had disappeared only hours before.

June stopped only briefly, taking this in, then charged up the pile of dead grey bodies, meaning to dig through them with her bare hands, but something caught her eye about halfway up the pile. With trembling fingers, she picked up a large swatch of a shirt, soaked with blood. A lot of blood, even after all this time still wet, smearing her fingers and wrist with blue as she turned it to and fro.

"Koen," she screamed, clawing her way to the top of the pile. "KOEN! FEORAS! ERRIGAL!" She pressed her face into the opening, her arm waving blindly into the cavern. "ARE YOU IN THERE? ANSWER ME!"

Silence.

June gave a primal scream of rage and anguish, sliding down the stack of Eid Gomen bodies as she collapsed in heartrending sobs, pressing the bloodstained cloth to her chest as hot tears slid down her face. She was aware that the sorcerers and maid had followed her outside and now watched her in a mix between curiosity and discomfort, but she didn't care. She was in her own private house of pain, doors locked, windows shuttered.

So she wasn't aware of a slight disturbance in the crowd, either, of someone approaching her, speaking her name softly, repeatedly, squatting down beside her. Only when that someone placed a hand gently on top of her head did she jump and raise her head, to meet eyes full of relief and love. Sea-green eyes, eyes she saw in her sleep.

With a yelp, she flung herself on his neck, and they both

tumbled over backward, June burying her face in his neck, a litany of thankful prayers spilling from her lips eventually de-evolving to her saying, "I thought you were dead," over and over again.

"It's okay, it's okay, *shh*," Koen said, holding her to him and stroking her hair. "We made it."

June's head jerked up suddenly, eyes wide. "The others, they're..." Looking over his shoulder, Errigal and Feoras stood, faces full of relief at a job finally done. Errigal was shirtless, and Feoras held his brother's blood-soaked, balled-up shirt to his side. "You're hurt," June said, getting to her feet and rushing over to him. "This is where the blood..."

Feoras nodded. "It's just a flesh wound, promise," he said evenly. "It's just bleeding a lot."

"Well, move it over, let's see," she said, pushing his hand with the cloth away to examine the wound. She pressed her hands over it, and within an instant, the blue blood smeared on his side was the only evidence he'd ever been wounded. "Everyone else okay?"

They all nodded, strange expressions on their faces as they looked at her. "What?" she asked, and Koen smiled like a man in a dream.

"You did it," he whispered, looking down the hill at the city, free of invaders and chaos. "It's over. You really did it."

June dropped her head, unable to meet his eyes, his exultant expression. How could she tell him it had all been a lie; that his best friend had died for nothing?

One of the purple-garbed sorcerers, with a wispy white beard, saved her from figuring out an opening line. "Was–did Queen Mab..." he asked, edging toward June, who nodded, "and she's..."

"Dead."

The sorcerer closed his eyes in relief, as Koen glanced at June, confused. "Queen Mab was in there?"

June took a deep breath and launched into the tale. The eyes of the Valforte widened, hardening with anger as they realized the magnitude of the deception they had all been operating under.

"That's sick," Koen said, and he looked nauseated, too, as did the others, as they processed this latest bit of information. "I can't–I can't even–"

"I'm sorry," said June, heartsick, and Koen looked at her in disbelief.

"What are you sorry for?" he asked. "You've lost more than anyone here–"

"It should have been obvious," she said, slamming a fist into the palm of the other hand. "The monks kept saying weird things...and it was just so goddamn hard to get the tablet pieces. You'd think they'd make something that would save the world a little more *accessible.* But of course it wasn't to save the world, it was to destroy it...and with all the other freaky things going on, these guys looking for us..." She gestured to the crowd of sorcerers clustered together, watching June as though she was a dangerous animal (at this moment not too far from the truth). "I just...should have questioned more."

"I don't want to hear you say anything like that, ever again," Koen said, controlled fury in his voice. "You damn near killed yourself trying to get here, to save a bunch of strangers. You were lied to by someone who gave you reason to trust her. And even though she had you backed into one hell of a corner, you still managed to outmaneuver her. You have nothing to be ashamed of."

June didn't agree, but didn't feel like arguing. Instead, she turned to the group of sorcerers, still staring at her dubiously. "So you knew about this, then," June said. "That I was being misled."

"Halryan was directly instructed by Queen Mab on the quest, excluding the rest of us, so we had no idea, at first, Your Highness," the wispy-bearded sorcerer who had spoken earlier said. "But he mentioned something about your mission to one of the stable boys. By the time the information worked its way back to us, you were in the wilderness, impossible to find. And of course we couldn't divulge all the details, so we concocted the kidnapping story, hoping someone would see you and turn you in."

The sorcerer fell silent, but his eyes flicked tellingly from Koen and back to June. Her little show of affection and relief hadn't exactly gone unnoticed, then.

June stepped over beside Koen and took his hand. "This is Koen," she said, chin raised defiantly. "My fiancé. And my friends, Errigal and Feoras."

You could have knocked the whole group over with the silly feathers sticking out of their hats, by the looks on their faces. June was too overwrought and too tired to care, though.

June nodded at the maid, who stepped forward anxiously. "Do you think you could find rooms for us?" she asked. "It's been a long, hard day, and I don't care what anyone says–before I do anything else, I'm taking a nap."

With a barely concealed smile, the maid bobbed in a curtsy and led them inside the castle.

~23~

Six months later, June woke up on a beautiful morning, cocooned in silk sheets, opening her eyes to the golden sunlight streaming through cracks in the heavy brocade curtains and the gauzy hangings of her canopy bed. She smiled and stretched, folding her arms behind her head and gazing upward, reflecting quietly, as she did every morning, on the days since her arrival in Prendawr City.

The sorcerers, also her advisors, staged the medieval equivalent of an intervention as soon as she woke up from her twelve-hour post-apocalypse nap, vehemently stating their stern opposition to her taste in men, loudly insulting the Valforte race and insinuating various weaknesses in her moral character (most of which she was proud to admit were true).

June, completely out of patience, fired them all.

After firing the advisors, June called for a scribe (actually, her words to a handy maid were, "Get me someone who can erase a law."). The scribe, a serene looking middle-aged man named Jan, complied with June's request to take all anti-Valforte legislation, especially the one about relations with Andrians, off the books without so much as batting an eye. Since June had just fired her advisors, and didn't have a clue what to do next, she asked Jan what he thought.

"Have a dinner, Your Highness," he said. "Invite all the upper-class men and women, a get-acquainted party. And make sure they know you will not bend, and you certainly won't break."

June looked at him thoughtfully. "How would you like a promotion?" she asked, smiling.

Jan was immediately very busy in his new post as Royal Advisor. He had a party to plan, plus the additional task of finding several other trustworthy individuals to fill the empty advisor posts.

The dinner was a success, and so were the advisors, especially since June convinced Errigal and Feoras to return with their families and fill two of the posts. A week later, June and Koen were married, and June was officially crowned Queen of Prendawr.

Working for equality for the Valforte wasn't actually as difficult as they'd thought it would be. The kingdom was in an uproar, initially, over the law changes and the relationship of their monarch with what Andrians viewed as an inferior race, but news quickly spread of the valiant efforts of the Valforte to bring their Queen safely to power, which caused most people to rethink their ideas. There were a few skirmishes, but June made it clear, by way of imprisonment, property seizures, and even one execution, that disrespectful behavior toward the Valforte would no longer be tolerated.

Life rolled on, busy and interesting and divinely happy. June had been afraid Koen would get bored, sitting around the castle, but in fact he was very happy to be actively involved, behind the scenes.

Despite his race, he quickly became a public favorite, and was June's right hand regarding public concerns, ferreting out problems, talking to the people, and coming up with innovative solutions to their dilemmas. And of course, he was her rock, her shoulder to cry on, the post she leaned on to hold herself up.

June stayed busy herself, establishing a new system of government. She didn't like this whole absolute monarchy thing, so she set up public elections, four candidates nominated by the people from both the Valforte and the Andrians, for a total of eight representatives, to decide on matters of legislation. She herself was a member of the House, but only served as a tiebreaker, if necessary.

She cleaned up the judicial system, and established public health, education, and assistance programs. She also hired Dukso, a liberal young sorcerer, to tutor her in magic.

One of her prouder moments, though, was making good on her promise to the dragons, setting aside protected lands for them, with heavy penalties for anyone caught trespassing or harassing a dragon. Tokesh's amazement that she'd kept her word made it all worthwhile. So did the promised midnight ride with Rakoz.

June sighed, blinked, and turned her head to find Koen's eyes open and watching her. "Reminiscing again?" he asked, and she rolled into him, snuggling her head under his chin.

"I can't help it," she said. "It's still such a novelty to have something nice to look back on."

"I know," he said. "And you've done so much, it's amazing."

"Well, I've had a lot of help," she said, reaching around and squeezing his butt. He returned the gesture in kind, causing her to roll on her back again to avoid his playful grip.

"I mean it, you know," Koen said, grown serious. "Andrians and Valforte, working side by side...I mean, I knew you'd change stuff, make it harder for them to antagonize us...but I had no idea something like this was possible."

"We lead by example, Koen," she said. "They'd never seen an Andrian and a Valforte together before. How could they have imagined it?"

"Well, they're going to see a new version of togetherness in a few months," Koen said, smoothing his hand across the satiny nightgown covering her abdomen, where a new roundness had begun pushing outward. Already, June had been forced to hang some of her dresses up in the back of the wardrobe, hoping she'd be able to fit back into them once the baby came.

June smiled again, covering his hand with hers, and Koen pressed close, kissing her neck in the way he knew drove her crazy. "We got our happy ending, didn't we?" he whispered between kisses.

June opened her eyes, looking around, at her husband in her arms, the baby inside her, and all of them together, changing a world for the better.

"Yeah, we did."

THE END

Jacquelyn Sylvan lives in Palmerton, Pa. A graduate of Northampton Community College, her life revolves around her husband, Martin, her pets, and her love of reading and writing.

In her spare time, Jacquelyn can usually be found tromping through the woods with her husband and dog, enjoying movies and diner food with friends, or simply having a night off with some Discovery Channel, wine, and Cheez-Its.

Jacquelyn's writing journey began at age four, when she wrote her first poem, and her infatuation with the written word intensified throughout the years. Her favorite authors and greatest inspirations include J.K. Rowling and Stephen King, whose examples she hopes to follow.

Surviving Serendipity is her first novel.

Printed in the United States
201616BV00001B/10/P

9 781590 805862